The Last Light of Dusk

JOANNE LOCKYER

Copyright © 2014 Joanne Lockyer
www.joannelockyer.com

All rights reserved.

ISBN-10: 0992536200
ISBN-13: 978-0-9925362-0-6

Cover design by Gareth Lewis
Cover photography by Nikita Pere, Gareth Lewis
and Joanne Lockyer
Cover wardrobe by Carol Lockyer and Antonia Lai

Copy editing by Liz Jacobsen

This book is a work of fiction. References to historical people, events, establishments, organizations, or locations are intended only to provide a sense of authenticity and are used fictitiously. All other characters, and all incidents and dialogue, are drawn from the author's imagination and are not to be construed as real.

No part of this book may be reproduced, scanned or distributed in any printed or electronic form without permission. Please do not participate in encouraging piracy of copyrighted materials in violation of the author's rights. Purchase only authorized editions.

First published ebook and print July 2014

Published by Lion Heart Media Pty Ltd
Brisbane, Australia

DEDICATION

To my gorgeous mum, Carol Lockyer.
For every phone call answered. For every long chat.
For every one of those times you said, "You don't need to
say thank you. That's just what mums do."
I love you.

ACKNOWLEDGMENTS

REACHING THIS MOMENT HAS SPANNED eight years, five continents, three places of employment, and the making of many new and much loved friends.

Every time I've looked around, I've found an incredible team of friends and colleagues, old and new, in Australia and across the world, who have supported me on every front. I never expect help, or, at least, I'm always overwhelmed when people offer it, and when you all rush forward with open hearts, excited, cheering, and so generously offering your time, skills and support, my heart fills with wonder and immense gratitude. I can't imagine having done this—or wanting it—any other way.

Thank you to my earliest supporters, especially Sarah Martin, Rebecca Knol, David Browne and Steve White. You joined this journey from the first. To amazing colleagues and friends who have since jumped aboard and enabled me to live my wonderful writing, working, traveling life, especially Christopher Doig and Barton Napier; your support, friendship and wisdom these past years has echoed through my life time and time again. Thank you for understanding everything. Thank you, too, to new work mates, who are just starting to see what they've got themselves into with me!

To my Romance Writers of America Golden Heart sisters, the 2012 Firebirds and 2013 Lucky Thirteens, I am so privileged to be a part of such inspiring and talented groups of women.

Thank you to my dear friends and beta readers: Catherine Rull, Wendy La Capra, Rosemary Potter and Camille Kirby. And to Bernie and Max too, for inspiration!

To the team at the Popular Romance Project, especially Laurie Kahn, Bill Anderson, Joseph Friedman and Daniel Brooks: *thank you*. For nearly five years, you have walked alongside me and have helped to make this experience unique and so special. Laurie, by offering me the opportunity to be part of the *Love Between the Covers* documentary film project, you have given me a life experience that will remain with me forever and that has been beyond anything I could have ever dreamed.

To my fabulous cover team, Gareth Lewis, Nikita Pere, Andrew Flint, Emma Jones, Scott Hamilton, Katherine Stevenson, Mark Williams, Katie Davidson, Nicole Gibson, Alan Whittaker, Antonia Lai and Debbie Pevitt: thank you from the bottom of my heart.

To friends, just because you're always near, if not in person, then in spirit. You never fail to put wind in my sails: Sarah Ross, Briana Van Tilburg, Sharon Lowe, Máire Claremont, Anne Calhoun, Heather Ashby, Paul Lockyer, Shawn Roberts, Tydus Meadows and Phil Rubin.

Helen Breitwieser, thank you for finding me all those years ago, for friendship and long-time support, and for offering your wisdom in books and life.

To my copy editor, Liz Jacobsen, I am truly the luckiest girl alive to have benefited from your enthusiasm and expertise. You have understood this book so well and drawn my attention to all the right places. Your input has truly helped make it sparkle. It's beautiful! Thank you.

To my indispensable critique partner, Elizabeth Essex, I never did get to say these words in a Golden Heart award speech, so I shall say them now: thank you for being fierce and funny and a damn good friend.

Rebecca Lumley and Yolekha Mallier: there are times in one's life when people walk out so that new people can walk in. Twice life turned, you have each walked in. What a deal I got! Bec, I know no one who does more meaningful things for their friends. Yols—you know why this is special.

To my dad, Glen Lockyer, for keeping my car running, lawns mowed, and generally fixing things I don't notice require fixing. And for helping plot action scenes.

Carol Lockyer, my darling mum, your message is on the third page.

What more can a girl ask than to have this kind of love in her court?

Finally, thank you to you, the reader, who has found your way to this novel. As Clarissa Pinkola Estes has written, "What does the soul want? . . . The soul wants stories."

I hope, very much, that you enjoy this one.

PROLOGUE

The Rice Coast, West Africa
August 1805

HORIZONTAL WELTS SCORED THE INSIDE of his wrists. Deep, raw and blistered, the twin wounds throbbed. Shackles might have done similar work—such apparatus were common enough in these parts. But the damage borne by his body was burns.

Burns that, when healed, would leave vicious scars to serve as even stronger reminders.

He could still hear the searing hiss of the hot iron. His skin recalled the moment of its touch. Yet even at that moment, the fury he had carried for months flared hotter. That fury remained, lodged and burning inside.

Jaw clenched, expression hardened, the young man raised his head. His linen shirt stuck to skin damp with sweat. Above, the merciless sun bore down to sap all it could, while below, his boat shifted at anchor. The raucous din of cicadas emerged from the jungle to pervade the motionless air.

Just up the river, drenched in daylight, the fortress—the severe, white-walled beast that it was—bedazzled, while in the broad river estuary beyond, a dozen becalmed ships waited at anchor.

On the pole above the fortress gate, the new British flag—new enough at least, what with the British Parliament having added the cross of St. Patrick of Ireland some four years past—hung like a limp, sun-bleached shroud. The outpost's chief agent lived at the fortress, occupied it with his officers as though it were a grand English castle and he the overlord of the land.

Indeed, this overlord could be proud of his cleared patch in the unrelenting jungle, his land of misery and scourge. For trade in these parts wasn't in oats, wheat or sugar beets.

At Bance, the staple commerce was slaves.

The young man's lips curled with soul-searing disgust. Aye, he'd received the answers he'd come for. Answers he'd heard time and time again at every British port down the African coast.

The very best you want? Then there's only one choice. MacArthur and Sons of London.

Aye, from England to Africa and the Caribbean and beyond, the MacArthur name was synonymous with this trade. It signified power, too. Reprehensible power.

Eyes burning, the young man's gaze shifted to the becalmed ships—and stopped to rest on the largest ship of all.

CHAPTER ONE

The sea. Love her always. Distrust her equally.
—*The Memoirs of Rhys Cavanagh*

The English Channel
October 1816

"For God's sake, what are you waiting for?" Jonathon Lecky roared. "Get over here and grab her, man!" Cleaving to the safety line with one arm, bracing the young woman who'd swallowed too many pints of English Channel with his other, Lecky waited for the rich nob he'd fished from scattered remnants of shipwreck a quarter hour before to realize he bloody needed help to get the lass and himself out of the water and onto the deck. Time was crucial. His swift attempts to purge the water from her airways had failed.

The lash of Lecky's voice roused the other man to action. The blanket that draped the nob's shoulders dropped to the deck as he lurched forward to the sloop's bulwark, knees buckling and hands grappling as the boat rocked in the swell. Clinging to the bulwark with one hand, he leant over the sloop's side and groped for the woman's spencer. Another wave clapped Lecky in the face as the man struggled to grasp hold. Lecky tasted salt and gritty, wet filaments of hair. He spat out both and blinked water from his smarting eyes. "Got her?"

The other man fumbled, then his fist closed around the collar of her spencer, behind her neck. "Yes!"

"Heave!" Grabbing a handful of wet dress where it cinched

below her breasts, Lecky thrust upwards. The roll of the sloop's hull lent aid, lifting the woman partway out of the water as the other man dragged her limp body up the boat's side and over the bulwark. Lecky waited for another break in the swell, then—every muscle in his arms, chest and back slaving—hauled himself hand over fist up the short safety line. He ground his teeth as he levered an elbow over the bulwark, then kicked out with his legs and swung himself up and over the side.

His hands and knees found purchase on the deck as the buoyant, wriggling form of Morgan, his collie, slammed into his chest. "Down. There's a girl." He ruffled her neck as he pushed her away, sliding on his knees for expediency's sake the short distance to where the nob had laid the woman out, skirts tangled around her.

The nob was sitting helpless, staring. His whitened fingers dug like the grappling hooks of a Port Royal pirate into the deck.

"Do you know this woman?" Lecky forced his way past. There was limited room left on the aft deck with two men, a prone woman, and a dog onboard.

For a split second, the nob looked shocked to have been addressed thusly. "I . . . I don't know."

"Your name?" Lecky demanded.

"Rossum. The Marquess of Rossum."

Lecky scraped away strands of hair sticking to the woman's mouth and nose, then tipped back her head. Prying her jaw open, he made sure she wasn't about to choke on her tongue. "I don't give a blasted damn if you're a marquess or a master gunner. Not very good in a crisis, are you?"

From the way the nob reared back, one would think the man had never received a flaying before. "The ship I was aboard just sank!"

"That was my point. What's yours?" Lecky glanced at the man crouched beside him, then lowered his head and breathed into the woman's mouth.

The Marquess clenched his fists against his thighs. "What—" he began.

"I would move back if I were you," Lecky warned, between breaths.

He felt the woman's throat constrict and hastily pulled away. Shifting position to get his hands beneath her right shoulder and knee, he rolled her onto her side as she started to gag. Then, holding the lass's sides, he helped lift her weight up on her elbow as her body convulsed and she began to retch.

She gagged again and vomited on the deck. Regurgitated seawater splattered the knees of the Marquess's already sodden breeches. Lecky had given the nob fair warning. Face drawn, the Marquess's hands splayed on the deck as he shuffled back too late. Lecky continued to hold the lass's sides as she swam back to consciousness, her body gulping in air with great, shivery, desperate gulps that, as the seconds passed, gradually grew less wrenching.

With each of those gulps, a modicum of Lecky's firmly harnessed tension eased. *That's it, lass. Breathe. That's it.*

Cupping her narrow ribs, he felt her trembling begin, her body's unconscious realization of just how close she had come to death.

"I'm sorry," she managed, as though she could somehow have prevented her plight.

Her voice, though roughened, was distinctly feminine, a mix of upper class and something softer, more accented.

Across from Lecky, the Marquess went still.

She raised her head a notch, blearily focusing on Rossum's knees. Slowly, she craned her neck to look up at the Marquess. Loose strands of hair from her bun plastered her pale cheeks and throat.

"I'm sorry," she repeated. Then, body slackening as though her anchor had been cut, she passed out in Lecky's arms.

The Marquess drew in a sharp breath. "Is she . . . has she . . . ?"

"She's unconscious again but breathing at least." Lecky lowered the woman's body back to the deck, out of the way of the watery vomit that dribbled across the planks with each roll of the swell.

"My God." Distress imbued the Marquess's tone. "Will she be all right?"

"Should know in a few hours. The near-drowned sometimes still die, even after you get them breathing again." Lecky crouched back on one heel, resting one fist against the deck for balance. In the shadow cast across the Marquess's face by the boom, Lecky saw the man's aristocratic features contort.

The nob levered himself up, groping for—then achieving—a hold on the cabin behind him. "You've witnessed this?"

"More times than I like to count."

The Marquess sucked in another breath. "What can I do?"

The chill in the air had increased sharply since the sun began to dip. Amid the wet, jumbled yards of gown, the lass was a shivering heap. Lecky clambered to his feet. "Keep an eye on her breathing."

"Keep an eye on . . . ." Lecky's suggestion seemed to alarm the man. He twisted wildly in the direction of Lecky's receding steps, his tone urgent. "Wait! Where are you going?"

"Just watch her!"

A few steps conveyed Lecky to the sloop's hatch. He swung down the companionway into the cabin. Quickly considering his options, he dug three fresh shirts and three pairs of trousers from an overhead locker and several blankets from another. He tossed the lot on his bunk. Then, after dragging his wet shirt over his head, he kicked off his trousers and donned a dry set of clothes. After pulling on his boots and coat, which he'd thrown down the companionway earlier when he espied Rossum off the port side, he returned to the sloop's aft deck.

Rossum had inched closer to the woman. His head was lowered over her chest, one hand placed on her ribcage. Lecky might have given the man credit for listening to the lass's breath but for the explorative passage of his thumb and fingers along the band of her short spencer. The buttons of the jacket had come undone sometime during her struggle and wet cambric sculpted every curve—including the tight, dark, budded circles of her nipples peaking above her stays.

The Marquess's head jerked upright at Lecky's approach.

Oh, for Christ's sake. One would expect a marquess to have seen his fare share of bosom. "Don't tell me you're one of those," Lecky said, pushing by the man.

"One of what? You asked that I monitor her breathing."

Lecky slung the woman's arm over his shoulder and scooped her up. Her head lolled against his neck, her skin wet and chilled. He avoided the boom of the mainsail as he maneuvered past the

Marquess. "Indeed, I said watch her breathing. Not salivate on her tits."

"What? No!" The Marquess's response was quick, harsh. "Mr. . . ." He flailed for a name. "Sir, you mistake me."

A smile breached Lecky's lips as he reached the hatch, a smile the Marquess didn't need to see, given the skepticism in Lecky's voice. "Of course." Lecky braced his weight as the boat's deck pitched with the swell.

Rossum half-shuffled, half-crawled his way closer. "The girl . . . she's young, isn't she? And quite lovely?"

For the love of.... Of all the topics the man could be concerned with. "What the lass 'is' is soaked through. God above." Lecky waited for the Marquess to arrive at the hatch. "I know you lords are partial to your Wordsworth and Byron, but save your odes to pouting peach lips and soft swelling breasts till later, hmm?" Lecky angled the woman toward him. "Hold her, then hand her down to me."

The Marquess made no move to help. Instead, his fingers fumbled for the side of the cabin. Finding the grab rail, he levered himself up, once again in a kneeling position.

By the angry press of the nob's lips, the deep pucker of his brow, Lecky anticipated the clash of his eyes, the deep glitter of fury. But as the Marquess lifted his chin, jaw clenched and determined, his gaze failed to align with Lecky's.

The Marquess's gaze passed *through* him.

Lecky went still.

Well, well, Jonathon. That just taught you.

The Marquess's voice had an edge, until-now unseen mettle. "You have my gratitude for your aid. But don't think I will tolerate your contempt. I won't abide it again. Do we understand each other?" A vein pulsed in his jaw.

Lecky took a moment to appraise the man—or rather, reappraise the man. He'd been so intent on the lass's rescue, he'd failed to properly assess the cold yet conscious man he'd dragged aboard.

Amateur, Jonathon. Very amateur.

Uncharacteristically amateur in fact.

By the gods; the man he'd rescued was blind.

Blind but capable. Uncowed, albeit insulted. And rightfully so.

Watch her breathing. The gods be damned. Lecky staved off a rueful laugh. It was no wonder the nob had been alarmed.

The lass meanwhile was a mass of shivers in Lecky's arms.

"You're right; I did mistake you." Lecky spoke into the silence. "Now I'd have your help, if you'll give it."

There was a pause. Then, with a minuscule—yet discernible—relaxation of tension in the Marquess's shoulders, the man across from Lecky said, "Yes. Tell me how."

"Hold her."

A large man, Rossum easily took the lass's weight, clasping her in his arms when her body touched his chest. Lecky could see too that, unless instruction was given, nothing short of a twenty-foot wave would rip the woman from the Marquess's hold. Even then, Lecky doubted the Marquess would let her go. The man's expression—now he had care of her—was almost fearful.

Who had he been traveling with?

Almost certainly, they were dead.

Morgan bounded down the companionway ahead of Lecky. Lecky clambered halfway down, then turned to retrieve the woman from Rossum. "I've hold of her. I'll take her again now."

The Marquess allowed the lass to slide into Lecky's arms.

He deposited her on his bunk. Morgan, sitting on her hindquarters and leaning her body against the wooden drawers and paneling below the bunk, took up watch. Quickly, efficiently, Lecky began tugging the woman's arms from the wet, clinging spencer. He cast a glance over his shoulder at the Marquess, whose body blocked the little remaining light coming through the hatch. The expression the man wore was uncertain.

"The hatch is eighteen inches wide," Lecky said. "The companionway comprises six narrow steps to the deck, with grab rails on either side. Once you reach the deck, there are bunks on either side, with drawers built into their bases and lockers overhead. Beyond the bunks, there is a small galley and a table that converts to another bunk. Watch out for the stacked crates on your left and right. Space is tight, but there's enough room for you to descend and change out of your wet clothes. I have a fresh set waiting for you."

"Thank you."

"No thanks are necessary." Lecky dragged the lass's spencer loose and dropped it on the deck.

Cautiously, the Marquess negotiated the steps. He paused at the bottom of the companionway. "Here," Lecky said, grasping a spare shirt and pair of trousers, and slapping them against the man's chest. "Take these dry clothes."

The Marquess grasped the clothes, but made no other move. "What are you doing?"

Deftly, Lecky raised the lass up, loosened her dress at the back, and began stripping it off her. "Getting her warm," he said.

After a moment's pause, the Marquess said quietly, "She is a lady, isn't she?"

"Why say that?" Lecky tugged the gown past her hips. The shift she wore beneath finished just below her knees. Slender calves came into view.

"Cambric skirts, very fine weave. Lutestring spencer, with ruffles of Belgian lace trim about the wrists and collar."

Lecky's hands briefly stilled. *Ah. Lesson number two. Remember that, Jonathon, next time you judge a man's straying hands.*

"And she has a filigree comb caught in her hair," the Marquess continued. "I . . . I felt a cluster of pearls."

The Marquess was right. For a split second, Lecky's gaze skidded to a stop. Well, now.

There was a comb tangled up in the lass's half-destroyed bird's nest of wet braids and bun. And it did feature a cluster of pearls.

Five round, perfect Tahitian black pearls. The most prized kind of all.

She was lucky they'd got stuck in her hair and weren't consigned to the deep.

With a grimace, he tossed her wet gown on the pile with the spencer, flicked several long, wet strands of hair back from his own eyes, and straightened.

He turned his gaze to the Marquess. The man before him was clean-shaven, manicured, and well-tailored—if one ignored the dunking he'd got in the Channel. Aye. The Marquess was either as rich as an old London banker up to his balls in the slave trade or, like many of his ilk, busy staving off creditors to maintain what he thought amounted to wealth. Sight or no, the man had the type of face and strapping build attractive to the ladies. In every likelihood, he excelled at the piano, housed the next Derby winner in his stables, and owned a dozen renowned pieces of art in addition to a God-awful, gloomy string of dead ancestors' portraits.

When it came to knowing where one descended from, Lecky had always thought blindness would be bliss.

He put the Marquess around seven or eight and twenty. One year, perhaps two years, younger than Lecky himself.

"Aye. She's a lady." Lecky turned to unlace the lass's stays.

"And you?" The Marquess's voice came low, weighted by wariness. "What are you?"

What was *he*? A smile curved Lecky's lips as he dug his fingers between the lass's laces, quickly working the soaked spiral lacing loose. "Well, for one," he said, "I've no qualm about admitting when I'm wrong. Marquess, my condescension toward you was undeserved. Beyond that, I could invite you to feel my chest, to see what you might learn. However, I can tell you already, you won't find it so fine."

He glanced over his shoulder and saw one end of the Marquess's lips quirk. The man was capable of humor, at least. Still, as Lecky watched, the quirk faded, and his expression grew perturbed as his gaze turned questioningly—but unseeingly—toward the bunk.

Lecky sobered. Blind mayhap, but the Marquess clearly sensed much. "When it comes to shipwreck decorum," he said, turning back to his task, "I can assure you of this. My sea-roughened hands are changing her clothes, not hiking up her skirts, unbuckling my breeches, and impeding her marriage prospects." The lass's laces came free. Lecky slid the shoulder straps down her arms. Stays joined cambric gown in the sodden pile on the deck. "Stop worrying about the lass and get changed." Lecky extended his arm. "Here's another blanket to dry yourself." The first one he'd supplied lay above-deck, where it had fallen when the Marquess helped drag the lass aboard.

At his blunt words, a little of the English Channel chill appeared to have gotten the better of his guest, freezing—nay, hardening—the Marquess's expression from inside out. "Thank you." The Marquess took the blanket under one arm, then, with fingers fumbling at first, groped along the overhead lockers and moved further into the cabin.

Lecky turned back to his charge. The lass's stockings came off next, then shift, then drawers. She'd lost her shoes in the sea. The only sound was the slap of the swell against the hull as Lecky brusquely dried her body with a blanket. Multiple bruises of varying sizes and various purplish-blue shades had begun to mottle her skin, particularly around her knees, elbows and hips. Morgan lifted her wet, twitching nose to inspect the woman's hand, splayed palm up over the bunk's side.

"Like her, do you?" Lecky asked.

"Excuse me?" the Marquess said.

"I was speaking to my dog." Lecky ruffled the fur on Morgan's head, then grasped the remaining set of shirt and trousers he'd deposited at the end of the bunk. The garments were far too big for the lass, but better she wake up dressed than naked on a strange boat with two unfamiliar men onboard. With a little neat juggling, he got her pale, bruised, goose-pimpled arms into the shirt, buttoning it down the front, then slid slender legs into the trousers. Her small, arched feet were cold in his hands.

Jiggling open one of the drawers below the bunk, he rummaged for a pair of woolen socks. Why any man preferred stockings, he didn't know. His search ended empty-handed. He looked at Morgan, then about the cabin.

One limp sock peeked out from between several wooden crates.

"Do that while I was ashore last night, eh?" he said gravely. "I thought we spoke about that."

With mouth slightly opened in protest, the collie put her ears down and thumped her tail on the deck.

Casting his dog a skeptical look, Lecky shook several blankets out over the woman. Then, leaning over her, he carefully untangled the pearl-adorned comb from her hair. Morgan's gaze tracked him. He gave a jerk of his head toward the bunk. "Up you get. Since you've slobbered on my socks, you'll have to stay here and warm her feet."

The lass's shivering would still take a little time to subside, but the heat of the collie's body would help.

Morgan immediately leapt up to settle beside the lass.

Lecky looked at the Marquess. The man was struggling out of his wet attire and into Lecky's dry clothes as he tried to brace against the swell. His face was grim, his jaw clenched. But it was not an expression of frustration. No—the Marquess's face showed pain. The tight-reined grimness of grief. Though he'd said nothing, Lecky knew there was every chance the man's valet had died aboard the wreck. His valet—at the least.

Lecky reached up to remove a ship's candle lantern and flint from an overhead locker as the Marquess drew Lecky's shirt down over his head. Lecky balanced the lantern on a companionway step as he slid open the lantern's back door and lit the candle. "Once you're done dressing, there's a small space at the table. Or you might prefer to stretch out on the deck."

"Thank you," the Marquess said again. "Wait—are you taking us to shore?"

Lecky moved further into the cabin to string the lantern up. "Thought I'd ransom you. Seeing as you're now conveniently aboard."

"What?" The Marquess's dark blond brows snapped together. He grasped the edge of the small table.

Lecky gave a snort. "It was a joke, Marquess. People aren't my trade. Now, I've hung a candle lantern on the beam above the table, in case the lass awakes. The barrel on the table contains water; there's a mug there, too. Help yourself. Oh, and here." He set the pearl comb down on the table and slid it forward to lightly bump the Marquess's fingers. The man's hand jerked, then his fingers closed over—feeling, recognizing—the comb with its telling cluster of pearls.

Whoever the lass was, she was valuable.

"Don't worry. You'll get to land soon enough." Lecky pulled back. "But first, we're going to run transects to see if any more ill-fated souls from your ship survived."

RACHEL CAVANAGH OPENED HER EYES to darkness. Water sloshed nearby, very close nearby. She could hear its wash on the other side of timber. Her body—no—the padded surface on which she lay, pitched beneath her. She held her breath—heave, then fall. The pattern became regular, distinct. She was on a boat, she realized. A boat at sea. A boat under sail, carving through swell.

Intuitively she knew it was not a large boat.

She swallowed. She lay beneath heaped blankets. Her throat was parched and sticky and dry. Lord, to swallow burned. Burned in a coarse, inflamed way that felt as though the inside of her throat had been roughed by the teeth of a wood file. To swallow was not a good idea.

The darkness wasn't absolute, but light was scant. Disoriented, she fought to free an arm from the cocoon of blankets, then lifted a hand to rub her eyes as they slowly adjusted. Pale, luminous, her sleeve billowed in front of her. The wide cuff slid down over her wrist. She froze—staring. It was a shirt sleeve. She was wearing a man's shirt.

The thought was cut off as a warm, solid lump moved against her legs. The boat dipped, and her heart pitched painfully against her chest. *What was it?* Stifling her dread, she pressed experimentally with her leg. First gently, then harder. The lump made a disgruntled, huffing sound, then unfurled and flopped out alongside her. Oh God, it was an animal. *A dog*, she realized, by the slight, yet unmistakable scent of damp fur that suffused the air.

Whose boat was she on?

She pushed up on an elbow. Pain partially smothered the anxious sob that sprang from her throat as her eyes registered the sight of the blankets. Albeit warm, the cloth was like nothing she had seen before, with panels of dark, woven, geometric patterns that stood out in contrast to an ivory background. Or what she gauged was ivory in the low light.

Wood creaked loudly at the other end of the cabin as though someone, out of sight, had come to their feet. Instinctively, she sucked in a breath. What little moisture remained in her throat dried as her every muscle tensed. Long seconds passed. She heard the rough squeak of a hinge, then an amber glow spread out to illume the dark wooden planks of the ceiling and graze the tight confines of the bunk. Stowage lockers hung above her head, and a companionway and half-opened hatch lay to her side. The cabin couldn't have space for much more than a couple of bunks, a table and a small galley. That was as much as she could register before footsteps lurched her way, the lantern swung directly in front of her, and bright halos swam in her vision.

She recoiled. Her hand clenched the blankets as a dark shape loomed above her. She blinked as the halos conjoined, then faded, and looked up into a face so classically handsome it could be sculpted and entitled Apollo.

A lock of rich, honey-blond hair rested against his temple. He stared down at her. Something about him seemed vaguely familiar. It was almost as though she should know who he was. "Please, do not fear," he said, then twisted away to present her with the clean-shaven underside of his jaw. He called out through the half-opened hatch, "She's awake!"

He had a powerful neck. Precisely the sort of neck that belonged on a well-built man. Her younger sister, Faith, would be agog. Aunt Ariene on the other hand—

Oh, God. Her lungs constricted. She could barely breathe. Where was Ariene?

Lord, she was still having difficulty adjusting to the light as the man's head swung back her way.

"Please," he said, "you mustn't be alarmed. You're safe."

Safe? Alarmed? How could she not be alarmed? Where was she? She registered his tone—crisp, aristocratic. To add to her confusion, his elegant hand strayed hesitantly toward the woven blankets. At the last moment he pulled back, as though encountering an invisible wall of etiquette.

Still, she could just make out his slight, somewhat bashful smile. Somehow, it seemed incongruent with the rest of his too-handsome features. The dog lying by Rachel's legs—a Welsh collie, with a black mask and saddle, and white legs and muzzle—sat up on its elbows and raised a back leg to scratch behind its ear.

At first, the animal's move seemed to surprise him. Then, with a choked-off chuckle, he reached out to stroke the collie's coat.

"You are a faithful friend, aren't you?" he said. "Helping to keep the lady warm."

Rachel stared at him, trying to make sense of the situation. She still couldn't place him.

Her gaze jerked upward at the sound of footsteps crossing the deck above. The dog by Rachel's legs inched forward along the bunk on its forelegs and began to thump its tail.

"Our host," Apollo supplied, attracting her quick, squinting look. "He's coarse, but not treacherous."

'Our' host, he'd said? Was that to say Apollo was a guest onboard, too?

Again, her gaze shot upward as their 'host' slid the hatch fully open. Silhouetted in the moonlight, he swung down the companionway in a movement of easy familiarity. Boots came first, then a dark broadcloth coat over white shirt and dun trousers.

With one hand still gripping the hatch, he leant forward, braced his opposite forearm on the stowage lockers above the bunk, and rested his forehead against his arm.

Unbound, chin-length dark golden brown hair, tangled by wind and the spray of waves, fell forward around his cheeks and jaw. Affixed to several different strands of hair, three—no, four—small silver beads glinted at varying heights around his cheekbones.

This time her stomach pitched—but she couldn't attribute it all to the boat. He was coarse. Rough. By appearance, strong. But his was a fierce, elemental kind of strength—palpable, physical, born of earth and wind and sea. The strength of a man who knew nature.

He'd not shaved—at least not for a few days. Thick brows ridged eyes she could tell were both sharp and quick to take measure. Whether they were blue or gray, she couldn't tell in the light. Yet the lines at their corners implied a mouth that curved often. That laughed a lot.

The lantern shone blindingly in her eyes again, and she raised her hand to shield her eyes from its glare.

His lips, as she suspected, were quick to curve. "Rossum dazzling you?"

"Rossum . . . ?" Her voice was a croak that hurt like the devil. She didn't have a clue what he was talking about.

"Rossum." With forearm still braced against the overhead lockers, he indicated Apollo by pointing one finger. "Beside you. Helping to care for you."

"What . . . ?" She remembered the white shirt.

This man's shirt. It had to be—the other man too was a guest. Oh, Lord.

One of these men had undressed her. The blond Apollo—or him?

"The Marquess will explain. Welcome aboard, my lady." He turned to ascend through the hatch.

The Marquess? What—

"No! Wait. I'm not . . . that is, it's Miss." The words abraded her throat as her hoarse voice emerged. It made him pause, one boot raised on the companionway steps. "Please, where is my aunt, that is, Miss Cavanagh? We were onboard—"

The memory imploded on her, splintering with the force of tall masts torn asunder, crashing inward from the outer regions of her consciousness. Her hands began to tremble. Oh, God. The brig she had been traveling on had hit a shoal and sunk. The debris in the water . . . . She had clung on. Then she was drowning. And after that . . . . She didn't remember after that.

These men . . . this man . . . had plucked her out? Somehow revived her? But what—

Terror seized her, just as it had done in the water. She was clenched in its paralyzing hand, forced to watch the last of the ship break up against the shoal. Forced to hear the keen of the *Castalia's* timbers, the snap of spars, the thwack of rigging as it crashed into the water.

No, please, they couldn't be dead! Not Ariene, her father's younger sister, only fourteen years older than Rachel herself. Not Rachel's maid Mary—precious, bubbling Mary—promised to marry her sweetheart at Christmas.

Lord, she had swallowed more than just sea. Tentacles of dread climbed up her throat to choke her. "Oh, God! Ariene! And Mary!"

"There were three in your party?" The man, Rossum, asked. She still couldn't place him.

"Three?" Her thoughts were so scattered, it took her a moment to focus on what he'd said. "Yes."

He had used past tense. There were three in your party. She wasn't ready for past tense.

Oh, God. What if they had died? What if they were *dead*?

Their host met Rachel's gaze as he stepped away from the companionway. His eyes were regardful, but his expression was otherwise unruffled by her emotional display. "We are still in the area, searching for survivors, Miss . . . ?"

Still searching. She grasped those words as though they were oars, bobbing on the water's surface and able to keep her afloat. If she had survived, if the other man, Rossum, had been saved too, perhaps—

It was October. The Channel was so cold.

Hers was a maritime family. She knew well the risks of the sea.

"Cavanagh." She again found her voice. "I am also Miss Cavanagh. My aunt never married. Please, how many hours have passed since . . . since . . . ?"

"The ship went down?" her host replied. "Four, perhaps five. I came upon you—half an hour?—after the accident. Does that sound right, Marquess?" He glanced at Rossum. The other man nodded. "It's dark now," he said, "but we're still finding wreckage. There is still reason to hope."

As though to concur, the collie inched forward to snuffle Rachel's hand with its wet nose.

The small canine gesture of condolence loosed another knot of emotion. "Sir, your crew—"

"Just myself."

Her eyes widened. Just him? But he would be manning the tiller as well. "Is there no one else on deck to help search? I have to help," she said. "I have to look."

"Miss Cavanagh," Apollo—Rossum—said, "you very nearly drowned. You mustn't feel compelled to go anywhere."

His voice was gentle. She understood he spoke from concern. Yet at that moment, there was no question. It didn't matter how exhausted she felt or that she had almost drowned. It only mattered that others might still need help, and the more able to search the better.

She had to search.

"Sir, were members of your family or friends aboard that ship?"

A muscle leapt in the man's jaw and immediately she regretted the question.

He again turned his head aside. "My valet was aboard. He . . . he is gone."

There was grief in his words. And anguish. Both pain and regret were writ on his face.

"I am sorry," she said.

Their host said nothing as he watched the exchange.

These men, she sensed, would cast her in the role of dainty, fragile miss. She couldn't allow that to happen.

"Please . . . I didn't see my aunt drown, or Mary, my maid. I can't stay down here. Not when they could still be out there, alone." She looked toward their host. "Is there a safe place on the aft deck? I'd like to help keep watch."

His glance flicked to Rossum, then returned to her. Far down in the depths of that blue-or-gray gaze, she detected a bare speck of mirth. Did he find her insistence amusing, or was it that he understood her need to assert herself?

Her eyes had better adjusted now. Enough to see his coat was dark olive. He didn't wear a neckcloth; just a knotted leather cord strung beneath the deep vee collar of his shirt. Throat to sternum, his tanned, bare skin lay exposed. He reminded her of the type of men who had worked for her grandfather. Men that Rachel's mother, Lady Georgiana, made certain never came anywhere near Rachel or her sisters.

"You're welcome on the aft deck," he said.

She was grateful she wouldn't have to insist. The tight pressure in her lungs eased. "Thank you."

"No need." He drew back from the bunk, again turning to the companionway. "It's cold out. Get bundled up. But don't be surprised if you need to dash for the chamber pot. The seawater in your guts will want to go through you."

Heat again stung her cheeks. He was blunt. Rossum's grimace suggested the other man found their host's warning crude. Meanwhile, the collie gazed up at her with its intelligent brown eyes, no doubt well versed in what drinking too much seawater was like.

"Sir," Rachel said. "I couldn't help but notice you were remiss when you said you had no crew."

Her words stopped him dead on the steps. His head, with all

that unkempt, dark golden brown hair, turned in profile.

"Your first mate," she continued, "the one warming my feet. Does he—or she—have a name?"

She glimpsed his grin as it formed, a sudden, white slash across his strong, unshaven face. Then he looked over his shoulder, his eyes glancing over her; and the wide, sweeping stroke of that look struck all the way to her stomach.

"She, Miss Cavanagh," he said. "The lady's name is Morgan, and she's honored you asked."

With a chuckle he turned, and—like a sword being pulled from her stomach—the struck feeling was gone. Except, that was, for the breathless shock of it.

"And the name of the man we must thank for taking us aboard?" she managed.

To her surprise, Rossum stilled also, then tilted his head in the direction of their host.

The man in question grasped the hatch above. His lips twitched. "Thank Morgan. She saw you."

The devil was surely teasing her. She persisted. "I will. Sincerely. But perhaps, you will share your name?"

"Good Lord." This time, he glanced toward Rossum. "She's barely been conscious five minutes. Marquess, has she been this demanding with you?"

As Rachel opened her mouth to protest, she realized she should have been ready this time. She should have braced herself for that devastating grin.

"Lecky," he said. "My name, Miss Cavanagh, is Jonathon Lecky."

CHAPTER TWO

The sea became accustomed to her quota from me.
—*The Memoirs of Rhys Cavanagh*

JONATHON LECKY'S BOAT WAS NOT a large one, Rachel confirmed, as she climbed through the hatch onto the deck. In fact, it could hardly be compared to the ships her father—and before that her grandfather—had sailed. Her father's final post before his death had been HMS *Theseus*, a seventy-four gun, third-rate ship of the line; her grandfather's vessel, the *Artful*, a sixteen gun, one hundred and ten foot brig. In size, Jonathon Lecky's boat was more akin to a harbor pilot's cutter.

A ship's candle lantern, secured to the backstay, threw light from the tiller over the small aft deck toward the hatch. The aft deck was roughly ten feet by ten feet, although the width tapered at the stern. A sunken well in the center of the deck provided seating and a place to man the tiller, with the deck protected on each side by one-foot-high bulwarks.

"Mind the boom." Seated at the tiller, Jonathon Lecky lifted a hand to hold the foot of the sail as Rachel, garbed in loose-fitting shirt and trousers and a blanket about her shoulders, skirted beneath.

She settled by the port-side bulwark. She'd had to roll the trouser cuffs up six inches to keep from tripping and, without stays, felt as self-conscious in the shirt as she might have done wearing only a shift. Doubly grateful for the thick blanket, she clutched the bulwark, tucked her bare feet up beneath her on the bench for warmth, and craned her neck to view the unfurled sails that stretched up and up, large silver fins in the night.

The vessel was Bermuda-rigged—a sloop—with a large triangular mainsail set aft of the mast and a single jib to the fore. Thirty feet, Rachel estimated, from transom to bow, though perhaps a couple of feet more overall, if the boat featured a bowsprit.

It was not a dark night. The bright harvest moon hung low, reflecting silver on the swell and illuming wisps of cirrus cloud. The ship's candle lantern served as a beacon to potential survivors, rather than necessary lighting for those aboard.

Years ago in Wales, Rachel, her two brothers, her grandfather, and Ariene had walked up Snowdon by the light of a harvest moon. Without Ariene at her side, the memory bit raw and painful. Swiftly, Rachel pushed the thought away.

Hope. She had to hope.

The blond man, Rossum, had followed her onto the deck.

"Marquess, take the starboard rail," Jonathon Lecky instructed.

This time, the boat captain's words triggered recognition that had not come before. Oh God, of course. *The Marquess of Rossum.* She had seen him at a distance, across crowded ballrooms. She'd read of him too. His achievements were often remarked upon, and newspapers printed excerpts of his speeches in the House of Lords.

He was known throughout Britain.

Because the Marquess of Rossum was blind.

Belowdecks, she hadn't noticed. When she woke in the cabin, she'd been confused. Suddenly his movements, his cautious feeling of his way across the deck, took on new significance. She became very aware of her surroundings; the sea spray on her face, the pitch and bob of the sloop's small deck, the snap of the breeze in the sails, the creak of the deck.

When the brig started to go down—

She could not imagine for him what it would have been like.

The cry of the *Castalia's* crew member still echoed in her mind. *Shoal off the starboard bow!*

"Go on, enjoy the sea breeze," Ariene had encouraged Rachel hours earlier, as she flopped down on the passenger cabin bunk. Two weeks of balls, soirees, and dinners with Ariene's best friend and her Belgian husband in Brussels had taken their toll. "I intend to sleep my way to England."

Still, as Rachel turned to leave the cabin, it had come as a surprise when Ariene had rolled onto her side, propped her head in her hand, and said, "Rachel, I have been thinking. I know I promised to accompany you to Alexandria to visit James next August, when you turn one and twenty. I also said I would help to deflect your mother's marriage schemes again this season. But I think... when we return to London... I would like to go to America. Just for a few months." Quite aware of how momentous this admission was, Ariene offered a tentative smile. Rachel had dared not speak as she waited for her aunt to finish.

"Rachel," Ariene said, "I think... finally... I want to meet my mother."

Ariene wasn't the sort to welcome exclamations or gushing. And, in this, Rachel's aunt was more than a little vulnerable. For five years, she had refused to respond to the letters that arrived from New York from the woman who had chosen to give up her newborn, illegitimate daughter to return to her American husband and four older children.

Now, though, the need for understanding had begun to outweigh old hurts. Rachel had leant back against the bulkhead and smiled. "I think you should go to New York."

"I will be back well before August," Ariene assured. "I will just miss part of the season. I would love for you to come to New York with me—"

But they both knew Lady Georgiana would never permit Rachel to miss the London season. Of course, once Rachel turned one and twenty, Lady Georgiana would no longer hold sway. Then, Rachel could travel to Alexandria, to see her father's final resting place. She could visit all the places—in Egypt and Greece and the Levant—that she had read about and that her grandfather had spoken about. Places to which Ariene had promised to accompany her.

"You must go to New York," Rachel said again.

As she made her way to the upper deck, her heart had filled with lightness, a sense of well-being. She could manage her mother, if it meant that Ariene would finally meet hers. It was Ariene's mother Rachel had been musing about when the sudden, jarring impact of the ship splintering against the shoal had thrown Rachel to the deck. At that point, panic erupted. As she staggered back to her feet, it quickly became apparent that, while the sailors on the Cavanaghs' own ships were trained for such an event, the same could not be said of the sailors on this vessel. On the *Castalia*, 'emergency' meant every man for himself.

And Ariene and Mary were below.

She had tried to fight her way down from the forecastle as the brig began to list. She'd slipped, fallen, pulled herself up, slipped, fallen again. How many times she couldn't hazard a guess. Yet her body could still feel every bruising fall and the fierce fear it drove up through her. Standing was impossible as the deck pitched—twenty, thirty degrees, while around her, the crew scrambled for holds, grabbing halyards, fife rails... anything still nailed down, still affixed. Waves battered the hull, washed over the deck, great forceful hands lunging, grasping, terrifying the petrified crew. Oh, those hands hadn't been choosy. It mattered not whether each powerful swat toppled men directly into the water or simply dislodged their grip to drag them away in the wash as their frightened cries crescendoed—then were smothered.

Such was the wave that took her overboard.

Rachel sucked in a deep, calming breath, battering the memories back.

Now, vast and empty, the expanse of swell stretched out in the moonlight, immutable as only nature could be when it chose to claim life. None aboard attempted to speak. In the tacit sea of silence, each piloted private, inner thoughts. Thoughts Rachel— perhaps the Marquess too—needed to steer alone.

The silence of their host wasn't quite the same. No, she thought, as she turned his way. Holding the tiller with one hand, opposite elbow resting on his raised knee, Jonathon Lecky's silence was another kind, deliberately unobtrusive.

Morgan, his collie, lay companionably at his side. They looked comfortable together, their pose likely a familiar one. Still, Rachel had spent enough time on boats to sense the expert hand at the tiller, the tiny adjustments to heading that kept the sails between luff and stall, that allowed them to pass over the edge of the swell without slowing.

Feeling her gaze upon him, the boat captain looked her way.

THE LASS'S DARK EYES REGARDED Lecky from across the deck.

She's quite lovely, isn't she? Rossum had asked.

Aye, Lecky had to acknowledge Miss Cavanagh was the sort to turn heads all right. All coffee-brown gaze beneath coffee-brown brows that contrasted with hair the color of butterscotch. She was unruly sea, not heaven's ether. And her eyes were the kind to demand much from a man without her ever speaking a word.

"Your vessel is fast to windward, Mr. Lecky," she said. "How many feet is she?"

Well now, that was unexpected. Plenty of folk—men and women alike—couldn't have told him the difference between windward, leeward and wind shear. The Marquess, clutching the starboard rail, had pricked his ears. "Thirty feet overall, four and twenty at the waterline," Lecky replied. "You know something of sailing?"

"I've picked up some." She allowed the hand she had been using to hold back her hair to fall. Fleetingly, her lips curved as she looked back to the swell. "Sailing has been a popular pursuit of the men of my family."

Cavanagh was an Irish name, yet the accent she spoke with was Welsh.

Cavanagh.

Tahitian black pearls.

Good Lord. *Rhys* Cavanagh.

"You're a Welsh Cavanagh, from Cardiff."

She glanced at him again. "You know my family?"

Was she trying to make him laugh? The question was not who *knew* her family, but who did *not*? Certainly none of the southern England and Wales' sailing fraternity. Lecky felt one end of his mouth creep up. "'Plunder for crew, plunder for crown. She'll be an *Artful* day, indeed, when a Cavanagh ship bears down.'"

The canny flash in the lass's dark eyes showed perfect comprehension.

Sailing had been a popular pursuit of the men of her family?

Lecky could hardly contest it. He might have a marquess on board, but among the men Lecky knew, a descendant—even a female one—of licensed pirating royalty was a far more impressive coup. From Southampton to Swansea, Scarfskerry to the Isles of Skilly, the name Captain Rhys Cavanagh held a certain . . . how might one say it? . . . *notoriety.*

The Marquess had turned, a slight crease between his brows. "You're related to Captain Rhys Cavanagh, the privateer?" he interposed.

The captain of the *Artful* had made himself and his crew a monumental fortune under the authority of his letter of marque, capturing an incredible one hundred and one foreign ships.

He had gone on to live the remainder of his life—for Lecky had heard Cavanagh had passed on—at a luxurious estate overlooking the Glamorgan coast.

Of course, privateering didn't have quite the same respectability it had a century ago. Not since the esteemed Lord Nelson made his disapproval of the practice known. For all his riches, Rhys Cavanagh had never succeeded in subduing society's tongues as he had American merchant ships with his open gun ports full of loaded cannon.

Instead, the ornery old devil had published his memoirs—and laughed all the more, as piles upon piles of his critics' pretty gold guineas poured their machine-struck selves through his door.

The lass's gaze diverted from Lecky to the Marquess. "He was my grandfather."

Across from Lecky, the Marquess was still adding branches to the lass's family tree, a tree Lecky could already tell him had plenty of knots and gnarls. Hell, it might well have more knots and gnarls than Lecky's own.

"Your mother is Lady Georgiana Cavanagh, the daughter of the fifth Earl of Whittlesey?" the Marquess asked.

Those velvety eyes came back to Lecky, eyes he now saw shone with a good measure of her grandfather's cleverness. One coffee-brown brow arched. The corner of her mouth lifted, mirroring his. Dryly, she quipped, "'No one can whittle the whiskey like Whittlesey.'"

A thread of warmth wove through him. He laughed. The lass

had a sense of humor. Her mother's father was near as well known as her father's. Everyone knew the last Earl of Whittlesey had died a debt-ridden drunk. The lass's wordplay had been tripping drinkers' tongues all across England for years.

"Yes." She addressed her comment, and her attention, back to the Marquess. "My mother is Lady Georgiana. And both sides of my family have a penchant for attracting verse."

Devilish humor, Lecky decided, as with hand on tiller he corrected their heading.

Rumor had it Whittlesey's daughter had married Rhys Cavanagh's son for his money. But then, to be fair, the same would have been said of any woman, given the extent of the Cavanagh coffers.

Cavanagh had written about his son, James, in his memoirs. Like his father, James Cavanagh had gone to sea. First on his father's ship, then as a Royal Navy officer. Because like his father, James Cavanagh had been proud. There had been a shipping empire lying in wait for him, but first he would walk on his own, outside his father's enlarged shadow.

He had been killed in Egypt, together with twenty-seven of his comrades and his captain, in a chance artillery explosion as their ship was preparing to sail. Cavanagh had written of his son with pride—and with love and loss too, the depth of a father's pain, when his son had died.

It was Rhys Cavanagh's brutal, searing honesty in retelling both weighty and ridiculous elements of his life that made his memoirs so popular. Few private libraries lacked a copy.

Besides his son, Rhys Cavanagh had had one other child—an illegitimate daughter to an American woman. *The lass's aunt.* The woman the lass feared for now. Lecky's stomach turned over. Damn, but so far as stories of seafaring dynasties went, this was hardly one a man wanted part of. Aye, he'd found two survivors. But odds weren't good for a happier ending.

The sea cared naught for authority or entitlement. She didn't care how many years service one had given, how many miles sailed, how many victories attained. Nor did she care about the reserves a man held within himself, although she could all too quickly expose those a man was missing.

THE LAST LIGHT OF DUSK

No, the sea rolled on, every one of her thousand moods inscribed with its own eons-old permanence, her own unfathomable concerns. One did one's best to read her, know her, fit with her, and—when necessary—pit oneself against her. But never did she care whether one rose to the challenge or not.

One didn't go to sea to challenge her. One went to sea to challenge oneself.

Low surface waves were superimposed on the swell. Reveal and conceal and reveal again; such was their nature. As he'd hoped from the path of the currents, signs of wreckage, fragments of the ill-fated brig, were growing denser. Miss Cavanagh's expression grew pinched at the sight of the amassing devastation. The Marquess sensed it, perhaps, from their terse silence.

"What do you see?" Rossum asked, both hands clenching the bulwark.

"Debris," Lecky replied.

Cork barrels, fractured timber, mangled rigging, a section of broken mast. Several capsized rowboats too, their bobbing hulls pearly-white.

Lecky brought the sloop's bow up into the wind and dropped the tiller in the comb. He cupped his hands to his mouth. "*Ahoy, Castalia!*"

"*Ariene! Mary!*" Hoarse, pained, Miss Cavanagh's voice joined his, over and again.

Flotsam spread out on either side. No voices were heard. No call came in return.

They drifted near a section of broken mast. Morgan, standing to Lecky's starboard by the bulwark, released a low whine.

I see too, girl. Lecky ran a hand through his hair. *Shit.* How many travelers were like to have been aboard that brig?

"What is it?" The faint note of distress in Rossum's voice brought Miss Cavanagh's attention round. "Is it... one of the crew?"

Lecky's gaze flicked toward Miss Cavanagh before he responded. "A woman. Caught in the mast's rigging."

Miss Cavanagh immediately pushed forward, ducking beneath the boom to cross to the starboard rail. "A woman? Let me...." She leant over the bulwark beside the Marquess. "Oh, God!"

She wrenched back, hand pressed to her mouth, her voice as strangled as a sailor struck through with a sword. "Oh, God."

Rossum, sensing her unsteady move, reached out blindly and grabbed her shoulder before she toppled overboard.

"Who is it, Miss Cavanagh?" Lecky demanded.

"It's . . . it's Ariene."

"You're certain?"

As Rossum tentatively released her shoulder, she looked at Lecky with glazed eyes. "The pelisse she's wearing. It's Ariene."

Lecky pressed his lips together. Normally, he would leave sailors to their watery grave. But Ariene Cavanagh was no sailor. She was Captain Rhys Cavanagh's daughter, and Lecky's boat was only several hours from land. He looked at the Marquess.

"Miss Cavanagh, please return to the port rail while the Marquess and I fetch your aunt aboard."

The Marquess gave a start as the lass blinked in shock. "Y-you would . . . ." She grasped his instructions like a lifeline. "Thank you . . . I can't tell you how much."

Lecky gave a nod. As she slipped from Rossum's side and ducked beneath the boom, Lecky turned to survey the remnants of mast, drifting ten yards off the starboard side.

Her aunt's body was well entangled in the rigging, which was probably the only thing that stopped the woman sinking once water filled her lungs. Fetching her was going to be messy.

Lecky reached for two lines he kept near the stern. He flaked each into neat rows on the deck to ensure there were no snarls in the line, then tied an end of each to separate cleats on the starboard bulwark.

"How can I help?" the Marquess asked.

Lecky could well imagine how helpless the man felt. "I've attached two safety lines to the boat. One is for me, the other is for Miss Cavanagh's aunt. I'll show you where they are in a moment." He shrugged out of his coat, pulled his shirt over his head, then sat down and dragged off his boots and socks. He threw the lot down the hatch. The deck was cold and wet and slick beneath his feet.

He reached for the vest he'd fashioned from hemp rope and cork—clever idea of the French—which hung over the backstay. An icy breeze stole across the deck as he slid his arms through the sleeves. Next, he looped the first safety line over his shoulder, across his chest, and beneath his arm and knotted it securely, then looped and knotted the second, ensuring it was easier to free.

He checked the knots at the cleats again and turned back to the Marquess. "Sit here." He guided the Marquess into position and placed the second line in his hand. "Don't worry about my line; it's located to your left. Haul in Miss Cavanagh's line when I tell you. We don't want to lose her to the deep once she's free of the rigging."

"The specificity of your instructions leads me to think you have worked beside blind men before," the Marquess observed.

"I've led a good few back to their ships after a wild night at the tavern, if that counts."

"Good enough." The Marquess's smile was faint. "You're ready now?"

"Aye." Again, Lecky glanced at the lass. His blanket enveloped her shoulders. Her knuckles were white where she clenched the blanket close to her throat.

The breeze plucked at her hair, whipping thick strands in her eyes. Her lips quivered fleetingly—a specter of acknowledgment one couldn't call a smile—as Lecky met her gaze. Her expression otherwise was drawn, complexion paler than the plumage of an arctic tern.

Lecky swung his legs over the bulwark and for a moment sat perched on the edge of the deck.

Here goes.

He slipped into the dark, moonlit water, releasing a small grunt at the stab of the Channel's thousand small, chill needles. The Gods knew two dips a day was cruel. But there was kindness, perhaps, that they had found Ariene Cavanagh at all.

He swam toward the rigging, keeping a careful eye on both swell and broken mast. The last thing he needed was the damned thing rising up and coming down on his head. He tugged the safety lines to keep them untangled from the other wreckage and lifted canvas sails out of his way.

Ahead, the woman's hair billowed in the darkened swell. She was young, he saw, as he came alongside. Young enough to be mistaken for Miss Cavanagh's elder sister. For while Ariene

Cavanagh's features were sharper, the two women shared the same slightly wild beauty. The water sloshed around Lecky as he paused to pass his wet hand over her face and draw her sightless eyes closed.

It took nearly ten minutes to extract Ariene Cavanagh from the rigging, haul her securely back to the boat, instruct Rossum how to raise her up over the side, and lay her body out on the deck by the starboard bulwark. Lecky was about to haul himself up into the boat again, when the Marquess extended a hand over the bulwark. "Take my arm?"

Surprised, Lecky hesitated at first, then he gripped the Marquess's forearm and accepted the proffered help.

On the deck, silent tears wrought parallel streaks down Miss Cavanagh's cheeks as she held a blanket out for him. It was the one the Marquess had dropped earlier when they'd dragged the lass aboard. As Lecky took it and wrapped it around his shoulders, the lass's gaze went to her aunt, laid out on the starboard decking. Lecky stepped back. Recognizing the opening, the woman he'd rescued slid onto her knees by the tiller. A sob caught in her throat as she clasped one of Ariene Cavanagh's cold hands between her own, then buried her face against the woman's shoulder. Her own shoulders shook as pain loosened within.

Lecky felt her open sea of desolation in his gut. He looked down at Morgan, who looked up in return, her eyes soulful and ears pressed back.

The Marquess had slid backwards from his seat near the cleats to lean against the cabin by the hatch. His head was propped between his hands. Lecky knew by the man's silence that the sound of Miss Cavanagh's anguish reflected the Marquess's own.

Lecky had seen drowning take more folk than he cared to count. Sailors of His Majesty's ships, men of the merchant class, fishermen and far too often their children. For a long time now, he had expected it to be his own fate. Those were simply the odds, the risk he took when he sailed.

Ariene Cavanagh was fortunate she had someone to cry over her.

Yet some pain needed to be expressed alone.

Lecky shifted toward the Marquess. The man sat a little

straighter, detecting Lecky's presence. "Miss Cavanagh needs time to grieve," Lecky said quietly. "And I need dry clothes. Let us go below."

KNEELING, HANDS IN LAP, RACHEL stared unseeingly at her aunt. Within, she felt wretched, gouged, cried out. For a long time after Jonathon Lecky and the Marquess brought Ariene on deck, the hurt that swelled in Rachel's throat, that felt like a solid, crushing mass in her chest, had been intense. Now, a strange hollowness settled over her.

The men had left her alone. Alone that was, except for the quiet presence of the collie, who lay by the tiller, head resting on her paws. She'd not followed her master. She'd stayed at Rachel's side. And at that moment, Rachel was grateful.

For without the canine empathy emanating from the collie's warm brown eyes, the hollowness would be too much.

The creak of the deck brought her attention round.

Jonathon Lecky. Returning.

His long hair, loose about his face, was still damp from the sea. In his hands, he carried a folded up canvas.

She knew what that canvas meant, and the hurt in her throat, in her chest, returned full-blown.

Oh Ariene. This is wrong. So utterly, utterly wrong. Surely this can't be.

"May I?" he asked.

She shifted back toward the tiller, taking refuge beside the collie, out of his way. In the cramped space, the dog's body pressed against her, coat slightly damp from sea spray.

Her host crouched down on one knee. She watched him unfold the canvas sheet. Then his hands stilled, and he looked toward her, in his gaze a question, ascertaining whether she was ready to proceed.

She was not. She never would be. Nevertheless, she returned his look, assent in her eyes, if not on her lips.

Neither spoke as he laid the canvas out alongside Ariene's body and lifted Rachel's aunt onto the middle of the sheet.

Oh Lord, she looked so pale against all that white. So cold. So unbearably cold. Yet dignified in a way only Ariene could look.

Rachel pressed her fist to her mouth as another choking sob rose.

"Here."

Jonathon Lecky pushed a small bag, some six inches wide by twelve inches long, across the deck toward her. His ditty bag. Rachel sat forward, then reached for the bag. With unsteady fingers, she opened it to find sailmaker's needles, a small knife, thimbles, and a ball of twine inside. Grateful to have something to focus on, she selected a needle and threaded it.

Jonathon Lecky leant forward to wrap Ariene's feet in the canvas, then held out his palm. In it, Rachel placed a thimble. He took the needle in the same hand, holding it between his forefinger and thumb. He leant over the canvas.

"Ariene is . . . was . . . I've never been closer to anyone."

He stilled at her words. She couldn't blame him. Even she couldn't say why she spoke them to a man she barely knew. She swallowed, painfully, as his gaze lifted to hers. Held hers in somber exchange. His mouth gave a little twitch of commiseration. Then he looked away, flicking his hair back from his eyes as he bent forward to insert needle into canvas.

She watched for a moment, saying nothing, then rose to her feet to unhook the lantern from the backstay. Settling beside Jonathon Lecky once more, she held the light to deflect the shadows that fell across the area where he worked.

Again his glance flicked up, acknowledging her gesture.

Clearly no stranger to mending sails, he worked quickly, creating a long row of flat stitches that held the sheet together from Ariene's ankles to neck.

Rachel focused on his hands. It was easier to do that than to allow her thoughts to rest on the true purpose of his task. Easier to watch him puncture the thick cloth with needle and, with the long draw of his wrist, pull the twine through.

At some point, watching that movement over and again, she became aware of his scars.

Thick and puckered and lacking pigment, they were old now. Still, the uneven bands that marred the undersides of Jonathon Lecky's wrists stood in stark contrast to his deep olive-tanned skin.

They weren't cuts, but burns.

Her gaze shifted to his face, partially illumed in lantern light. Her grandfather used to say, common or otherwise, every man had a story.

Scarred wrists, beads affixed to his hair, woven foreign blankets, a sloop with no crew. Whatever this man's story, it wasn't common.

He rethreaded the needle, ready to sew the sheet closed over Ariene's face. It was then Rachel stopped him.

"Please. Let me."

He looked up. Said nothing. She wasn't required to explain. He understood that this was a matter of honor, and of love. He relieved her of the lantern and swapped places with her.

She squeezed her eyes shut against sudden vertigo. *This could not be happening. Could not be real.* The situation, at this moment.... Lord knew, it was not an intimacy she could have imagined sharing with anyone.

Yet she was here. Irrefutably.

There were so many things. Things Ariene had left to do. Things she and Rachel were meant to do, *together.* Ariene had yet to meet her own mother. Ariene was to travel with Rachel to Greece, the Levant and to Alexandria, where Rachel's father, Ariene's half-brother, lay buried.

Now, Ariene would see James Cavanagh, above.

Rachel took a breath and began.

Unused to sailmaker's needles or sewing canvas, the trembling that claimed dominion over her hands hampered her already slow efforts. The needle and thread were well waxed, and she stubbornly forged on, the words *don't think, just sew* a rolling litany even as her vision blurred.

One ... two ... half a dozen large salty splotches spilt onto the canvas as she painstakingly stitched the sheet closed over Ariene's mouth, her nose, her perfect flawless brow.

Finally ... *finally* ... she was done.

She slumped back. The hollowness returned.

Jonathon Lecky took the needle and thimble from her slack fingers, tied off the twine, then sat back on his heels beside her. "It's just temporary, until you reach shore."

"Yes." Weight pressed her chest, crushed her heart. Every part of her felt ragged. Stormed. Wrung out. "Thank you."

A moment passed. Their knees almost touched. Almost, she could feel his body's warmth in the cramped space.

"There's no shame if you wish to go below," he said quietly.

She turned her head his way. What had he seen in life, she wondered, to respond to another's grief this way? With solemnity, with patience? And not a speck of judgment.

But then, what sort of man sailed with only a Welsh collie for crew?

None of the impressions she had formed when he first descended into the cabin had changed. The man had a potency, an awareness in his eyes, that only made his coarse looks more compelling.

Which elemental force did she owe tribute to for placing Jonathon Lecky in her path?

Would she even *be here* if he were anyone else?

The latter was too much to contemplate—not something she could think about right now. Calling on the strength she *did* have, she dragged a shirt sleeve across her wet cheeks.

"Thank you," she said again. "But I cannot. There is still Mary."

CHAPTER THREE

I never did like the sight of a shattered ship: splintered wood and other flotsam floating atop ocean foam. Shattered ships are like shattered dreams. If one must send a cannon ball in their direction, far better that they are just damaged a bit.
—*The Memoirs of Rhys Cavanagh*

LECKY'S SLOOP WAS SILENT. EXHAUSTION had finally claimed the *Castalia's* two survivors in a net of sleep. Lecky had left the Marquess in the cabin below. The man had drifted off while Miss Cavanagh was alone on deck, and Lecky had chosen not to wake him. Rhys Cavanagh's granddaughter had fought that net longer, her dark stare fixed on the moonlit swell. Yet even against her vast store of obstinacy, physical and emotional exhaustion triumphed in the end.

No good news surfaced. The *Castalia* had been smashed to pieces. Materials that had once comprised the brig spiraled out across the surface of the Channel, refuse thrown back from the shoal. Lecky had maneuvered his sloop in close to scour each. Sometimes, they found nothing. Other times, evidence of Ariene Cavanagh's shared fate was all too stark. Bodies—crew for the most part—draped over flotsam sloshing about in the swell. Where conditions allowed, Lecky freed those he found to sink. The weight of their descending souls tugged on his own. Miss Cavanagh had looked aside, her arms crossed, fingers clutching elbows, and dry, coffee-colored eyes red-rimmed.

Now she slept, seated, legs to one side, head propped in her hand, elbow resting on top of the low cabin roof three feet from the hatch. Her feet were tucked up beneath the blanket she nestled in for warmth. Long, dusky eyelashes fanned her cheeks.

She'd not uttered a word about the shirt and trousers or how she'd come to don them. Nor had she backed away from the search, despite their grim findings. Yet at that moment, the ashen, predawn sky at her back and the dark shadows grief wrought beneath her eyes combined to give her a deep, almost haunting air of vulnerability.

Ariene Cavanagh, Lecky gathered, had been far more than an aunt. *I've never been closer to anyone.* The lass looked as though she'd been torn from her moorings. Still, she'd done her best to remain staunch.

"We're sorry for her, aren't we, girl? The Marquess too." He ruffled Morgan's coat. The collie lay on the deck at his side, her head resting on his thigh.

Rain was approaching. He could smell it.

He was tired himself after a day and a night without sleep and the unanticipated events in between. But rest would not come anytime soon. He had a ship to meet. Winter was waiting for him. And now, given recent findings and the time that had passed since the *Castalia's* wreck, there was little more here he could do. Little more, that was, other than convey the Marquess and Miss Cavanagh safely to shore.

Positioned opposite the tiller, she slept directly in his line of sight, her breathing soft as the sloop ploughed on. Behind her, the sun emerged over the horizon to sit low and lucent beneath the clouds. Reflected off the water, dawn's glow framed her with a warm, shining backlight, while the light breeze played with the loose strands of hair around her face.

The Fulani blanket, one of several Lecky had brought back from the Rice Coast, slipped down her shoulder as she slept.

Exhausted. She was exhausted. In a just world, Lecky thought, only the fairest of dreams would penetrate such slumber.

Over and again, he found his gaze returning to her. Earlier, he had moved her aunt's canvas-wrapped body to the foredeck where he had lashed it securely. The decision had been a sound one. For all the lass's courage and the brave face she put on, there was only so much a wounded heart should be forced to bear. The way she had borne up impressed him, but the constant reminder posed by that sewn canvas shroud was too much.

Respite. When he looked at her now, respite was what he saw. Respite with the barest whisper of something more, something not so much sighted as sensed.

A tingle skittered across the surface of his skin.

Whatever its source, it wasn't like the Leveche, the hot, dry, red-dust-laden wind that blew from the Sahara to the Spanish coast, heralding storms and heavy rain. No. This was the gentle graze of the zephyr, with soft promise of coming warmth, replenishing and—perhaps for the first time in his life—somehow nearer to peace.

He dug his fingers into the long hair of Morgan's coat. "Ah, but we know peace, don't we, girl?"

Friendship and company a man could find plenty of ashore. It was alone at sea one learnt who one was and what one was capable of.

That was peace. Peace he knew each time he clung to the tiller all day and night through a vicious storm and his whole body ached and his fingers came away bleeding. Peace he knew each time the sea carried him wildly off course or too close to rocks and he had to fight Poseidon himself to right it. The uncontainable sense that began, deep in his chest, of his heart spreading out, spreading through him, then... *settling*, leaving repletion, somehow transcendent, that lived within, sometimes for moments, sometimes for days. That was peace.

It was Notus, god of the south wind, dangerous to mariners and friend to thieves, to whom the Leveche belonged. His hot, abrasive blast had called to Lecky all his life. And though Zephyrus, from the west, blew too at times, he called for something different, something that had never been in Lecky to give.

Lecky gently pried Morgan's head off his leg. The collie gave a little grunt of protest. "Come now," Lecky said. "No complaints. I have to tend to our guest." A glance at the sky above the horizon suggested the woman in question would be better off below.

Morgan stretched out her front paws. She gave a yawn and sat up to watch as Lecky placed the tiller in the comb then slid several feet closer to their guest.

But as he reached out a hand to wake her, he came to a stop.
So beautiful.

It wasn't those butterscotch locks or gently arched brows or the soft appearance of her skin. No—it was the blend he had witnessed, the coalescence of bravery and vulnerability, heart and determination. It was that which again brought a tingle, a susurration that skated his senses along with one word that held all the sheerness and clarity of the waters of the Spanish Mediterranean on a clear day.

Special. This one was special.

If he woke her now, she would again fight the notion of sleep. She would put her exhaustion second to the needs of others. He had seen enough of her character to know that.

He hesitated too long. Sensing his presence, those long lashes fluttered and drowsily opened.

He dropped his hand to his thigh. "You were dozing."

"Was I?" She gazed at him for a moment through a sleepy haze.

No, not demanding, Lecky thought, looking into those eyes. He had been wrong to think her demanding. This one didn't need to demand. *Those eyes were unwitting coffee-brown coercion.*

"It's time to go below," he said. "Rain will soon be upon us."

"No, I—" Grasping the blanket that threatened to slip down her arm, she quickly scooted her bottom closer to the cabin and sat up straighter. "I'm fine. Truly, I didn't mean to fall asleep." Releasing a breath, she looked beyond him to the surrounding sea. "It's light. Perhaps . . . perhaps now we have a better chance."

There was no easy way to deliver the news. "There are no more chances."

She stared at him for an uncomprehending moment. Then, grief-stricken, she shook her head, voice hiking. "No . . . You can't mean . . . . *No!*"

"I wouldn't say what I have, if I thought there was more we could do."

That panicked, searching, all-too readable gaze, told him the moment she realized he was sincere.

"Oh." She pressed her hand to her mouth and squeezed her eyes closed. "Oh, Lord, surely—" She didn't finish. He didn't offer help. Just gave her time to filter each of her thoughts.

Her voice was low when it emerged. "I just can't believe the Marquess and I . . . that we were the only two souls to survive."

Discomfort rippled through him. Poseidon had held her in his palm—she *and* the Marquess—only to relinquish them both at the last second. Lecky drew his knee up to his chest and rested his elbow upon it. "It is far more difficult to believe," he said truthfully, "that *anyone* survived."

Her gaze jerked up. Abyss-like eyes collided with his. "Goodness, you mean that, don't you?"

He did. And he could see the knowledge shook her.

She looked away, out to sea. "You . . . you will take us to shore now?"

"I will."

"Mary's fiancé works for my family. They were planning their wedding. If I had so much as thought it would end this way—" Her voice cracked.

"You couldn't know."

"I would have insisted she stay," she said softly, vehemently. "I *should* have insisted she stay."

"Sometimes we're not meant to have those choices." Too many times, he had learned that.

"Is that how you felt when you came to our aid?" she asked. "You don't fear—as some sailors do—that by saving a life yours may be claimed instead?"

He knew men who believed that. "I've always accepted that could be the cost of my inability to stand by and watch another person drown. But you're right. Perhaps I should have given it more thought. Especially as everyone knows a woman aboard a boat is a curse." He smiled ever so slightly at her sharp, surprised look. "Tut-tut, Miss Cavanagh," he teased. "'Tis just another superstition."

"I take it you are not superstitious, Mr. Lecky?"

"Dastardly unlucky to be superstitious." Her still-reserved look coaxed a grin from him. "No, I'm not superstitious. But I pay careful attention to those who are."

"You believe superstitions are dangerous," she observed.

"Superstition is fed by fear. Man's inability to control his fear endangers him and the men in his company."

"Is that why you sail alone?"

"I sail alone because I enjoy it. Besides, I'm dreadful company for long durations."

She regarded him with a somewhat dubious expression, and he found he enjoyed the opportunity to distract her. His grin edged toward a smile. Lowering his knee and resting back on both hands, he conceded, "I've spent time enough aboard larger vessels. This life suits me better."

"Royal Navy or merchantmen?" she probed.

"Do I look like the Royal Navy type?"

"No. But nor do you look like you've stepped off an East Indiaman." She glanced down at the woven blanket enveloping her and rubbed the cloth between thumb and forefinger. "This blanket isn't from the East."

"I acquired it in Africa a long time ago."

"Africa?" A trace of amusement replaced her frown. "Ah," she said, as though that explanation made more sense. "Will you tell me of these?" She leant forward to raise her hand to the beads in his hair.

Like a boom sweeping across the deck under wind-loaded sails, the accidental graze of her fingers against his cheek caught him unawares and damn near knocked out his breath.

Women rarely touched him—not in this way. Not with gentle curiosity.

Her hand froze—her eyes met his. There was realization there, and startlement, at the boundary of intimacy she had just crossed. It was a slip on her part, of that he had no doubt. Nothing had been normal for her these past twelve hours. She was vulnerable, and he had rescued her and made her feel safe. It was easy to understand the lapse of her guard. Still . . . she didn't drop her hand. The very sky itself, carrying moisture's scent, seemed to be holding its breath.

"Are these . . ." Her glance flicked nervously to the beads. The slight quiver of her wrist told him that his equilibrium wasn't the only one unbalanced. Of the two men onboard whom she could attach herself to, whom she could let her guard down with . . . . The lass was mad to let it be him.

"Are these from Africa, too?" she asked.

Her soft words drew attention to even softer lips, and the hot blast of the Leveche ripped through him, a fierce, swift, brutal reminder of how long it had been since he'd lain with a woman. *Devil plague it, not now, damn it.* Because with the reminder came a vivid image of *this* woman: stripped of the blanket—hell— stripped of everything bar his shirt, her back against the deck, legs encircling his hips, and hands pressed to his chest as he kept her body warm by an entirely different method.

Gods above. He'd berated Rossum for slavering over her. *You hypocrite, Jonathon.*

Yet the lass's swift, startled glance, the inquisitive brush of her fingers, whispered to him that to lie with this woman would be to be enmeshed with the Leveche at its hottest, it's most searing—only to be released in the end to the soothing care of the zephyr.

Such was not for him to know.

"Yes, they're from Africa." Damn but he wasn't used to feeling this off-balance on his own boat. He brought his hand up to capture hers. It was small, clasped in his own. He conducted it safely back to rest on her thigh, then for a moment imprisoned it. Just long enough for her to understand where that hand should stay. Long enough to remind her that, of all the things he was, rescuer included, a blood relation he was not. And he still had some knowledge of proprieties.

Understand she did, by the faint rise of color in her cheeks.

Yet as he began to release her, she wove determined fingers through his. The rose in her cheeks deepened that little bit more. Her brown eyes implored. "Please... don't misunderstand me. I need this... your companionship... just for a moment." Then, with no other contact between them except her hand holding his, she blushingly turned her face to the sea—unaware, perhaps, that he may as well have been accosted by Barbary raiders by the way she'd left his heart slamming in his chest. Slamming as the breakers did along the cliffs of southern Morocco, with the same violence, the same almighty crash of sea.

He wasn't a lothario, but nor was he a eunuch. He just hadn't been in the mood for a mindless tumble for a while. Rhys Cavanagh's granddaughter didn't need fear he misunderstood her actions—but holding her hand was a bit bloody different to patting his dog, no disrespect to Morgan.

Yet somehow as he sat, serving up this unknown kind of comfort, the wild crash in his chest receded to become something gentler. Something that encouraged stillness and quiet. *I need this ... your companionship ... just for a moment.*

And somehow, as the sun's warm light softened the sea and backlit her profile and simultaneously turned those delinquent butterscotch strands to gold, his mind responded unbidden, with a whisper.

A moment only? I may well need you *for a lifetime.*

Like the unexpected bite of a lash, instant shock swept through him.

What the hell? A whisper mayhap—but a damned crazed thought. A damn sight *more* crazed than any challenge Lecky and the sea and the south wind god had *ever* wagered upon. Even so, as he attempted to thrust it away, he felt the twist of it in his breast—the three sharp points of Poseidon's trident.

Behind them, the steps of the companionway creaked.

Miss Cavanagh gave a start. Quickly, she slid her hand from Lecky's and buried it in her lap. Of course, the Marquess couldn't see her hand in Lecky's, but that didn't stop the guilty flush that spanned her cheeks.

An awkward, discernible silence hung over the deck as Rossum emerged from the cabin, fumbling for the handrail. In his other hand, he clutched Lecky's pewter mug—sign he was growing more familiar with his surroundings. The Marquess detected the pregnant pause on the deck as he gained his grip. A moment passed before he spoke. "Is aught the matter?"

Ah, but a fine question. *Notus and Poseidon be damned, what game are you playing?*

Lecky leant back on one elbow, raising his other arm to shield his eyes as he squinted up at the Marquess. What the man lacked in sight was likely compensated for by his other senses, not to mention a high dose of intelligence.

And determination.

"The likelihood of finding anyone alive has passed," Lecky said. "I'm returning you to shore."

The Marquess drew a long, almost pained breath. "Miss

Cavanagh's maid . . . ?"

"Mary Thacker," Miss Cavanagh inserted quietly. "Her name was Mary Thacker." Her glance flicked up at the Marquess. "She's—" She closed her eyes, shook her head and looked away. "No."

The swift knot of the Marquess's brow suggested the man felt Miss Cavanagh's loss just as he did that of his own servant. The man's voice was raw. "I am sorry."

"Yes. I—" Visibly, she swallowed. "Thank you."

Her fist pressed deep into her lap, small and stiff, yet assailable. And suddenly, Lecky wanted to be the one who defended her and enclosed that small hand inside his own.

He pushed to his feet. "You'll be on land in three hours."

"Thank you," she repeated. But he could tell she was once again retreating into herself to tend her grief.

The Marquess was still frowning as Lecky brushed past him enroute to the bow. With one hand gripping the handrail, the Marquess twisted as Lecky reached the starboard side-deck.

"Mr. Lecky." His words were low, pitched with courtier's precision to drop between them—and only them.

Lecky stilled.

"She may be a privateer's granddaughter on her father's side, but Miss Cavanagh is the granddaughter of an earl on her mother's."

No, the Marquess's perceptiveness lacked for nothing.

"State your point clearly," Lecky said.

There was a pause. The Marquess clenched Lecky's mug in his hand. "Your cabin is stocked with half-ankers, Mr. Lecky. I am aware what that means."

Ah. More precisely, the Marquess had already decided what the presence of those small, four-gallon, easily transportable barrels meant. It seemed the Marquess was guilty of making snap judgments, too.

"That I enjoy wine?"

"That much, do you?" The Marquess's tone was as dry as the rieslings Lecky carried from Alsace.

It was true that being caught with such barrels had sent more than a few lads to the gallows. Lecky had no reason to be one of them, but the Marquess could make whatever damn judgment he liked. Lecky didn't much care. He had no need to justify himself. But he would put the man's mind to rest on one matter.

"Marquess, I will say this, because I appreciate the gentleman in you demands you speak up and because we do not know each other. I'm not the kind of man to take advantage of a woman in need, no matter her beauty, connections, or riches. Rest easy on that."

RACHEL CLASPED THE BLANKET CLOSER to her throat as the Marquess lowered himself to sit beside her. She would have been naïve not to detect his sudden suspicion of Jonathon Lecky. Yet their host had done *nothing*. *She* had touched *him*. And though the boat captain's eyes had revealed how startled he was when she raised her hand to his hair—a reaction that surely mirrored her own—he had not for a moment misconstrued what she had done.

Not that she entirely understood it herself.

The Marquess cleared his throat. "I thought you might like this." He held a pewter beer mug in the air in her direction and added, with a slight smile, "It contains water."

A blind man had thought of *her* thirst? The Marquess was fitting his popular image. If his consideration was an indication of the type of man he was, he *was* a good man.

Rachel accepted the mug. "Thank you, my lord. Though I am sure many folk in our position would prefer it were spirits."

"To forget their sorrows? Are you that type, Miss Cavanagh?"

"No, my lord, I'm not that type." Absently, Rachel twisted the mug in her hands. Her fingers brushed the engraved mark near the lip. *The Lord Nelson, Gravesend*, it read.

She raised the mug to her lips. After several sips she lowered it, to cradle the pewter in her hands. An awkwardness took root in the silence.

"You must be exhausted," the Marquess said.

"Yes." She *was* exhausted. But she couldn't succumb now. "I can rest later, when we're ashore."

When she knew everything had been done to tend to Ariene and ensure Ariene went home.

"Did you join the *Castalia* in Antwerp?" the Marquess asked.

Rachel was aware of Jonathon Lecky moving around the bow. "Yes. We...we were visiting friends." They had gone to see Ariene's best friend, Celia, Countess Davignon, and so that Rachel could meet Baroness Gisele de Bauer, a Belgian travel writer whose work on Egypt and Greece Rachel very much admired. Of course, neither Rachel nor Ariene had told Rachel's mother, Lady Georgiana, of their plans to meet the Baroness.

"You're friends live in Antwerp?" the Marquess asked.

Thinking about Ariene suddenly made elaboration very difficult. "Brussels, actually. Count and Countess Davignon? The Countess was once Lady Ravensdale, but sadly, Lord Ravensdale was killed at Toulouse. Perhaps you know of her?"

"I do. I have conversed with Lady Ravensdale—the Countess—once or twice."

Rachel nodded. Celia's circle of acquaintances was large. "And you, my lord?"

"I came to purchase several pieces of art."

"Oh?" The Marquess's admission caused only slight surprise. Rachel's grandfather's grizzly old quartermaster had lost his sight. And yet, he had continued to carve much-prized little boats and ships for Rachel, her brothers and sisters, and the children in the village near the Cavanagh estate. "I hope none of your purchases were aboard the *Castalia*," she said.

"One. Just one."

She smiled humorlessly. The regret that underscored those words exposed much. "I don't think I want to know the painter."

"Sculptor," he corrected, leaving Rachel with another sliver of insight. This time, it was the Marquess's smile that held no humor. "I must say I'm relieved, because I don't think I could bear to tell you."

He didn't exaggerate, she realized, studying his face. Their circumstances cut him deep.

His expression sobered and his voice dropped as though he had no wish to be overheard. "Miss Cavanagh—" He was interrupted by the sudden reappearance of the collie, who brushed up against him and inadvertently slapped Rachel with her tail as she wheeled happily about.

Her owner returned to the aft deck, directing a glance towards the Marquess as he moved from side-deck to tiller. The Marquess tilted his head to follow the sound of their host's passage.

"You began to say?" Rachel asked the Marquess.

His expression shuttered. "Yes," he said. "Mr. Lecky." He cleared his throat. "Which port do we make for?"

The response that came was brusque. "Dunkirk."

"Dunkirk?" Rachel sat straighter. She had assumed—she had *hoped*—their rescuer would take them to England. Of course, the crossing between Dover and Dunkirk was scarcely longer than that between Dover and Calais. Still, to put them ashore in *France*? "You ... you won't take us to England, Mr. Lecky?" It would only take a few hours under the right wind conditions.

"I'll take you to Dunkirk." He seated himself by the tiller. "It's the closest port. Obtaining another berth to cross the Channel will be straightforward from there."

The collie darted back to his side as disappointment uncurled through Rachel. She wanted—needed—Ariene's body to be returned home safely. And for some reason that lay deep in her heart, she instinctively trusted Jonathon Lecky, with his thirty-foot sloop and Welsh collie for crew, to get them there. "Would it be ... terribly out of your way, to take us home?" she asked.

Beside her, the Marquess stiffened.

"That is to say," she hurriedly continued, "we lost everything aboard the *Castalia*, and in France, without bills of exchange, access to funds is ... difficult. If you could take us to England, I know my family will see you properly compensated for any inconvenience caused."

"The last thing I need is to be 'compensated', Miss Cavanagh." Their rescuer almost sounded amused.

"Please then, if it's no trouble—"

His gaze softened and searched hers. For a moment, she thought he would relent.

"Miss Cavanagh." The Marquess spoke. The quiet authority in his voice snapped Rachel's attention his way.

His jaw was firmed. The difference in him was startling. For the first time, she truly saw the peer of the realm. Their brush with death, the moonlit search, meant they had met on a footing far removed from the gilt assembly halls and wallpapered drawing rooms where they might otherwise have formalized an acquaintance.

"We will arrange passage from Dunkirk," the Marquess said. "Please, do not fear for funds. I will ensure we are both promptly reunited with our families."

"Thank you, my lord," Rachel said. "But will you not also appeal to Mr. Lecky?" She looked back at Jonathon Lecky. "Please, in the time it will take to sail to Dunkirk, it cannot be *that* much further to England? We could hire a conveyance from Dover, if London is too far."

Jonathon Lecky's gaze shifted from Rachel to the Marquess. The soft look had disappeared, to be replaced by something knowing in his eyes, something grimly amused. It was almost as though he was waiting to see what Rossum would do.

The Marquess too seemed to sense it. He swiveled his large body in Rachel's direction, and his knees accidentally knocked hers. She jumped.

"Miss Cavanagh, with the exception of the bunk upon which you were recovering," the Marquess said, "the cabin below is filled with half-ankers. Mr. Lecky is a smuggler."

The air rushed from her lungs as though she had once again been knocked to the deck. For a moment she was breathless. *Oh.*

Oh.

She had noticed the stacked crates, of course. Noticed but not registered. The total sum of her thoughts had been focused on Ariene and Mary. Her head whipped in the direction of their captain.

He was watching Rossum with an expression of grim amusement. Something—some knowledge he chose not to share—played at the corners of his mouth. He leant back against the stern of the vessel, then drew one knee up and rested his elbow atop it.

Her gaze travelled over him, seeing him again. There was something in his manner, in his pose, that set him apart. But whether it was lawlessness, she didn't know. Somehow, from all she had observed so far, that impression didn't quite sit . . . right. He was settled back at the tiller in his dark olive-green coat and white shirt with a relaxation few men she knew possessed. Nor could she think of many men who could wear silver beads in their hair, yet whose masculinity was still unquestionable.

Wherever he had come from and been to, she sensed at this moment he chose to be here, with his dog and his boat.

"I am certain," the Marquess continued in a low voice, "our host does not want to encounter English authorities should he take us to shore."

Once again, she caught sight of that grim, silent flicker of amusement. And yet, Jonathon Lecky did not deny it.

Oh, God. Another thought occurred to her. Surely the Marquess wasn't the type to turn another man over to customs? Not a man who was the sole reason she and the Marquess were alive? A man who had *taken her aunt's body aboard* so Ariene might be farewelled and buried? Perhaps it was Rachel's privateer blood, which in that saw no benevolence, no justness.

No, she realized as she studied the Marquess's impassive face, she couldn't be sure *what* he would do. Not because he showed vindictiveness; rather, she sensed Rossum was a man who believed it his obligation to do right, according to the law.

She looked again at Jonathon Lecky. The breeze lashed his long hair about his unshaven face as his gaze shifted to her. There was no apprehension in those depths, no concern. But there was perhaps a mutual understanding—a common reading of the Marquess.

And that grim trace of amusement that raised questions and unsettled her senses.

Had the transport of contraband always supported Jonathon Lecky's life?

Rachel found at that moment she didn't care. Not enough to risk him being taken in as reward for saving their lives.

Dunkirk, he had proposed.

"Very well," Rachel said. "Dunkirk it is."

CHAPTER FOUR

The breath of the wind and the flow of currents direct a man far more than he would like.
—*The Memoirs of Rhys Cavanagh*

DOUR AND SHABBY, THE JETTIES and warehouses that lined the inner channel of the port of Dunkirk presented like old, worn-out household servants. A few brigs and schooners berthed along the jetties' lengths; but for the most part, the moored vessels were fishing ketches and smacks. As Jonathon Lecky's sloop passaged up the channel, Rachel watched the workers on the shore set down their tools and retreat from the encroaching weather. A year on from Napoleon's defeat, the French port of Dunkirk had an air of lost productivity and languishment that the drizzle peppering the channel and soaking the jetties only served to emphasize.

Refusing to be cowed by the weather, Rachel clutched the thick cloth of Jonathon Lecky's blanket over her head as a hood. The Marquess sat directly across from her by the starboard bulwark. His expression was impassive. The knuckles of his hand were white where they gripped the bulwark. Soon, both she and the Marquess would be ashore in France.

Her chest began to tighten, squeezed suddenly by panic. Her breath became shallower. The drizzle had begun to soak through the blanket and spread damp across her shoulders. *She didn't want to be left here.* Too quickly, the world had changed.

"Are you all right, Miss Cavanagh?" Their host's voice came from behind to pierce the grip of her thoughts.

She turned toward Jonathon Lecky. Seated by the tiller, he

seemed impervious to the drizzle dampening his hair and beading his coat. The weight of his gaze was upon her. She opened her mouth, but her throat was clogged. Nothing emerged.

She must have looked a fright, because his eyes once again softened as though he understood what she couldn't say. She felt panicked. Stranded. His lips gave a little twitch at the corners in a look she was coming to understand as empathy. For whatever reason, it calmed her a little and made her feel not quite so alone.

He turned his head and squinted through the thickening drizzle to scan the larger vessels. His gaze sharpened, then became a look of satisfaction, as it came to rest on one. *The Essex*, Rachel read on the brig's prow.

"Marquess, Miss Cavanagh," he said. "You can rest assured you won't be in Dunkirk for long."

TWO HOURS LATER, RACHEL PACED before one of the guest room windows of the Hotel Patrice and the view it offered of the jetties. Gray clouds crowded overhead, while water pooled on the street. The jetties remained deserted. The men, who had gone to see the captain of *The Essex*, had bid Rachel to stay at the inn to eat and to refresh. The first was impossible; her loss of appetite was near absolute. She had, however, bathed. She'd needed to wash the salt from her hair and the shipwreck from her skin. She'd needed to feel clean, even though her cambric dress was still crumpled and soiled.

If Rachel's mother, Lady Georgiana, was here, she would tell Rachel to sit down and be patient while Rachel awaited the return of the two men. But that was impossible given how unsettled she felt. At home, she would have made the arrangements herself.

She returned to stand by the window and hugged her arms over her chest.

She saw them then, making their way back to the inn. Both men had a presence. The hotel proprietor had provided the Marquess of Rossum with a cane, and with one look, one knew the man was well-born. Conversely, the man at his side was more difficult to pick. Jonathon Lecky had an air of authority; he moved on land with the same relaxed assurance he had on his boat. One instinctively knew he was a man with whom one could joke, but he wasn't a man with whom to trifle. He possessed the space he moved in.

In that respect, he reminded her of her grandfather, Rhys Cavanagh.

And just as she had felt with her grandfather and with Ariene, when Jonathon Lecky turned his gaze on her and his eyes softened, on some deep level she felt safe.

Safe to demand that she help search for survivors.

Safe to grieve.

Safe to be afraid.

From the street, he looked up at the window to where she stood behind the glass. His look was intent. There was something there. Some element she wasn't able to describe, yet which pulled her toward him. Whatever that pull was, it ran between them now. And right now, she wanted to take refuge there.

Then he and the Marquess passed out of sight below, as they approached the inn's heavy oak door.

ARRANGEMENTS HAD BEEN MADE, THE lass and the Marquess's passage to England secured. Already, Lecky and Captain Napier of *The Essex* had had Ariene Cavanagh's body transferred to the London-bound brig. Yet as Lecky stepped into the tap room of the Hotel Patrice, the feeling that lay low in his gut wouldn't budge. It wasn't that he felt Rhys Cavanagh's granddaughter would come to harm if he moved on. These days, he listened to those gut feelings unquestioningly. No, she would be fine. This was different. This was something within him. Something unsettled.

The gods knew that, when she asked that he take her home, he'd been sorely tempted to say yes. But ferrying Miss Cavanagh and the Marquess to Dover was not the same as ferrying the pair to London, which *The Essex's* captain, Napier, could do in half the time and greater comfort. No, this way, Lecky could still meet his commitments to Winter. He needed to move on.

Yet, as he'd approached the hotel, he'd caught a glimpse of her through rain-speckled glass. Some bedamned voice inside had begun to whisper that no one should look after her but him.

"You've taken good care of the mademoiselle?" Lecky asked Patrice, the hotel's namesake and proprietor.

"*Oui.* Camille has tended her. She has bathed but is still too shaken to eat." Patrice's eyes flashed from Lecky to the Marquess, who stood silent at Lecky's side. "A room has also been prepared for the Marquess to freshen up."

"I must speak to Miss Cavanagh first," Rossum said, "to inform her of the arrangements that have been made."

Patrice gave a nod. "Camille will show you the way." He signaled to the French serving woman, who came forward to take the Marquess's arm. As the Marquess and his attendant disappeared upstairs, Patrice turned his attention to Lecky.

The Frenchman and Lecky had known one another since the days that Patrice had worked for Lecky's associate, Winter, in the nearby French coastal city of Boulogne-sur-Mer. "Captain Lecky." Patrice shook his head. "If there is a shipwreck to be found, you will find it."

Lecky gave a little snort. "This one found me, Patrice."

"*Oui.* Lucky for your survivors."

"It's just a shame there weren't more."

"The Englishwoman. She is beautiful. Surely you do not plan to leave her with the blind one?"

"He seems quite capable to me," Lecky said.

"Ha! But you are her rescuer."

Her rescuer indeed. Rescuer of dark, unguarded eyes, apricot lips and endless lashes. Lashes that he could still picture drifting open in the dawn light as Lecky sat at her side.

Lecky returned the Frenchman's look. "She's a lady. The Marquess is appropriate company."

"*Approprié*? Bah!" Patrice made a sound of disgust. "Captain, has the blind one journeyed into the Moroccan desert to save our men? Has he negotiated the ransom of our mariners with the Arab tribes? When does Captain Lecky get his reward, hmm? The Englishwoman owes you her life. Let her worship at your feet. Forever darn your socks!"

Lecky smiled and slapped Patrice on the back. "How matter of factly you see things, my friend." Although really, Lecky's years in Africa had naught to do with it.

"You should go upstairs," Patrice said. "Do not allow the blind one a head start."

There was no race, as far as Lecky was concerned. He gave Patrice's shoulder a squeeze. "I'll keep that in mind."

The lass's voice filtered to him as he reached the top of the stairs. "Thank you again, my lord," he heard her say, "for informing me of the arrangements."

"Of course, Miss Cavanagh," the Marquess replied. "I knew you would wish to know right away."

Lecky paused at the top of the stairs as the Marquess exited the guest room on the opposite side of the landing. The gaze of the serving girl, Camille, flickered to Lecky, and she gave him a little smile as she escorted the Marquess down the hall.

The guest room door remained ajar. Lecky stepped forward and gave a knock.

"Come in," the woman he had rescued called.

As he pushed inside, his heart gave an involuntary lurch.

So far as possible, her appearance had been restored. She stood before the banked fire with shoulders straight and hands clutched together. Her hair, dressed high upon her head in a braided bun, looked clean and soft. *She* looked clean and soft, yet at the same time overwhelmingly vulnerable in the stained, resurrected dress in which she had survived the shipwreck.

Before, when she was unconscious and the white cambric wet and clinging, admiration of her feminine attributes had been the last thing on his mind. Now, not even stained cambric could detract from her loveliness.

Those stains showed she had survived.

"The Marquess said we will depart in two hours," she said. "He said Ariene's body is already aboard *The Essex*. He said you know the ship's captain and that you have arranged for his wife to be my chaperone."

Lecky had known the captain of *The Essex* for a long time. "Yes. Captain Napier is a friend, a good man. He and his wife, Mrs. Napier, will see you reach London safely."

"Thank you," she said. "You've done so much, so quickly. I didn't expect we would sail so soon."

"It's fortunate Captain Napier is in port."

"Yes." She drew a breath and caught her lower lip between her teeth.

Gods above, she was lovely.

And fragile. The sooner she was surrounded by the arms of family, the better.

Visibly, she straightened her shoulders and drew herself together. "Are you . . . leaving now?"

"I am. An associate awaits me."

He found his gaze locked on hers. Really, there was nothing more to say and certainly nothing more he could do. And yet, abiding in the space between them, something held them both motionless. A shimmer of reluctance. Was it his only? Did she feel it too?

Let her worship at your feet.

Poseidon, you old sea god, be damned, he thought. You know that's damned impossible. *Get your ass out of here, Jonathon.*

"I wish you all the very best, Miss Cavanagh." Politely, he turned to leave.

"Wait!"

She stepped within a scant foot of him, drawing his attention back around. He smelled the light soap from her bath and the slightly damp, yet clean scent of her hair. The brush of it against his senses was a sudden, unexpected balm, and he doubted that anything else in the world at that moment would have felt as soothing—and as uncharacteristic—as sliding his arms around her shoulders and comforting her in his arms.

"Please . . . how will I repay you?"

"There's nothing to repay."

The little shake of her head was denial. "You saved my life. Such is no small act."

Do you want to darn my socks? he almost asked, then squelched the impulse. He had never wanted a woman to wait on him. Not in the sense of caring for him and certainly not in the sense of watching land or sea for his return. For years, the risks he took could have seen him die any day. Leaving Morocco hadn't changed that. Even in Europe, there were men enough who wanted him dead.

"Lives are saved every day, Miss Cavanagh." In Morocco, that had been his focus. "Thanks is plenty enough."

"But—"

This time, he shook his head. "*No.*"

She fell silent. For a moment. "My grandfather taught me a debt should never go unpaid."

"As I said, there is no debt. You owe me nothing. You have no obligations."

The uncertainty in her eyes showed he had failed to reassure her. "But what if . . . I have need to contact you?"

Contact him? Given the disparity between their lives, as the Marquess had so felicitously pointed out? Reluctant or not, Lecky would be doing them both a disservice if he allowed that. "I can't imagine any circumstance, Miss Cavanagh, in which contact would be necessary."

She flinched. Too late, he realized his words—though softly delivered—had struck a blow. For Poseidon only knew what reason, she had let her guard down with him.

"I . . . of course." She drew a steeling breath and took a half-step back. He felt the distance open between them; but before he could speak and perhaps repair the situation, her chin notched up. She stuck out a determined hand as though to shake his. "Then there is but one thing left to say."

Given his reaction to their hand-holding on the boat, he hesitated to touch her. But if Rhys Cavanagh's granddaughter needed some formal gesture of closure, he wasn't going to stand in the way of her ability to put tragedy behind. He accepted her hand. "Safe travels?"

He was gifted with a small smile. Again, she shook her head. "I'm sorry. In that case, I must revise. There are two things, and safe travels is the second. Mr. Lecky, I would like you to know my name." The look in her dark eyes turned solemn and warm. "It is Rachel. Rachel Anwen Cavanagh."

A warning, not unlike many that had served him in the past, split loose from internal moorings. She raised his hand in a gentle yet firm way, just as a lord might do for a lady. On some level, he understood the meaning. Protest leapt forth. "You don't need—"

She held his gaze as she grazed his knuckles with her lips—a gentle touch that may as well have been a gale that shook him from stem to stern. He wasn't used to wrestling this type of storm.

"I do," she said.

She looked into his eyes with a gravity that was uniquely hers, and he knew that he had just received a gift, one generously and wholeheartedly given.

A gift, stunningly, of regard.

"Thank you, Jonathon Lecky, for my life."

His throat had damn near closed over, as though *he* was the one near-drowned. His voice was rough. "You're welcome."

She searched his features, and he knew damned well he was exposed. Even a blind man would see she'd brought him undone with her soft words, softer touch, and the brush of her lips.

She'd given her name as well as her thanks. She knew that he'd heard it. More importantly, that he'd *felt* it. Awareness arced between them, awareness of life, sensual as much as sexual.

Ever so softly she smiled again and turned his hand over. This time, he had to close his eyes as blood pooled in parts of his body it oughtn't to as she pressed a kiss to his palm. She held his hand between hers for a moment, then curled his fingers closed over the spot.

"Thank you."

His palm tingled in the place she had kissed. She was fortunate the guest room door was wide open to remind him they lacked privacy. She was fortunate that the lines he'd drawn for himself as her 'rescuer' weren't so matter of fact as old Patrice's. Because now, what he suddenly wanted was to bury his fingers deep in those butterscotch coils and find out every other sensuous thing she could do.

"Well." He cleared his throat, closed his hand in a fist and withdrew it from hers. "As thanks go, that was decent enough from you, I suppose. But I'll expect a bloody lot more from Rossum."

His words stunned a laugh from her, and the sound made him want her more than ever.

DESPITE HIS JOKE, INTENDED TO lighten the moment, Jonathon Lecky had not laughed with her, Rachel realized. His gaze had become intense, unreadable. She grew silent again.

To press her mouth to his hand—perhaps she had been too forward. But she had had to do *something* to convey how she felt. To show by tangible means what his actions had meant. And Jonathon Lecky *had* understood. His eyes had told her as much. So too the roughness of his voice.

She swallowed and again clasped her hands together. "Your associate will be happy for your arrival?" she heard herself ask lightly.

A flicker passed over his features, another of his private thoughts.

"Always," he said and stepped forward.

The tide of her breath stilled as his hand came up and two bare fingers lifted her chin.

Two fingers only, yet still she felt his touch all the way to her toes. Suddenly, the opposing currents of good sense and unformed, foolhardy questions collided to form a mighty whirlpool that swirled in her stomach . . . and in her mind.

Lives are saved every day. Yes, and they were lost every day too.

Perhaps he lived closer to that knife-edge than she. Perhaps he understood such things in a way she did not. But what now lay between them—

The muted clink of glasses and a round of laughter drifted up from the taproom below.

Gray eyes, she registered suddenly.

Jonathon Lecky had gray eyes.

But not the dark, swirling, stewing, converging, congesting gray of late afternoon showers banding across the sea. His were the diffusing cloudbanks after such a storm had passed, illumed by the soft majesty of dusk.

His thumb grazed her chin. Almost, almost touched her bottom lip.

Oh, there was no denying he was coarse. But the powerful sense of individuality he conveyed, his strong features, his gaze—that of a man who told the truth as he saw it—

Jonathon Lecky *was* handsome.

Not in the fabled way of Greek myths and fairy tales.

Certainly in the way that could encourage a woman to bed.

The turn of her thoughts brought a swift rush of heat to

her face.

Men were interested in her. She was reasonably fetching and possessed an impressive dowry, in addition to the infamy or fame attached to her grandfather's name. But the way Jonathon Lecky was looking at her now? She couldn't remember a man ever looking at her that way before. Not with that combination of tenderness and intensity and admiration. Admiration not for her appearance, but for something more. *Her.*

He drew the pad of his thumb across her chin. "I enjoyed meeting you."

His touch was light. *So light.* Yet coupled with the low tone of his voice, there wasn't a place she didn't feel it.

"You are a woman with no shortage of courage, Rachel Anwen Cavanagh," he said softly. "Every one of your grandfather's crew would be proud. I wish you the very best of fortunes. Truly I do."

This was his way of saying goodbye, she realized.

But she couldn't stop him.

Nor could she compel him to look back as he walked away.

CHAPTER FIVE

When a man sinks in the marshes of grief, Herculean is the effort to lumber his way back to terra firma.
—*The Memoirs of Rhys Cavanagh*

ARIENE CAVANAGH WAS BURIED AT the side of her father, Rhys Cavanagh, in the cliff-top cemetery of the family's Glamorgan estate, which overlooked the Bristol Channel. Across the water, the easterly wind blew harsh and cold. Bordering the grounds of the Cavanagh estate, on a small holding of land all of its own, Ariene's cottage stood dark and empty.

The family, except Rachel's younger brother who was at school, had returned to spend the customary three months' mourning in Wales. Under the circumstances, there was nowhere else in the world Rachel wanted to be; yet here on the Welsh coast, she was also faced with the aching knowledge of all that would no longer be.

She and Ariene would no longer while away the hours in Ariene's cottage. They would no longer escape Rachel's mother and sisters' long discourses on the latest London fashions by taking Ariene's curricle to the village. Then there were the snippets of old conversations—the looks, the jokes, the smiles—that lived along every stretch of the Cavanagh estate paths. To walk those paths was to catch a glimpse of Ariene's shade, to hear echoes of her dry wit and observations and, through the trees, the flittering sound of her laugh. It was to feel, with acuteness, her absence.

Weeks passed. Weeks of nothing and everything, during which Rachel wanted to do little more than find a dark hollow in the

Cavanagh woods and curl up inside it. Clear winter days that, any other year, would have enticed her outside now saw her struggling to rise. She slept late. She had no energy, no drive. There were days it took effort enough to extract herself from the deep leather confines of her grandfather's favorite armchair, where she sat for hours, an unopened book in her lap, in order to take herself outside. Such lassitude wasn't like her. She wasn't the lazy, self-pitying type. Yet she could focus on nothing. Time just . . . passed. The future stretched before her, empty and strange, where once it had been full and familiar.

Ariene was gone and so too were Rachel's direction and the plans of which Ariene had formed part. Plans to skirt Lady Georgiana's matrimonial campaigns until Rachel reached her age of license, then visit the places of which she'd dreamed—places Rhys Cavanagh had described in his memoirs, as well as others where no Cavanagh had ventured before.

But of course, these were plans only she and Ariene had discussed. Neither had shared them with the other members of Rachel's family. Lady Georgiana, for one, would not approve. The expectations Rachel's mother held for her second-eldest daughter were very different.

And so for the rest of the family, life went on, albeit without Rhys Cavanagh's vivacious, spinster daughter. Occasionally, Rachel would find her elder sister, Juliet, standing in one of the upstairs window alcoves that overlooked the estate, brushing back tears. "I miss her," Juliet would say, and she and Rachel would end up in each other's arms until talk and tears brought welcome memories and the sisters could part, if not happy, then at least consoled by a laugh.

It was a time when Juliet should feel naught but happiness. The baronet, Sir William Kersley, had expressed his affection—feelings that Juliet reciprocated. What might otherwise have led to a swift courtship slowed on account of the Cavanagh family's mourning.

The staff missed Ariene and also Mary. Both Mary's family and her fiancé were members of the Cavanagh staff. It had hurt so much to recount what had happened. It had hurt so much to see the grief in their eyes. "It was a tragedy, miss," Mary's sister, Ruby, had reassured her. The young woman had stepped into the role of

THE LAST LIGHT OF DUSK

Rachel's maid. Her family didn't blame Rachel but still... Rachel had come home. Mary had not.

Something that was clear to Rachel now—following countless hours of reflection—was that the women's expedition to Belgium had been *for her*. They had gone to Brussels to see Ariene's best friend, Celia, yes—but in essence, Ariene had proposed the trip so that Rachel might meet the Baroness Gisele de Bauer, whose exploits Rachel so much admired. And Rachel and the Baroness *had* had a wonderful time.

And now Ariene and Mary were gone. Such knowledge was not easy to bear.

Then there was Ariene's will. The family had assumed Ariene's wealth would flow back into the family's coffers. And it had. Ariene, after all, had owned fifty percent of the Cavanagh's shipping interests. However, Rhys Cavanagh's daughter had settled her assets upon Rachel and her brothers and sisters individually. Individually, but not equally.

In addition to a handsome portion of Ariene's personal fortune, Rachel had received sole title to her aunt's cottage and a twenty-five percent share of the Cavanagh family's shipping interests. Her younger brother, Andrew, also received a twenty-five percent share. Rachel would gain control of both cottage and funds at the age of one and twenty. Her older brother, Hugh, would oversee Rachel and Andrew's share of the shipping interests until each reached the age of five and twenty.

The disproportionate terms of Ariene's will did not please Rachel's mother. She didn't understand why Rachel and Andrew should receive half each of Ariene's share of the family's shipping interests, rather than Hugh and Andrew. But for Rachel that mattered for naught. How could she think about her personal change in circumstances in light of Ariene's death? She didn't *want* benefits. Not when Ariene was gone.

One thing she was forced to think about was the Marquess of Rossum. The Marquess was a topic that excited her mother and sisters particularly, thanks to the broadsheets that linked Rachel's name to his. As the only two survivors of a shipwreck that had claimed the lives of one hundred and sixty passengers and crew, their story had become a popular one. It contained, after all, the types of things the broadsheets loved: shocking tragedy coupled with potential intrigue, a blind hero and the Cavanagh family's infamy and connection to the sea.

Rossum had, of course, earned the highest praise of Britain's journalists. The Marquess stood, according to the broadsheets, "as testament to the challenges that a man with will and determination could overcome" and had once again proved "it is not title nor wealth that defines a man", but his "stalwartness and valor in dire exigency". The public, the papers assured, should have "no shortage of confidence in such an accomplished and admired member of the House of Lords".

Rachel, meanwhile, had been described as "a dashing Cymric beauty", with "courageousness of spirit", "surpassing bravery in the face of peril," and "indefatigable pluck", which she had apparently inherited from her "daring and fearless ancestor", the privateer-adventurer, Rhys Cavanagh.

Apparently, there was every reason for romance to spark between the two souls that fate had so cruelly thrown together.

Lady Georgiana certainly believed so. Indeed, nothing pleased her more than the arrival of another London paper that speculated on a match between Rachel and the Marquess. "Your popularity shows no sign of waning," she told Rachel, one morning at breakfast.

Her 'popularity', as Lady Georgiana called it, hardly seemed important compared to the dozens of discarded, handwritten pages strewn across Rhys Cavanagh's former desk, pages on which Rachel had tried, time and time again, to find the words to inform Elizabeth Wilston of New York that the daughter she had never known, yet so dearly wished to meet, was dead. Those pages took Rachel back to the *Castalia*, to the look of vulnerability on her aunt's face, when Ariene said she wanted to meet her mother. Those words were almost the last Rachel had heard Ariene say. Then, those words had filled her with lightness. Now, that knowledge was a vice that gripped and squeezed her heart.

The letter to Elizabeth Wilston took Rachel a long time to write.

Then, there was the matter of her rescuer. The newspapers, society, Rachel's family, their friends—all believed that a French fisherman had come to Rachel and the Marquess's aid. While it felt wrong not to give credit where credit was due, Rachel had agreed with the decision of Rossum and Captain Napier aboard *The Essex*. Their true savior would not want his involvement known.

Even so, there was a second, more private reason why Jonathon Lecky's name remained locked inside. In the days since Rachel and the Marquess's rescue, she had been over those events hundreds—no, *thousands*—of times in her mind. Still, she couldn't resolve how she felt.

Lives are saved every day. Every day she lived was *because of him.*

Yet to divulge too much would inevitably lead to judgments about Jonathon Lecky, the free trader, the smuggler.

She didn't want to hear those judgments. She didn't want to hear him impugned.

Yes, he was coarse, but she'd seen and sensed so much more. He'd braved freezing waters to retrieve Ariene from the channel. He'd provided the dignity of the sewn canvas shroud. And at the inn, she had felt the gentleness of his touch.

You are a woman with no shortage of courage, he had told her.

Such words from the man who was responsible for the lives of the *Castalia's* survivors meant far more than any newspaper that sought to commend her 'pluck'.

THE MARQUESS OF ROSSUM ARRIVED in Wales unexpectedly, a month after Ariene had been laid to rest.

"I wished to offer my condolences and to see how Miss Rachel has fared," the Marquess told Rachel's mother, as he stood before the Cavanagh women in the drawing room of the Glamorgan estate. "I cannot imagine the past month has been easy."

"It has not," Lady Georgiana agreed. "We miss Ariene terribly, of course."

Still, that did not stop her apparent pleasure at the presence of one of England's most eligible bachelors standing in their midst.

"Did you travel to Wales on estate business, my lord?" Lady Georgiana asked.

"This visit brought me to Wales," the Marquess replied, and Rachel's heart gave a pained squirm. She glanced toward Lady

Georgiana with concern. "I had a sudden opening in my calendar," the Marquess continued, "and admit to coming on a whim. I apologize for not sending word."

"Oh!" A satisfied smile spread across her mother's face. It was a smile the Marquess could not see but could surely hear in Lady Georgiana's voice. "We are only too pleased to welcome you, my lord. I'm certain the past month has not been easy for your household either. To think how close they came to losing you! I am sure you and Rachel will have much to talk about."

As she took the Marquess's arm and guided him to the sofa near the hearth, she proceeded to invite him to stay.

THE MARQUESS OF ROSSUM WAS an intelligent man, accustomed to the fawning and platitudes his position and eligible-bachelor status evoked. Even so, for Rachel, it took less than twenty-four hours for Lady Georgiana's barely veiled expectations to become too much.

"Just look at how far he has travelled to see you," Lady Georgiana pointed out. "And on a *whim*. Rachel, this is your chance."

Her *chance*? She could barely bring herself to *open a book*, let alone look to her future. The contrariety between herself and her mother was so vast she could scarcely comprehend it. "Mother, we are in mourning."

"Phoo!" Her mother waved her concern away. "Rachel, such customs are hardly reason not to form an attachment."

She didn't know whether to laugh or be horrified. A thousand questions crowded her tongue, not least whether Lady Georgiana had felt the same way when Rachel's father had died. But to say such a thing would be hurtful and cruel, a wounded response to her own pain. Rachel remained silent.

When Lady Georgiana not so subtly suggested Rachel take the Marquess to the orangery the following afternoon after discovering Rossum enjoyed gardens, Rachel acceded, but not for the reason Lady Georgiana may have thought.

The orangery was one of the grandest buildings on the Cavanagh estate. Twenty-seven tall, uniform Venetian windows stretched along the facade of the building, which was some three hundred feet in length. Elaborate plasterwork, depicting honeysuckle vines and ornamental lamps and griffins, decorated the interior, which consisted of east and west pavilions separated by a long arcade. The temperature inside was warmer than outdoors by several degrees, on account of the row of fireplaces and heating flues that lined the rear of the building. A path ran down the center of the arcade, between dozens of orange and lemon trees that rose up in large pots. The scent of citrus burst upon visitors as soon as they stepped indoors.

The scent was likely stronger still for a man who relied on smell to compensate for what he lacked in sight.

"Goodness," Rossum said, as Rachel led him through the east pavilion and into the arcade. "How many plants do you keep?"

"We've three dozen orange trees and a score of lemon trees," Rachel responded. "This is my favorite building on the estate." Favorite, and yet, she had barely set foot in the orangery in the past month. The realization gave her pause.

"Why is it your favorite building?" the Marquess asked.

"The light," she replied. "And the beauty. The orangery was my grandfather's retreat. He wrote his memoirs in the library in the west pavilion. I feel close to him here." She could picture him still, emerging from the library to sit in the arcade. He would wear his private smile—the one that announced whatever he had just written was likely to send society scrambling for their smelling salts or, better yet, Lady Georgiana into a fury. Rhys Cavanagh and Rachel's mother had always loved to hate one another.

"I had heard of your grandfather, of course, but I was unfamiliar with his memoirs until this past month."

"This past month?" Rachel echoed, surprised.

"Yes. My cousin Sophia has been reading them to me. I see now what has made his work so popular. Your grandfather was unique. Captivating, in fact. Nothing escaped him."

"No, nothing did." Neither enemy ships nor the way he could read people. Still, she felt surprise that the Marquess would read Rhys Cavanagh's memoirs *now*.

As though sensing her unspoken thoughts, the Marquess said, "I felt ignorant of your family, Miss Cavanagh, despite all the broadsheets have said. Your grandfather's memoirs have helped."

He smiled, ever so slightly. "They've also provided a much needed distraction."

She felt a pang at the wistfulness in his tone. "I'm glad you are enjoying my grandfather's memoirs. They've always been very important to me." She paused to take a breath. Lady Georgiana's expectations were a heavy weight, and there was no easy way to begin to unburden herself. "My lord, you mentioned the broadsheets. I presume you are familiar with the speculation?"

"It has come to my attention, yes."

Rachel gave a nod, which she realized he couldn't see. She summoned her nerve. "My lord, if you have not already detected, my mother holds fairly typical aspirations for her children. She wishes to see each of us married, and married well. I appreciate your visit, but in light of the broadsheets, I fear that by traveling to Wales you have encouraged in members of my family the hope that an attachment may form between us. I am terribly sorry if that gives rise to any . . . discomfort."

The Marquess stilled. "Are you always so direct, Miss Cavanagh?"

"I am not, my lord. However, the circumstances are hardly usual. To ignore the speculation would be like ignoring the presence of an African elephant in one's drawing room. I am a Cavanagh and, like my grandfather, not very good at overlooking the obvious."

"It is my experience, Miss Cavanagh, that a great deal of what is obvious remains unsaid. People will speculate regardless of what we do. I know that you mourn your aunt, and I hope that I have not created, as you say, discomfort. I hoped only to further our friendship."

Relief should have been her overriding response, but reluctance threaded through her. His words didn't make her mother's expectations any easier to manage, and the truth was that she didn't have the energy to try. Her hesitation was brief. She took a breath. "May I be frank, my lord?"

"Of course."

"I am exceedingly touched that you traveled to Wales. Please believe me when I say your friendship is not unwelcome. However, I must decline. I haven't anything to give. I barely have enough for myself."

She felt awful, but she also knew she was doing the *right* thing. She could not accept anything that she could not return; and right now, she needed every ounce of strength for herself, to overcome the dark, hard knot of pain that remained, a suffocating mass wedged inside.

He was silent for a time. Then, "I appreciate what you are saying, Miss Cavanagh."

"I know you are sincere, my lord. I must be also. I'm sorry."

"Please, you mustn't be sorry. I do understand." The Marquess paused to draw an unsteady breath. "My valet died aboard the *Castalia*, Miss Cavanagh. Peter served me for fifteen years, since we were boys. Before that, we played together as children. He became my guide when I could no longer see. He was at my side when I learned that my parents had died."

Rachel's heart constricted at the realization of the true extent of his pain. *Oh, Lord.* She had known he mourned the loss of his valet, but she had not understood the depth of their friendship. "My lord, I am so sorry."

Shaded by sorrow, his smile was a mere wisp. "I lost both my family and my sight for a second time, Miss Cavanagh, when the *Castalia* went down. No one describes the world quite the way Peter did."

Oh. With sudden alacrity, Rachel realized, "He became your sight."

"For everything I did and didn't want described, yes. Including Lady Gardner's hats."

Lady Gardner's hats were monstrous. A little smile pulled on Rachel's lips. "I am sorry."

"As am I," he said. "I do not think my life improved for knowing what Lady Gardner wears on her head. But," he added, before Rachel could speak, "I tell you not for your sympathy. Miss Cavanagh, I appreciate your honesty. I appreciate it more than you can know."

The following day, the Marquess of Rossum departed the Cavanagh estate and, in turn, Wales.

IN THE THREE MONTHS THAT followed, Rachel received letters, surprisingly amusing letters that were written—or rather dictated—by the Marquess. Usually, the missives made light of some newspaper article that referred to them both, and they always ended with the note that he had shared the snippet for her amusement only and did not expect a response.

By the feminine hand, she suspected they were written by his cousin Sophia.

At first, she didn't respond. She had explained how she felt. Yet, as the weeks passed and her mother and sisters once again began to formalize their plans for the season, she found she enjoyed the Marquess's letters. He surprised her with his willingness to share the lighter, more private side of himself and to reach out without the expectation of anything in return. She appreciated that. She especially appreciated it given his position and the fact that he was constantly surrounded by people who sought things from him.

She surprised *herself* the day she handed her maid, Ruby, a letter in return. Finally, she felt as though she might return his offering of friendship. "Ruby, will you please post this?"

Thus, when the London season of 1817 commenced, the Marquess of Rossum became a regular visitor at the Cavanaghs' Hanover Square townhouse.

RACHEL HAD HOPED THAT INTEREST in the story of the shipwreck would have waned by the time the Cavanagh family returned to London. The opposite was true. Society had simply been holding its breath, counting down the months of mourning to see what the Marquess would do. A number of dramatic odes detailing their miraculous survival had been added to Rachel's family's already dubious collection, and there was even talk of a *play*, "inspired by true events".

Their celebrity was unavoidable. Their names sold newspapers. *Mountains* of newspapers. Not a week went by that the broadsheets did not report on Rachel and the Marquess's attendance at the theatre, soirees and balls.

Speculation grew as the season advanced. Was Miss Rachel Cavanagh the perfect marchioness for the much-adored Marquess of Rossum? Or would she prove unsuitable on the grounds of her family's 'black' reputation?

Would their story culminate in a grand wedding at St. George's, Hanover Square? Or in the equally appealing notion of a scandal?

It was fortunate, Rachel thought, that both she and Rossum were able to laugh about such speculation. And equally fortunate that they both seemed to ignore it the rest of the time.

"Dare I ask how much attention we are attracting today, Miss Cavanagh?" Rossum asked.

"You may dare." A smile tugged on Rachel's lips. She looked about Hanover Square, the address of the Cavanagh family's townhouse, as she strolled beside the Marquess. Her arm rested upon his, although in truth, it was Rachel who were their guide.

They had not gone far today. Rossum never failed to attend Parliament, and the last session before the summer break was that afternoon.

"The good Mrs. Watson and Mrs. Bartholomew have stopped to chat on the opposite side of the square," Rachel observed. "Their bodies are angled our way. And Lord and Lady Goodrem are about to pass by in their barouche." Rachel inclined her head to the baron and his wife, who returned the courtesy, speculation rife in their eyes.

"My, Hanover Square is quiet this afternoon," Rossum said, and Rachel smiled again. He was being ironic. Rachel had just named the square's four biggest gossips. "Was Lady Georgiana pleased with how events went yesterday?" he asked.

"Exceedingly," Rachel replied. The day before, Rachel's elder sister, Juliet, had wed Sir William Kersley. Sir William's courtship had quickly resumed on the Cavanagh family's return to London, leading to Sir William's proposal.

Juliet's wedding was precisely what Rachel had needed. She had *thrown* herself into helping with Juliet's plans. Or rather, she had thrown herself into the *distraction* of Juliet's plans—if she were to admit the truth to herself. She had fixed on the present and blocked out past and future. Anything else lodged too great a wad of pain in her chest.

Rossum was in the same position. He too felt the absence of his oldest, closest friend. And while neither could substitute for what the other had lost, common ground had brought them together.

In that common ground, friendship had grown.

Now, with the season coming to an end, the months stretched ahead... blank and no longer possible to ignore. She would, of course, study the family's financial ledgers and educate herself on other aspects of the business, but thanks to numerous discussions with Ariene over the years, she was already largely familiar with those. It was also four years until, at five and twenty, she would wield any real influence.

The travels she had planned with Ariene seemed so distant now, as though her dreams had belonged to someone else.

"Rachel, you seem quiet today. Is aught the matter?"

Her first impulse was to say no, but on reflection, she *had* been quiet today.

"Yes," she conceded. With the whirl of wedding preparations and then the wedding itself, this morning was the first time in days, if not weeks, that the Cavanagh women's diaries were relaxed. Her elder brother, Hugh, had been free to read the paper without interruption. Faith had sat curled in the window seat with the latest edition of the *La Belle* Assemblée, the women's fashion journal. Her younger brother, Andrew, had left for Wales with school friends. And Juliet had a new home with her husband. Rachel would miss them both. She saw too little of Andrew, who was four years younger than herself. Her mother had been pregnant with her younger brother at the time James Cavanagh was killed. Rhys Cavanagh had been the only 'father' that Andrew had known. She felt a closeness with her younger brother that she did not feel with Hugh. In fact, she felt a closeness with her younger brother that she did not even feel with her sisters, especially Faith. But he was so rarely home.

Is aught the matter? Rossum had asked. Rachel strolled alongside him for a time before she answered. "With the end of the season and Juliet now married, I cannot help thinking about what is next."

"There is Atherton Court, for a start."

Rossum's words were light and intended to draw her smile.

And they did—a small one. "Of course," she agreed. Next week, Lady Georgiana, Rachel and her younger sister, Faith, would be attending a house party at Atherton Court, Rossum's family seat in Kent. She gave his arm a reassuring squeeze. "I was thinking... *beyond.*"

"Not next month," he said quietly. "You mean next year. The year after."

"Yes."

For a time, Rossum said nothing. "I heard Percy Shelley has published a new work. An account of his travels through France and Switzerland."

"Yes. It's titled 'A History of a Six Weeks' Tour'."

"You've read it?"

On the surface, it seemed like a lightly phrased question, but the truth the Marquess dug for was deeper.

"No," she said.

She couldn't.

Her love of travel narratives had begun at her grandfather's knee. Until the shipwreck, she had read every one she could get her hands on. Published journals, maritime diaries, natural histories, memoirs such as her grandfather and the Baroness Gisele de Bauer had written.

She had also kept a journal herself.

Now it lay at the bottom of the Channel, and she couldn't bring herself to replace it. Or read the work of Shelley or any other travel author.

Several months ago, she had confided as much to Rossum. His question now, and the answer she gave, told him that nothing had changed. She had thrown herself into the here and now of the London season and her sister's wedding and had pushed away thoughts of the future. Now, the future had all too rapidly crept up on her.

"We could give them their happy ever after," Rossum teased.

His words drew a reluctant smile to her lips. "Can you imagine?" Rachel said. "Where does the betting stand at White's at the moment? I daresay one of your contemporaries is set to become very rich."

Rossum smiled. "I can imagine. I would be happy to make

someone rich. My life would be . . . if I shared it with you."

His words, their meaning and the drop in his tone took several moments to sink in.

All thought slowed.

She slowed and came to a halt. Unconsciously, she had withdrawn her arm from his. Suddenly, she was gripping the handle of her parasol with both hands. "My goodness. You're serious."

"I've surprised you."

"I . . ." She sucked in a breath. "Yes. I mean . . . a *little*."

As much as they always made light of it, it was impossible to *completely* ignore the speculation. Lady Georgiana, for one, needed only to *look* at Rachel to convey her expectations. Expectations that Rachel had been able to brush off, so long as Rossum also brushed them off.

"Rachel," the Marquess spoke. "I think both of us have been contemplating . . . *beyond*."

Yes. But there was a vast difference between Rossum and herself. As Marquess, the man before her *knew* his path. Every week, he balanced estate, House of Lords, magistrate and family duties. He took his every responsibility seriously and, determined never to be found lacking because of his blindness, worked twice as hard as his peers.

Rachel was foremost expected to make a good match, at least as far as Lady Georgiana was concerned. If Rachel's mother had her way, she would also have Rachel sign over permanent control of Ariene's shipping interests to Hugh.

There was no doubt the Marquess was an exceptionally good match. Quite apart from his much-coveted title, Rossum was simply one of the best men Rachel knew. He was kind, thoughtful, and dedicated. And yet . . . .

"There is . . . easy familiarity . . . between us," he said.

"Y-yes," she stuttered. "Of course. Yes."

Still, Rossum knew her well enough to sense he'd disconcerted her. His tone was almost rueful. "I haven't chosen the most opportune moment for this discussion, have I?"

With the too-rare blue sky of London above and the multitude of foot, horse and carriage traffic trundling through Hanover

Square? No, when they had stepped outside the Cavanagh townhouse, she had not expected *this* conversation.

"Rachel, forgive me," he said. "I had not yet intended to speak."

Yet. Her mind fixed on that word. It meant, at some point, he *did* intend to speak.

"When . . . ?" The word was no sooner out than hot prickles heated her cheeks. How gauche. *He had just told her that he wished them to wed, and she responded by asking* when *he intended to speak?*

"At Atherton Court," he said.

She had wanted the possibility of a match between them to remain in the distance, where no decision was required of her. Because she cared for Rossum's company and friendship. The entirely sensible decision stood right in front of her.

"Caius . . . I . . . I don't know what to say." His given name slipped from her tongue. He stood stiffly before her, and she suddenly realized she'd left him alone in darkness, with only her voice as guide to her reaction. She started forward and grasped his hand. "My goodness, now I'm making a botch of things!"

He wove his fingers through hers. "No, Rachel, you couldn't. Do you know how rare it is for people to be honest with me? For my title, my blindness, not to influence their actions?" He took a breath. "Do you remember that day in Wales?"

He referred to the day she'd declined his friendship, when she'd told him she had nothing to give.

"Yes."

"Who I was didn't matter to you. You weren't prepared to offer something false. Rachel, I trust you as I trust only a handful of other people in this world. My uncle. My cousins Sophia and Alexander. And Peter, before the *Castalia* went down."

Rachel's throat closed over. Rossum's uncle, who was next in line to inherit the family's title, had had the most to gain if his young, blind, orphaned nephew was declared unfit to be Marquess. Yet it had been his uncle's unflinching support that had seen Rossum, at the age of twelve, receive the title. To be held in standing anywhere near Rossum's uncle was a wrenching compliment indeed. Unable to find words, Rachel squeezed Rossum's fingers between hers.

"I believe you trust me, too," Rossum continued. "I know I have little to offer"—Rachel made an instinctive sound of protest even as Rossum pressed on—"I rely on others," he said, "far more than other men. With your own fortune, you have no need for mine, and my title isn't even an enticement. Rachel Cavanagh, you make measuring up quite difficult for a man."

His admission stunned her. Was that how he saw himself? Saw *her*?

Did he not see all that he was? His intelligence and determination and kindness?

"Everyone relies on someone in one way or another," she said. "Caius—"

He again cut her off. "I know that we made light of the speculation at first. Neither of us expected anything to come of it. A traumatic experience hardly need result in a lifelong commitment. But Rachel, as we've come to know each other, I've grown to realize how important you are to me."

Lost for the words to reply, she again gave his fingers a squeeze. His words echoed the way she felt. Even so, he sensed her uncertainty in her silence, as she knew he would.

"Rachel," he coaxed, "you need not respond now. Come to Atherton Court next week. See if you can imagine it as your home. If you wish, I'll take you to each and every one of my estates." He took a breath. "Please, consider this form of 'beyond'."

Beyond. Married to Rossum. It was so different from everything she had envisaged when Ariene was alive.

An image flashed before her. Wind-filled sails, the bright glint of the sun reflecting off sea, the sheen of sea spray over the rail, the cry of gulls overhead. The pink- and dove-colored hues of a foreign port, lying just across the water.

Closer still, gray eyes full of mirth, intelligence and calculated spontaneity. Breeze-lashed dark golden-brown hair. A devastating smile. The roll of easy laughter on the wind. In spirit, her rescuer reminded her of her grandfather. And Ariene. Of a life lived by different rules.

She pushed the thought away.

"Yes," she said. "Yes. Of course, I will consider it."

Then she was on his arm again, and an uncharacteristic silence descended for the remainder of their circuit around the square.

They arrived back at the Cavanagh townhouse to find Rossum's new valet, John, waiting by the Marquess's carriage.

"I won't come inside again," Rossum said, as John opened the carriage door. The Marquess had paid his respects to Rachel's elder brother, Hugh, Lady Georgiana and Faith an hour before, when he arrived.

"I understand." Rachel stood, once more gripping her parasol. Tightness had invaded her chest.

"Please pass on my farewell to Hugh. I understand he is returning to Wales tomorrow?"

Rachel swallowed. "He is."

Rossum gave a nod. "We'll speak again in Kent."

"Of course."

The tightness in her chest rose to her throat and turned choking as he boarded the carriage. So much lay between them now. Their friendship, which she valued immensely—

She stepped forward suddenly. "Cauis. I... my reaction... please don't—" He stilled in his seat despite the verbal jumble that spilled from her mouth. She clasped the window frame of the carriage with one gloved hand. "For all the talk of you and I marrying, I never assumed... I have never given it the consideration I should have."

"I know you haven't, Rachel."

He smiled softly and with far more understanding than she wished to see.

That understanding shook her, because as the carriage began to move and she was forced to release the window frame and step back, it made her wonder whether, although blind, the Marquess of Rossum saw her better than she saw herself.

CHAPTER SIX

Why is it the nature of man to heed so little the ways in which we might inflict pain?
—*The Memoirs of Rhys Cavanagh*

"Rachel, dearest, you have me intrigued. Pray tell, what is so interesting about the dirty brown Thames?"

Rachel jerked her gaze away from the view outside the carriage window to look at her younger sister, Faith, who was seated opposite her. One of Faith's brows was arched, and her amused glance flickered to the Gothic novel that lay open in Rachel's lap. A little smile played along her lips. "Interesting in comparison to reclusive French marquises, that is?"

"Yes, do tell. I am also interested to know." Lady Georgiana's gaze lifted from her needlework, and she sent Rachel an assessing look from beneath her lashes. Unable to abide a carriage ride with her back to the direction of travel, Rachel's mother was seated on Faith's left. Despite the bumpy ride, a beautiful sampler was emerging beneath her fingertips. It was a gift for Juliet and Sir William to mark the occasion of their moving into their new home. "Rachel, you have barely spoken a word since we departed London."

"There is no great mystery. I've had nothing to say," Rachel replied.

Faith, dressed to perfection in her new traveling dress, regarded Rachel dubiously then turned to Lady Georgiana. There was a teasing light in her eyes. "I see what the problem is. She has realized that she *should* have come to the modiste with us last Monday."

Rachel gave an indelicate snort. Now *that* was amusing. "As I told you last Monday, I have absolutely no need for another riding habit to wear in Kent. I've barely worn the forest green velvet that was delivered two months ago."

"And as I told *you*," Faith returned, "designs are already favoring more frogging."

"I agree with your sister," Lady Georgiana said, and once again, Rachel was on the receiving end of one of her mother's pointed looks. "We will shortly be among the Marquess's most exalted acquaintances. Both my girls must present as 'belles of style.'"

"We will be among Rossum's closest friends and family," Rachel corrected, "and it is Faith who wishes to be the vanguard of fashion, not I. Mother, I have met the Marquess's relatives before, and I assure you, I will not be judged overly harshly for wearing a riding habit sewn in *May*."

Lady Georgiana's lips pursed. All knew this argument was a circular one. Between Lady Georgiana and Faith, *hours* were spent in the Cavanagh household poring over fashion plates and debating whether one or two or three festoons of satin about the bottom of one's evening dress would constitute 'the thing' the next month or—as the case might be—whether July would see more frogging on the bodice of one's riding habit.

If Faith was not so very determined to *set* fashion, she could write the columns of *La Belle Assemblée* and the other monthly journals herself.

The latter, however, was not what Faith had in mind. To achieve the kind of influence that enabled one to determine the month-to-month popularity of colors, gemstones, and flounces, Faith Cavanagh needed to make a very fine and very impressive match.

Rachel didn't doubt her sister would succeed, if through force of will alone. Beneath the veritable picture of white-laced confection Faith painted in her new, profusely trimmed, white satin Marlborough spencer, fetching cambric gown and jaunty little hat—beneath all that—James Cavanagh's youngest daughter was craftier than a pirate from Port Royal. And right now, Faith was not of a mind to be diverted.

"Really, Rachel; you seem so distracted. It's almost as though—" Faith cut off, but Rachel sensed what her sister had been about to say. *It was almost as though they were back in Wales in the weeks after Ariene had died.* Faith's pause showed she was reconsidering her words.

"I thought you were looking forward to seeing Rossum's estate," Faith said finally. "We've spoken of this visit for weeks."

Rachel had been looking forward to it. The visit felt very different now, knowing that she could become *mistress* of the estate.

"Distracted?" Lady Georgiana shot Rachel yet another glance as she completed the final stitch of a rose leaf. "Faith, your sister is never 'distracted'. There is always something unfolding in that mind of hers. She has been studying every boat braving that soup of a river as though she were making an inventory. Rachel, what on earth do you expect to see?"

Rachel drew a harsh breath. Her mother's words surprised her. *Had* she been making a study of the boats on the river? She didn't think so, but . . . she didn't really know *what* she had been thinking. "Given the provisions of Ariene's will, you cannot be surprised that I would take an interest in Thames shipping." Some Cavanagh trade took place at the London docks, although with the bulk of the family's interests now in raw materials, most Cavanagh shipping was handled in Liverpool and Bristol.

Ariene's will remained a sore point with her mother. "Hugh takes care of those matters," Lady Georgiana said dismissively.

Faith was still regarding Rachel, her expression unconvinced. "Something is bothering you."

"No."

"*Yes.*"

"Faith, *nothing* is the matter." Not if she pushed Rossum's offer of marriage from her mind.

What was she to do? Was that to be her life? Should it be her life? For the past two days, since her stroll with Rossum in Hanover Square, those questions had weighed heavily on her mind. Questions and uncertainty and a strange feeling a little akin to panic had built in her chest and stuck in her throat when she imagined standing before a vicar with Rossum and exchanging vows. But she couldn't talk about it. Not to her mother nor to Faith. Not in a thousand years would they understand her confusion. Not as Ariene or Rhys Cavanagh would have done.

If Rossum had been strolling in Hanover Square with Faith that day, he wouldn't have made it back to his carriage without first being dragged to the nearby parish church of St. George to set the wedding date.

"Has something happened between you and the Marquess?" Faith asked.

Rachel sighed. "Faith—"

"Oh!" Faith's eyes widened, and she clutched their mother's arm. "She suspects the Marquess will declare himself!"

Lady Georgiana's piercing gaze immediately fixed on Rachel, while her needle poised in the air.

Faith had always had the senses of a shark. It was all Rachel could do not to react. "Faith, you are sailing the wrong tack."

Her sister shook her head. "It would be perfect timing."

"I couldn't agree more," Lady Georgiana said. She shook her arm free of Faith's grip, then proceeded to dip needle into cloth. "Rossum's family will be present, together with his closest friends. He will have the opportunity to introduce you to his estate. It is the perfect time to make an offer."

Again the subject of that assessing gaze, Rachel pressed her lips together. She didn't trust herself to speak.

"You *are* perfect together," Faith said. "Whenever you speak, he smiles. Everyone wonders what makes you both laugh so."

It was true that Rachel could make him smile. That was because she described the little details that Rossum's other companions did not. The merging of happiness and terror on a shy debutante's face after a dandy requested a dance. The aggravating swoosh of a matron's purple hat feather in her long-suffering husband's face while the woman blathered to her circle of listeners. The odious manner in which an old, puffed-up English baron was ranting about "how we blew those bloody Frenchies to bits in Spain", oblivious to the growing indignation of a visiting French dignitary who stood five feet to his left. An old dowager surreptitiously stealing sweetmeats each time her sour-faced companion's back was turned.

Years of reading travelogues had schooled Rachel well. Those small moments were precisely the kind of detail she had hoped to record on her travels. They were precisely the moments she had written about and sketched in her journal, now lost at the bottom of the English Channel. Moments that showed the texture of places. The texture of people. Their unique strengths and quirks. The things each did in the moments they thought no one was watching.

Moments the Marquess of Rossum never saw.

"It is as the newspapers say," Faith continued. "Rossum and yourself, the only two survivors of a shipwreck. Even you must acknowledge it *is* a romantic story."

"There is scant romantic about a shipwreck, Faith."

A little scowl formed between Faith's brows. "That's not what I meant."

"No?" Rachel said dryly.

Her sister persisted. "A bond has forever formed between you."

Of course, Faith was correct. A bond *had* formed between Rachel and Rossum. It was a bond that had developed slowly, that had begun with honesty and had been secured through friendship. But what would Rossum's offer mean? What would it change?

Thought of her rescue conjured another face to mind, one very different in cast to the Marquess's.

"Truly, Rachel," her mother said. "I cannot understand why you pretend to be oblivious. Rossum has doted on you for months. Now I understand a blind husband is not ideal—"

Rachel was horrified that her mother thought such a thing would matter. "The fact that Rossum is blind has nothing to do with it!"

"Then I cannot imagine what other objections you might have, hmm?"

And that was precisely Rachel's dilemma. She cared for Rossum deeply. He was honorable, thoughtful, deeply accomplished.

Silent, she again looked out the window.

This time, she was careful not to inventory the boats as the banks of the Thames rolled past.

FAITH GAVE A SIGH AND tapped her fan impatiently against the blue-clothed table at which the Cavanagh women sat taking refreshments. Outside the dining parlor, in the yard of the Gravesend coaching inn, their carriage horses were being watered.

"Surely we can be on the road again soon?" Faith asked. "It will be dark before we reach Gillingham."

They planned to spend the night in Gillingham, enroute to the Marquess's estate near Canterbury. "It will be dark," Rachel pointed out, "because we departed London late after waiting for your delivery from the modiste to arrive."

Faith's blue gaze—inherited from their mother—snapped to Rachel. Even so, humor lurked there. Rachel's younger sister set aside her fan. "Now that you have seen my new hat, I think you simply must agree it would have been a travesty *not* to wait." She picked up the teapot. "Oh, we are out of tea." She signaled to the serving girl to bring another pot.

The dining parlor in which the women sat was quite pretty. The walls were decorated with pale-blue, flock wallpaper and several paintings of ships and sea, while small white vases containing sprigs of marigold decorated each table. Besides their own table, four were occupied with travelers.

The serving girl arrived to balance a tray on the edge of their table. "Your tea," she said, before carefully lifting the fresh pot and setting it down on the table.

Rachel's attention shifted to the tray. Suddenly and quite dramatically, her heart pitched in her chest. "Oh, my God."

A pewter mug sat in the middle of the tray. '*The Lord Nelson, Gravesend*' was engraved near its lip.

The memory of a similar mug surged through her. More overwhelming was the memory of the man who had owned it. In her mind, she could still see the slash of his grin as he first told her his name. So too the stunned look in his eyes and the way his lips had parted and he'd grown so quiet when she'd pressed her mouth to his hand.

Had Jonathon Lecky come here once? *More* than once? Was it possible that he was known here? Might one of the servants know where to find him?

"Rachel, what is it?"

Lady Georgiana's question was sharp enough to still her ricocheting thoughts. "It's...I...." Rachel looked up at the young, blonde-haired, blue-eyed serving girl who stood beside the table. Rachel blew out a breath. "I'm sorry. What is the name of this inn?"

"It's the Lord Nelson, miss."

That confirmation only worsened her jumble of thoughts. Was it possible she could contact him?

I can't imagine any circumstance, Miss Cavanagh, in which contact would be necessary.

But it *was* necessary. *This* was the circumstance. Every fiber of her being suddenly told her that was the case. Her pulse sped up.

"Rachel, why do you need to know the name of the inn?"

She had to fight hard to concentrate on Faith's question. She had to grope for a response. "It struck me as...familiar. Perhaps from one of grandfather's stories?"

Rhys Cavanagh's stories had found selective audience with Faith. As it was, mention of their grandfather was a swift means by which to lose both Faith's and Lady Georgiana's attention.

"Oh," Faith said.

"Would you like me to pour your tea?" the serving girl asked.

"No, thank you. You may go." Lady Georgiana lifted the teapot off the table to refill their cups.

Rachel's mind was busy. *Just because Jonathon Lecky possessed a similar mug didn't mean he was known here.* It was *just a mug*— not the answers to the mysteries of all mankind. Still, she had to ask.

She felt jittery, aware every passing minute brought the time of their departure closer.

Lady Georgiana and Faith's conversation turned to the entertainments that Rossum might have planned for the upcoming week.

Rachel's foot started to tap beneath the table. She forced it to stop.

Suddenly, she pushed up from her seat. "Are you done? I'll pay our account."

Lady Georgiana looked shocked to be interrupted mid-sentence. "You could just call the girl over."

"It's fine." Rachel abandoned her chair and crossed the room, leaving no further opportunity for discussion.

The serving girl also looked surprised and somewhat concerned by Rachel's approach. "Would you like something else, miss?"

Yes. Do you know where I might find a boat captain by the name of Jonathon Lecky?

Suddenly, the questions she wanted to ask seemed ridiculous. Jonathon Lecky could have obtained that mug a dozen years ago and never been back.

The young woman was still looking at her.

"I'd like to pay our bill, please," Rachel said.

"Certainly, miss. It will be one shilling."

Rachel dug in her reticule, all the while admonishing herself. It didn't *matter* whether the question was ridiculous. What if the answer was *yes*? She placed a crown in the young woman's palm. "Have you worked at the Lord Nelson long?"

"Since my father became innkeeper three years ago, miss." The young woman glanced at the coin, brushed a golden-blonde strand of hair back from her face, then fished about in her apron pocket for change.

Rachel mustered her nerve. "Excuse me. Can you perchance tell me—"

A heavy-set man with a thick beard appeared behind the serving girl. "Pa!" The girl twisted to look up as the man set his hands on her shoulders.

But his attention was directed at Rachel. "Beg your pardon. You are Miss Cavanagh, are you not? Your party is traveling to Gillingham tonight?"

"That's correct. We are," Rachel replied.

"Miss, may I urge you to hold over and make a clear run through in the morning? There's been highwaymen on the road these past nights. Four carriages have been stopped so far."

Hold over in Gravesend? Her heart beat faster. "How awful." *How convenient.* "I hope no one has been harmed?"

The innkeeper shook his head. "No. But one of the coachmen—the brother of my stable master—was fired upon. And the blackguard that did the deed got away with a goodly portion of money."

Lady Georgiana and Faith drew up beside Rachel. "Is aught the matter, Rachel?" her mother asked.

"Highwaymen, Mother," Rachel replied. "On the road to Gillingham. A man was almost shot."

At Rachel's side, Faith made an indignant noise.

Outwardly, Rachel knew she appeared calm. But inside, her heart was clamoring. *If they were to stay overnight, she could make enquiries....* "None of us wishes to be endangered for the sake of a few hours delay, do we, Mother?" Her mother, fortunately, was not partial to being separated from the family's money or valuables. Rachel turned back to the innkeeper. "Do you have rooms? We have a large party." They were traveling with two carriages, carrying luggage and coachmen and maids.

"Aye, miss. Rooms enough."

"Then we must thank you for your warning. We will stay." She cast a 'no argument' look at her mother and sister and knew, for the second time in her life, she was grateful for men with an affinity for lawlessness.

THE EYES THAT WERE NARROWED on Jonathon Lecky across the table in the inn's public room glittered with a disturbing mix of hatred, suspicion, and a desire to kill. But then, Lecky knew the man before him presently inhabited manifold pits of hell.

"What reason," Joseph Blackburn growled, "do I have to trust a goddamned thing you say?"

"I don't expect you to trust me. Not on such short acquaintance." An alliance based on mutual enmity did not trust make. That was certainly the case with a man like Blackburn, as it was with a man like himself. "You'll understand I feel the same. However, I heard you were a man with a desire to inflict damage." Lecky slid a folded sheet of newsprint across the table. He tapped two fingers on an article at the top. "Given the nature of your target, I know precisely where you can hit the hardest."

Blackburn's gaze dipped to the newspaper. Both men were already well aware of what the article said. *Damage to The Helena, English Schooner.* The vessel, owned by Messrs. Jonas and Chaloner MacArthur of the trading and shipbuilding firm MacArthur and

Sons of London had blown aground in a storm off Cascais, Portugal, en route to Cadiz, Spain. While the ship itself was recoverable, her cargo had been lost at considerable cost.

Of course, any misfortune suffered by MacArthur and Sons was always welcome news.

Blackburn's gaze lifted. The man was not considered especially influential or particularly upstanding. In truth, Blackburn was considered a jackal. The man's eyes narrowed again. "Griffiths told me your story."

As though sensing his name had come into the discussion, the innkeeper, Owen Griffiths, looked their way. Lecky briefly met his gaze. He knew exactly what Owen had said. The innkeeper had been coached before he ever mentioned Lecky's name to Blackburn.

"Then you'll understand my interest," Lecky said.

Blackburn's look scoured his face, his expression one of substantial distrust. "I'm not so sure about that."

"Let's just say you're not the first to suffer at Chaloner MacArthur's hand."

Blackburn had a jackal's smile, too. It came sharp and fast, before it hardened to a sneer. "Suffer?" he repeated. "*Suffer?* The man destroyed my business. More than that, the son of a bitch took my *daughter*."

"A son of a bitch he is not," Lecky corrected. "The bad blood comes from the father. However," he continued, as Blackburn's sneer turned vicious, "I am well aware that the lives of others mean little to Chaloner MacArthur."

Blackburn slammed his hands palm down on the table. "'*Little*'? God damn right they mean '*little*'! Do you understand, Mr. Lecky, that my daughter threw herself off the goddamned London Bridge, rather than tell me what MacArthur had done to her?"

Shock punched through Lecky. *By the gods, that was news.* It must have been a recent turn of events. He'd known Chaloner had got to Blackburn's daughter, but he hadn't known the girl was *dead*.

Chaloner, you heartless, contemptible dog.

"I'm sorry."

Blackburn saw Lecky's shock, but the man's anger had been

unleashed. He burst from his chair to plant his fists in the table. His eyes flashed—hatred, suspicion. Underlying it all, Lecky recognized the wildness of grief.

"The only reason, the *only goddamned reason*," Blackburn snarled, "we are talking is because Griffiths vouched for you. He said you got him out of trouble in Africa. He says you're the reason he's here today."

Blackburn's sudden move had brought Owen's attention around again. Lecky shot the innkeeper an 'I've got this' look. "That's true." He had gotten Owen Griffiths and his crew mates out of trouble in North Africa. But that wasn't the reason he and Blackburn were here today.

Lecky looked back to Blackburn. "You want MacArthur dead."

"My daughter is dead! Blast it, yes, I want the cur dead!" For a split second, the wildness in Blackburn's expression betrayed a man teetering somewhere between a powder keg exploding and a father shattered by grief, then dissolved into equally dangerous nothingness. "But don't mistake me. I want to see Chaloner MacArthur suffer first. I want MacArthur to know what he's done. Quick is too good for that bastard."

Chaloner MacArthur *always* knew what he did. But the man had never given a damn. Nothing Blackburn did would change that. But Lecky agreed. Quick *was* too good. Anything that could thwart or impair Chaloner MacArthur was worthwhile.

His look didn't waver. "Then you might want to take your seat again, Blackburn. I'm glad to hear you like doing things slow, because I've just the answer you're looking for."

"Didn't think you'd get through to him for a while there," Owen Griffiths said, when Blackburn was gone. "That was a big gamble, Jonathon."

"Mayhap. But you know better than most that my gambles usually pay." With a pointed look, Lecky lifted his mug in mock salute. "Cheers, my friend. For your good word." He took one long, last swallow, only to set the remainder of his ale down as his mouth filled with the bitter taste of sorrow.

Poor lass. *Dead.*

If anything, Blackburn's daughter's fate was vindication he was doing the right thing. He'd turned his back too long. That made him just as culpable.

"You've had a haircut, Jonathon. It looks good," Sarah, Owen's daughter, remarked as she whisked by en route to the counter.

"Indeed. Thank you, Sarah." He'd needed the clean cut style to meet with his associate Winter's investors the previous week. It had been a few years since he'd worn his hair short.

"More ale?" the young woman asked.

"Not tonight."

"Not any night, it would seem." Setting down two empty tankards on the nearby counter, Owen's daughter indicated to her father that she needed a refill, then swept a loose, golden-blonde strand of hair back from her face. "You know, Jonathon, I can't remember a single time I've ever seen you falling down drunk. Not like that lot. That lot are always sniffing the floor." She gave a toss of her hand in the direction of a table of burly patrons, then turned to her father. "Have you, Pa? Ever seen Jonathon drunk?"

"Oh, aye." Owen's blue eyes lit on Lecky with no shortage of knowledge. "There's been occasions when he's had something particular to celebrate."

Aye, there had been plenty of those nights in Mogadore, at the British Vice-Consul's quarters, after a successful expedition down the Moroccan coast or into the desert to ransom a shipwrecked sailor from the Arab or African tribes. In some cases, Lecky's party had been able to reach the survivors quickly. Other men and women had been enslaved for six months or more before the Vice-Consul received word and was able to send Lecky or another contingent to negotiate their release.

Rescuing British and European sailors and their passengers had been dangerous work. It was work Lecky had done for eight years. But Owen had the right of it, for after all, Owen knew first hand. Regaining a man his freedom was indeed something to celebrate.

Celebrations tonight, however, with respect to Blackburn would be premature. Lecky gave Owen a wink, then slid the folded page of newsprint back across the table. As he did, his glance caught on the second article of interest, printed lower down the page.

Privateer's Granddaughter Marries Baronet.

Lecky knew what that article said, too. Three days before, Juliet Cavanagh, the eldest daughter of Lieutenant-Commander James Cavanagh and Lady Georgiana Cavanagh, had married Sir William David Edmund Kersley at St. Georges, Hanover Square. After detailing the nuptials, the article predictably closed with speculation about a potential match between the second daughter, Miss Rachel Cavanagh, and the Marquess of Rossum, who was said to have been in attendance.

If Lecky were in a mood for more drinking, he'd say cheers to them, too.

"Did I mention we have quite illustrious company under our roof tonight?" Owen asked.

Lecky eased back to rest his elbow on the table. "No. And for that matter, I'm always skeptical when you use that term. There seems to be a vast discrepancy between your definition of 'illustrious' and mine."

"Oh, you won't disagree with me tonight." A sly grin spread across Owen's face. He refilled a tankard, set the ale down on the counter, then gave a nod towards the newsprint. "The family of Rhys Cavanagh, the privateer."

Well, damn. Lecky went still. That was like being doused by a bucket of water from the Baltic.

In newsprint, Rachel Cavanagh was one thing. In Gravesend, in the Lord Nelson Inn, separated by walls rather than miles, she was entirely another.

By Owen's snort, Lecky's surprise must have showed.

"Ha! See? I've got you." Owen looked damnably pleased with himself, despite knowing nothing of Lecky and Rachel Cavanagh's acquaintance.

"Very well, I'll grant you that one," Lecky said. Of course, there was the chance his arabica-eyed survivor wasn't among them. "Which members of the family?"

Owen set the second tankard to the tap. "The drunken Earl Whittlesey's daughter, Lady Georgiana, and two of the daughters. The one from the shipwreck they all say will marry the blind Marquess and a younger one."

Well, there went that hope.

"I served her in the dining room earlier," Sarah put in, grasping a refilled tankard in each hand. "So pretty, she is. And so *gracious*. Oh, I do hope she marries the Marquess. It's so easy to imagine her as marchioness."

No, it wasn't. Lecky's every thought rebelled. *Not Rachel Cavanagh; not the girl he had met.* She didn't belong in a world of formality and duty and expectation. A world of mahogany desks and cold, echoing, centuries-old halls and estate management. No, where Rachel Cavanagh would be *most* alive was amid open seas and sea winds and fair weather. Exploring bustling ports and quaint villages and marveling at desert flowers. She was an earl's granddaughter perhaps, but her blood ran to Cavanagh.

With a contented little sigh, Sarah sagged against the counter. "After such a tragedy, all those lives lost, it's nice that she and the Marquess will have a happy ending."

Owen gave an affectionate snort. "You've got your mother's soft heart, my girl. But, aye, it's quite the love story, all right."

"Isn't it just." Suddenly, Lecky was in no mood to laugh. The smoke in the taproom was cloying. He wanted some damn air. He pushed to his feet. "Excuse me while I duck out back."

He exited through the foyer to the yard and found himself pacing. He locked his hands behind his head as he came to a stop to look up at the heavens.

The gods be damned.

He hadn't forgotten her. No, the memory of Rachel Anwen Cavanagh stirred each time the light brush of the west wind caught his sails. He could close his eyes and see her still, curled up tight against the side of his cabin with the lucent dawn behind and his blanket slipping down her shoulder.

When that image arose, he wanted to wrap her in his arms and keep her warm against his chest. To hell with hand-holding.

But the way things had developed, it seemed that was the Marquess's business now.

Let it go, Jonathon. She's not your path. You crossed paths; that was all.

He leant against the brick wall of the yard and tipped his head back. Somewhere up there, above the taproom, behind the first- or second-floor windows, was the woman he had rescued.

Not the *first* woman he'd rescued. But it hadn't left him, that feeling that she was special.

What is it you actually *want to do, Jonathon? Mosey on up there and say hello? Meet her mother? Convince yourself she* isn't *as lovely as you recall? Or remind yourself that she* is?

Good, Jonathon. An excellent idea. Inflict that *upon yourself.*

Another patron staggered out the door to the foyer and lurched toward the privies. Brawnier and heavier than Lecky, the man cast Lecky a sullen, drunken glance before thumping into one of the stalls.

Damn. He could read about Rachel Cavanagh later, in newsprint, when he had again put miles between them and his arrangements with Blackburn had been taken care of. He needed to walk away now.

But his body wouldn't move. He tipped his head back, closed his eyes, and sighed.

Because all he could think about was butterscotch coils and solemn dark eyes.

Gravel crunched. *Too close.*

His senses burst into action—

Too late to prevent the fist that ground into his side.

BUSTLING AND LIVELY, THE TAPROOM of the Lord Nelson Inn swelled with patrons. There were no paintings of the sea here, no pale-blue, flock wallpaper. Instead, dark timber panels stretched from floor to ceiling. Travelers and locals congregated at sturdy wooden tables and relaxed in the brown armchairs arranged by the fireplace. Although there was no fire—it was high summer—Rachel could imagine how quickly a fire would warm the room at the weather's turn.

Upstairs, Lady Georgiana, Faith, and their maids slept in their rooms. Rachel had waited until the sliver of light beneath each of their doors was extinguished before slipping downstairs.

The blonde serving girl from the dining room spotted Rachel standing on the threshold to the taproom. Holding two large tankards, the young woman came to a surprised stop. "Miss Cavanagh." Her glance took in the reticule Rachel clutched in case money loosened tongues and the traveling dress Rachel still wore. "Is everything all right, miss? Can I help you with something?"

Rachel's hands were perspiring. She intended to be swift. "Yes, thank you. I'd like—I'd hoped—to speak to your father?"

"Of course." The young woman nodded, clearly anxious to please, but her hands were full. She glanced back over her shoulder. "He's by the counter. I can fetch him—"

"A few steps is no trouble," Rachel said. "Please . . . continue."

The young woman nevertheless hesitated. "You're sure—"

"Of course. Please, go ahead." Rachel cast her a reassuring smile. She pretended to be oblivious to the glances she received as she crossed to the counter.

"Miss Cavanagh." The innkeeper, like his daughter, appeared surprised to see her. "Is all well?" he asked. "You're satisfied with your accommodation?"

"Oh, yes. Thank you again for your warning about the highwaymen." Her nerves were on the rise again. So too her feeling of ridiculousness. What did she think—

She could only ask, she reminded herself. *He would say yes or no.*

She drew a breath. "I'm seeking information about a man who may be a patron of the Lord Nelson."

"Oh?" Her words clearly came as a surprise. He set his hands upon the counter. "That's a wide net, miss. We've all sorts that come through here, but I'll try to help. Who's the chap?"

"He's a boat captain." Rachel's glance flickered sideways as the serving girl appeared by the counter, minus two tankards.

The innkeeper was diverted by his daughter's arrival, too. "Miss Cavanagh is looking for a chap she thinks might be a patron, Sarah."

"Oh!" His daughter's look turned inquisitive. "What is his name?"

The name of her rescuer had been stuck inside for so long, dislodging it was like scraping hardened barnacles from a ship's hull. To speak of him made her feel bare and exposed—as though it were all too clear what his involvement in her life had meant.

"His name is Lecky. Mr. Jonathon Lecky. He has a dog. A Welsh collie called Morgan."

The innkeeper's brows shot up faster than a sailor looked to the crow's nest when 'Pirate!' was called. "Wait—Jonathon *Lecky*, you said?"

His daughter appeared equally dumbfounded. The girl's astonished glance went to her father.

They recognized his name; that was what their looks meant. Questions rose in Rachel's throat as the tempo of her heart surged.

The innkeeper cleared his throat. "Beg your pardon, Miss Cavanagh. Don't take this the wrong way... but why is a lady like yourself looking for Jonathon Lecky?"

"You know him?"

"Aye. I know him, miss. Though it surprises me that you do."

"He did me a great service once," Rachel said. "Do you know how I might find him?"

"He did you a great service?" He exchanged a look with his daughter, the meaning of which Rachel couldn't quite fathom. "What did he do? If you don't mind me asking."

Suddenly, Rachel was sick of withholding the truth. "Nine months ago in the English Channel he saved me from drowning. The Marquess of Rossum and I both."

The innkeeper's jaw dropped. His daughter's eyes turned to saucers as she gaped.

They stared at her. She stared back through their stunned silence.

Finally, the innkeeper cleared his throat. "How very like Lecky."

Was it? Rachel didn't know.

"Quite common for him to save women from drowning, is it?" she asked.

The older man gave a bark of laughter and another meaningful glance passed between father and daughter. "Drowning women I'm not so sure about, but let's just say that I know a few folk that Jonathon Lecky has helped." Puzzlement shot through Rachel. Before she could speak, the innkeeper asked, "So, you want to find him do you, Miss Cavanagh?"

Yes. No. *Yes.*

What was she thinking?

Was she *seeking* a plank to walk, as her grandfather used to say? Because *this* path felt equally mad.

She kept her features schooled, afraid of what she might reveal, as the innkeeper studied her. "I would like to know how to contact him."

Like the crawl of the sun over the horizon, canny eyes lit and an amused grin broke over the innkeeper's face. "Well, Miss Cavanagh, I daresay we at the Lord Nelson Inn can help you with that." Suddenly, the man standing before her looked ready to have a jolly old time. "Your valiant boat captain will be back in a minute."

CHAPTER SEVEN

Every lass should be taught to wield a cutlass.
—*The Memoirs of Rhys Cavanagh*

FOR A MOMENT, RACHEL WAS certain she'd misheard. Did he say... had he said....

"Back in a minute?" she managed to stammer.

"Aye." The innkeeper pointed to the untended mug that sat in the center of the table behind her. "That's his ale right there."

Rachel's stomach took a sudden, roiling, nervous plunge.

"Truly, he shouldn't be long," the innkeeper's daughter added, as she was summoned by a patron. "He just had to duck out back."

Rachel faced the innkeeper, speechless, as his daughter slipped away.

He seemed to intuit some of her thoughts or perhaps her obvious lack of them. "If you'd like a moment of privacy, there's a little foyer located off the tap room. There, just through that door. Folks pass through there on the way back from the yard. Lecky should be passing that way in a minute."

"Thank you." She slipped from the taproom, relieved to have a moment to collect herself.

She braced against the wall, clutching her reticule. Her palms were damp. *What would Jonathon Lecky do when he saw her?* She shot a glance at the half-propped-open door that led to the yard. Darkness lay beyond.

It was then she heard it. A crash, followed by a throaty growl—only just audible over the hum that flowed from the taproom.

Both sounds had come from outside. And she knew, *just knew,* with stomach-deep certainty, where her boat captain was.

Swiftly, she moved to the door. Outside, two men grappled in the yard. The larger man—a Goliath, heavier by at least sixty pounds and perhaps three inches taller—had his opponent trapped against the wall. Rachel flinched as Goliath drew back his fist, then drove it with savage force into his opponent's gut.

His opponent's breath whooshed out. Rachel saw the white flash of teeth—vicious and gritted and angry—as he sagged deep into the shadows of the wall.

Then, the grit of those teeth twisted into a smile that could have burst straight from her memories.

Except that this time he was real. He was here before her in the flesh.

"I'm beginning to take this rather personally," her one-time rescuer said. Then launched himself forward, only to be stymied by Goliath, who used his weight to slam them both back into the wall. Jonathon Lecky released another grunt.

Rachel pressed her fist to her mouth to stifle her cry. She could go for help or—

Her eyes fell upon the empty brass umbrella stand near the door. Quickly, silently, she lifted it.

Her breath caught in her throat as she slipped through the door and inched forward. Neither man saw her.

Jonathon Lecky landed a blow to his assailant's side but, with limited mobility, lacked the power to throw his assailant off. His second jab proved just as futile.

Goliath thrust out an arm and caught Jonathon Lecky by the throat, his thick fingers digging into Jonathon Lecky's jaw.

Rachel swung. *Hard.* And connected with the back of Goliath's neck, at the intersection with his shoulders. Her grandfather had always said she had a good aim.

With a shocked grunt, Goliath staggered. His grip on her rescuer's throat slackened.

The boat captain was quick to take advantage. He wrenched away from the wall, fisted his hand and delivered a shattering blow to his assailant's jaw.

Goliath's head snapped round. Thrown off balance, he staggered to the side, swayed precariously... then toppled like lopped timber and pitched into the dirt. His overlarge body lay still.

Rachel allowed the umbrella stand to slip from her fingers. It hit the dirt with a thump as Jonathon Lecky turned, rubbing his neck where his assailant had squeezed.

Stillness crossed his face—his hand froze—as his look stopped on her.

Stopped on her and took her in. Swiftly and thoroughly.

No, she needn't have feared that he wouldn't remember her.

But what he was *thinking*? She hadn't a clue.

She opened her mouth to speak just as he drew a breath. A pained grimace twisted his features, and he raised his hand to his ribs.

Rachel took an involuntary step forward. "Are you—"

"Bruised. There wasn't anything shy about the bastard's fists. *Damn*." His gaze focused on her again. "What are you doing in the yard?"

I was looking for you.

She couldn't say that. She found at that moment she couldn't say anything at all.

His dark golden-brown hair was different. Cut shorter, it emphasized his handsomeness. With that exception, he was just as she remembered, in his dark brown trousers and unbuttoned-at-the-neck navy blue shirt. In the dim light shed by the lantern above the inn door, his gray eyes regarded her, piercing and intense.

She had to tear her gaze from his. She cast an anxious look at his attacker. The man hadn't stirred. "My mother, sister and I are staying at the inn this evening," she said by way of explanation. "Do you know that man?"

"As a matter of fact—no." His gaze too broke off. He leant down to grasp the collar of the man's shirt.

"Why was he attacking you?" She had to take a quick step back as he began dragging his assailant across the dirt. The man's barely audible groan was at least reassurance that he wasn't dead.

"That," her rescuer threw open the door to one of the privies, "is something I would like to know myself."

"Perhaps...." She momentarily lost the direction of her thoughts as she watched Jonathon Lecky grasp his attacker again.

"Do you want me to fetch someone? The innkeeper—"

With a grunt from the strain placed on his ribs, Jonathon Lecky rolled his attacker into the privy and, with a few good shunts, forced shut the door. "What I *want*—" He swung back around, then fell silent as he stared at her. One might have mistaken her for an apparition by the way he was looking at her. He ran a hand raggedly down his face. "Bloody hell. *Bloody hell.*"

Rachel blinked as he strode past her back to the inn.

At first, she stood rooted. *What on earth?*

She spun and followed him. She caught up with him in the taproom of the inn, just as he lifted his mug, threw back his head and finished his ale with several long swallows. He slammed the mug down in front of the innkeeper. The innkeeper's gaze shot from Jonathon to Rachel with shock.

"One of your bastard patrons formed the view that it's polite to drive one's fist into a man's side on the way back from taking a piss."

The innkeeper's gaze wrenched back to the man who had saved her. "*What?*"

Whether the man was more shocked by the language Jonathon Lecky had just used in front of her or by the information the boat captain had just imparted, Rachel wasn't sure.

"It wasn't Blackburn?" the innkeeper asked.

It was then Rachel realized Jonathon Lecky was angry. Deeply, furiously angry. His eyes glittered, fierce and dangerous. "No. He was with them." With a jerk of his head, he gestured toward one corner of the taproom.

The innkeeper's attention shifted to the group and narrowed as he catalogued those present. He gave a groan. "Ah, damn." His gaze came back to Jonathon Lecky. "The one in the yard. He was a big, brawny chap, about so tall?" He indicated with his hand.

Something shifted in the boat captain's eyes—a minute release of tension? He gave a slow nod.

"Knust." The innkeeper's look again flickered to Rachel, as though he were uncomfortable speaking in front of her. "Knust's woman left him a sennight ago. Most like because of his fists."

Again, Jonathon Lecky's eyes narrowed.

"Where is he now?" the innkeeper asked.

"Still in the privy."

The innkeeper grimaced. "Not dead?"

"No. I wouldn't bring that trouble on you."

The innkeeper took a breath and spaced his hands on the counter. "I'll get one of the lads to fetch him."

Jonathon Lecky gave a nod. He slapped his hand down on the counter, and some unspoken understanding passed between them. "We'll talk again soon."

"Yes." The innkeeper returned his nod, although the glance he sent Rachel was quizzical.

Jonathon Lecky was *leaving*, Rachel realized.

Oh, God. He *couldn't* leave.

"Wait! You're going?" She swiftly stepped forward as he turned.

He regarded her. And for the most fleeting of instants, she thought she saw something beneath the layers of anger—an infinitesimal hint of something else, some other emotion.

Whatever she'd glimpsed was gone as he pushed off across the room. "Quite right, sweetheart. Privies aren't safe around here."

That was *it?*

She understood he was angry. He'd been assaulted. But he was just going to *go?*

"You won't spare a moment?" she blurted.

He reached the main entry to the inn and rounded on her. "Miss Cavanagh, it has been an unexpected surprise to meet you again. Truly unexpected." His gaze skated over her again, before he turned and wrenched open the door.

She realized she had just become the focal point of half the room as the door swung shut behind him. The innkeeper and his daughter in particular looked aghast. Rachel felt the flush of chagrin and gritted her teeth. Irrespective that she'd just saved his hide, his actions were *rude*.

She strode forward and shoved through the inn's front door onto the narrow, cobbled road outside. The inn stood in the center of Gravesend, closed in by shop fronts and townhouses on either side. A few lanterns cast distantly spaced pools of light along the street. Jonathon Lecky whirled around as the inn door slammed closed.

She heard his hiss of frustration. "Notus be damned, what are you doing? You need to hurry back to your room before someone spots you out here."

She was aware of that. Her trip to the taproom was supposed to have taken a moment. But if he walked away . . . .

If he walked away now, it would be too much like his departure in Dunkirk, when he left her in the guest room still with questions in her throat.

"Stop, please! So we can speak."

"Everything was said in Dunkirk."

"That was months ago!"

"Then I should think," he said, "you would have well and truly put those matters behind."

His words knocked her breathless. More than a fist to the stomach, so too they exploded in her chest. Pain unfurled.

Put those matters behind. That was what everyone expected. They all thought she should have 'put those matters behind' by now. Her mother. Faith. Society with all its speculations.

Damn him. Damn him to hell.

Damn him for making her feel just like everyone else did. Lost. Like she was a failure. Like there was something wrong with her.

He took a breath. Perhaps he could see that he'd hurt her, that he'd scored a direct hit on something raw, because his voice dropped a notch. "I don't know what you think I can do for you, Miss Cavanagh."

Pain solidified into sudden, vicious, choking, hurtful anger. Anger that spread through her *everywhere*. Hot. Furious. She stared at him.

In some disjointed, still-aware part of herself, she knew he personally hadn't done anything to warrant this fierce a storm. Not entirely. But that didn't matter right now.

"You might at least say bloody thank you!" she exploded.

For a split second, her words surprised him. She saw his shock.

Then the expression in those gray eyes shifted to send her tumbling back through the months, back to those moments on the aft deck of his sloop, when his eyes had softened with a look that *understood*.

"Of course," he said, after a pause. "This time you came to *my* rescue."

He stepped closer in a move that surprised her.

Despite her anger, something changed in the air—became charged. Her skin prickled. It was like Wales—the tang of late afternoon storms, the laden current that permeated the air when lightning sheeted above the Bay of Bristol and the Glamorgan coast.

Jonathon Lecky's scent came back to her—the same combination of salt and sea and male that clung to the blanket he'd loaned her that night nine months ago, aboard his sloop.

Suddenly, his body crowded hers.

"I don't claim to have your manners, Rachel Anwen Cavanagh. Nor do I claim your finesse."

He captured one of her hands. Her heart, fearing that he intended to make mockery of the tribute she'd paid to him in Dunkirk, gave a pained cry. But Jonathon Lecky didn't raise her hand to his lips.

He dragged her whole body against his, and his mouth crashed down on hers.

It wasn't an admirer's kiss or a lover's kiss.

It was a stolen kiss. The kiss of a marauder. A buccaneer. Swift and smacking, claiming for one split second everything it oughtn't.

In that same moment, he held her hand in his, pressed against his heart.

He released her as quickly as he had approached, then stepped away entirely. "Thank you, Miss Cavanagh, for your deft use of an umbrella stand."

She could barely breathe, let alone prevent her jaw from dropping. The man had just *kissed* her.

"If it weren't still lying by the privies, I might use it over *your* head," she managed.

His look was sharp, but her words elicited his grin.

Oh, she knew as her stomach plummeted that she was a fool to elicit that grin.

And then it faded, and his expression once more became grave.

Naught but cobblestones lay between them.

Cobblestones and silence. And space she couldn't force him to cross.

"Speak with me."

She thought, perhaps, she whispered it.

An eternity passed, so long she wondered if she'd not spoken at all. He didn't move.

Finally, his gaze flickered over the facade of the inn before returning to her.

"We'll want privacy then," he said. "Come say hello to Morgan."

CHAPTER EIGHT

When a man becomes lost, give him the helm. If not paralyzed by fear, serving as master of his own destiny in a well-lived adventure usually leads a man home.
—*The Memoirs of Rhys Cavanagh*

AHEAD, A BARK SOUNDED AND Morgan's black shape leapt from Lecky's sloop and bounded forward as Lecky and his unexpected guest reached the pier, located just a few short blocks from the Lord Nelson.

"Down, girl," Lecky commanded, greeted by thirty-five pounds of happy, prancing collie and a series of short, enthusiastic whines. Unfazed by Lecky's dismissal, Morgan fell back. It was then she took note of his companion. Did Morgan remember her? His collie hesitated, clearly considering the same question, then bumped up against Rachel Cavanagh's legs with the little yip reserved for people she knew.

"Hello, Morgan." Rachel Cavanagh paused to give Lecky's collie a pat. Thus rewarded, Morgan fell into a trot at her side.

She'd been quiet on their walk to the pier. So had he.

They had a little time. Owen had seen her follow him out of the inn. Owen would know he'd keep her safe. But he wasn't looking forward to his old friend's questions.

Women like Rachel Cavanagh did not leave inns with men like him.

They came alongside his sloop, and Lecky stepped from pier to deck. He turned back to Rachel Cavanagh and, without speaking, held out his hand. Her gaze went to his hand first, before she placed her own hand in his and accepted his help to step onto the boat.

They released one other as soon as she gained her balance. Once aboard, she looked about. Her gaze traveled over the decks and up the mast to the night sky beyond.

This was his home. He trod these boards every single day. But for her, to step aboard, to stand on this deck, was to be cast back in time. And not to a very easy time.

The night was dark, a half moon only, with plenty of cloud in the sky besides. That darkness turned Rachel Anwen Cavanagh's eyes darker still, the expression within passionate and pensive and disquieted. Her face was a little leaner than it had been nine months ago, and her lower lip trembled as she absorbed their surroundings. The flicker of memories played across her face.

Damn, but part of the tightness that wrapped his chest came from just looking at her.

She was more beautiful than he remembered. Softer too, when he'd pulled her body against his in the street.

Finally, she looked back at him.

There was something more in that leaner face, reserve he'd not seen before, not so much permanently etched as nebulous. Akin to a night like tonight, it crossed her face in the same way that broken clouds crawled before the moon; and, for moments of time, the depth of shadow intensified.

"I've thought of you," she said.

Unexpected, her words were a jolt to his core, one far more surprising than a drunken lout planting a fist in his side.

Oblivious of the way she could affect him, she continued. "I have thought of what you did for me, and you say I owe you nothing. I've tried, but I can't find peace with that."

The reserve, her disquiet.... This was not the lass the newspapers presented. He didn't care what ballrooms she'd graced these past months. But suddenly, he wondered what previously unexplored paths Rachel Cavanagh had walked inside.

Again, he said, "You don't owe me anything. But, rest assured, if you did, your ability to wield an umbrella stand was more than adequate recompense."

His comment lured a smile. "You were simply fortunate

someone thought to place that stand in the foyer. *And* to invest in brass."

"Oh, I don't know. We could take that rationalization further. People's aversion to the rain, for example. Umbrella stands would not exist without umbrellas, after all. Truly, humankind fabricates the need for the most amazing things, then seeks to give those things more status by decorating them."

Her mouth twitched with amusement.

More dangerous was the warm rapport he could feel spring between them. "How long will it be until your mother and sister realize you are missing?" he asked, and her gaze slid away. Suddenly, she seemed more interested in Morgan.

She crouched down to stroke the collie's side. "I don't know. Not 'til morning, I should expect."

He raised his brows. "You don't plan to be back 'til morning?"

That brought her attention back to him. Color flushed her cheeks. "I didn't mean . . . ."

Suddenly, her lack of chaperone struck him. "Wait. You were downstairs at the Lord Nelson Inn, *alone*?"

Her eyes widened. She buried her fingers deeper in the thick fur of Morgan's coat, as though his question distressed her.

Something was amiss.

"Surely you're concerned for your prospects?"

That struck home. Those eyes again flashed to his, riled and defensive. "Yes, of course."

Yet her actions were passive. Or rather, they were passive *now*.

She had been reckless to call to him across the public room of the Lord Nelson, with Owen's burly patrons watching on. She had been reckless to follow him out of the inn. Then there was this. The fact that she was here on his boat, when everyone in England from parlor maid to prime minister knew she was a hair's breadth from marrying the Marquess.

The lass who had searched through the night for *Castalia's* survivors had not been reckless. Nor had she been passive. That woman had been *determined*.

There was a world of difference between reckless and determined. The gods knew, in North Africa, he'd practiced both for long enough to know. Right now, experience told him that

Rachel Cavanagh's guiding compass had been snatched from her hands.

"What happened after you left Dunkirk?" he asked.

"What do you mean?" His question clearly surprised her.

"You returned to London with Captain Napier. Then what?"

"Captain Napier and the Marquess took me to my family's townhouse on Hanover Square."

"Then what?"

"My older brother, Hugh, took over arrangements. He had Ariene transported to Wales, where we buried her alongside her father—my grandfather. My family went into mourning. Convention decrees that three months is appropriate for one's aunt."

"Three months is not very long."

The shadow of a smile crossed her features. "Some would argue that it is far *too* long."

That shadow, those words, told him much. Three months had not been long enough for her.

He lowered himself down to sit by the tiller. "Go on."

She was still crouched beside Morgan. Her fingers wove through the collie's fur. Unconsciously, she sought warmth, touch, the closeness to another that helped comfort one's self.

"My mother, sisters and I remained in Wales until Christmas," she said. "Hugh returned to London to settle Ariene's affairs and to open our London house for the season. We followed when our mourning period was over. The balls and morning calls and match-making must go on." There was an ever-so-slight brittleness to her short laugh. "My elder sister, Juliet, married last week."

Lecky studied his guest. "Are you not happy for her?"

"What? Of course, I am." For a moment, she genuinely looked shocked, then her brow creased in a frown. "I'm very happy for her."

Lecky suspected that frown was directed at herself.

"The newspapers say you are all but engaged to the Marquess of Rossum."

"You read the newspapers?" An expression—part discomfort and part alarm—flickered across her features. Her reaction surprised him—made his pulse skip a beat. Hers wasn't the expression of a woman in love.

"They've done nothing but speculate as to our relationship since we returned to English soil," she said.

"Oh, I don't know." He injected a light note of chiding in his voice. "I recall reading a story or two about luddite attacks and poor harvests." He watched as she relaxed a notch and smiled at herself, realizing he was teasing.

"Quite right," she conceded. "They've published other stories, too."

"So there's no truth to what they say?"

Suddenly, Rachel Anwen Cavanagh had trouble meeting his gaze. Which meant, most likely, there was *some* truth to it, albeit not such simple truth as the newspapers portrayed.

"We spend a great deal of time together. He came to Wales after Ariene died. Rossum and I—" Her look slid to Morgan as she sucked in a breath.

His collie was apparently easier to confide in.

"My family is on the way to Rossum's estate near Canterbury, in fact. To attend a gathering of his close family and friends. Before we left London, he asked that I consider...consider whether I would like his estate to become my home."

So Rossum *had* proposed. The man rose in Lecky's estimation. At the same time, he felt a clench in his chest.

"I see," Lecky said. "Hoping you'll buy the place from him, is he?"

"No." Her lips curved, telling him that she appreciated his stab at humor. She slid her arm around Morgan. "The Marquess still intends for it to be his home, too."

Lecky raised his knee and rested his elbow atop it. "You said you're on your way to Rossum's estate?"

Appearing discomforted, she looked away again. "I am."

He debated for a moment how much he should say. How much he should delve. "I can only imagine there are many women clamoring to be in your situation. To receive an offer of marriage from a marquess."

"I am in a very fortunate situation."

Yet still, she couldn't bring herself to look at him. Her words were little more that a murmur, the belief she spoke, forced.

In a moment or two, he would figure out why that made him so damn angry.

"Are you?" he demanded. "*Why?*"

Astonishment, confusion, and perhaps a little fear lit coffee-colored depths as her glance swung back his way. "Why would you even ask that?"

How could he *not*? "Mayhap it relates to the contradiction I see."

Oh, the lass had had her compass snatched, all right.

"What do you mean?"

The uncertainty in her voice was perhaps indication that she *did* know his meaning, on some gut level at least.

Damn. Suddenly, he was angry. *Why was he angry?*

He was angry because Rachel Cavanagh was fooling herself. She was floundering under the belief that she should want the same things that everyone else did. *Had* she grown to care for the Marquess? He didn't really want to know. But clearly, she didn't want to receive the man's proposal.

He took a breath to rein himself back in. Schooled his features to something more controlled. Then chose his words carefully. Because it seemed at that moment, she lacked anyone else in her life willing to offer an outside opinion. And it was rather evident she needed one.

"What do I mean, Miss Cavanagh? One thing I've learned in life is that it pays to keep as close an eye on one's associates' actions as an ear to their words. So when I look at you, I remember a woman nine months ago who knew exactly what she wanted. Who, despite near drowning and discovering her aunt was dead, still searched through the night for Mary Thacker, her lady's maid. I remember a woman determined to see her aunt home. Hell, an *hour* ago, she was even determined to speak to *me*. So you will understand, then, that I see a contradiction when that same woman isn't champing at the bit to get back to her very impressive fiancé-in-waiting. Or to explore her future home."

Her face had leeched of color as he spoke. She stared at him, her expression startlingly, heart-wrenchingly vulnerable.

"Where is the woman who was on my boat nine months ago?" he said. "What happened to her?"

A shutter had come down over her face, which, like the shell-money he used to trade in North Africa, was pale and porcelain-like and still. For a split second, it reminded Lecky of the expression on his mother's face, the day her eldest son, Lecky's brother, had betrayed her. Had betrayed the beliefs that mattered so much to her. Lecky had looked on, helpless and furious. Yet his father's apathy had been worse: the fact that he'd pretended to care and yet had done nothing.

Lecky's father had never *seen* his mother. Oh, he'd loved her, been obsessed with her, but he had never understood her. He'd never *listened* to her. Instead, through his actions, he'd chipped away at everything she was until, finally, all the fight in her was gone. Whether his father realized the damage he had done, Lecky never knew. But he'd learnt that it was possible to love a person and still be bad for them. That it was possible to demand they sail in one's own direction, rather than set course for themselves.

Rachel Anwen Cavanagh needed to set her own course.

Her expression was frayed. Behind it, he could well guess what was transpiring. Fibers were snapping in the strands of beliefs she'd woven together. Beliefs strung like mooring lines that held her to a landing that might be safe enough but might never put wind in her sails.

It was a hard thing, to be caught in that place. To have one's lines wrenched in both directions, with the ebb and flow of the tide. Like the breaking up of sea foam on the tide, more of his anger dispersed.

Lecky glanced toward Morgan. The collie had her ears pressed back. She gave him a concerned look. "Miss Cavanagh will be all right, won't she, girl? She just needs a little time."

A harsh, cut-off, unladylike laugh emerged from his guest's throat. "Time? What *time* do I have? As soon as my family realizes that an offer has been voiced, they will be relentless. And why should they *not* want that for me? Rossum is a wonderful man. There is no reason I shouldn't marry him."

Quietly, Lecky said, "Seems to me you haven't done grieving."

She shook her head and so too shook off his words. "Ariene has been gone nine months. Everyone expects—"

"That you are ready to be swept off your feet?" Lecky smiled humorlessly. "Of course, they do. Rossum is a *marquess*. There is no better cure for heartache than adding an honorific to one's name."

She was too distressed to detect his subtle gibe. "You don't understand. Rossum and I... everyone told me. *Everyone* speculated. But in my mind—" Her panic was growing.

Oh, but he did understand. He suspected he understood very well.

"Tell me," he said, "about Ariene."

HIS ABRUPT CHANGE OF SUBJECT brought her every thought to a standstill, as though he'd tossed a bucket of Thames water over her head. "*What?*"

He sat across from her, leaning against the stern, one arm resting on his raised knee. Was it possible that she had imagined the whetted edge to his words just moments ago? He'd accused *her* of being a contradiction. But what of him? Where did *that* contradiction lie?

Within him... or her image of him?

He was blunt in speech. Rough in appearance. But coarse in thinking? No.

No, no, no.

An unknown world of thoughts lay behind those gray eyes. Thoughts she was sure would tie her up in a dozen clove hitch knots if she attempted to guess them all.

She didn't want to know his opinion of her.

She cared too deeply about the answer.

Where is the woman who was on my boat? What happened to her?

None of her family—not her mother, nor Juliet, nor Faith, nor Hugh; no, even Andrew—had laid down that challenge. Ariene would have, of course. Her aunt would have been every bit as direct as Jonathon Lecky.

"You told me that you had never been closer to anyone."

She had told him that. She'd hardly expected him to remember. It came as a shock that he did.

"You miss her," he continued. "Tell me what you miss."

Her chin jerked at his words; her throat constricted. What did she *miss*? So much. *Everything*. Ariene's humor, her comfort, her glow. Lord above, she could barely speak for the tightness of her throat. "I hardly know where to start."

"It doesn't matter. Just start."

Uncertain of his motives, she hesitated. It felt intensely private to speak of Ariene. Yet to not speak of her . . . .

Lately, everyone—her family, even the household staff when they were in Rachel's vicinity—seemed to think it for the best. As swiftly as passing mention was made, it was swept away, hurried out of mind as though memories were shards of broken china or glass liable to cut somebody. Liable, in particular, to cut Rachel.

The meaninglessness of Ariene Cavanagh's death was too tragic a subject for any to dwell upon. And not only for its own sake; rather, it dredged up Rachel's father's death, too. Lost not in battle, but in a chance explosion. Villagers and sailors alike whispered that, for all the years Rhys Cavanagh had sailed the high seas, she'd claimed his offspring for her toll.

Where had Ariene Cavanagh's unconventional life got her? That was the underlying nature of Rachel's mother's words about Ariene. Lady Georgiana had never understood how Ariene could be happy.

Jonathon Lecky would.

Vivid came the image of the boat captain touched by lantern light, leaning across white canvas with needle and twine in hand. Vivid, too, was the memory of his scars each time he completed a stitch. They were etched in her mind, just as they were etched on his wrists. How had he come by them?

Those wrists were turned away from her now, strong hands casually resting.

He was waiting.

"Ariene was . . . she never cared what others thought. In that respect, she was very much her father's daughter." So often, Rachel's aunt had shaken her head, bemused by the social aspirations of Rachel's mother. Ariene had never understood how, given the vast array of interests the world offered, Lady Georgiana could be so completely fixed on so few.

"Ariene was interested in *everything*. The lives of people from all walks of life. Places, travel, business.... She was extremely good at business."

"She managed your family's shipping interests?"

"Her share, yes." Ariene had been every bit as sharp with numbers as Rhys Cavanagh had been with his wit. Rachel hesitated for a moment, unsure of how much she should say. Yet she wanted this man to understand. For that, she had to explain the whole.

"My mother was never particularly enamored of the fact that Ariene took such interest." Lady Georgiana had always been divided between the aristocratic beliefs of her birth, which looked down on men in business and trade, and the security afforded by the empire that Rhys Cavanagh and his children had built. "She—many of our acquaintances, in fact—found it difficult to understand that Ariene could be so happy, so *content*, despite being unmarried. Ariene was strong, and independent, and yet so kind. Her spirit wasn't so much restless as light." Except, of course, when it came to the matter of her birth mother. Then, that lightness had gone, turning to fierce, raw hurt deep inside.

"I suspect"—Rachel took a breath—"I suspect they were actually intimidated by her." For many, it would have been more comfortable to feel sorry for her, to attribute her failure to marry to her illegitimate birth, rather than accept that the life of a spinster was Ariene's choice.

"Tell me about the ways she was strong."

His words showed he was listening. Rachel wrapped her arms around her knees and leant back on the cabin. "For one, she didn't allow the judgments of others to hurt or influence her. 'Judgments,' she often said, 'showed more about the values of the person making the judgment than about the subject being judged.' Ariene knew what was important to her, and that was enough. She was wonderful at putting things in perspective."

"You miss her perspective."

"Yes." She missed it *so* much. She missed the comedy in Ariene's eyes when Rachel invariably reported on the latest of Lady Georgiana's plans. With just a few words, Ariene had been able to make Rachel laugh. "When I was with her, I felt... unburdened."

"There is no one else in your life like her?"

There had been Rhys Cavanagh, of course. But he had been

gone these past five years."

"No one." She looked out over the sloop's bulwark to the dark expanse of river beyond, flowing out to sea. It was as though all her uncertainty, the depth of her despair, had been lodged just beneath the surface, submerged where no one could see it, and she too could pretend it wasn't there. Yet this man appeared back in her life and dislodged it all. She whispered, "She used to say I should trust myself more."

Jonathon Lecky was silent. Then he asked, "Do you really need her voice to tell you that?"

Rachel closed her eyes. The pressure was building in her chest. "She was far more perceptive than I."

"And she had, what, a good dozen years' experience on you? I suspect you are far more perceptive than you give yourself credit for. Take tonight, for example. What made you take the risk of venturing onto my boat?"

She understood his inference. This visit had the potential to ruin her, to deem her unsuitable—unworthy—to be the Marquess of Rossum's bride. It could all too easily be the tragic twist the newspapers and rumor mongers longed for.

Some weak part inside her couldn't help but wonder if that would be an easy solution. Easier than searching inside. Easier than telling Rossum no and disappointing them all.

"Seems to me, Miss Cavanagh, that you're not sure what you want." Jonathon Lecky paused. "I am going to ask you a practical question. Is there any financial reason you should marry the Marquess *now*? I know women must weigh such factors. Your aunt fortunately did not need to. But need *you*?"

In a month, Rachel would turn one and twenty. She would gain control of Ariene's cottage and the money Ariene had left her, while Hugh continued to oversee her shipping interests until she turned five and twenty. That thought, as it always did, led to a painful clench of her stomach. A prickling in her throat. "No." The word was forced.

He propped his head on his hand and considered her. "Tell Rossum you need more time. *Ahh.* I see." At his suggestion, some thought—feeling—must have reflected on her face. "That's not all—is it?"

She pushed thoughts of Ariene's fortune away and turned to another track, one equally true. "I can't do that to him. I can't make him wait like that."

"But is he *prepared* to wait?"

Rachel swallowed. She knew—just knew—Rossum would wait as long as she asked.

Jonathon Lecky read as much in her silence. "So, the man is as handsome as our kind comes. Unfortunate about his blindness, but I think that makes his determination all the more impressive, no? I doubt a woman he cared for would want for anything."

It was true. She saw the way Rossum cared for his uncle, his cousins. She knew how he would care for a woman. His *wife*.

"Grief aside, what is it you fear?"

His question froze her. Turned her blood to ice from her extremities to her heart. It was a question that struck to the very core of her uncertainty. What did she *fear*? Things she didn't want to think about, let alone name.

She feared she would never love Rossum the way she sensed he might come to love her. That no matter what she willed, some part of her heart would remain closed.

She feared giving her life over to becoming the perfect hostess, the perfect marquess's wife.

She feared the distant places she had grown up hearing about, reading about, imagining would remain ever that. *Distant*. The experiences of others, never hers.

"Have you read my grandfather's memoirs, Mr. Lecky?" she asked.

"I have."

"My grandfather used to regale my brothers and sisters and me with his tales. He was not, however, a simple man. He thought deeply. Even when we were young, he spoke as often of the difficulties and pain that came with his choices as he did of his victories. He used to say the greatest adventure was not exploring foreign ports and meeting new people. The greatest adventure came from what that exploration taught a man about himself. In my heart, I have always wished to understand his meaning for myself."

"Do you have plans to go exploring yourself, Miss Cavanagh?"

"I *had* plans. Ariene was to come with me when I turned one and twenty. We were going to go to Alexandria and then to the Levant."

"Alexandria?" His gaze became quizzical, then comprehending. "Your father was killed in Alexandria. Buried there, too, I presume?"

"Yes. I was four years old when he died."

"You wish to visit his grave."

"I wish to see what he saw, stand where he stood. I hoped that that might—" The tidal surge of reasons that she wished to go all flooded back. Old discussions with Ariene. Solemnity and laughter and hours spent scouring maps.

"Might what?"

Rachel released a shaky breath, jolted by her rescuer's prompt. "Might acknowledge his sacrifice. Perhaps, in some way...help me to feel closer to him. I can remember things about him. I can remember his smile." She looked toward Jonathon Lecky, only to discover his hooded eyes made his thoughts difficult to gauge.

"And the Levant?" he asked.

"I have read many travelogues besides my grandfather's memoirs. We intended to make our way to Aleppo, to the end of the Silk Road. My family's mercantile connections provide links to the British Consul there." Her rescuer's eyes narrowed ever so slightly at mention of the British Consul, perhaps drawing connections. "I didn't want to spend my life imagining such places based on the descriptions of others," Rachel continued. "I wanted to feel them, *experience* them, for myself."

Surely he would understand?

He did, she discovered a moment later.

He spoke. "Well, it's little wonder that you find yourself here, Miss Cavanagh. I've spent time in North Africa, and if you feel you should go—then you should go. There is no substitute for your own experience. But tell me, would Rossum not wish to travel to such places with you?"

The questions that had leapt to her throat at his mention of Africa were cut off by his question.

"He has many responsibilities—*important* responsibilities. To the House of Lords. His tenants. His family. I have seen how hard he works." Rossum's sense of duty ran deep.

"I'm sure. But you haven't answered my question."

It was not something she and Rossum had ever discussed. Perhaps he could depart for a month. But three months or six? The thought provoked an overriding sense of discomfort. "I do not think the Marquess would feel comfortable leaving his duties in England for so long."

"Not even for you?" One end of Jonathon Lecky's mouth curled up. "Are you certain of that?"

Was she? She considered. "Yes."

"Would he stop you from journeying to your father's resting place?"

She presumed the boat captain meant if Rachel were to become Rossum's marchioness. "No . . . ." At least, she didn't think so.

"And beyond Alexandria?"

Rachel's gaze shot to his. The husbands of some women would refuse outright. After all, what sort of wife would wish to travel to Egypt or to the Levant, without her husband's company and protection?

The sort that most assuredly became a topic of speculation for London tongues.

However, as she considered Jonathon Lecky's question, she realized she *did* know the answer.

Rossum would weather the speculation. He would surround her with protectors—but he *would* let her go. He would feel he must, as repayment of a kind, for the fact her life would be more burdened with duty once aligned with his. Yet at the same time, she knew he would worry. How could he not, when his own parents were killed in Italy by brigands?

She remembered his soft smile of understanding in Hanover Square. Rossum *would* bear those worries for her.

But how could she *let* him? How could she take more than she could return?

She was afraid she would not love him *enough*.

"Rossum wouldn't stop me," she replied. *But under such circumstances, she would stop herself.*

Another part of her mind played devil's advocate, questioning whether the experiences she yearned for—*had* yearned for until

Ariene died—were truly what she wanted?

Of course, the answer was simple. She would not know unless she sought those experiences. And although she had scarcely been able to face such thoughts these past months, the prospect of burying those dreams *forever* sent the chill of winter sweeping her, as though a torrent of snow and ice cascaded to settle and freeze around her heart.

"Sometimes it is not only the loss of a person that hurts, Miss Cavanagh. It's the gap than opens up between the life we envisaged and the life that is waiting for us."

His words were like a thunderclap over the dark waters.

"What are you going to do?" he asked, as she reeled from that thought.

What was she going to do? Could she blot this conversation from memory? Thrust it to the farthest reaches of her mind?

No, not since he'd loosed those questions: *Where is the woman who was on my boat? What happened to her?*

It's the gap that opens up.

The *Castalia* had not only taken Ariene and Mary. It had claimed a part of her, too. Or, at least, part of her was forever changed. As to her questions and the answers she needed?

She knew, with gut-deep certainty, that the road to Canterbury would not provide a supply.

Jonathon Lecky was right. She didn't need Ariene's voice to tell her to trust herself. *She* had to do that.

She set her hands on the deck. The grain of the wood lay beneath her palms. Here at the pier, she could feel the slight chill in the night air, smell the salt of the estuary, see the lights of Gravesend. The sloop rocked gently on the water. She understood what life awaited her at Rossum's estate. No, if she had any hope of determining what she truly desired, she needed something different.

She hadn't sailed on the open sea since the *Castalia* went down. The thought stoked sudden fear—her chest tightened. But the alternative of never setting foot on a boat again was worse. She carried Cavanagh blood. The blood of seafarers. The death of her father had not confined Ariene and Rhys Cavanagh to shore. Nor would it her. She gathered her will. "Where are you sailing next?"

"Boulogne-sur-Mer, on the coast of France."

"Take me with you."

His brows lifted. He leant back to rest his elbow on the tiller.

She waited. He regarded her.

After a moment, he lifted a hand to rub his brow, as though he were developing a headache. "Miss Cavanagh, you will have to rationalize why you would want to do such a thing with a man you recently saw attacked. Not to mention a man who, less than an hour ago, also claimed liberties with your person he should not have taken. Rationalize—please—how remaining on this boat constitutes a good idea?"

He was right, of course. She had no idea what danger she was placing herself in by wishing to remain in his company. And there *was* that smack on the lips. She wasn't prepared to call it a kiss, but the thought still made her cheeks flame.

"What is your purpose for going to Boulogne?" she asked.

"I've a few matters to attend to."

"Those matters . . . they don't involve . . . smuggling?"

He stared at her for a moment, then gave a bark of laughter and shook his head. "You're a prime one, Miss Cavanagh."

"Do they?" she pressed.

"I'm not a smuggler, Miss Cavanagh, regardless of what you and the Marquess may have inferred."

"You didn't deny it, last October. You let us believe you were."

Of course, that impression had not sat right with her, even then.

"I didn't feel like explaining myself. Nor did it change the fact that I had a rendezvous to keep. One I was in danger of missing due to the *Castalia's* misfortune."

"But the half-ankers? Why were they aboard your boat?"

"My associate trades wine. I was returning to Boulogne from Amsterdam with samples for him that had been transported up the Rhine." While she absorbed this information, he gave a groan. He tipped his head back and rubbed his hands down his face. "Poseidon, dear god, what are you doing to me?"

Heat rose in her cheeks. As angry as she had been, it was a little embarrassing that she had followed him out of the inn. Dignity demanded she not beg or cajole. She would ask once, and if he said no, he said no.

Please don't say no.

"Mr. Lecky." Her voice was soft. "Please. I want to be certain whether it is right for me to desire something different."

For long moments, he made no move. Just sat with palms pressed over his eyes. Unsure whether he had heard her, she found herself holding her breath.

In the silence, her heart began to sink beneath the waters of the Thames.

Again, finally, he ran his hands down his face and gazed at her from across the deck.

Then she didn't know *what* to feel: sinking hope or something else entirely.

This could be a very bad idea after all.

The thought had nothing to do with her physical safety.

It had *everything* to do with the effect of those sharp gray eyes and the unnerved, slightly flustered feeling that developed in her stomach.

"Five days," he said.

Her heart reacted with a lurch. "Five days?"

"Five, possibly six, days. That is the general duration of a return trip to Boulogne. You need to understand, though, that's an estimate. Not a guarantee."

He was *agreeing?* This was a *yes?*

"I don't want guarantees," she said quickly.

He smiled humorlessly. "Do you want to leave a note for your family?"

"I do." Not that she knew what she would say.

"I'll get you a quill pen and paper. Then I'll take it back to the inn. That is, unless you'd prefer to leave a note in your chamber and collect more things?"

Suddenly, the enormity of what she had proposed rushed in. She had to consider Rossum, her mother, and Faith. "I need a moment to think."

He nodded. He moved across the deck to the hatch and crouched down. But instead of descending the companionway steps, he reached out. Her lips parted in surprise as his fingertips gently but firmly brought her jaw around, so that her gaze met his.

"We'll find that woman again. The woman I met on my boat." Soft gray eyes searched hers.

She managed a small nod; and, with a final, scrutinizing look, he released her.

Her eyes fluttered closed.

She released a pent breath as he disappeared below.

CHAPTER NINE

Some sailors believe bringing a woman aboard one's ship is bad luck. I say the lack of warm, sweet company is a blasted lot worse.
—*The Memoirs of Rhys Cavanagh*

THERE WAS NO TIME OF day, Lecky thought, that the fresh scent of earth and estuary pierced a man as sharply as it did during early light. The air circulating off the Thames in the predawn was cool yet promised to warm as the sun rose unimpeded over the horizon. The intermittent splash of a leaping fish, the distinctive, piping 'kleep-kleep' cries of the oystercatchers, and the passage of fishing boats down the river—with the occasional gruff banter bellowed between crews—gradually began to fracture the early morning quiet. Above the river, the thick banks of night-time cloud had dispersed to leave remote patches of cumulous cloud.

After their brief return to the inn, Lecky had untied the sloop's dock lines from the pier and moored in the Thames off Gravesend overnight. Then he'd sent Rhys Cavanagh's granddaughter to rest in the cabin below, while he caught a few hours' nap on the deck. The arrangement was for their security, he'd said, which was partly true. Mostly, he had just needed time to reconcile *what the hell* he'd just done.

Because what he'd just *done* was madness, pure and simple.

He'd smuggled her back into the Lord Nelson without notice and smuggled her out by the same method. She'd brought with her a small bag containing several changes of clothes. "Does the letter say anything I ought be aware of?" he'd asked in relation to the missive she had left for her family.

Her eyes when she returned his look had been solemn and dark. "I did not mention you."

It was only right that his old friend Owen Griffiths be ready for the barrage that was sure to be directed his way when Rachel Cavanagh's absence was discovered. An unconscious lummox in the privies was no trouble compared to a missing 'miss'.

"She's coming with me," Lecky had informed the innkeeper. "I'll have her back in six days."

"You'll have her back in *six days*?" Owen had not been happy. "By the devil, Jonathon, you've got some explaining to do."

"You know I'll watch out for her." He would make sure there was nothing to connect her to him. Nothing his adversaries could use.

Harshly, he'd quashed the niggle of a whisper. *Jonathon, six days with her could be your undoing.*

"I think," Owen gave him a pointed look, "when it comes to Miss Cavanagh, you've already proven tonight that I don't know a bloody thing."

True. He'd never spoken to Owen of the *Castalia's* wreck. His gaze had remained steady. "Trust me. She needs this."

And so do you.

Again, that whisper.

No. This trip was for *her*. Rhys Cavanagh would want his granddaughter to soar and—damn it—she just needed a little help.

Owen had regarded him for a long moment. Questions had hovered in the depths of the former sailor's eyes, but in the end, the innkeeper had loosed a ragged sigh and had run a hand through his hair. "Yes," he said, "But only because you already have my trust. You always will."

Aye, he'd earned it, eight years before in Mogadore. He'd earned it when he'd led a free Owen Griffiths and his crew mates out of the desert.

Lecky weighed anchor an hour before dawn. He was still trimming the sails when his passenger awoke. She emerged on deck with a blanket around her shoulders and hair refixed in a loose bun at her nape. Taking a seat near the cabin, she crossed her arms over her chest, her posture less indicative of being cold than it was of apprehensiveness. The dark flash of her glance all too easily conveyed her thoughts and the question whether, in the hours between darkness and dawn, Lecky had come to regret his decision.

In all bloody likelihood he would. Just as she might regret having made the request. He was blasted if he knew how they would negotiate his thirty-foot sloop together, let alone its ten-foot-by-ten-foot aft deck.

The breeze gusted up between them, catching and flapping the edge of the sail. Her fingers dug into her elbows, betraying her nerves. Perhaps, Lecky thought, the hours between darkness and dawn had spawned doubts in minds other than his own.

He gave a nod towards Gravesend as the distance widened. "The town is not out of sight yet. You can still go back."

"No!" Her expression turned stricken. "Please... I wish to remain."

In other words, any doubts she had were still outweighed by the thought of getting back in a closed carriage to Canterbury. Lecky squinted toward the horizon. "From here, we sail the estuary toward Ramsgate," he said. "Then, we'll fix a heading almost due south to Boulogne-ser-Mer. With winds as they are, we should reach France by early tomorrow afternoon."

Her question came after a pause, so soft it was almost whipped away by the breeze. "Why did you agree?"

Because he was bloody mad? He looked at her sitting so ramrod straight.

He didn't pretend to misunderstand. His first inclination *had* been to say no, but some damn part inside—the part that had never liked to see a man shackled—knew that the notions that bound her like locks needed breaking. Rachel Cavanagh needed a taste of freedom.

"Maybe you just need a few days to remember what you're capable of."

Her lips parted in surprise, although in no other way did she move.

The gods be damned, he'd be lucky if *her* freedom didn't come at the cost of that coffee-brown gaze slapping *him* in irons.

Another gust snapped the sails.

"Time to relax, Miss Cavanagh," he said. "Worrying about your decision now won't change a thing. The damned main mast is less rigid than you. Although on the positive side, if it gets knocked down en voyage, at least I'll have something with which to replace it."

His statement eked a guilty-as-charged smile from her lips. She was like a windlass loosening to half-turn as her shoulders relaxed and she set her hands on the deck. "And I'm sure, if the boom should snap, I would make an excellent stand-in for that too."

She looked across at him from beneath her lashes, and blast if that smile didn't explain why the memory of all that unruly beauty stayed fixed in a man's mind long after it should.

JONATHON LECKY WAS RIGHT, SHE thought. She was wound tighter than a capstan and needed to relax. She'd made her decision and did not intend to go back on it.

Please let her mother and Faith follow her instructions. To do so was in *all* their best interests. But if they chose not to . . . .

If they chose not to, she would just have to be prepared for the consequences.

She'd left the note propped on her bed at the inn. In it, she'd asked them to travel on, to continue to Atherton Court, Rossum's estate, and tell Rossum that she'd encountered an old friend in Gravesend with whom she'd decided to visit for a few days. He wouldn't believe it, of course; he would fear—somewhat correctly—that their last conversation had driven her away. She hated to cause him pain. She hated to cause *any* of them pain. Yet by doing this, she knew that she would.

In her note, she had written that she was safe, that she was sorry to vanish, but that her decision had been sudden and was for the best. The end of the season had resurrected memories of plans she'd had with Ariene, and she needed a few days alone. She asked that her mother send the coachman back to Gravesend to collect her in six days, at which time she would rejoin her family at Atherton Court. *Don't worry*, she'd implored. And *please* don't cause alarm.

Then there was Jonathon Lecky. She had woken that morning

in the same bunk she had slept in nine months before—the day her world had changed. The reality of what she'd done struck home.

In part, she was embarrassed. But more so, she'd feared to emerge on the deck and discover he'd changed his mind. Because knowledge had solidified in her heart: she *needed* this. No matter the consequences, *she needed it.* And he'd proved again with that whetted silver-gray gaze that she didn't need to speak for him to understand.

"There's a small basin and soap in the cabin, for when you'd like to freshen up," he told her, and even that small offer of thoughtfulness, directed towards her comfort, touched something inside.

Ahead, the wide reach of the Thames stretched out. As the sky lightened, the features of the estuary were becoming more distinct: its banks, bird life and the other patrons of the water. It was a world of physical work and nature. Of fishing and laboring and boat making. So close to and yet a world away from London. The city had always provided her with plenty to contemplate. What thoughts and tasks filled its inhabitants' days? The same applied here, yet the lives of men and women who lived along these tidal stretches had a different texture.

As her tension lessened, the nature of the silence between her and the boat captain changed, grew comfortable. She could simply watch and relax. Small figures went about their business on the banks. Thames sailing barges, ketches and smacks plied the waters. There were so many people, every one a small piece of something larger, built on the backbone of the wide spread of water and marshes and the inevitability of seasons and tides. It was not an easy life, here in the dawn light.

The estuary gradually widened as the river's Gravesend Reach joined the Lower Hope Reach, then Sea Reach. She slipped below then, to sponge herself clean and to carefully look around the cabin for the first time. Nine months before, it had not been foremost on her mind.

There were no half-ankers, as Rossum had detected. But she did notice the rolled up drawings that stacked the small table to the fore of the cabin. Curious, and at first wondering if they were charts, she spread one open across the table. Her breath caught. Beneath her hands lay the finely wrought plan of a ship. An original plan.

All the drawings were plans of ships, she realized, gingerly sliding her fingers along their edges and half-unrolling several more. Among their number lay deck plans and hull plans and sail plans, all intricately drawn.

No shipbuilder had signed them. She caught her lower lip between her teeth as, slowly and thoughtfully, she rolled the plans back up and returned to the deck.

Clean and feeling refreshed, she sat once more by the cabin, beneath the boom, directly opposite Jonathon Lecky at the tiller. Several large ships passed—East Indiamen, brigs and a British Navy corvette—piloting in from the Queen's Channel on high tide.

To the north lay Cavney Island on Essex's southern coast. To the south lay the Hoo Peninsula, on the northwest coast of Kent. It was along the Hoo that the North Kent marshes spread, carrying their foul vapors and transmitting recurrent fevers. Even so, there were no signs of unwholesomeness today, with the sun beaming down, its tepid warmth punctured by the crisp breeze that blew across the water. It was possible to feel a world away from one's concerns, Rachel thought, when sunlight and fresh air and new places were upon one.

They passed the British Army barracks at Sheerness by midmorning. They were still some four to six hours sailing from Ramsgate. How many times, Rachel wondered, had Jonathon Lecky sailed the Thames? What constancies constituted the fabric of his life?

"Are these your home waters, Mr. Lecky?" she asked.

"I no longer have home waters, Miss Cavanagh."

"You have nowhere you call home?"

He smiled. "Besides my boat? Not really, no."

"Then what brought you to Gravesend?"

"Owen," he said. "The innkeeper of the Lord Nelson is a friend."

A small part of her had wondered, when she saw that pewter mug. "Have you known each other long?"

"Eight years, or thereabouts."

"And Boulogne? What takes you there?"

A look crossed his face then, one she was learning to recognize. A look that spoke of amusement but couldn't rightfully be called a smile or a grin. No, the greater share of that humor reflected in his eyes. A hint played along his lips, too, although they barely moved. "How many questions do you have, Miss Cavanagh?"

"I'm not certain yet. It really depends on how short your answers are."

He gave a bark of laughter.

"I'm trying to understand, Mr. Lecky, if you are not a smuggler, who you are?"

"My, that could lead to a rather philosophical discourse."

"Could it?"

His eyes laughed at her. "I bloody well hope so. Very well, Miss Cavanagh, let's see. Who am I? Do you want strengths or weaknesses?"

"Strengths *and* weaknesses."

"Well, that will save me some thought, because they're probably one and the same."

There was something endearing in his look as his eyes grew serious and his jaw firmed. She still wasn't entirely used to the change in his appearance—his short hair—although she liked it. For so long, her rescuer had looked different in her mind.

This was all new. She was learning new things about him.

"Miss Cavanagh, I'm not a man to cross, but I can be relied upon in a scrap. My friends know that."

Yes, on some level, she knew that too. She'd sensed it nine months ago, when, after the shipwreck, she'd begged him to return them to England. And while in the end he'd not taken them there himself, he'd made sure that she and Rossum had safe passage.

"What else do your friends know?" she heard herself ask quietly.

He regarded her. "About my weaknesses?"

She gave a nod.

"They'd say I have a penchant for playing the rescuer."

Her brows rose. "Playing the rescuer?"

"Aye." He flicked his wrist towards her, then towards Morgan. "Drowning heiresses. Half-starved hounds."

Although a smile tugged on one end of his mouth as he looked towards his collie, Rachel couldn't help but feel he was making light of something that ran far more deeply through his fabric.

The collie lay three feet away, head raised and nose twitching in the wind. She had spent most of the morning dozing. "Have you had her since she was a pup?"

"A youth. I found her in Swansea during a storm. Hunkered down under timber at the dock, trying to stay out of the rain, weren't you?" he addressed the collie, who swung her soulful eyes his way. "Wasn't doing you much good, though, was it? Ground was flowing like a stream. Any bloody deeper and a man could have thrown in a line and tried to hook a fish. Didn't matter which way the poor girl turned, it was still wet, inescapable misery. She was as skinny as the chain on my spare anchor. Reminded me of a—" he cut off, and Rachel wondered what he'd been about to say. "In any event, I brought her on board the sloop and got her dry," he said.

"She wasn't afraid? She didn't try to attack?"

"I think she was beyond caring. It was almost too late to matter." He reached out and placed a hand on Morgan's back leg. It was the type of gesture that one made to reassure oneself that a loved one was all right. The collie twisted toward him, ears back, mouth slightly parted, and thumped her tail.

Rachel's heart twisted in response to the fondness between the two seafarers. She felt a sudden, unexpected urge to capture the moment. To bind in the quick lines of a sketch the depth of the attachment she saw.

What? Where had that come from? For months, the thought of even picking up a pencil had turned her stomach over and left her heart gripped and frozen with panic.

She swallowed. Still, she sensed the skittishness of that urge. She took an inward step back, afraid to rush toward it lest it scurry back into the shadows. Be calm, caution told her. Don't force. Don't grab. Allow those feelings to gain trust and emerge on their own.

Across from her, Jonathon Lecky straightened at the tiller.

"We got some food into you after that, didn't we, girl? Spent some time fattening you up, 'til you started to look more like the chain on my main anchor. I tried to convince her that she'd be a happier Welsh collie on land than at sea. Even offered to find her a new owner, some lucky chap with whom to walk over hill and dale. I thought she might get restless aboard. I couldn't persuade her, though. She doesn't like sheep."

Rachel stared at him, bemused. "You are just saying that."

It was quite an image: Jonathon Lecky standing in the middle of a country road, trying to convince his collie to take up with a grizzled old Welsh farmer.

"I'm quite serious. She doesn't like sheep. I think it was what got you into the mess at the dock in the first place, right, girl?" He reached out to ruffle the collie's coat. Morgan, who seemed to understand her character was in question, gave a slight whine then pursed her mouth, as though trying to decide whether it was better to give a another whine, a huff or a bark.

Oh, Rachel could see why the Welsh collie refused to leave him. She too knew what it was like to have Jonathon Lecky to thank for one's life.

Surely this time spent with him would help? Mayhap coming to know him better would help to reduce the inner turmoil she felt on account of him saving her life?

Conversely, she was beginning to fear that coming to know him better would only increase her fascination.

"How long ago did you find her?"

"Two years, or thereabouts. We've come to tolerate one another, haven't we, girl?"

There was more than tolerance there. What man and dog shared was affection.

Once more, Rachel settled back against the cabin to watch him. He was at ease. Yet she knew he was as quick to delve deep as he was to humor.

Not even with Rossum had she been able to discuss their rescuer. On the few occasions she'd gathered her resolve and veered their conversation in his direction, she'd sensed... *something*... from Rossum, something in the Marquess's manner, or mayhap something in what the Marquess *didn't* say, that made her pull back from the topic.

Yet the man before her had known of the speculation about Rossum and herself in the newspapers. Which meant—

Oh, God. Neither she nor Rossum had mentioned him in the account of their rescue because they had believed he was a smuggler.

"Mr. Lecky." She suddenly felt the need to explain. "The Marquess of Rossum and I, we never spoke of your involvement in our rescue. The newspapers, even my family, believe it was a French fishing boat that came to our aid. I've always felt terrible not to give you credit—"

He cut in. "Miss Cavanagh, I've no desire to see my name in the newspapers. No words need be said. Truly," he added, detecting that she still felt torn despite his response.

His certainty set her back for a moment. "I cannot recall if I have ever met a man who cares so little for thanks," she said.

He gave a shrug. "In the end, what does it matter, if a man knows within himself that he's done the right thing?"

"Lack of recognition can cause pain."

"True, it *can*. But that depends on what one seeks from an exchange."

For a moment, Rachel didn't know what to say. "You are quite singular, Mr. Lecky."

He laughed. "I hope not, Miss Cavanagh. I hope there are many men who see things as I do."

She felt a smile work its way across her face, until finally she too couldn't help but laugh. "So do I."

And then, warm with shared mirth, her eyes met his, and she felt the sudden flare of something conscious, *cognizant*.

He cleared his throat and averted his gaze, just as she averted her own.

She heard his quiet chuckle as she battled another blush. That chuckle was directed at himself, she knew. Directed at the fact that, whatever had just flared between them, the ruggedly handsome boat captain, who had planted a kiss on her less than twelve hours ago, had just done a terrible job of pretending he hadn't noticed.

Far better that she pretend nothing had happened either—and

that *included* last night's kiss. Because if there was one thing *she* was doing a terrible job of at that moment, it was keeping her hypothesizing mind from wondering what a real kiss from Jonathon Lecky—the rugged boat captain who rescued starving dogs and drowning heiresses—would be like.

POSEIDON BE DAMNED, LECKY THOUGHT ruefully. This *had* been a mistake. Rachel Cavanagh was about as effective as a fire ship set among an enemy fleet when it came to getting a reaction out of him. The heady gaze of those dark eyes was like spark to tinder. Bloody dangerous on a boat.

But he'd made his bunk, so he'd damn well have to lie in it. He'd remind her of broader horizons with a taste of Boulogne, then return her to Gravesend safely. Still, would partaking in recent female companionship have been effective defense against the narrow strip of black lace that acted as a band around the very high waist of her gown, he wondered? Because before today, he would have assumed that trimming first had to be knotted around a man's neck for it to slowly choke his air supply.

As the day warmed, she had removed the blanket from about her shoulders and folded it to sit upon. Whether the color of her gown was fashionable, he didn't have a clue. Champagne, he supposed it was called. Not that any man would give a fig. Its light shade and snug fit, with the high waist and more black lace trimming around her shoulders and high collar, drew the eyes to slim arms, a lovely bosom and smooth throat. And that thick ribbon of black lace about the high waist helped keep them centered there. No. Recent female companionship wouldn't have made a bloody scrap of difference where Rachel Cavanagh was concerned. She was lovely. She brought a smile to his mouth.

She *shouldn't* be on his boat.

Not when she looked so strangely right in her tailored clothes, leaning against his cabin.

"Have you been to Boulogne before?" he asked.

She shook her head.

"The Old Town is located on the top of a hill, within the original Roman walls. The new town stretches from the base of the hill to the port area. There is a large fishing fleet and quite a decent beach."

A quizzical little smile crossed her features. "Do you enjoy the beach, Mr. Lecky?"

"You make it sound as though that is a surprising concept, Miss Cavanagh." What was she imagining? he wondered. Lecky with his boots off and sand between his toes while throwing a stick for Morgan? Maybe he would just have to show her.

Surprisingly, a light blush colored her cheeks. "I just haven't imagined— That is . . . ." Her flush increased.

Hadn't imagined what? Or perhaps, what *had* she imagined?

Because the image that came to his mind involved loose butterscotch curls and warm dark eyes and a deliciously sweet helping of smooth, bare, moonlight-lit skin.

God damn, toe the line, man. Toe the line.

"Thank you," she finished. "Thank you . . . for seeing that I needed this. I must seem very inexperienced to you."

What she was proving was very *dangerous* to him. He hadn't noticed how much luster the sea had lost until she stepped aboard his boat and made the journey between Gravesend and Boulogne sparkle again. Even the breeze that skimmed the water seemed more effervescent, more lively.

"I'd say more uncertain than inexperienced," he said. "But we both know why that is."

Her dark eyes turned solemn. "How often do you do this?"

Find myself with a willful, adrift Welsh beauty on my aft deck? Never. Except for you.

He didn't pretend to misunderstand. "I was thinking about placing an advertisement in *The Morning Post*, actually," he said. "Business has been good the past couple of weeks, but I'm certain there are more heiresses who need help escaping prospective engagements to eligible English marquesses."

His light teasing earned Rachel Cavanagh's self-deprecating smile. "Well, it is a fine vessel for it. How long has she been yours?"

"I built her," he replied. "Five—nearly six—years ago."

"Oh." Her lips parted, and he watched as she again looked over the workmanship of the boat, taking in the smoothness of her timbers, the sturdiness of her tiller, her sleekness of shape and the way she rode over the waves. "That perhaps answers another one of my questions."

"What question was that?"

"The ship plans on the table in the cabin."

"You wish to know who drew them?"

"Yes. They're beautiful."

"Thank you, Miss Cavanagh."

"You designed this boat?"

"Designed and constructed." Shipbuilding ran in his blood. It was one aspect of his past he hadn't turned his back on. Instead, as the years passed, that pull had grown stronger. "I wanted to sail something I knew intimately." He set his hand on the decking. He had planed and laid every board himself. He had wanted that connection.

"Have you built other vessels?"

"I'm building one now," he said. "A brigantine in Boulogne."

"You're building a *ship?*" Clearly, he'd surprised her.

"Overseeing the construction, yes. One can't simply go about rescuing drowned heiresses all the time."

That brought her up, with a self-deprecating smile. "I'm glad you don't have to." Still, he caught a glimpse of her little shiver before she asked, "Is one of the designs in the cabin the ship you are building?"

"One of the designs is, yes."

"What is she?"

"Ninety feet overall, seventy-three at the keel. She'll weight around two hundred and thirty tons and require a complement of around seventy."

"How far advanced are you?"

"We laid the keel eighteen months ago. She's progressing well. We're hoping to have her in the water by next spring."

"'We're' hoping?" She looked at him inquiringly.

"Winter and I. The man I'm building her for."

What would Elijah Winter make of Rachel Cavanagh, he wondered? Or, more to the point, what would Lecky's business partner make of the fact that Lecky had brought Rachel Cavanagh with him at all?

He could see he'd got her thinking, and he could almost read the play of thoughts across her face. "Did you think my existence devoid of responsibility, Miss Cavanagh?" he asked with a light note of teasing. "Empty days, with naught to do but sail back and forth?"

"I'm not sure. I haven't known what to think."

That didn't particularly surprise him. He was amused that the Marquess and Rachel Cavanagh had thought him a smuggler. He'd taken many roles during his years in Mogadore: sailor, skipper, trader, negotiator, ransomer, expedition leader, informant. Roles that came to him naturally enough. He'd done his share of human smuggling, he supposed. The result had been men's freedom.

Vice-Consul's representative or not, the work he'd done in Morocco had been dangerous. Too easily, the Arab or African tribes might decide that the Vice-Consul's man was more valuable than the ransom he offered. He'd run plenty of risks and received recompense for it. Not least, in several instances, true friendship.

Across from him, Rachel Cavanagh drew a breath. "You design ships and are overseeing the construction of a brig. You sail a sloop you built yourself. Is there more that you do, Mr. Lecky?"

"I act as ship's agent on occasion." Given her family's interests, Rachel Cavanagh would, of course, be familiar with the responsibilities involved. Essentially, an agent facilitated the smooth arrival, the unloading and loading, and the departure of a foreign ship in port. Lecky watched as she observed this information.

"Do you do that often?"

"When it suits me." It suited him for most of the transactions in and out of Boulogne. However, he and Winter simply put alternative arrangements in place if he needed to be elsewhere.

Rachel Cavanagh regarded him, her coffee-colored gaze intense. "Sir, I think you prompt more questions than you answer."

Lecky laughed. "That is not my intention."

"Perhaps not. But it is your effect."

The devil in him was tempted—suddenly—to ask her whether there were any other effects he had?

Quickly, he quelled the impulse. *For the love of the gods, Jonathon. Avast!* That there was a dangerous channel.

"Are there any other questions pressing on you, Miss Cavanagh?" he asked.

She smiled, ever so slightly. "This sloop. Did you name her?"

Ah. Of course she would wonder that, this seafarer's daughter. She would know the traditions; she would understand that they meant something to him.

"Aye, my lady was christened. Her name is known to Poseidon and me, recorded for all time in the Ledger of the Deep."

"Do you not speak her name?"

"Do you wish to know it?"

She regarded him as though it were a trick question. It wasn't.

"Only should you wish to share," she said.

He smiled. "Perhaps I might bestow it as an honor, after we conclude our adventure?"

"As an honor?" Her lips pressed together in an amused smile. "In that case, perhaps so."

As she turned her gaze back to the sea, Lecky wondered whether—all other matters between them moot—Rachel Cavanagh and the Marquess of Rossum bantered so easily.

Then he realized it wasn't an answer he desired to know.

CHAPTER TEN

Free is the man who has the luxury to visit foreign shores for no reason but curiosity.
—*The Memoirs of Rhys Cavanagh*

THE SEA BREEZE PICKED UP, the temperature dropped slightly, and the weather otherwise blended into a perfect summer evening for sailing.

That breeze carried Rachel back in time. Not to the memory of her last haunting passage on the English Channel. No, its graze reminded her of the long, playful summer days her family would spend in Wales, bobbing from dawn to dusk in her grandfather's sailboat on the Bay of Bristol. In those days, she would sit at her grandfather's side as he taught her to sketch, as he showed her how to capture the glint of the sun off the water and the catch of the wind in the sails and her siblings' laughing figures. She had always been awed by her grandfather's ability to capture humanity at sea, the essence of shipboard life, in both his drawings and his journals.

Those summers spent skippering the dinghy were many years ago now, but the evening breeze stirred the passage of days to carry their indelible print across time. Rachel had wanted an escape. Now, instead of conjuring pain, this excursion felt like a tribute to Ariene and to the man who had been Ariene's father, Rhys Cavanagh.

The sloop passed Ramsgate. Rachel watched late afternoon segue to evening, then evening segue to night. The first stars began to shine, small individual glints against the cerulean sky. Each grew stronger and was joined by a myriad more as the sky darkened to navy.

The breeze in the sails and the lap of the swell against the hull were the only sounds. Although only one day's sailing from Gravesend, she might have been a world away, so far was she from horses and carriages and servants and aristocrats, gardens and coppiced chestnut woods, medieval manor houses and family parties. That was the world she was supposed to be part of right now. Instead, in stark contrast, the dark, empty swell stretched out.

This was where she wanted to be. She needed to be out on deck, beneath the stars and sky. She turned to Jonathon Lecky.

He'd placed the tiller in the comb and sat in his casual way with one knee raised, his arms draping his leg. He always looked eminently comfortable seated that way.

"How do you sleep when you sail alone?"

He regarded her from beneath his strong brows, his gray gaze shadowed by the mainsail, which blocked the fall of the moonlight across his face.

"Short bursts and often," he replied after a pause. "Never more than an hour at a time when under sail. More commonly, twenty minutes or thirty with one ear open. So if I nod off on you, Miss Cavanagh, you'll know why."

"I won't take offence." Sleeping while on open water provided challenges enough, but the concentrated number of vessels in the English Channel increased their chances of collision. "Perhaps, tonight, I can take the tiller while you sleep?"

He arched a brow. "You're proposing to take the role of first lieutenant and sit the night watch?"

"Am I not already first lieutenant?"

"I don't know. Morgan might contest you." The boat captain glanced toward the collie, who was stretched out on her side, replete from the meal of dried beef that Rachel had fed her earlier. The collie was sleeping. "Then again," Jonathon Lecky said, "perhaps she's taking the evening off. Very well. Over here with you, Miss Cavanagh."

She slid closer, aware that she entered his space.

"Does the first lieutenant know what she is doing?" he asked.

"The first lieutenant has been sailing boats since she was *two*." Albeit when she first began, she'd been seated on her grandfather's knee.

"Not my sloop, she hasn't."

"She *is* competent."

Jonathon Lecky's lips twitched. She was coming to understand when he was teasing.

"We'll see." He unfolded from his position and maneuvered around her, to free the place by the tiller. Rachel slid into the space.

"If you hold this heading we shouldn't have a problem."

"I can hold this heading," Rachel said.

"Good." He set one hand on Morgan's flank. The collie cracked an eyelid, regarded him for a moment, then emitted a huff before she promptly returned to her snooze. With a small snort of amusement, Jonathon Lecky slid further along the edge of the recessed deck, to the spot near the hatch where Rachel had been seated moments before.

He swiveled, then lay out flat on his back with one knee raised. He settled his shoulders into a comfortable position against the deck, then closed his eyes and clasped his hands together over his chest.

Abrupt as it was, that was it. That was how he intended to nap.

The minutes slipped by. Yesterday, she had been trapped in a carriage. Tonight, she had responsibility for the tiller. Her very soul expanded to fill with a sense of wonder.

She was under no illusion that they were presently at risk. With the fine weather and good visibility, they would spot the sails of other boats long before they came close. Nevertheless, at that moment she was charged with three lives in a small boat, bobbing atop a stretch of water that over centuries had witnessed the passage of *thousands*. Romans, Bretons, Christians and naysayers, invaders and traitors. Foreign envoys and armies, including those returning home.

Even though this water had claimed Ariene's life, Rachel's aunt would still have understood Rachel's wonderment. Ariene would have liked her company, those early pilgrims and adventurers and mercenaries who also hadn't returned to shore.

Like the click of a cogwheel, the reason for Rachel and her brother's disproportionate bequest in Ariene's will slipped into place. It was not that Ariene had loved Hugh, Juliet and Faith less.

In fact, Ariene had known that Hugh would always control the other fifty per cent of the Cavanagh's shipping interests, in the same way she had known that Juliet and Faith would do as Lady Georgiana wished, and that would make them happy.

Ariene had known it would not be the same for Rachel.

By granting Rachel part of her personal fortune, as well as a stake in the Cavanagh's shipping interests alongside Andrew and Hugh, Ariene had assured Rachel's freedom. Rachel would give it all back in exchange for Ariene's life.

Yet, for the very first time, the thought of Ariene's gift brought something other than a feeling of constriction from clawing grief abrading her throat. No, what brimmed from her now, what spread from her heart, looking over those moonlit waves and up to a banner of stars, was a warm, boundless well of gratitude and awe and love.

She felt the hot sting of tears at the corners of her eyes. Happy tears. Grateful tears. If she experienced nothing more in the next few days, already this feeling was worth it. This moment was enough.

It was the boat captain, her rescuer, who had helped her to have this. Who saw that she needed it.

He lay recumbent before her. With his face in profile and eyes closed, his chest rose and fell softly with his breaths. She had been serious when she said he prompted more questions than he answered. He was like nothing—and yet like everything—she had expected. He was a shipbuilder. A craftsmen in his own way. Yet she knew, when he said he was overseeing the brig's construction, that he would be alongside the shipwrights himself, bending the timbers and setting them in place, just as he had done with this vessel. He was that kind of man.

Earlier in the day, he'd left the tiller in the comb, made a meal for Rachel and himself, sponge bathed as she had done, and donned a new set of clothes. Now, his taupe-colored trousers hugged thighs that rivaled those of any of her grandfather's fittest and burliest men. His shirt, which today was white, was unbuttoned at the neck with sleeves rolled up to his elbows. She had not before had the opportunity to study him like this. Unintentionally, her gaze drifted back to his thighs.

She nearly leapt from her seat when he spoke, his eyes still closed.

"A man can only take so much ogling, Miss Cavanagh. Keep looking at the captain like that and before long the first lieutenant will be flat on her back, demonstrating what other varieties of tillers she might competently handle."

A fire arrow could not have set her cheeks alight faster.

"But," the boat captain continued, "I don't think those are the skills she wants to demonstrate. Not on this voyage."

And with that he rolled away from her onto his side, positioning his arm as a pillow beneath his head and leaving the conflagration that burned across her cheeks to cool like embers in the night.

JUST AS JONATHON LECKY HAD described, the French city of Boulogne-sur-Mer, with its elevated Old Town, straddled rolling hills at the confluence of the Liane River and the English Channel. Unlike empty Dunkirk during their brief stop nine months before, the port of Boulogne teemed with vessels, most of which belonged to the city's fishing fleet, although a score of larger ships anchored in the harbor besides.

Rachel's attention, however, was drawn to the dry docks and the ships being built there as they entered the mouth of the river. "Is one of those yours?"

Jonathon Lecky followed the direction of her gaze. "The leftmost dock, yes."

And there was his brig, albeit at such a distance, it was difficult to make out much detail. "It appears the hull is finished?" Rachel asked.

"It will be shortly. Soon, we'll begin the caulking."

In other words, forcing oakum into the seams between the planks, which would be covered over with hot pitch or tar to ensure the watertight integrity of the hull. Following which, the hull would be filled with water and searched for signs of leaks.

All the while, the shipwrights would be busy laying the decks.

It was a mammoth undertaking, to build a ship. Rachel could only imagine how it must feel, to lay one's hands upon the timbers after they had been planed and bent and fastened into place. It was awing enough to know the sloop they sailed on now had been built by his hand.

She hoped he would show her the brig up close.

"How satisfying it must feel," she said, "to see your plans come to being."

"It keeps a man's days honest."

Still, something in his eyes belied the lightness in his tone as he looked upon the dock, and she knew: *this was important to him.*

"This vessel; do you yet know her name?"

"This one? Aye," he spoke quietly. "I've always known the name of this one."

His words thrummed through her, but before she could form her next question, his attention settled on something over her shoulder.

"Ah, look. We're about to have company." She twisted to see he nodded toward the approaching customs boat. "I'll list you as my sister on the manifest, if anonymity is preferable?"

"It is," she agreed. It was a relief that he thought to protect her that way.

Effortlessly, he switched to French to hail the custom's officers, who in turn greeted him by name.

"You speak French well," she observed, after the customs boat had pulled away.

"Yes." He smiled as though amused by her surprise.

They sailed the short distance up the Liane River to the bustling quay where they waited another fifteen minutes for the commissaires to inspect the vessel. While they waited, the boat captain pointed out the Customs House, the Chamber of Commerce, and the various hotels and boarding houses that extended along the quay.

It was apparent, too, by their relaxed nature and jovial greeting, that the commissaires knew him and knew of his ship too. Rachel waited as Jonathon Lecky spent several minutes on the quay chatting and answering the men's questions about the brig's progress after the inspection was complete. When the commissaires moved on to the next vessel, he turned back to the boat to extend his hand to Rachel. "Ready?"

Gathering her skirts to one side, she reached out to take his hand. "Yes." She placed a foot on the bulwark, and he hauled her up beside him onto land.

Unbalanced, she tottered and staggered against him. He caught her, his fingers warm where they closed around hers.

His voice was warm too. "Steady?" he asked, and she looked up into his face. His lips were slightly curved. A playful sparkle lit those cloudbank eyes.

This close to him, she wasn't steady at all.

"I am," she lied.

Releasing her, he tilted his head in the direction of the main esplanade. "In that case, Miss Cavanagh, shall we?"

RACHEL CAME TO A STANDSTILL at the edge of the Boulogne-sur-Mer market square. Dominated at one end by a church, every inch of the square overflowed with people and produce-filled stalls, many of which were sheltered by red and blue awnings. The clucking of hens and bleating of goats punctuated the constant babble of French and provincial tongues.

Excitement unfurled within her. She loved the sights and smells of produce markets. "You knew this would be here?" she asked Jonathon Lecky.

"Yes," he replied. Morgan had come to a stop by his legs. "It's Wednesday."

"Is the market always held on Wednesday?"

"Wednesday and Saturday. We're a little late. It's better to arrive before noon."

Presumably, stalls at that hour still had plenty of stock. "And the church? What of it?" The building's stone facade rose above the marketplace. Visitors teemed around its large oak doors, exchanging coins for candles before they disappeared inside.

"That's the parish church of St. Nicholas, the patron saint of sailors."

"Truly?" She liked that thought. "Mr. Lecky, have you been known to light a candle inside?"

"I have. On occasions when I thought doing so might mean something to a friend."

She felt a stab of sadness. Men who were lost or injured, she imagined he meant.

"Perhaps you'd like to spend an hour here while I meet with colleagues?"

His question immediately caught her attention. *An hour to simply drift among the stalls*? To browse the wares and watch the vendors and customers? She'd not been able to do that since....

Since last September, when she and Ariene had traveled to Belgium. Her mother considered produce stalls to be the domain of the staff, not the domain of her daughters.

"Yes," Rachel agreed, "I would like that."

"They'll accept English coins, should you wish to make a purchase. Mind the pickpockets, though. Boulogne's boys put the London lads to shame. I'll be at a nearby inn, the Le Magnifique." At her expression, he smiled. "It's not as salubrious as it sounds. I'll find you here when I'm done."

"And should the hour grow late without your return?" Rachel asked.

"It's unlikely. But should that happen, you recall the route we just walked?" He looked at Rachel for confirmation. "Good," he said, at her nod. "Morgan and I will meet you back at the boat."

He surprised her then, by leaning in close. His breath brushed her ear. Amusement brushed his lips. "Go forth, Miss Cavanagh, and *explore*."

By the time she recovered her wits, he was already moving down the Grand Rue.

Morgan, sticking close to his heels, looked back over her shoulder to see whether Rachel was following. Realizing Rachel hadn't moved, the collie came to a complete stop and stared back. But as the distance between man and dog widened, she turned and dashed after her master.

Rachel turned to face the marketplace. Except for the long walks and rides she took across the Cavanagh estate, this was perhaps the first time in her life she had stood in public without a companion or escort present. Always, *always*, she was accompanied.

Now, on the edge of a square of people, she was alone.

And she had never experienced more freedom.

"WAIT BY THE DOOR," JONATHON Lecky instructed Morgan as they arrived at the tavern entrance.

The collie did not look pleased. With mouth slightly parted in protest and ears pressed back, she took a grudging seat on her hindquarters. Lecky sent her another pointed look. She settled on her stomach with a grumble and tucked one front paw beneath her chest.

Stepping inside the tavern, Lecky's eyes took a moment to adjust to the murky interior. However, what Le Magnifique lacked in ambience was countered by the taste of the ale, which made it Winter's preferred drinking hole.

Lecky's business partner was seated at one of the low tables toward the back wall. Their French supplier, Winter's soon-to-be brother-in-law, Bertrand Mercier, sat at Winter's side. The Mercier family numbered among the oldest and wealthiest families of Boulogne.

The Merciers had long been in the business of supplying British society with its beverages of choice, be it Burgundy or cheap brandy. Whether traders, such as Lecky and Winter, or the coastal smugglers of Essex and Kent facilitated that supply didn't much matter to the Merciers. As it was, the family's interests stretched from Britain to the southern coast of Spain.

Winter, the black-haired, black-eyed devil that he was, looked up as Lecky approached. "Ah, we were just speaking of you. It's about time you arrived."

Mercier, French and thus more graceful, stood to grasp Lecky's hand. "Jonathon, it is good to see you."

"And you, Bertrand. I understand we will be raising our glasses to you in two nights' time."

"*Oui*." A smile spread across the Frenchman's face. It was the worst-kept secret in all of Boulogne that Bertrand and Winter's half-sister, Martine, would announce their betrothal at the Mercier family's forthcoming dance. "You will be joining us, I presume?"

"You can count on it. I wouldn't miss an evening at the Château de Boulogne-sur-Mer."

The men took their seats. "I take it all is ready for the *Shearwater*?" Winter asked.

The *Shearwater* was due in Boulogne the next day, and neither

Winter nor Lecky had had prior dealings with her captain. "I've a few loose ends to tie up in the morning, but otherwise yes," Lecky said. "You mentioned reports on Lawrence were favorable?"

"He ticks all the boxes according to Napier. Steady, reliable and determined, without excess pride. Napier was happy to recommend him. This should be a good test."

Lecky gave a nod. Napier was a good judge. Ultimately, Lecky and Winter were looking for a captain for the brig, once construction was complete.

Winter's glance flickered towards the counter. For a second, his eyes narrowed on one of the tables, then the expression was gone. He lifted his hand to signal the barmaid as his attention returned to Lecky. "You want an ale?"

"No. I can't stay long."

"Oh?" Winter's look was questioning. Wednesday afternoons at Le Magnifique were an institution.

Lecky crossed his arms on the table and leant forward. His look encompassed Bertrand, as well. "I need a favor from both of you. It concerns a woman."

"A favor for you involving a *woman*? This territory is new." Lecky's business partner waved away the barmaid's attention as he lowered his hand. "Who is she?"

"Important enough to ensure her reputation is protected."

Winter's brows lifted. "Interesting. Continue." His glance flicked to Mercier, who also gave a nod.

"Rachel Cavanagh, the granddaughter of Rhys Cavanagh, the privateer."

Uncharacteristically, Winter missed a beat. "The lass you rescued."

"Aye, the very one."

"I thought she was going to marry the English marquess."

"Apparently, she's not as enraptured with the idea as England's newspapers are. She's here in Boulogne with me."

Winter gave a low whistle and leant back in his chair. "How, precisely, did that come about?"

"Damned if I know."

Winter was looking at Lecky as though he thought Lecky *might* know. And truth be told, he did. The gods had thrown her in his path . . . *again*. With an umbrella stand.

"Her family was staying overnight at the Lord Nelson in Gravesend. Encountering her was . . . unexpected. The lass needs time to think. She's under pressure to marry."

"So you offered a jaunt to Boulogne."

"I didn't offer, precisely."

"Lecky, let me assure you, if a man were ever to sail alone with Emily or Martine across the Channel, I'd have his bloody head."

Oh, he knew. "Winter, I'd like to think that Emily and Martine's relationship with their family is such that if they ever felt pressure to marry, they would never need to come to me with that request."

His words scored a hit. Winter was, and always had been, protective of his sisters. He also prided himself on caring for them.

"I see your point," Winter said. "But you *are* planning to take Miss Cavanagh back?"

Lecky returned the Englishman's gaze. "Of course." Yet as he spoke, he felt an unwonted stab that belied his words. "The lass isn't running away. She just needed a reprieve."

Still, Winter wasn't fooled. It didn't help that Winter had sensed, all those months ago, that a certain bruised, battered shipwreck survivor had gotten under Lecky's skin.

"I see. And *you* needed . . . ?" Winter's lips curved in the Englishman's incisor-sharp smile.

With just the right amount of incisor-sharp insight, his question hung in the space between them.

"I'll return her to England after Bertrand and Martine's celebrations." Lecky shot Bertrand a questioning look.

Bertrand gave a nod. "The *mademoiselle* is welcome to attend, of course."

"Thank you."

"Miss Cavanagh is now as famous in her own right as her grandfather, since you so 'secretly' rescued her," Winter said. "I presume that was the favor you wanted? An invitation for Friday?"

"It's one part. I need Emily."

"Emily?" Once more, he'd caught Winter by surprise. Emily was the oldest of Winter's two younger sisters. She was also Winter's full-blooded sister; both she and Elijah had been born to their father's first wife.

"Is she in Boulogne?" Lecky asked.

"She is."

"I'd like to introduce her to Miss Cavanagh. I'll be tied up with business tomorrow when the *Shearwater* arrives, and I'd like her to show Miss Cavanagh more of Boulogne."

"Where is Miss Cavanagh now?" Again, Winter's glance skimmed the nearby tables. His brow creased in a frown.

"In Dalton Place. Exploring the market."

"Thus the reason for your short stay. Very well." Winter half-raised his tankard. He looked at Lecky over the rim. "Come by this evening. There are other matters we need to discuss."

"Oh?"

His business partner's gaze didn't waver. "Blackburn."

Hot and sharp, a spark of anger flared. He bit down rather than bite out. *Winter, don't go there.* Blackburn was not Winter's concern.

A beat passed as each regarded the other. "Comrade, I suggest you back away from that line."

Without dropping his gaze, Winter took a swallow of ale and set his tankard down. "You and I can discuss later where that line is drawn."

One end of Lecky's lips curved. It would be a cut-and-dried conversation. "Very well. We'll do that."

"I'll let Emily and Martine know that you and Miss Cavanagh are coming. And that discretion is required."

"Thank you." Lecky set his hands on the table and moved to stand.

"One more thing. Don't be obvious," Winter said. "The older fellow seated two tables over. His interest in our party increased when you walked in."

Had it? Lecky gave a nod.

"Until this evening," Winter said.

"Yes. And Bertrand. Friday, yes?"

"*Oui.* Friday." There was a sparkle in the Boulogne man's eye. "I look forward to meeting your *mademoiselle.*"

"Miss Cavanagh, you mean." He spoke with a smile, but his message was clear. *She's not mine, my friend.*

Perhaps not, *but you want her to be*, the voice inside whispered.

"*Oui*. Miss Cavanagh." Bertrand nevertheless took his meaning.

Lecky's gaze sliced to the nearby table as he departed. Winter was right. It seemed he'd drawn some interest.

The man Winter had spotted had the look of a sailor, with his deeply weathered skin and tan, the likes of which lingered for years. In his forties or perhaps fifties, his unshaven face bristled with gray stubble. Yet it was the look in his eyes—a look that went beyond idle curiosity to shrewd and downright assessing—that brought Lecky to a stop.

"*Trouvez-vous quelque chose d'intéressant?*" Lecky asked. Do you find something of interest?

"*Non, non.*" Seemingly unfazed by Lecky's directness, the man lifted his ale to his lips. Still, his eyes were sly. Sly in the manner of being privy to a private joke. It was not a look Lecky trusted.

Lecky strode on. Morgan leapt up to fall in at his side as he exited the inn.

SHE WAS IN FRANCE. RACHEL stood in the midst of market stalls while a stream of French and other local variants flowed around her, imparting their exotic charm.

She drifted between flower stalls thick with scent and overflowing with blooms. She ambled by vegetable stands filled with peas and haricot beans and new potatoes. She wandered past smock-clad field workers haggling over cages of poultry and uniformed household staff spending their employers' coins on eggs, flour and butter.

The fruit stalls were particularly impressive, with their plentiful supply of apples, chestnuts, pears, currants, walnuts and plums. The smiling, ruddy-faced fruit seller noted her interest and fired a question at her in one of the provincial tongues.

When she failed to respond, he switched to heavy-accented English. "The lady is a visitor to Boulogne?"

His grin was infectious. She smiled. "Yes. I was admiring your stall."

"Ah!" He gave a nod, then pointed to the plums. "You see? *Produits français*. And these?" He led her along the stall to point out the figs and dates. "*Algérie.*" Detecting her interest, he continued on, telling her of the various nations and regions from which his produce originated and showing her the fruits he had grown himself. "You wish to buy?"

"Just admire."

He took no offence and seemed happy to entertain her until the next customer arrived.

When he was called away to serve, Rachel again turned to look out over the sea of colorful stalls. With the large, flat facade of the church rising above the canvas shades, it was a vista that could have been taken from the pages of *Ackermann's Repository*. She could picture the colored illustration it would make, complete with the title, *Market Day in Boulogne-sur-Mer*, and the subtitle, *Looking Toward the Church of St. Nicholas*.

And then there would be the accompanying article, describing the provincialism of the marketplace and the flow of people among the stalls. In England, she would have pored over both illustration and article. Dreamed about being immersed in it and dreamed of the day when she would be able to discover such places herself.

Never would she have imagined herself being in such a place, in the company of one rather rugged boat captain.

Just as it had on Jonathon Lecky's boat, when she'd been watching man and dog, that quiet urge stole over her again. The urge to *sketch*.

She stilled, wary once more of the feeling. She sucked in a breath. *Are you real? Are you there? Have you come back?* She sent out a tentative, testing, inward inquiry. The urge inside didn't scurry away. It was there, nervous, yet holding its ground.

Her journal lay at the bottom of the Channel. She hadn't been able to bring herself to replace it. Now, she felt braver.

She turned back to the fruit seller. "Please. Do you know where I might purchase a book to write in?" She made a scribbling motion with her hand.

"*Oui.*" The fruit seller pointed to a row of shops lining the street opposite the square. "*Libraire.*"

Rachel identified the sign above the door. "Thank you!"

The fruit seller smiled and gave a nod.

Small bells jingled above the bookseller's door, and the wooden floorboards squeaked as Rachel stepped inside the shop. The young, bespectacled man behind the counter briefly looked up at her entry. His glance dwelt on her before he quickly looked away. Several respectably dressed customers browsed the long, tall sets of shelves.

She hunted along shelves lined by French titles until she reached the section that stocked writing materials. Thankfully, they stocked manuscript journals. Of course, Boulogne was a long way from London—or Paris, for that matter—and the selection in the provincial French city was limited.

She picked up a journal with a red leather cover. Turning it over, she stroked the small section of gilt lettering that identified the journal's manufacturer. It was a common make. She hesitated. It didn't feel quite *right.*

Her attention shifted to another bound volume with a patchwork cover, sewn from a mix of pecan- and rosewood-dyed leathers. She set the red journal aside and picked up the one bound in mixed leather. She could feel the raised stitches beneath her fingertips. She flipped the journal open to touch the crisp, blank pages inside.

Yes, this one felt right.

Next, she chose a pencil. She could sharpen it using the pen knife she carried in her reticule.

She emerged from the bookseller's with both purchases and heightened nerves. A hard lump was back in her throat. Now that she carried the tools to sketch in her hands, the urge had once more turned skittish. It was fear, she realized. *Rachel, you're afraid.*

What was she afraid of? she had to ask herself. It was a question she had *avoided* asking herself.

A little voice inside whispered in response. She was afraid it would be too hard, that it would never be as it once was.

She quashed the worry down as she examined the marketplace from several different angles. The view from the fruit stalls was preferable, she decided. The fruit seller saw her return and, to her surprise, produced a stool. "You wish to sit?" He smiled broadly and mimicked her scribbling motion.

She laughed, warmed by his thoughtfulness. She showed him her pencil, then swept her arm toward the view of market and church. "I am going to draw."

"Ah." He gave a nod and again offered the stool. "*Mademoiselle*, please. *Sit.*"

She smiled at his insistence. Grasping the stool, she indicated toward the place she wanted to set up, out of the way of the foot traffic. "May I take it over there?"

"*Oui, oui.*" He motioned 'go ahead' with his hands.

"Thank you." Still smiling, she carried the stool a little way, then settled down.

With a deep breath, she creased open the journal and stared at the crisp white paper that lay beneath her fingertips.

It had been so long. *She could do this.*

She steeled herself with another deep breath, then lifted a critical eye to her surroundings.

She was quite skilled at portraits, but landscapes had always been her forte. She had a natural eye for perspective, especially when depicting architecture. She could see what she needed to do.

She had to begin.

Her hand was unsteady as she put pencil to page. She caught her bottom lip between her teeth as she mapped a few light lines in the shape of the church and its relation to the market. Perspective and size: she needed to get those elements right first.

At first, her strokes were uncertain. But as the outline of the church emerged and the lines she drew grew more confident, so too did contentment begin to flow back into her pores. The contentment that came from holding a pencil in her hand. From capturing the life she saw.

But there was something else, too. Something that welled in her chest and rose suddenly, threatening to spill over, as with each stroke the picture began to take form. It was something that, in that moment, was more consuming than contentment.

Relief.

Abiding, overpowering *relief.* She bit her lip hard. *Yes, she could still do this.* Her heart swelled, and hot, happy tears sparked at the corners of her eyes. She blinked them back and carried on. The line of stalls and layout of the market took shape as her pencil skated across the page.

A rough sketch of a French market did nothing to resolve

matters with her mother or Rossum. But for the first time in months, this was *her*. This was what she did. What she'd done before. What she'd hoped to do.

This is you.
For now, it was enough.
It was enough.
And she was grateful.

CHAPTER ELEVEN

Every man needs another whose words he doesn't want to hear.
　　—*The Memoirs of Rhys Cavanagh*

LECKY EXPECTED TO FIND HIS wayward adventuress exploring the stalls that crowded Dalton Place. Instead, amid the surging market goers, it was Rachel Cavanagh's very stillness, seated on a stool beneath an awning with pencil and notebook in hand, that drew his eye.

Or maybe it was just *her*.

She glanced up at the church, then back down to the notebook. He realized, by the quick movements of her wrist, she was sketching. Her expression was unguarded and intent. Unconsciously, she tucked a wayward butterscotch curl behind her ear.

The sight of her was so damn lovely it made his chest hurt.

Morgan gave a little yip and tore forward.

"Morgan!" She bent over to give the collie a pat. Then, looking up, she spotted his approach. "Hullo," she said, with a small smile. As she straightened, she again tucked that wayward curl back.

He had the strongest urge to lean in close and brush his mouth against the delicate curve of her ear.

That line, Jonathon. Toe it.

"Hullo." He glanced down at the notebook that lay open in her lap.

There, a sketch of the marketplace emerged. She'd captured the facade of the church, the large, flat expanse of alternating dark and white-washed brickwork, and the figurative sculpture of Christ the

Judge, which stood in the recessed portal above the doors. She'd begun to render the market stalls, too, with their produce-laden tables and mill of customers beneath the canvas awnings. But what was more remarkable was the way she'd captured the market's vibrancy and movement with a few quick strokes of her pencil.

She was talented. Perhaps as talented as her grandfather, whose sketches had been published with his memoirs and who might have been an artist, had he not dedicated himself to the life of a privateer.

Lecky could produce a sketch too; but his skills were generally confined to sailing vessels and far more technical in nature.

"Impressive." Lecky looked up from her notebook. She'd gone quiet. The hesitancy in her eyes surprised him.

"I haven't drawn in a long time. I . . . I haven't wanted to."

Ah. He had a sudden suspicion. "When was the last time?"

"Belgium. Last October."

Belgium. Before the *Castalia* went down.

Belgium. Before Ariene Cavanagh had died.

This sketch was significant then.

He studied her. "Spend as much time on it as you want. We're in no rush."

"Are you certain?"

By the gods, if she looked at him too many times with those rich, expressive, coffee-brown eyes, all the cork on the Spanish coast wouldn't stop him from sinking.

"We don't need to leave," he reiterated, "until you are done."

Those eyes only became more captivating when gratitude brimmed in their depths. "Thank you, Mr. Lecky."

Jonathon, he had the urge to say. "Miss Cavanagh, it's nothing."

Still, as she looked back to her sketchbook, he couldn't shake the feeling that she was thanking him for more than just an extra half hour.

RACHEL CRANED HER NECK UP at the mansion residence Jonathon Lecky had led her to in the heart of Boulogne's Old Town. Thick rows of white mullioned windows contrasted with the building's dark brick and hinted at the elegance within. Elegance she had not been prepared for, when Jonathon Lecky said he was taking her to meet a friend.

"Whose home is this?"

"It belongs to the Winter family. Mr. Elijah Winter and his sisters, Emily and Martine."

"They are English?" Rachel asked in surprise.

"Elijah and Emily are, yes. The same goes for a good quarter of the population of Boulogne. Martine is half-French."

"How are you acquainted?" Rachel asked, as Jonathon Lecky rapped with the door knocker, then took a step back to wait. Morgan perched on her hindquarters by his feet.

"We have interests in common. Rachel"—his demeanor became serious—"you can trust these people. I wouldn't bring you here otherwise."

Her throat went dry. It was the first time he'd called her by given name alone.

Coupled with his concern, it had a rather unsteadying effect.

A maid opened the front door. Without hesitation, Morgan streaked past her legs.

"Morgan is a regular here," Lecky told Rachel, as the maid laughed and showed them through to a rose-colored salon.

Inside, Morgan was already garnishing the attention of the room's only occupant, a striking, raven-haired woman who glanced up at their entry.

The woman greeted them with a smile. "Look, Miss Morgan, your owner has caught up! Hello, Jonathon." Her bright eyes shifted to Rachel as she came to her feet. "And Miss Cavanagh, I presume? Elijah said you would be accompanying Jonathon this evening. I am Miss Winter, but please, call me Emily."

"It's a pleasure to meet you, Miss Winter—Emily."

"I heard Morgan is here!" A second, raven-haired young woman appeared in the doorway. She smiled at Rachel.

"Martine," Emily said, "this is Miss Cavanagh."

"Oh! Miss Cavanagh, I am so excited." The young woman came forward to squeeze Rachel's hands. "How wonderful that you will be joining us for my engagement celebrations!"

Her *engagement celebrations?* Rachel blinked. "Oh, yes . . . I beg your pardon?" She cast a wild look at Jonathon Lecky. *What on earth?*

She had *no* idea what she had just walked into. She suddenly felt very unsettled. This was not the type of company she had expected Jonathon Lecky to keep.

Martine laughed, while Emily cast the boat captain an exasperated, if affectionate look. "Has Jonathon not told you? Miss Cavanagh, my sister, Martine, is recently engaged. The formal announcement will be made this Friday eve at the Château de Boulogne-sur-Mer. Our family and the family of Martine's intended, Bertrand Mercier, are holding celebrations."

"Indeed, we are!" Martine dropped into a crouch beside Morgan, who immediately cuddled closer for a scratch. The look the second Winter girl cast Jonathon Lecky was full of devilry. "A medieval ball in a medieval castle, Jonathon. Do you not think it's perfect?"

Jonathon Lecky stood with his arms crossed over his chest. He was grinning. "You plan to make Bertrand dress up as your *knight*, Martine?"

"Jonathon, *everyone* shall be dressing up. Yourself and Miss Cavanagh included."

It was impossible not to respond to the girl's mock imperiousness. "I would be delighted," Rachel said. "I cannot tell you how much I have always wanted to attend a medieval-themed ball in a French castle."

Martine Winter's eyes sparkled with humor as she recognized an ally in Rachel. "You see, Jonathon?" she teased. "It is every woman's dream to be surrounded by princes and knights and champions. Even that of Miss Cavanagh."

"That may be so, Miss Martine. But not all of us fit that bill. Some of us are just ordinary men."

"You, Jonathon? Ordinary? How funny. I can't think of another person *more* qualified to rescue a damsel in distress."

On account of his penchant for rescuing starving dogs and drowning women, Rachel wondered? Did the two Winter women know the role Jonathon Lecky had played in her life?

Jonathon Lecky appeared amused. "I don't know, Martine. I haven't rescued *that* many damsels." He looked across the salon to give Rachel a wink.

Sitting on the floor by Martine, Morgan produced an indignant huff.

"There now, beautiful one." Martine reached out to scratch Morgan's neck. "Jonathon, Morgan thinks you are forgetting her. Beautiful one, he is *not* forgetting you, I promise." The collie inched closer and stretched her nose towards Martine's. Martine cupped her furry jaw. "But you must tell me, Morgan sweet, what *you* wish for in a boy collie? A lad who will fight for you? Care for you? Protect you? You should wish for those things, Mademoiselle Morgan." She stroked the collie's face. "You are a true belle."

"A belle maybe, but also a pat-strumpet," a man's voice interrupted. "Look at her. She's anyone's for a pat."

"*What?* A *pat*-strumpet?" Martine hugged the collie tighter. Morgan flattened her ears and looked back over her shoulder at the newcomer. "How could you say such a thing, Elijah?" Martine demanded, then turned to Morgan soothingly. "Do not listen to him, *mon cher*; my brother says bad things."

By the playful, devilish glint in Elijah Winter's eyes, Rachel suspected it wasn't unknown for Martine's brother to *do* bad things either. Here, Rachel thought, was a man who knew precisely what feathers he could ruffle and for how long. Rachel's grandfather, and later Ariene, had taught her how to recognize that sort. Rhys Cavanagh, after all, had been one of them.

"Miss Cavanagh, please meet our brother, Elijah," Emily said.

"A pleasure, Miss Cavanagh."

She smiled charmingly. "I hardly know whether to say the same, Mr. Winter. I too am quite partial to Morgan. I am still trying to decide whether I should be enraged on her behalf."

Elijah Winter's brows arched before he caught her humor and laughed. She could see she'd risen a notch in his estimation. "Let me assure you, it *is* my pleasure to meet you, Miss Cavanagh. You may side with Martine if you wish." He turned to Jonathon Lecky.

The boat captain still stood with arms crossed, but his gaze rested on Rachel. His gray eyes were warm. A little smile played at his lips. A secret thrill passed through her at the possibility of having risen in more than just Elijah Winter's assessment.

"Jonathon, a moment?"

At Winter's request, the mood of the room immediately

changed. Even Rossum, without the benefit of sight, would have been able to detect the tension that had sprung up between the two men.

"One," the boat captain replied.

"Ladies," Elijah Winter said, "please excuse Jonathon and I for *one* moment."

"So," Lecky said, as they stepped inside Winter's office, "Martine intends for us to dress as knights and medieval maidens and dance the galliard."

"*I* shall dress as a knight," Winter said. "You may dress as a maiden if you wish. I doubt anything would amuse Bertrand more. Or me, for that matter."

"Mayhap my performance of a tassel kick in women's skirts?"

"I would pay to see that." Winter closed the door and crossed to his sideboard. "Drink?"

"No. Thank you." Lecky sat down.

Winter poured one for himself, then crossed to take the seat behind his desk. "The Cavanagh girl. I can see why she has you tied up. Poetry, isn't she? With those dark eyes and caramel locks?"

She was precisely that. There was good reason why she'd captured England's imagination, why she and the Marquess featured in all the broadsheets. Lecky understood Winter was curious. But the man didn't need to pay *too* much attention. "Careful. I requested Emily's company for the lass, not yours."

"Ha!" Winter looked amused. "This is something I haven't seen before."

"What is that?"

"You. Staking your territory."

"You've seen me stake my territory before."

"Yes. Besides myself, you're the stubbornest knave I know. But I've never seen you set up pickets around a woman."

No, because he never had. And even now, he did not for one minute think he *had* a claim on her. He had *no* intention to claim her. She wasn't for him. The circumstances of his life didn't allow for romantic attachments.

So who knew what the bloody hell he was doing.

Across from him, Winter's fingertips rested on the rim of his glass, the spirits inside untouched. A beat passed.

"Winter, you are straying remarkably close to matters that don't concern you."

"Am I? Let's talk about Blackburn."

"As I mentioned . . . *remarkably* close."

"Jonathon, what you do affects *me*."

"My dealings with Blackburn have nothing to do with you."

"When my business partner and master shipbuilder enters into 'dealings' with a jackal like Blackburn, it has *everything* to do with me. Don't bloody tell me otherwise. Who was the man at the tavern, Jonathon? Late forties, solid in appearance, unshaven. The one watching you?"

"He wasn't familiar."

"Surely that concerns you."

"It concerns me. But don't speak as though this comes as a surprise to you. You knew who I was when we went into this."

"Yes." Winter's eyes hardened. "Now we both have more at stake."

"Perhaps you do. My position hasn't changed."

"Hasn't it? Is that what you call manipulating Blackburn into striking the MacArthurs? Excuse me, but that's new."

"No." There was no warmth in Lecky's smile. "I recall doing that before."

"Yourself. Years ago. Years before the arrangement between you and I."

"Careful." He wouldn't give too many warnings.

"You and Blackburn plan to raze the MacArthur shipyard, don't you? That was the bait you supplied."

Notus be damned. Lecky had done his research, but it seemed Winter had, too.

"Blackburn wants his revenge, and I have no qualms—*none*—in helping him attain it."

"Damn it, Lecky! Blackburn has a mean streak wider than the Channel. He'll get his revenge regardless of whether you abet it. Keep your damn hands clean."

Lecky shot to his feet. His blood burned hotter than molten metal in a blacksmith's forge. "You say, do you?" He balled his fists against the surface of Winter's desk. "Do you know, Elijah, what happened to that man's daughter? The very same thing that has been happening *for years*. The only difference this time is that the woman Chaloner MacArthur chose to abuse has a father of some means, with a disregard for the law."

"I'm not saying what Chaloner MacArthur has done is right. I *am* saying you need to let it go."

That was precisely the problem. "I *have* let it go. I've let it go far too long. Do you know how many people he's hurt?"

"I'm aware he's a prime candidate for castration. But these things usually have a way of catching up with a man. Lecky, you don't need to be the conductor. Let MacArthur orchestrate his own doom."

"I'm surprised you of all people would say that."

Winter's gaze clashed with his. There was history there. History not often alluded to or spoken about. "I learned some things in the desert."

Lecky hadn't known Elijah before that time, but he knew the desert had tempered the man. The Elijah Winter who had walked into that land had not been the same man who walked out.

"Jonathon," Winter continued. "I fail to see how destroying that shipyard will prevent MacArthur from hurting innocents the likes of Blackburn's daughter. I should think a man with a character like MacArthur's would be more *likely* to fall back on his baser behaviors when under threat of ruin. He'll lash out at those who *can't* oppose him. That is usually what the weak do."

Lecky clenched his jaw. Castration would indeed serve, but he wanted something more. *He wanted Chaloner MacArthur to understand what it felt like to have nothing.* No control. No power. No lifestyle to which he'd become accustomed on the back of others' suffering. He wanted to strip MacArthur of everything the man had gathered and used to gauge his importance. He wanted Chaloner MacArthur to discover what a man felt like when his identity was destroyed.

But he didn't want that for Chaloner MacArthur alone. He wanted Jonas MacArthur, patriarch of MacArthur and Sons, to feel that pain too. It was, after all, Jonas MacArthur's blind eye that had allowed his son's actions to continue for so long. Above all else,

Jonas MacArthur cared for his profits. Above all else, Chaloner MacArthur cared for his cock.

Now, with the company's recent losses, MacArthur and Sons was heavily exposed. One act, timed to perfection, would bring the almost century-old business undone. Money made through company trade would not be enough to protect against damages sustained to the MacArthur's shipbuilding division, particularly if the company was forced to renege on contracts. The recent damage to the schooner *The Helena* assured of that. Such were the vulnerabilities that anyone who made a habit of studying the company would see.

MacArthur and Sons had weathered the blow of the end of the British African slave trade ten years earlier by diversifying and strengthening its ties with Cadiz. Now, the company was part of the band of English merchant houses that continued to provide their counterparts in Spain with the necessary goods for their Iberian neighbor to continue its own, still-legal traffic of human merchandise out of Africa.

Now, the Spanish too were considering bringing an end to the trade.

It had been a condition long ago, when Lecky partnered with Winter, that the goods Winter shipped had no origins in slave labor. French wine, brandy and tobacco, yes. Never Caribbean rum. It was a request Winter never contested. For Winter, too, such experience was too close to home.

Apparently, Lecky's business partner had decided he'd given Lecky enough to think about. He came to his feet. "Regarding Miss Cavanagh. She is welcome to stay here in the company of my sisters, should that serve better than a hotel or aboard your boat. I imagine you're concerned about propriety?"

"I am. I was going to ask. Thank you." Depending on his mood and his needs, Lecky slept on his sloop or in his office at Winter's warehouse or at the sailor's accommodations at the dry docks, where he could oversee his men. His alternative was to establish Rachel Cavanagh in a hotel. Emily and Martine Winter's company was preferable. Now that she'd met Elijah's sisters, he knew she wouldn't object.

"That line, Jonathon?"

Lecky's gaze settled on Winter as his business partner opened the office door.

"You can be as silent as you want, Jonathon. But in this room, there is no line. Besides, you might also find you'd enjoy your time with the delectable Miss Cavanagh more, if you weren't forever watching your back."

"Here she is," Emily Winter said. "She's coming along wonderfully, is she not?"

The dark-haired Englishwoman offered Rachel a smile, then rested her parasol against her shoulder as the two women came to a halt inside the Boulogne-sur-Mer shipyard where Jonathon Lecky's brig was being built.

The vessel extended before them, her keel resting on extensive log-bed foundations. The planking of the hull appeared finished. At once the vessel looked large, yet sleek, compact and fast.

In a move that sought to protect Rachel's reputation, a servant had been sent to collect Rachel's things from Jonathon Lecky's boat the previous evening, and Rachel had remained at the Winter residence overnight. It was now morning, and her English companion had led Rachel on a tour of the city. First, they had stopped inside the Château de Boulogne-sur-Mer to check on the progress of Martine's engagement preparations. To Rachel's surprise, the celebrations were to be held in the open air of the castle's courtyard. From the château, Emily had guided her through the Old Town's maze of narrow, cobbled streets to the ramparts of the Old Town's walls. Now, following a short traipse, Emily had brought her to the shipyard, to see the vessel being constructed for her brother.

Beyond, the mouth of the River Liane spilled into the English Channel, while the Straits of Dover formed a glittering expanse in the sunlight.

The day was clear, the breeze stiff enough to keep haze at bay.

"I know Elijah cannot wait to take possession of her," Emily said, in reference to the brig. "He's long wanted to own his own vessels. Jonathon hopes she will be finished by next spring. They're looking for her captain now."

"Have they a man in mind?" With her family's own contacts in shipping, they heard of plenty of men aspiring to a new command.

"Originally, Elijah hoped that Jonathon would sail her. But that's not Jonathon's interest."

"Is it not?" Such news surprised her. After constructing and sailing his own boat, he did not want to sail his own ship?

The wind lashed loose strands of hair to her face. She combed them back with her fingers, curious to hear Emily's explanation.

"No. He loves the freedom of captaining his sloop. But when it comes to ships, his love lies in their building and design."

"This is the first ship he has constructed, though?"

"Yes. But I should be surprised if it were the last. I know Elijah wants to build more. He has plans to extend our trade."

"Emily," Rachel realized suddenly and rather embarrassingly, "we were so busy speaking last night about Martine's engagement, I don't even know what your family trade!"

Good Lord, she thought. *Ariene, you left me a quarter of the company. What sort of custodian am I?*

Simply, she'd been busy enjoying new female company.

Emily didn't seem to mind. "Ah! That's true! My brother stocks London's drawing rooms. Champagne. Burgundy. Bordeaux. Brandy. French tobacco. He has acquired some very important clients."

"My family are in trade also," Rachel said. "Raw materials principally—"

"Have you been affected by the corn laws?" Emily interrupted.

"Some. Thankfully, our principal interest is not in wheat." Rhys Cavanagh and later Hugh had been canny, capitalizing on Britain's booming trade with Ireland during the war. But coming back to Jonathon Lecky....

How had he come to meet these people? Rachel wondered. And as their shipbuilder and ship's agent, he seemed to enjoy great freedom. After all, she realized somewhat guiltily, he still had to return her to England.

"Your brother does not mind that his master shipbuilder comes and goes?"

The breeze snatched up Emily's laugh. "Rachel, no. Not when the ship agent in question owns half the business."

Her rescuer owned ... *what?* Jonathon Lecky owned *half* of Winter's company?

Emily's words left her stunned. Dumbstruck.

The Englishwoman noticed. Her eyes shimmered with amusement as again she laughed. "Did you not realize? I thought Jonathon would have told you. Rachel, Jonathon is my brother's silent partner. With the exception of building this vessel and occasionally acting as ship's agent, he has little involvement in the day-to-day running of the business, which is an arrangement that suits both Jonathon and Elijah just fine. Not, of course, that overseeing this," Emily swept her hand towards the brig, "is any small undertaking."

"Emily, I'm still trying to...." Wrap her mind around the discovery? She couldn't say that without looking like a fool.

How had a man who appeared to own nothing more than a thirty-foot sloop come to hold a fifty percent interest in a trading company?

"Emily, how did Jonathon Lecky and your brother meet?"

That question shocked another laugh from the Englishwoman. "Goodness, my favorite boat captain really has been tight-lipped. Why, they met in Morocco. Jonathon freed him."

Rachel blinked. *Morocco?* "I beg your pardon ... Jonathon *freed* him?"

"Yes. For six months, my brother was held captive by a Moorish tribe. Jonathon Lecky led the party sent by the British Vice-Consul in Mogadore to secure his release." Her glance settled on Rachel, the depth of her feeling suddenly evident within. "Martine and I are very grateful to him. If not for Jonathon ... without our brother ... our lives would be very different."

Rachel drew a breath. All the air had vanished from her lungs. For the second time that morning, Emily had managed to confound her. "But ... how? When ... ?"

"Three, no, four years ago? But my brother was certainly not the first man Jonathon freed. He spent eight years in Morocco with the British Vice-Consul, repatriating lost men." Likely, Emily could see Rachel's mind crowding with questions. The Englishwoman smiled, almost apologetically. "I'm sorry. I've overwhelmed you.

"It's quite a story, isn't it?"

Quite a story? Rachel was still grappling with the barest pieces. "I had no idea."

"How would you, if Jonathon never said?"

How would she indeed? *Lives are saved everyday*, he had told her in Dunkirk.

I can't think of another person more qualified to rescue a damsel in distress, Martine had said last night.

It cast Rachel's own story in a somewhat different light to discover she was just one of many whose lives Jonathon Lecky had so significantly touched. But instead of that taking something away, somehow *lessening* its import, it made her *more* grateful. More awed. Her gaze came to rest again on his ship.

Why her? How was it *she* had been bestowed this fate? How was it *this* man had come to be placed in her path?

And Jonathon Lecky. What of him? Eight years, negotiating the release of lost men? What did that involve?

Risk, she thought. *It involved a great deal of risk.*

Emily, quite intuitively, gauged the direction of her thoughts. "I can see that you want to know more, but it's Jonathon's story, so better that he tell it. I believe he's meeting a vessel this morning. You should ask him when he returns to the house this afternoon."

"I will."

She would, because, the devil help her, she wanted to know everything about him.

Her heart had risen to her throat. "Emily," she said, "thank you."

"Mr. Lecky, I presume? It's a pleasure to meet you." Ian Lawrence, captain of the English schooner *Shearwater*, grasped Lecky's hand in a firm shake.

"It is," Lecky said. "And I you."

He'd been watching Lawrence for a good twenty minutes while the ship drew alongside. Lawrence's interactions with his crew were direct and authoritative, without sign of arrogance, just as Captain Napier had said. One could see too, that he cared for the handling of his vessel.

Lawrence was perhaps in his mid-thirties. Fair but not overly tall, he certainly looked fit enough to hold his own against any marauders of a mind to grapple his ship.

"First time to Boulogne?" Lecky asked.

"Third. But the first time for the Winter Trading House, as you know." Lawrence flipped open the satchel he was carrying and removed a set of documents, which he passed to Lecky. "The ship's papers."

"Thank you. When we're done with the commissaires, I'll take you to the warehouse. Mr. Winter would like to show you our operation."

Their new captain nodded. "I'd be pleased to see it."

"Good." Neither Lecky nor Winter had indicated to Lawrence that they had him in mind to be their own captain; they'd wanted to evaluate the man first. "I'll see if I can hurry up the officialdom," Lecky said. He strode off to find the commissaires.

The following hours were busy. He dealt with the French authorities, made arrangements for loading the *Shearwater*, and spent a good amount of time establishing a feel for the man that he and Winter thought might captain their brig. Lawrence wasn't a showman. He was steady. He was the kind of man Lecky liked. The kind Lecky wanted in charge of his ship.

Even so, there were moments when his thoughts strayed.

Rachel Cavanagh had accepted Elijah's invitation to remain beneath the Winter family's roof. The decision was for the best, from a propriety *and* a sanity point of view. Typically, even when in port, Lecky anchored offshore overnight to avoid troublemakers. That meant seclusion, which Notus knew would not have been a good idea with Rachel Cavanagh aboard. Lecky wouldn't have slept a damn wink. As it was, hours had passed during which he'd lain on the deck, arm behind his head and the gentle rock of the boat beneath him, and stared into the night.

Of course, last night was hardly the first time he'd thought about Rhys Cavanagh's granddaughter before he fell asleep. He'd read plenty of newspaper articles, after all.

And more than a few times, the zephyr had blown over the bow.

It was different to have her this close.

It was different to know her marriage to Rossum was not a *fait accompli*.

Come late afternoon, with introductions at the warehouse completed, Lecky left Lawrence in Winter's company and returned to his business partner's home. He found Emily and Martine poring over the final guest list for the following evening.

"I took Rachel to the docks to see the brig today!" Emily told him, after the sisters had clucked over Morgan.

"I thought you might," Lecky said. In fact, he would have been surprised if she had not. "Where is Miss Cavanagh now?"

"We just took tea at the Agnès Café," Emily said. "Miss Cavanagh remained behind to sketch the château. She should return shortly."

The coffee house Winter's sister referred to was located just down the street, directly opposite the château. "I'll find her," Lecky said. And he did, seated at one of the cafe's outdoor tables, wearing a deep pink colored dress and a shawl draped over her arms.

She looked up and smiled at his approach. "I'm almost done."

"Once again, no rush." He took a seat beside her. Meanwhile, Morgan veered closer, lifting her nose to sniff at a plate hosting the remnant crumbs of a French pastry.

"I'm so sorry, girl; it's all gone." Rachel gave Morgan an affectionate scratch behind the ear. "You've had a productive day?" she asked Lecky.

"Yes. But I'm not here to distract you." He motioned to her journal. "Carry on."

With a glance, she realized he was serious. She turned her attention back to her sketch as Morgan settled at her feet.

She worked for some time more. He watched as she rendered the large, medieval stone château, with its high walls that stretched between multiple, tall round towers, all of which was surrounded by the château's moat.

He looked for signs that his attention to her work made her uncomfortable. He saw none. Instead, on one or two occasions, she looked his way and smiled. He felt the simplicity of that smile thread through his soul. And it struck him that he simply felt . . . *comfortable* . . . just to sit at her side.

It wasn't a feeling that rushed over him. Rather, it settled in place, just as an anchor came to rest on the seabed. Steadying. Grounding. Restful.

Damn but that was a dangerous heading for a man's thoughts.

After a time, she closed her journal. "Done." He could see how pleased she was. She looked at him expectantly. "Shall we return to the Winters?"

To the Winters, who had shared her company all day? No. At that moment, he wanted the glow of her happiness all to himself.

"I shouldn't say yet," he replied.

CHAPTER TWELVE

God and I have long had a debate about chance. Speculate as I might, I daresay the answers are his.
—*The Memoirs of Rhys Cavanagh*

RACHEL RAISED HER BROWS. "You have something else in mind?"

Her rescuer leant forward in his chair, set his elbows on his knees and his chin atop clasped hands. The directness of his gaze had nearly the same potency as the slash of his grin. Her heart tripped and sped up. There was so much she still didn't know about him.

"Yes," he said. "Are you interested?"

"I don't know. I don't know what you have in mind." That wasn't true. He could suggest a trip to collect dog food for Morgan, and still she would be interested.

With a smile, he came to his feet and offered his hand. "Nothing that will get you into trouble. In fact, it requires no great exertion at all, other than a preparedness to take a stroll. Trust me?"

She felt a smile tug her lips. "I've been able to so far." She slid her new journal into her reticule and accepted his hand to rise. "First, I should tell the Winters where I'm going. Emily may worry if I don't return soon."

"Emily and Martine know I came to find you. It will be fine. Come."

Once more, Jonathon Lecky led her through the maze of the Old Town.

Yet instead of heading south, he deviated west. "I thought you might have been taking me to see your new ship?" she asked.

He shook his head. "I heard Emily provided a tour today. No, I have something else in mind."

Shortly, they had passed beyond the city limits, following a road that ran along the bluffs, high above the coast. Then, Jonathon Lecky turned off the road to lead the way down a narrow, well-worn, switchbacking path that descended the bluffs.

Low waves battered the beach below. The sun, long past its zenith, sat just above the horizon. Although light was still plentiful, the shadows cast were long. When they reached the base of the bluffs, Morgan, who had danced with impatience during their walk, broke away to tear across the damp sand, barking and prancing and wriggling as the tide crashed around her paws. Here, the smell of sea and wet sand was much stronger than it had been in the Old Town.

Jonathon Lecky sank into a crouch to remove his boots. He nodded towards Rachel's half-boots as she stepped onto the sand. "Not going to wear those, are you?"

"No." She crouched too, her fingers moving to unknot the laces. Jonathon Lecky pulled his boots off and set them aside, then sat to roll his trouser cuffs to just below the knee. The dipping sun at his back cast his features in half-shadow. He looked relaxed. At peace. As though there was nowhere else in the world he would rather be.

He also had, she couldn't help but notice, a very fit, very handsome pair of calves.

She felt the sting of a blush and quickly dropped her gaze.

Stop it, she admonished herself, willing the blush away. A nearly impossible feat, thanks to the little flip-flop effect the man had on her stomach.

He sat for a moment waiting for her to finish removing her boots, then pushed to his feet.

"Pass your boots here," he said. She handed them over, and he tied her laces to his and slung both pairs over his shoulder. "Ready?" She gave a nod.

They walked down the waterline. The sand, wet where the tide had retreated, felt cool beneath her feet. "Morgan!" She laughed and swept her skirts out of the way as the collie chose that moment to bound toward her and shake.

As she scraped breeze-lashed strands of hair from her eyes, she glanced at her companion. He tilted his head in the direction of the long, empty expanse of beach that stretched north from the mouth of the Liane. "Walk, shall we?" he asked.

Again, she gave a nod. Morgan hung back for a moment to trace scents across the sand, then sped ahead of Rachel and Lecky to settle into a contented trot.

They spent the first minutes walking in silence, barefoot at the edge of the tide. The water rushed up, then retreated around her ankles and stole the sand from beneath her feet. The last time she had stood on a beach had been in the midst of winter, in the cutting wind, beneath the sullen sky, on the Cavanaghs' Welsh estate in the months after Ariene had died.

Now, she walked in the late afternoon light, her deep pink colored skirt gathered to one side to keep the hem from the tide, while her shadow and Lecky's spread long across the sand.

The quiet felt easy. Her spirit felt full. She liked walking beside Jonathon Lecky to the lulling batter of waves.

"Your ship is very beautiful," she said. "Her lines are very sleek."

"Thank you. Did Emily show you the half-model?"

He referred to the scale model of one-half of the vessel, which he and his shipwrights used to determine the dimensions needed to construct the ship.

"Yes, I saw that too." Emily had taken her into the shipyard office where the half-model, built from his plans, was housed. "How long did it take you to design her?"

He cast her a look. "She's still being designed every day, in many ways. But eight years, on and off."

Eight years spent *where?* So many things made her curious. "May I ask you a question?"

His lips wore the trace of a smile. "Go on."

"You said you were building the ship for Winter. But you own half of it? Emily Winter told me you are a silent partner in her brother's business."

"Ah," he said, after a time. "Did she tell you also how we met?"

"Yes. But only the barest of details. She assumed I knew. When she realized I didn't . . . she said it was your story to tell."

"True. In that case, Miss Cavanagh, what would you like to know?" His lips curved when he saw her expression. "Ah. Everything."

"Please. I barely know *what* to ask. Put the pieces together for me."

"The pieces . . . I suppose there are a few of those." Wryness tinged his smile. "Very well. I left home at the age of seventeen. The gods, the winds, the fates—call it what you will—called me to Africa."

"At *seventeen*? Why Africa?"

"Seventeen because I was brash and angry and impervious to Berber daggers and African throwing knives. Africa because, like you, I read a lot. There were things in Africa I needed to see."

"What sort of things?"

Her father's death and grandfather's journals called her to Alexandria. She wanted to know what had driven him.

"I have a particular dislike for the deprivation of freedom."

A beat passed. Rachel said, "You speak of slavery."

"I speak of the deprivation of freedom—whatever its form."

She frowned. She wanted to be sure she correctly understood. "By form you mean . . . ?"

"Irrespective of color or sex or ownership papers. There are many ways and many grades by which a person can lose their freedom."

How did Jonathon Lecky and your brother meet?

Why, Jonathon freed him.

Did that mean . . . "Was Elijah Winter a slave?"

"Elijah's ship was wrecked off the coast near Sidi Ifni, two hundred miles south of Mogadore. He and a dozen crew survived but were captured by a passing Moorish tribe. He and the men were enslaved," he confirmed.

The man she'd teased the night before? The man who had called Morgan a pat-strumpet?

It seemed unbelievable. And yet, both Emily Winter and Jonathon Lecky said it was true.

"We didn't hear about the ship's loss in Mogadore for several months," her rescuer continued. "Often, that was how things worked. The Vice-Consul would hear of the wreck of a Christian ship some days or weeks after the fact, and I or another member of staff would lead an expedition to locate the crew. Depending on where the wreck was, we would either sail or travel overland. Speed was of the essence. If survivors were enslaved and taken into the desert... recovery became more difficult. The desert presents barriers. One's contacts become crucial. So does luck."

Her mind conjured the image of a nomadic tribe's desert camp. "But you recovered Winter and the crew."

"By the time we got there, we recovered Winter."

"Oh." Rachel swallowed as his meaning sunk in.

"The tribes' treatment of slaves is often harsh. But no more harsh"—a hard tone entered his voice, a hard tone with a sharp edge—"than the treatment of African slaves by white Christians."

The same hardness reflected in his eyes when Rachel's gaze met with his.

Year after year, he'd followed one dangerous commission with another.

In between those commissions, he'd designed boat and ship plans and constructed his sloop.

Her image of the type of life he had lived and the risks he had taken grew stronger.

"It was hazardous work for you, too. You might also have been captured and enslaved."

"There was that risk, yes."

"How did you come to be on the British Vice-Consul's staff? Did you deliberately go to Mogadore?" Many were opposed to slavery, but fewer took such active steps to see men freed.

"No." Tension seemed to leave him. "Mogadore was a stop on my return voyage from the Rice Coast. I sailed in for one night and stayed for eight years." He gave a little snort. Shook his head too. "It was a chance meeting, Miss Cavanagh. A chance meeting on an evening when, for a hundred reasons, I might never have slowed down and, for a hundred more, I might have been more guarded. But the sun had just set; and from the minaret above, the call to prayer had begun. I stopped by the main doors of the mosque to listen. I wasn't the only one to stop that evening. A conversation was struck." He gave another little snort. "Had I passed through the medina five minutes earlier or later, I might have sailed out of Mogadore the next day."

She sensed, as he lifted his head to stare down the beach, how much he felt the course of his life had hinged on that moment. "Who did you meet?"

"A former slaver. Enrique Barillis. He was Spanish. He'd been enslaved himself, after his ship was wrecked. He'd just had his ransom paid by the Vice-Consul. We paid all Christian ransoms," he added, "irrespective of nationality."

"And was Enrique on his way home?"

"No." Jonathon Lecky shook his head. "He was staying. He wanted to rescue other men like him." Her own rescuer seemed to consider his words. "Given his less than commendable history, he would have lost my attention had he only held his own captors in contempt. I would have sailed on from Mogadore without a backward glance. But Enrique had seen himself in the men who had held him. He realized he'd been just the same."

"When I saw Enrique Barillis," Jonathon Lecky said, "I saw atonement. What he felt . . . I could see it was more than apology. It was understanding that went to core of his being. Until then, I hadn't believed people could change."

He took a breath. "I wanted to understand his experience. That was what led me to the Vice-Consul. Now, there is another impressive man." He looked along the beach, but Rachel sensed he was looking back, across a continent and through time, perhaps remembering the day they had met. "By then, I had been in Africa for over a year. I'd managed to fend for myself. The Vice-Consul saw something raw in me. Something he could use. I was young, hungry. I dared what other's wouldn't. I was perfect for what he needed. And back then, Mogadore was perfect for me."

"Why was it perfect?"

This time, by the little twitch of his lips, she knew he was looking into the past, seeing things that she could not.

"The winds of North Africa were in my blood. Doggedness was one thing I could give. I didn't back away from a mission. I learned the fate of every man, eventually."

"Is Enrique still there?"

"In spirit, yes. He was killed a few years later." Gray eyes settled upon her. "He died in a sandstorm."

Her heart squeezed. "I'm sorry."

"Thank you. He was a good friend."

Rachel took a breath. "How did you get from there to here?" She motioned towards their surroundings.

He understood she meant something greater. "It was time to leave."

"For any particular reason?"

"My imperviousness to Berber daggers and African throwing knives had finally worn off?" That little smile was back, the tug of amusement at the corner of his mouth. "Winter had a great deal to do with it, to be fair. But then, I also met him at the right time. The right time in here." He tapped his chest with his fist.

"The Vice-Consul paid well. Not overgenerously, but well," he continued. "And trade ties between Mogadore and Great Britain were strong. I made some small investments that had large payoffs. While my resources hardly rival the Cavanagh coffers"—his lips quirked—"they're decent enough."

"Winter saw my ship design one night as I was leading his troublesome behind out of the desert. He wanted to know if I could build it. By then, he'd had plenty of cold nights out beneath the stars to think about the life he wanted. He stayed alive by spinning dreams and envisaging his future. I told him I could build it. I also had funds to invest. By the time Winter was ready to leave Morocco, he'd made me an offer I couldn't refuse. He asked me to build a ship for him."

"It was that offer that drew you back?"

"Aye, though the wind had already been changing. I'd been leading expeditions for seven—almost eight—years. For a long time I pushed it aside, but the need to construct my own vessels had been building."

She could imagine that. She could picture him beneath ocean and desert skies, conducting transactions with Moorish and African tribes, then retreating to his plans at night, beneath the lantern in his tent.

She could understand it, too. It was not so different from the feeling that dwelled within her, the discomforting sense that it would be wrong for her to marry Rossum and surrender the journeys she'd planned.

"You're wondering why I kept my interest private," he said. "My interest is in shipbuilding. The attachment to the company itself is Elijah's. The day-to-day management makes his blood sing, not mine. It was clear from the beginning that I never wanted that involvement. I expect one day he'll want to buy my share. Until then, the arrangement suits us both."

"You must trust Elijah's judgment."

"In matters of business, yes."

She caught the distinction. "But not in other matters?"

He cast her a glance. "Other matters, too. But only those that concern him."

She watched as the man who had saved her life leant down to scoop up several pebbles, then sent one skimming across the tide.

With the remaining pebbles still cupped in his hand, he turned back to face her. The afternoon sun at his back had the effect of deepening the crinkles his smile caused at the corners his eyes. The sea breeze lashed his dark golden-brown hair about his temples and jaw.

Tanned. Coarse. Complex. He was a man who thought about and understood the reasons for what he did. Her stomach did another little flip-flop.

His decisions, his moments of chance, led to hers. The realization came swiftly of how easily things could have been different. *One moment* could have changed it all. *One moment* during all those trips into the desert, had an expedition gone awry....

One moment when he came upon the *Castalia's* wreck, had the waves obscured her from view....

One moment in the dining room of the Lord Nelson Inn, if she not seen an engraved beer mug.

Her chest felt tight. The slimness of chance was both frightening and incredible.

"There is no such thing as 'if', Rachel. Not when we look to the past," Rhys Cavanagh used to tell her younger self. "'If' doesn't exist. The only thing that exists is what *was*. And if it so happened that luck or some greater power was on your side? Well, then, you've got double the reason to be grateful."

Should she be grateful for this?

Should she be doubly grateful?

She knew now she had needed this. To break free from the life she knew, to glimpse what life might be. And so she stood here in the orange-gold light of the slow-dipping afternoon sun. Unchaperoned, miles from England, almost a year beyond Ariene's death. Barefoot in ankle deep water, the sand of a French beach between her toes. The man who had saved her life—saved many lives—beside her. The soft pound of breakers on the shore and the kiss of the sea breeze on her face.

No shipwrecks. No newspapers. No London society.

No expectations of what she must be.

The rest of her life and all of its possibilities spread out before her.

Yes. She was doubly grateful for this moment.

WHAT THOUGHTS HAD THEIR CONVERSATION stirred, Lecky wondered, as emotion played across Rachel Cavanagh's face.

"What is it?" he asked.

"Just that... you spoke of chance. What you said about Mogadore made me think how incredible it is we are here. In this moment. Walking together like this."

Mayhap it was the afternoon light that touched her skin, but he thought he detected her flush, a blush of color that swept her cheeks.

"What I mean is," she hastened to add, "when you rescued me, the chance of us both being there... then at the Lord Nelson, too... I can't help but think how easily things might have been different."

"I know." After Dunkirk, he'd never thought she would step into his world again. Not barefoot and sweet and beautiful, a perfect bundle of dark eyes and creamy skin.

Her eyes searched his. "Does life ever astound you that way?"

"Life astounds me all the time."

He wanted to kiss her.

He'd taken an involuntary step forward before he knew it.

Notus be damned. *Jonathon, no.*

He'd offered her a few days' sanctuary, not bloody seduction.

Still, the way she looked at him, with a soft kind of reverence that managed to summon just about every protective urge he had—

She wasn't immune to him. And Poseidon knew he wasn't immune to her.

The silence, the air between them, seemed to constrict, become heavy.

"You can be entirely too serious at times, Miss Cavanagh," he said.

He'd hoped to make her smile. Instead, he scraped something raw and all-too vulnerable.

"I'm afraid of that," she said softly, pulling her shawl slightly tighter over her arms. "Since Ariene died... some days I've wondered if I'll ever be lighthearted again."

With the honesty of those words, his heart went out to her.

He did the only thing he could do, short of kissing her. In a swift move, he dropped their boots on the beach, snatched her reticule and dropped it on top, then reached out and grasped her hand. She gave a small, startled cry as he dragged her toward him, scooped her up and slung her over his shoulder, his arm securing her behind the thighs. He caught a mouthful of skirts before their length trailed down his chest and past his waist.

Her hands brushed his lower back as she clutched his shirt for balance. He caught his breath as a tingle crossed his skin.

"Jonathon Lecky! What are you doing?" she half-cried, half-laughed. "Put me down!" She attempted to lever up, but already he had spun in the direction of the breakers. "No! Stop! What are you doing?" she laughed again, as he began to stride toward the water.

"Stop wriggling. You're as bad as Morgan!" Despite his teasing, she felt far too good in his arms, regardless of being inverted.

"You don't have Morgan slung over your shoulder!"

That was true; however, his collie's interest had been piqued by the curious sight of her master slinging one infamous privateer's granddaughter over his shoulder, and this brought Morgan dashing across the sand to yip and bark and generally get in the way of his feet as he splashed through the breakers crashing around his knees.

"Arghh! Jonathon Lecky, put me down!"

He was smiling. Releasing his shirt, she pounded on his back in protest, but the force of her small fists did little to deter him. "Here?" he asked, now submerged thigh deep. The hem of her skirt and the ends of her shawl floated on the water's surface. Morgan raced back and forth at the edge of the beach, barking.

"You devil!" His bundle laughed. Lecky was waist deep now. "Stop! Go any further or throw me in, and I'll . . . I'll . . . ."

"You'll what, Miss Cavanagh? Do I need to be afraid?"

"Yes! You do! Because I'll . . . Oh, Lord." She had stopped pummeling him and clutched his shirt again. She let her forehead fall against his back. "All the blood is rushing to my head."

By the gods, she could make him grin. More than that, she warmed him inside. He released his arm hold on her thighs a fraction. "Are you *sure* you don't want me to put you down?"

"No!" She gripped him tighter to stop from slipping toward the water. "No," she repeated. Then, once again, she was laughing.

THE MERCIER FAMILY HAD LONG known how to hold a party, and their eldest son's engagement was unlikely to prove the exception.

Greeted by the jaunty notes trilled by a piper, Lecky fell in behind the drifting procession of medieval-garbed guests descending upon the Château de Boulogne-sur-Mer. Ahead, knights, hunters, woodsmen and maidens glided beneath the large, decorative archway that led to the moat bridge. Lanterns placed along the stone sidings of the bridge provided a glowing pathway to the château.

Mercenaries sported leather brigandine vests over light chain mail. Women wore gowns made of rich brocades and velvets, featuring long sleeves, cinched waists and frontal lacing. Decorated hairnets abounded. As Lecky stepped into the courtyard, pennants flapped atop several marquees. Lanterns strung posts, and light spilled from the château's ring of first-floor windows illuminated the courtyard. Flamboyant and merry, the piper's tune flowed over the gathering. Food and flagons of wine were heaped on trestle tables, men congregated at benches with mugs of ale in hand, and the air carried the earthy scent of fire and roasting meat.

But it was Rachel Cavanagh who immediately drew his gaze. She stood with Emily Winter, just beyond the Mercier family's receiving line. Kept busy by the loading of the *Shearwater*, the questions of his shipwrights and the enquiries he'd made, this was the first time he'd seen her that day.

In the meantime, Martine Winter had had her way. Rhys Cavanagh's granddaughter had been transformed into one very fetching, very adorable, medieval peasant lass. A long, white-sleeved blouse with a smocked neckline dipped off her shoulders. Over the top, a dark burgundy underbust bodice scooped beneath her breasts to tie at the front with cross-lacing. Two layers of rose-and-cream-colored skirts revealed a hint of ankle.

She spotted him among the guests who stood queued in the Mercier family's receiving line waiting to greet their hosts. Her lips swept up and laughter lit her eyes at the sight of his costume.

He approached after greeting the Merciers.

"Are you what I think you are?" she asked.

He lifted the large cross strung about his neck on twine. "A good brother of the Order of Friars Minor?"

She pressed her lips together in clear sign she was fighting back the urge to laugh. "That is a very fine cross you have."

"Indeed. All the better to pray with." He fell silent as she considered the rest of his costume. The dirt-brown habit that hung to his feet, the hood pushed back over his shoulders. The length of hemp rope—an offcut from a line on his boat—knotted about his waist. There was a warmth in her eyes that, Notus help him, drew him in and made him want more. More warmth. More smiles.

"I expected to see you in a dress," Elijah Winter said, arriving at his side. "However, I thought it would be more colorful."

"I contemplated that," Lecky said, eyeing his business partner's deep hunter-green shirt, black hosen and cavalier boots. Black vambrances extended from Elijah's wrists to his elbows, and a dun leather belt looped his waist. "However, someone needs to atone for your outlaw behavior."

"Ha! Clearly you've become more contemplative since I last saw you." Elijah set his hands on his hips. "I am intrigued, however, as to the inspiration? Have you abstinence from anything particular in mind?" The play of amusement on his lips bespoke what he thought that 'anything particular' was, namely, one infamous privateer's granddaughter.

Emily dove to the rescue. "It's time to dance. Rachel, shall we?" To Lecky and Elijah, she added, "All the dancing tonight shall be that of long ago. No one is expected to know the steps. However, a group of us will begin with a *branle des chevaux*, so that others may observe and join in. I taught Rachel the steps earlier today."

Elijah raised his brows. "Your doing a *horse* dance?"

"It is a very *pretty* dance," Emily said. "Will you watch?"

"Of course. Go ahead." Elijah waved them on. "I have been watching the girl, you know," he added to Lecky, as Rachel and Emily joined six other young women in the center of the courtyard. "I've seen the way she listens when your name is mentioned. You intrigue her."

Lecky had seen that too. He said nothing. There was nothing he could say to the truth.

"Have you discovered anything about the man from Le Magnifique?"

"Aye." Lecky was grateful for the change of topic. "Henri Cox, lugger captain. New to Boulogne."

"Lugger captain?" Elijah's gaze narrowed. "Smuggler?"

Luggers were most commonly used to make the nighttime run across the Channel. "Looks that way. Apparently came to Boulogne from Le Harve. He's half-English, half-French, and tight-lipped, too, say the staff at Le Magnifique." A tight-lipped sailor didn't always make for a trusted one in Lecky's experience. There were things a man shared and things he kept to himself when he worked in such close and dangerous confines with others.

"Why is he interested in you?"

"I'm still making enquiries. Until I know more, the lads are keeping an eye on my sloop."

No, he hadn't trusted Cox's sly look, as though the man was enjoying some private amusement.

The wind manifested as the musicians struck the first bright notes. At the center of the dance floor, Rachel Cavanagh and Emily had joined with six other women, all dressed in pretty medieval gowns, to stand in a circle. With a shared glance, they began, relaxing into the music and smiles broadening as they took a series of sidesteps in a circle, first one way and then the other, punctuated by a little hop. Then, the dancers came to a halt to allow four of their number to dance into the middle, where they hopped and clapped and retreated again, before the other four followed their steps.

A ripple of laughter passed through the crowd as the rising wind made merry and snatched their skirts. Rachel, Emily and the other women gave little shrieks of surprise, then laughed, too, aware their male onlookers had no objection to the flash of ankles.

Elijah lifted a glass of red wine from a passing servant's tray. "You know, Jonathon, I've also been keeping an eye on you."

Lecky gave a little snort and folded his arms over his chest. "Of course you have."

"I wonder sometimes whether the nights you spend on your sloop are getting longer, perhaps colder, alone? Do they stretch out before you as the open sea does?"

They never had before. For him, the sea, even at its calmest, had never been empty. And yet the burgundy and rose bundle before him made him want something more.

There were things he needed to do. To see done.

Things that were long overdue.

Beside him, Elijah took a sip of wine. "We're a long way from Morocco, my friend," he said quietly. "I think you are wearing that habit because your filly has stirred thoughts of revolution. Thoughts that aren't compatible with your plans with Blackburn."

Lecky looked back to one beautiful, laughing, imitation peasant lass.

No. There was nothing he could say to the truth.

CHAPTER THIRTEEN

Bah! Admiral Lord Nelson, the old killjoy. Ban sea shanties? I never want my boys to stop singing.
—*The Memoirs of Rhys Cavanagh*

THE MEDIEVAL DANCING WAS A huge success. With so few guests knowing the steps, opportunity abounded for improvisation. The result was chaotic, lively fun, reflecting the merriment of a country dance rather than the formality of a ballroom.

"Where are you going, Rachel?" Martine called, spotting Rachel's attempt to slip away between sets. Emily's sister glowed. Her eyes shone with joy. "Stay for another dance!"

Rachel shook her head. "I need to catch my breath!" She laughed. "I've not had a moment's rest since the dancing began!"

Martine pulled a good-natured face. "Very well. But hurry back! *Oh!*" She and the women around her let out little squeals and laughs as a gust of wind blew through the courtyard to impudently snatch at skirts and sweep napkins off tables.

Rachel took refuge under the eave of a marquee. A moment later, Emily arrived at her side, looking flushed and happy. "I need to rest, too. I can't remember the last time I danced so much!"

"Or I," Rachel agreed, then made a grab to hold her skirts as another heavy gust of wind blew up. She exchanged a look with Emily, who had responded similarly, and both women laughed. Around them, men grabbed for their hoods and women their wimples and medieval veils. The tops of the marquees ruffled. Sheet lightning lit the dark gray clouds that had gathered high above the castle.

Emily craned her neck up, even as she held her skirts down. "A gale is coming."

As though to mark Emily's words, Rachel's skin tingled in response to the sudden, dramatic fall in air pressure. She could picture in her mind the corresponding drop of mercury in her grandfather's stick barometer. She too gazed up. "Do you think it will it rain?" A shower would bring a rapid end to the celebrations.

Emily shook her head. "I don't think so." She thrust her chin towards the sky as more sheet lightning lit the clouds. "I think it will just wage up there."

The musicians played on. In the courtyard, the wind manifested, blustering and brash, to snatch random notes from the air. Titters were occasionally accompanied by a happy shriek of laughter. More lightning sheeted above as rolling clouds moved over the castle.

Emily was right. This show would play out in the sky.

Rachel twisted to see whether Jonathon Lecky was watching. She spotted him almost immediately in the company of several costumed medieval soldiers she did not know. The group had moved closer to observe the dancing. Except Jonathon Lecky was not observing the dancing. His narrowed eyes were fixed on the sky.

As she watched, he turned and pushed through the crowd, flicking the remaining contents of his wine goblet on the ground as he went. He strode across the courtyard to the gatehouse. Rachel's heart tripped. Where was he going?

She looked to Emily, who had followed her gaze. Rachel saw the same confusion on Emily's face. "Excuse me, please?" she asked.

Understanding where Rachel was going, Emily gave a nod. Rachel pushed away from the marquee and wove through the crowd. Breaking through the throng, she crossed the clearing to enter the gatehouse. She came to a halt inside the gate passage, one hand braced against the old stonework.

At the opposite end of the moat bridge, beneath the decorative archway that led onto the bridge, Jonathon Lecky had also come to a halt. He stood with his back to her, his arms crossed over his chest and head tilted up. The wind tangled his hair and whipped the cloth of his habit as he absorbed an unimpeded view of the action playing out in the sky.

But it was the image of *him* that captivated her as snatches of notes were carried forth on the wind. Palpable, physical, he stood perfectly still, yet it was as though he too was part of the storm. Wind and lightning and man himself, all elemental in nature.

Her fingers curled against the old stones. Should she stay or go? Inwardly, she felt like an interloper who had just caught a glimpse of a private relationship. This man wasn't made to be closed in. Too easily she could imagine the younger version of him, the version completely at home in the foreign ports of North Africa, the version who would stop for a night—and stay for eight years.

He turned his head in profile, as though he sensed her watching, and she was immobilized again. Then he looked over his shoulder at her, and she was immobilized *and* exposed, illumed by the lightning.

She was drawn to him in the same inescapable way she was drawn to her grandfather's stories and all they embodied. Drawn not to plush drawing rooms but to places where she could feel the greater expanse of the world, its open-stretching skies, the connection between earth and wind and people and sea. She sensed Jonathon Lecky had felt that. He had experienced that. It was deep in his blood.

Inside the château, the notes of another country dance came to an end. On the moat bridge, neither she nor Jonathon Lecky moved. Her chest felt tight, her breath suspended. A charge lay thick in the air, while for long moments they stared at one another, all the intensity of the storm in his gaze.

She suspected all her hopes lay in hers.

The strains of music commenced again, a different tune, quicker and more flamboyant.

Then he was crossing the bridge toward her.

He said nothing as his hand locked around hers. He drew her back through the gatehouse passage, back toward the dancing. His grasp was strong and commanding. She almost tripped keeping up with the pace of his strides.

He cut through the crowd and brought them to the center of the courtyard, where all the other dancers were paired. He spun her to face him.

"Wait!" she said. "Do you know what you are doing?"

His hand tightened over and lifted hers. As he had done at the Lord Nelson, he pressed her hand to his heart.

"Not ever, when it comes to you."

Her breath caught, brought to a stop by his words, his gesture, by the beat of his heart beneath her palm. She'd been so distracted by his buccaneer's kiss outside the Lord Nelson—so convinced it had been a joke—she'd not realized more emotion lay behind it. Now, his storm-gray eyes, so dark and intense at that moment as to be part of the cells of storm clouds above, told her she had been wrong.

Her mouth went dry as, slowly, intently, he drew her hand up to rest on his shoulder. She could feel the warm, solid expanse of his skin through his habit.

Somehow, she found her voice as she met his gaze. "Nor do I, when it comes to you."

More sheet lightning lit his eyes.

He settled his sea-roughened palms around her waist, atop the underbust bodice. He spread out his fingers. Beneath them, her waist looked so small.

His glance had come to rest on her waist too. "Damn." The word came out on his breath. "*Damn*, Rachel Anwen Cavanagh."

Her name on his lips brushed over her senses, registering a longing that cut through every other thought. Her other hand came to rest on his shoulder as though of its own accord.

Then he was guiding her. His gaze held hers captive as he encouraged her steps, repeatedly lifting her by the waist and holding her suspended as he spun her around and set her down again, his strong thighs brushing hers. It was the way the dance was done—but whether the look in other men's eyes was as potent as Jonathon Lecky's, Rachel didn't know. It scarcely mattered.

Because she was learning about *him* at that moment. Realizing the things she'd not seen. She'd been too blinded by his coarse exterior, his lack of trappings, his often coarse words.

Jonathon Lecky was truly, madly, deeply, a romantic.

No one was driven to the extent of adventure-seeking or soul-searching as he was—or as her grandfather had been—without great passion, without idealism. He had donned the monk's habit in jest. But if it represented anything, at minimum, the qualities it represented were those.

There was so much more she wanted to understand. More she wanted to know. Not least, the thoughts that hovered there behind that storm-gray gaze.

The flamboyant tune wound out, out, out into the night. Then, reaching its apogee, wound back in again. The notes of the finale crescendoed, then—like the bluster of the wind abating—settled and dissipated.

Rachel did not know whether she or he brought them to a stop. But they did not immediately move apart. Silence lay between them even as laughter rose around.

TWO STORMS RAGED. THE ONE overhead charged the air. The second charged his blood. The musician's flutes and pipes had fallen silent; but inside him, their combined energy still pulsed.

He had no one to blame but himself. He had been the one watching as Bertrand's friends spun her around the courtyard to the tunes of the piper. He had been the one to draw her into the dance.

Her dark eyes shone luminous in the lantern light. Winter was right. She wasn't compatible with his plans with Blackburn. She wasn't compatible with him watching his back. But Notus be damned if he didn't want her in his arms.

Of course, those dark eyes were also a reminder she was vulnerable. Only days before, she had been at sea herself, not knowing which direction to sail between family desire and freedom. Lecky had given her the distance from England she needed—already she was happier—but such repairs weren't made in a few days. Tempered steel needed time to cool and set. And when that steel set, who knew what Rhys Cavanagh's granddaughter would want?

Not him, necessarily.

His hands were still on her waist. She was flushed and warm from their dance. *What the hell was he doing?*

"Attention, please! May I have everyone's attention?"

Perfectly timed to help a man direct his thoughts to a less

dangerous heading, Bertrand Mercier's father called out to the crowd. His wife stood at his side. A hush gradually fell over the assembly as guests realized it was time for the expected announcement. Lecky took Rachel's hand in his own and turned to listen.

Bertrand's father spoke in French. "Bertrand, will you join me? Perhaps you would also like to escort Mademoiselle Winter?"

Across the courtyard, smiles blossomed on Bertrand and Martine's faces. Bertrand took his betrothed's hand and escorted her forward, to stand at his mother and father's side.

"Two years ago," Bertrand's father told the assembly, "our family entered into a business arrangement with the Winter Trading House. Little did we expect then that the Merciers and Winters would unite as a family. Yet through our valuable business union, Bertrand found the right woman to stand at his side. A woman my wife and I shall be delighted to call daughter. We are therefore very pleased to announce the betrothal of our son to the beautiful Martine Winter."

Lecky released Rachel's hand to clap. *Damn, but he was happy for them.*

Martine glowed and Bertrand beamed as, around them, a round of cheers went up. Martine broke into a joy-filled laugh, and Bertrand wrapped his arm around her shoulder. Lecky's heart warmed. He glanced at Rachel Cavanagh, and she met his look with delight in her eyes.

"I would like to thank you all," Bertrand's father continued, "for being part of these very special celebrations. I hope you enjoy the rest of the evening."

"One more moment." Bertrand held up a hand to stay the crowd. "I have a surprise for my bride-to-be."

"A surprise?" Martine set her hand in the middle of her fiancé's chest, then peered up at him, her expression both eager and quizzical.

"*Oui.*" All the Frenchman's affection shone on his face. "You see"—he raised his voice for the benefit of those assembled—"my bride-to-be loves fireworks . . . so fireworks I have arranged."

A whoop of approval rose up from the crowd.

Martine's jaw dropped. "*Fireworks?* For *me?*"

"*Oui, mon cher*, for you." Bertrand laughed. "They will begin down by the quay, as soon as we arrive there. Any guest who wishes may join us, but none must feel they must come. We will return to the château afterwards to continue celebrations."

"Could you not hold this surprise at the château?" Bertrand's mother asked.

"And risk setting fire to the roof? I think not." Bertrand again wrapped his arm around Martine's shoulders and pulled her against his side. "Besides, between my mother and my oh-so-inquisitive bride-to-be, my surprise would have been sniffed out in a moment."

Oh, the Frenchman had Martine's measure, Lecky thought. He grinned, while laughter rose all around.

"For any who wish to join us, I'll be escorting my bride to the quay now," Bertrand announced.

Lecky turned to Rachel. "Would you like to see the fireworks?"

Her dark eyes glimmered with the same happiness as the crowd. "Of course."

And with that, they fell in with the laughing, flowing procession of knights, ladies, peasants and archers that again swarmed through the gatehouse passage and over the moat bridge, this time headed for the quay.

THERE WAS A MAGICAL QUALITY to the laughing flow of Bertrand and Martine's medieval-clad guests through the French city. It was a feeling Rachel wanted to bottle, to somehow capture and store, not just the sight but the sense of wonder. Had she been asked, one week before, whether she would be drifting down cobblestone streets en route to watch fireworks amid a host of knights and ladies, she would have shaken her head with bemusement. Yet here she was.

Was this what her grandfather had felt? The wonder of the unexpected, of true stories surpassing the make-believe?

The excursion was a distraction, too, from the dance she and Jonathon Lecky had just shared.

Each had been able to brush over his buccaneer's kiss. The dance was different. She didn't quite know what to say. An attraction every bit as mighty as a storm at sea lay between them. Now, it was as though that storm had breached a seawall and they both stood on the shore, futilely focusing their attention in every direction *except* the incoming flood.

Tail wagging, Morgan met their party on the quay, more than delighted by the unexpected host of visitors.

The fireworks had been set up on a barge in the river.

"Jonathon, may Bertrand and I watch the fireworks from your boat?" Martine asked.

"Of course, my lady." Lecky winked at Bertrand. The Frenchman positioned himself onboard, and Lecky took Martine's hand and helped her down into her betrothed's waiting arms. Bertrand gave the signal for the fireworks to proceed, then Martine burrowed against her fiancé's side as the pair took their seats, shrouded in the moonlit shadows of boom and mast and rigging.

The sloop was their own private world in that moment, even as their guests lined the quay. Rachel's heart warmed. It was thoughtful that the man standing beside her had granted it. Yes, Jonathon Lecky was a romantic.

An explosion rent the air as the first rocket released. It ascended high above the water, then burst in a shower of a dozen stars.

Around them, the crowd exclaimed. "How beautiful," Emily breathed. And so it was. On Jonathon Lecky's sloop, Martine gave a little cry of pleasure as more rockets launched and white, silver, turquoise and violet stars and sunflowers burst overhead. Beside Rachel, standing with his arms crossed over his chest and head tipped back, Jonathon Lecky's lips curved in a smile.

Medieval-garbed guests stood enrapt as showers of sparks above illuminated their faces. On the barge, a fountain of fireworks sparked to burn in a long row. The scent of gunpowder drifted across the water as tendrils of dissipating smoke streaked the sky.

She couldn't marry Rossum. She knew that unequivocally in that instant. Yes, they shared easy familiarity. Yes, he trusted her, because she had always been honest. She cared for him, *loved* him, but in her heart, she did not believe she was the *best* person to love him. Not as he deserved to be loved.

He deserved a woman with a full heart for *him*. Who shared his passions, who wished to serve at his side and, in doing so, serve the marquesate.

What Rachel needed, she would not find as his marchioness. She had no desire to hurt Rossum nor would her family like it. But her purpose was something different.

As the last rockets arced high overhead and exploded, the knowledge that such a decision was right settled deep and comforting in her heart, despite the challenges it posed.

Quiet reigned over the quay while all waited to see if the fireworks were over.

"By God, Bertrand. Well done, man!" Elijah Winter began to clap into the silence, and all around, jubilant cheers and applause rose up. On the sloop, Martine threw her arms around her fiancé and bestowed on him several kisses. "Back to the château!" Bertrand called as he struggled to stand with Martine wrapped around him. Jonathon Lecky moved to the side of the vessel to hand Martine up.

Smiling, Rachel and Emily turned from the water. Emily froze.

A man stood just along the quay, staring in disbelief at Emily.

"Lawrence!" Elijah called out. "I was wondering when we'd see you. Not that I can commend your costume."

The man wrenched his gaze from Emily. He was garbed handsomely in a navy jacket, waistcoat, buff breeches and high top boots. "Yes, I .... My apologies. I wasn't prepared for a costume ball."

"No matter," Elijah returned. "We're headed back to the château. Join us?"

Beside Rachel, Emily too looked as if she'd been struck. Rachel took another look at Lawrence. Tall but not overly so, the man was sandy haired and fine featured, in a very masculine kind of way. "Is everything all right?" she asked Emily.

"Yes .... No. I mean ... that is to say—" Rachel had never seen Emily so nonplussed.

Elijah waved a hand in introduction. "Emily, Miss Cavanagh, this is Ian Lawrence, our new captain. Lawrence, standing before you is my sister, Miss Winter, and our friend, Miss Cavanagh."

"How do you do, Miss Winter? Miss Cavanagh?" Lawrence asked.

Even though they appeared to recognize each other, Rachel couldn't shake the feeling that Lawrence was surprised to learn Emily's name.

"Very well, thank you, Captain Lawrence," Emily replied. She cast her eyes down as she dipped her head at the introduction. Rachel too provided a polite response.

Elijah motioned to Lawrence again. "Walk with me back to the château?"

"I... yes. I'd be pleased to." After casting another sideways glance at Emily, the new captain moved to join Elijah.

Martine arrived off the boat to loop her arm through Emily's and drag her sister's attention away. "Oh, Emily! Can you believe Bertrand organized *fireworks* for me? Was that not magical?"

"I can believe it," Emily said, "because your fiancé adores you that much."

"Are you coming, Lecky?" Elijah called.

Jonathon Lecky waved them on. "I need something from the boat. Go ahead. I'll be along shortly."

Rachel turned back to look at Emily and Martine as Lecky disappeared through the hatch of the sloop.

Emily saw her conflict. "You should wait for Jonathon."

"Are you certain?" She wanted to walk back with him, but there was Emily's strange reaction to Lawrence to consider.

"Yes. I promise. Meet us back at the château. And Rachel?" Emily hesitated for a moment. Her glance flickered to Lawrence and back. "I know the proper Englishwoman in me should not say this, but... sometimes opportunities happen so unexpectedly, chances are missed. The celebrations will continue for hours. You need not hurry back."

"Emily!" Martine squeezed her sister's arm and pretended to be aghast.

"Would you tell her otherwise?" Emily asked. "When Jonathon looks at her the way he does?"

Mischief shone in Martine's eyes as she suppressed a little smile. "No, Emily. I would not."

"Rachel," Emily said again, with a smile of her own, "we will see you back at the château."

CHAPTER FOURTEEN

She was spun from heaven's ether for someone else, but I wanted her all the same.
—*The Memoirs of Rhys Cavanagh*

BY THE GODS, LECKY WASN'T typically the type to retreat; but right now, he needed a moment to regroup. He dragged the heavy cross and monk's habit over his head as he moved across the sloop cabin. Bunching the habit in his hands, he tossed it on the bunk as he sank down on the seat at the small table. He dropped the cross on the surface of the table, then tipped his head forward to rub out the ache in his neck. A monk's costume indeed. If he had found out one thing for certain, it was that it didn't do a damn thing to keep impure thoughts at bay.

Rachel Cavanagh had been made for moonlight. Moonlight and showers of stars, what with those dark eyes, creamy skin, and soft form that a man ached to have pressed against him. Hers was the beauty of a moonlit ocean swell; the combination of shadows and shimmer. Not quite in the light, not quite in the dark—she was instead shades of laughter and complexity and intelligence and sensuality. And he wanted her. Oh, yes, he wanted her.

Not that that meant a bloody thing. There were plenty of things he'd deprived himself of before and never questioned those choices.

He jerked backwards as Morgan inserted her body into the space at his feet and lifted her nose to his, seeking attention. "There, girl. I know. I know." He grasped her sides and gave her a good ruffle.

Rachel Cavanagh was still finding her way. Conversely, the path he'd committed to with Blackburn was dangerous and long overdue. He wouldn't allow his choices to touch her.

"I don't want Chaloner to know a damn thing about her," he told Morgan.

That didn't change the fact that, like the damn dog cuddled up between his legs, a certain privateer's granddaughter had pirated her way into his heart.

He heard footsteps on the deck. He tensed and looked up. A shadow fell across the companionway as a figure blocked the hatch.

Rachel Cavanagh crouched at the top of the companionway in a billow of peasant skirts. "What did you need?"

The chance to breathe. That's what he'd hoped for at least.

His blood pulsed. For grip, he buried his hands in Morgan's coat. "Did you not go with the others?"

She shook her head, those glorious butterscotch locks, then climbed through the hatch.

Don't, he wanted to tell her. *Don't come any closer.*

She reached the deck of the cabin and leant back against the companionway, setting her hands behind her hips. "Who is Ian Lawrence?"

Lecky frowned, surprised by the question. "Our new captain. Why?"

"Do he and Emily have a history?"

Lecky blinked. "As far as I know, they've never met before. Elijah hadn't met Lawrence until a day ago. Why?"

"Their reaction when they saw one another. Both appeared stunned. And more than a little flustered."

"Did Elijah notice?"

"I'm not certain. Though it was fairly obvious."

"Did Martine recognize Lawrence also?"

"She gave no sign."

Lecky shook his head. "I have no idea where they could have met. Did Emily give no hint?"

"Not exactly. Though . . . she did say one thing."

"Which was?"

She caught her lower lip between her teeth, a sign she was considering her words. "She said sometimes opportunities happen so unexpectedly, chances are missed."

A beat passed as his heart shuddered to a brief stop. Recovering, he said, "For example, the opportunity for more medieval dancing. We should head back to the château."

Gently prodding Morgan out of the way, he pushed to his feet. All gorgeous, slender, searing flares and curves in peasant dress, Rachel Cavanagh was far too lovely standing in the well of moonlight that shone through the hatch. The cabin was rapidly becoming too small. As were his better intentions, the ones that questioned how much harm could come from determining, just for a moment, how smooth her skin would feel beneath his hands.

Softly, she said, "I don't think that's what Emily meant."

And, damn, didn't he know it.

RACHEL WATCHED JONATHON LECKY DRAW a breath and turn away from her, one hand set on his hip. With his other hand, he raggedly combed through his hair, then covered his mouth with his fingers. His sidelong gaze came back to her. Traveled over her smocked shirt and burgundy underbust bodice to her hips—to the place he had set his hands during their dance. Her skin was still warm with the memory of the spread of his fingers across her waist.

He'd removed the monk's habit, revealing the white shirt and tan-colored trousers he wore beneath. The lantern cast a warm glow over his dark golden-brown hair, heavy brows and firmly set jaw.

Her position blocked the companionway. *Move, feet*! she instructed. *Step out of his way.* She may as well have been nailed to the deck.

She shouldn't be doing this, she knew. Tempting fate and helping her chances of ruination along. Wanting, so very badly, for him to kiss her—this boat captain whose white slash of a grin had, from the very first, struck chords within.

He wasn't grinning now. He was waiting for her to move. To turn around and climb up the companionway for both their sakes.

"Rachel, I need you to step out of the way."

She didn't mistake the gravity in his tone. Her hands gripped the companionway step behind her hips. "I know." The darkness and the quiet that had fallen over the quay outside with the departure of Bertrand and Martine's guests added to their sense of seclusion. She didn't shift an inch.

Jonathon Lecky closed his eyes and pressed his fingers to his brows. He exhaled long and hard. "Fuck," he said.

She didn't know how to respond.

He looked back at her. "I need you to understand. I dance. But I'm not a man who teases and flirts. If I touch you, Rachel.... You shouldn't let me touch you."

"I know."

The twist of his lips almost constituted a grimace. "What do you know?"

"All the things you said."

Her voice sounded husky. Not at all like herself. *Were either of them breathing?*

He stared at her, then took a swift step forward. He crowded her as he braced one forearm against the step above her head. "Understand this, Rachel Cavanagh. I have never seen anything as beautiful as you. You have eyes a man can fall into. Wit to match. And a mouth... a mouth that's damn near torture for a man to spend too much time contemplating."

This time she *knew* she wasn't breathing. His words, his proximity, threaded a response through her whole body. Her breath caught, her pulse sped up. Longing suffused her.

Words didn't have to be whispered or poetic or filled with innuendo. Not when plain ones conveyed meaning just as well.

As for her thoughts... well, they had just scattered all about the cabin. Possibly, she would spend the rest of their journey collecting them.

"But we both know, Miss Cavanagh," Jonathon Lecky continued, "you're no tavern wench out for a quick tupping. Any debauchery where you're concerned, my sweet, is strictly your husband's prerogative."

Fueled by his terminology, the longing in her belly resolved into something else. Something that spread to sit lower, to throb in her abdomen, and higher, to ache in her breasts. Shifting away from the companionway became even more difficult. She knew behind his blunt, almost crude words, his thinking was anything but.

His actions had told her otherwise, when he'd held her hand to his heart.

Somewhere, she found her voice—and with it, her nerve. "*Debauching* me? Is that what you would be doing?"

Slowly, he drew his arm back and straightened as he read the soft challenge in her eyes.

"Hell, no," he said.

His hands came up to capture each side of her jaw. His mouth came down as he used his weight to trap her against the companionway steps. His lips met hers.

Oh, God. There had been Gravesend. But this . . . *this* was a kiss, open-mouthed and hungry, with the power to drag ships down. With his mouth on hers, his calloused fingers stroking her cheeks—she couldn't think. *He was dragging her down*, down into depths where all she could do was feel.

His arousal pressed hard against her belly. She felt a responding pull low in her stomach. She thought she might detect the taste of wine on his lips from the château, but no. She just tasted *him*. Salt and sweat and sea and man. And that was better than a thousand glasses of champagne at a thousand English balls or house parties.

His lips moved across her cheek. His fingers slid down her throat. Then they slid further, to stroke along the edge of the smocked neckline of her shirt. She shivered and let her eyelids drift closed. She brought her hands up to slide through his hair.

"You're mad," he breathed. "Rossum was right. Granddaughters of earls don't consort with rascals like me."

"Rascals?" She captured his head and forced him to look at her. "Jonathon. I'm also the granddaughter of Captain Rhys Cavanagh, the shameless privateer."

Something came into his eyes, something soft. He pressed his thumb to her lower lip for a second. "Courageous, sweetheart. Not shameless. And, oh, so beautiful."

Even as those words and that look quivered around inside her in the most wonderful of ways, he scooped her up and deposited her on the middle step of the companionway. But before she could revel more in him, he stepped between her legs and caught both her wrists. "What of Rossum?"

His question had a swift, sobering effect. She reared back in his grip to stare at him.

Subject to his weighty regard, she swallowed. How could she explain everything she'd come to understand? The things *she* needed?

She raised her chin and looked him in the eye. "A marriage between us would not be right. Not for him nor for me."

With gray eyes as penetrating as she'd ever seen them, he studied her face as though evaluating her resolve.

He released a breath she'd not realized he'd been holding. "Damned if I know if this is either."

He freed her wrists, and she released a little gasp as he drew her hips against his. His hands gripped her hips as he leant into her, his desire apparent even through trousers and skirts. His gray eyes were unabashed.

"I don't know whether to fall on you like a starved man or savor you slowly. Either way, Notus knows that touching you is only going to make the hunger worse."

Before she could ask what he meant, his mouth dipped to her throat. Her breath caught, and she immediately dropped her hands to cover his. His grip was hard, but, oh, so good, because it told her just as bluntly as his words how he felt. And that was what she wanted to know, wanted to *feel*. Covered by the smocked neckline of her blouse and thrust upward by her arched back and the cut of her bodice, her breasts ached.

With a low groan in his throat, he moved again to cover her mouth with his as he slid warm hands up her bodice from hips, to waist, to sides. While his kiss was fierce, his touch turned caressing. *Oh, help her.* She'd wanted this. If she was truthful, there had been times she'd thought about him in just this way in the months since he'd saved her from death. She could still see the moment when he'd swung down the companionway and into her life. It made complete sense to find herself in his arms, bracketed against these steps.

She lifted her hands to grip his shoulders. A little sound tore from her throat—her body gave a surprised jerk—as his palms came round to weigh her breasts through her blouse. This is what she had been aching for. But as he molded her breasts with his palms and teased the peaks, the ache only transferred, moved lower.

"Rachel." The way he spoke her name said much. He let go of her to drag his shirt over his head. As he tossed it to the deck, amber light fell across the expanse of his shoulders, arms, and chest. *Oh.* Rachel caught her breath. She barely had a second to absorb the sight of him before he wrapped one arm around her waist and dragged her against him, while he buried his other hand in her hair. Mouth to mouth, breasts to chest—she felt his hunger. Hot, damp skin over layered muscle encased her, muscle that bespoke strength and power.

His lips trailed down her throat. His shaven jaw was slightly abrasive, but heaven above, she didn't care. All she wanted was to hold on. To stay locked in his arms. And to touch him too. "You saved me from drowning. But I'm drowning again now."

He wrenched away with a short, abrupt laugh and stroked the bare curves of her shoulders, exposed by her smocked blouse, in a way that was full of care. "Sweetheart, we're going down together." His gaze heated again, still holding hers as his palms brushed lower, eliciting her shiver as he stroked the sides of her breasts. Boldly, his fingers reached for the laces that fastened the front of her bodice, which in medieval style was worn on the outside of her blouse. An inner voice whispered: *How far could she let this go? How far would* he *let it go?*

She held her breath. Heaven help her, she wanted him to see her, touch her. A series of deliberate tugs saw the knot undone, then each of the laces loosened.

His hands rose again to the straps of the bodice running over her shoulders. Watching her expression—a combination surely of vulnerability and desire—he pushed the straps down.

Her already shallow breathing became shallower as he encouraged her arms out of the bodice, then so too the long white sleeves of her blouse. The smocked neckline of her costume had allowed for no shift or corset beneath. He pushed the smocked neckline down, down, down so that blouse and bodice bunched at her waist, and her bare breasts and arms were exposed to his view.

They stared at each other, each uncovered to the waist. This time, it was his eyes that drank her in. And even though a blush fired her cheeks, she drank in the sight of him too. Her mouth went dry. His body was magnificent. Not smooth or lean, no. Nor was it unmarked. His beauty was fierce, a fighter's strength.

She drew a swift, surprised breath as he set one hand flat to her breast. "I've seen your body before," he said. "Then, all that mattered was that you survived. I didn't see you. This is different. You are . . . ." The muscles in his arms bunched as he shifted to cup both her breasts.

She couldn't explain . . . . His touch felt reverent and sensual. "Jonathon . . . ."

He leant forward to taste the curve of her neck where it met her shoulder, even as he continued to mold her breasts. She shivered at the nip of his mouth, the soft trail of his lips. Her feeling of longing grew heavy, yet at the same time, she felt light-headed, at sea, as though floating atop gentle, lulling, lapping waves.

Her hands again moved to his shoulders to revel in the feel of his skin. He took the opportunity to strip the loosened lacing from her bodice and discard the garment, then draw her blouse over her head. Any self-consciousness she felt was swept away as his lips returned to scorch a heated path down her throat.

She stroked downward across the breadth of his chest. He shuddered when she skimmed her fingers across the contours of his stomach near his waistband. A quick learner, she did it again.

"Ahhh." As he raised his head, his grin came swiftly; the grin that turned her inside out. He caught her wrists again. "Don't do that to me."

"What can I do?" she asked.

"What can you do?" He released one of her wrists, then glanced over his shoulder, first to the tight confines of the bunk, then to the cabin space beyond.

He took her by the hand and wove his fingers through hers, then drew her away from the companionway. With his other hand, he pointed to the hatch. "Morgan, out!" The collie pressed her ears back, looking unhappy at the instruction. "Out!"

On his second command, the collie obeyed.

With a glance towards the hatch, he crouched down, tugged the blankets from the bunk and spread them out across the deck. He grasped the pillow from the bunk and threw it on top.

"You can come here." He drew Rachel down and pulled her partially atop him. "How is that?"

Her hand rested on his chest. Her bare breasts pillowed against his side. Her thigh lay across his, to press against his arousal through her skirts. His skin radiated heat. She felt a smile nip at the corner of her mouth. "That's better than touching your stomach?"

"Yes. For now. Anywhere else. You can put your hands anywhere else." Then his hand was buried in her hair and encouraging her mouth back down to his.

He kissed her as though he would never tire of it. And nor, she thought, would she. His lips were firm and warm. As he coaxed her response, swept away her every other thought bar him, he wrapped one arm around her waist and slid his hand up the gentle arch of her spine, to splay his fingers across her back. She felt small in his arms. Feminine.

She wanted to touch him. Breaking off their kiss, she saw his body tense, felt the muscles leap beneath his skin as she tentatively skated her palm across his shoulder and down his chest. He was watching her, she saw, as her look slid briefly to his. Shyness rose in the form of a blush as she looked away again, back to the path her fingertips trailed across the expanse of his shoulders and upper arms. Would she find the sight of all men's bodies this wonderful? Or was she especially drawn to him?

Her gaze again drawn to his chest, she leant down to press a kiss to the flesh above his heart. She thought, faintly, she could feel its beat.

"Rachel." Her name was a word on his breath. He cupped her cheek.

"I like the way you feel." Her words emerged all by themselves, expressing a sentiment she had never guessed she would speak aloud.

Storm-gray eyes didn't waver. "Not as much as I like the way you feel."

The words kept coming. "I think, perhaps, just as much." Once again, she pressed her lips to his heart. Then, closing her eyes to employ only touch, she ran her palm across his shoulder, down his chest and over his ribs to stroke the smooth, bare skin above the band of his trousers.

He gasped, abdominal muscles clenching. Before she could think, he'd rolled over with one smooth move and straddled her. Surprise gave way to the realization that his weight above and the clamp of his strong thighs around hers felt delicious. Leaning over her, all bare chest and broad shoulders and storm-filled eyes, he pinned her wrists to the blankets.

"Sweetheart, I'll say again. Not the stomach. And not any lower. There's only so much a man can take." He looked down at her body, exposed above skirts that hung low around her hips. She was acutely aware of what he saw. Full round breasts. Smooth flat stomach and belly-button. Her small waist and the gentle flare of her hips. "Right now," his voice held a note of teasing, "you're testing it to the limit."

Releasing one of her wrists, he stroked his hand down her side from the curve of her breast to her hip. Her breath escaped as a shiver ran through her.

"Believe me, I want your hands there. But I don't think either of us is ready for the repercussions." He skimmed his hand along the flare of her waist again, eliciting another shivery response. "You make a man want to forget every one of his better intentions. In saying that...." His attention returned to her chest. Sliding his hand back to a breast, he leant over and took her nipple in his mouth.

Oh, Lord. Her back arched in sweet, unexpected shock at the nip of his lips, the sweep of his tongue. *Yes. It felt wonderful. He felt wonderful.*

A groan issued in the back of his throat, and he released her other wrist to take both her breasts in his palms. Driven by the need to touch him, her hands sought his shoulders and slid over his back. *Was touching or being touched better?* She didn't know. Either way, she didn't wish for it to end. She wanted to explore the comparison. With him. With this man.

He shifted his weight so only one thigh lay atop her. His groin pressed into her hip. He drew one hand down, lightly grazing the back of his fingers from her side to her navel, then across to her waist. "I love this," he breathed, as he grazed the same soft path again.

He continued stroking down, to find the hem of her skirts and slide his hand beneath to touch her smooth calf.

She wasn't the only one to catch her breath at his touch. She heard his catch, too. With a groan, he buried his face in her hair. She drew her leg up to place her slippered foot flat on the deck as his fingertips stroked upwards toward her knee. There, he encountered the cuffs of her drawers with their little silk ribbon. He cupped his palm to her calf. "Damn," he said. "*Damn.*" Then, as though he wanted to record her every expression, he lifted his head to watch her as he set his hand on the front of her thigh, atop her drawers. She caught her lower lip between her teeth. Waiting. Not quite sure what came next.

She jerked against him, reflexively pressing her legs together as he stroked higher, along the slit of her drawers.

"Jonathon—" His name caught in her throat, thick with everything she couldn't find words for, couldn't quite explain.

"Relax, sweetheart. Trust me."

Her teeth bit hard into her bottom lip. Breathing in, she did as he asked.

He didn't immediately touch her between the legs. Instead, he slid his hand around to the opening at the back of her drawers and grazed the curve of her buttocks once, then again. "You're incredible. You can conquer a man just by the way you say his name." She tensed as he brought his hand back to the slit of her drawers. Once more, he said, "Trust me?"

"Jonathon—"

She didn't know whether she was asking for something or not. She didn't want to lose her virginity, that would be too rash, but—

"It's all right." He shifted his weight again, put his arm around her and gathered her against his chest. "Poseidon help me." He brushed his lips over hers. "You can think of this, sweetheart, as 'not missing a chance'." His fingers slipped inside her drawers, found her slickness. The little sound that broke in her throat was echoed in his.

"Rachel." He stroked, then slid a finger inside her as he pressed his lips to her jaw. His breath came against her ear. "By the gods. You're perfect. So perfect." And then she was lost as his fingers dipped and delved and stroked and teased, responding with frightening swiftness to her slightest reaction, the slightest sign that with this touch he might bring her undone.

But it wasn't just that. It was the whole of him holding her. The warm scent and heat of his bare skin. The graze of his stubble and the brush of his lips. The lock of his strong arm around her. It was the fact that, at the inn and then at the château, he'd held her hand to his heart.

She whimpered against his throat as her body pulsed around his hand in a rush of sensation before now unknown. His arm steadied her, held her tight against his chest as she clung to him, firmly anchored and adrift and safe and exposed all at the same time. But most of all, safe.

Against her jaw, his breathing was as ragged as hers. At first, neither of them moved. Then, after a time, he slowly removed his hand from the slit of her drawers and drew down her skirt. With the weight of one thigh still atop hers, he hugged her closer and buried his face in the curve of her neck and shoulder.

"Zephyrus, you're playing with me." His warm lips brushed her bare skin. His hardness still pressed against her thigh.

Zephyrus, the Greek god of the west wind? His words made no sense. She squirmed beneath him. "What . . . ?"

"Woman, don't move." His instruction was sharp, forceful. Yet within it, she also heard care. And perhaps a trace of humor?

She stilled, waiting for she knew not what. Some sign that she could wrap herself around him as she wanted to do?

When he continued to say nothing, uncertainty began to creep in. "Jonathon . . . ?"

"Yes?"

"A guinea for your thoughts?"

His laugh was warm and full against her shoulder. "A guinea is generous. Calms seas, sweetheart. Windless days."

Calm seas? Her fingers curled around his shoulders as a little flush rose in her cheeks. Was that another way of saying . . . he was trying to bring himself under control?

She could feel the slowing of his breathing. Could feel the gradual slowing of his heart. She could lie this way with him forever, day after day, night after night. Uncovered and skin to skin. Her voice was soft. "There's more, isn't there?"

He levered up on one elbow to look at her, and once more her breath caught. All the turbulence of a storm breaking against the Welsh coast lay in his eyes. He wanted her. Soul deep, she could see his desire. For her.

Her throat clogged with the rise of her own feelings, and she shifted to link her arms around his neck. She felt his shudder, watched his eyes briefly close and his jaw clench as her breasts pressed against his chest.

He rolled his body to trap her beneath him.

"There is more," he said. "But not for us."

And then he kissed her.

CHAPTER FIFTEEN

*The break of the dawn is something a man realizes he should see
more often when he has not absorbed its quiet for a while.*
—*The Memoirs of Rhys Cavanagh*

AS SWEPT AWAY AS SHE was by his kiss, his words still penetrated her thinking. She placed her hand on the center of his chest and pushed him back to search his face. "Wait. What do you mean, not for us?"

He hesitated. For a moment she felt a stab of fear. Then, in a move that surprised her, he leant over, holding his weight on his elbows, and kissed her on the nose. "Call me insane, but four days ago you were considering marrying another man. I'm not prepared to deflower a beautiful woman who is still deciding what she wants. Even if she has determined what she wants does *not* include a marquess."

He was right. She didn't wish to lose her virginity. She wasn't ready for the repercussions—what it might mean to her marriageability. Still, that didn't mean she wouldn't wish to . . . with him . . . later. His consideration, in light of the fact she had been the one to bring this moment about, drew him that little bit deeper into her heart. "You understand?"

He traced his thumbs down her cheekbones. "We stay like this. I am going to lie here and hold you."

He shifted to roll onto his back and tuck her against his side. She rested in the crook of his arm, her head against his shoulder, her hand flat against his chest. He stroked her hair, the strands sliding through his fingers. They both stared up at the flicker of lantern light against timber. A week ago she could not have imagined they would be lying together like this. But then, the thought of even *meeting* him again had seemed unbelievable.

"What happened to the beads that were in your hair?" she asked.

"I kept them." He continued to stroke his hand through hers.

"What is their significance?"

His pause was so long she didn't think he was going to respond.

"Enrique," he finally said. "My friend, the Spaniard. During our expeditions, our parties would sometimes stay overnight in the Berber camps. On one of those evenings, during the storytelling, the women of the camp threaded the beads onto our hair. Diplomatically, we left them in. Funnily enough they became identifiers; they helped our passage. All the tribes came to know that the Englishman and the Spaniard with the Berber beads were the negotiators for the British. After Enrique died...." He turned his head. She felt his kiss against near her temple, against her hairline. "After he died, and I left Morocco, I just... left them in."

"Symbolic of your friendship?"

"Yes... perhaps. More so symbolic of Enrique."

"What changed?"

"Winter had an investors meeting that he needed me to attend. Besides, it was time."

She burrowed further into the crook of his shoulder. Content to just think.

"*Essaouria*," he said quietly into the silence a few minutes later.

She flattened her palm against his chest, uncertain of what he had said. "I beg your pardon?"

"*Essauoria*." The word he spoke was pronounced Essa-weera. "The name scribed in the Ledger of the Deep. The name of my boat."

He must have been able to sense the flutter of her thoughts, her questions forming, the name upon her lips, because he said, "It is the Moroccan name for Mogadore. The name given by the Sultan Sidi Mohammed Ben Abdellah when the modern city was constructed fifty years ago, on the site originally settled by the Phoenicians. Of course, we British persist in calling the city Mogadore."

Arranging a blanket in front of her chest for modesty, she pushed up against his chest to gaze down upon him. She tested the name. "*Essauoria.*"

"She was built there." He searched her eyes. "It means 'the beautifully designed'."

Her heart momentarily went still. "Oh . . . . How perfect."

His mouth turned ever so slightly up at one corner. "So I have always hoped."

More than his mouth, she loved his eyes. She loved the look they contained.

Oh, Lord. One might think his world small, if gauged by the size of his boat.

But that was wrong, so wrong, gauged by other measures.

Still, she understood nothing of whence he came. "And you—from where did you hail? You were born in England?"

"No." He once more lifted his hand to trail a strand of her hair. "South Carolina."

South Carolina?

Was *anything* about this man predictable?

She stared at him. "You were born in *America*?"

Her apparent surprise made him chuckle. "Yes," he replied. "To English parents." He raised himself up on an elbow so they were lying side by side, eye to eye.

"Is that where they are now?"

"My eldest sister married a South Carolinian, a business associate of our father's. I presume she is still in America. My mother died in England many years ago. The rest spend their time between England and Spain."

"The rest?"

"My father, brother, and four other sisters."

She blinked, surprised to learn he had such a large family. He'd never mentioned any of them. "Do you see them often?"

"Never. We are estranged."

She felt a stab of dismay. "I'm sorry."

His smile was swift and humorless. "I'm not."

Should she infer that the estrangement was at his instigation? She didn't feel comfortable asking for that detail yet. "How long has it been?"

"Twelve years."

"You've not seen *any* of your family in twelve years?" Of course, he'd been in North Africa for at least eight of those years. Still . . . .

"I've made certain of it. They are not nice people. But you, on the other hand . . . ." He reached out and tugged on her blanket.

She clutched the blanket tighter to her chest. He wasn't being deliberately dismissive but clearly had plans to divert her. "But they know where you are?"

He abandoned his quest for the blanket and instead set his hand on her hip and tugged *her* closer. "No."

His thighs pressed against hers through her skirts. "Do they *want* to find you?"

He rolled to trap her beneath him. "Oh, yes, sweetheart. They want to find me. Very much."

For a while, those words formed her last rational thought.

Which suited her fine, because rational thought brought thoughts of the morning.

And in the morning, England called.

FIRST, THEY RETURNED TO THE château. Hours had passed since the fireworks—the time had disappeared as she lay in Jonathon Lecky's arms—and the courtyard had emptied. Guests, flute and pipe players had gone. Rachel looked around as servants removed the last trays of food. Though she didn't regret stealing away, she did feel a little bit guilty for missing the rest of the celebration. "Surely the Winters will have returned home?"

Jonathon shook his head. "No. But I know where they will be. Come."

She followed him into the château and up four flights of tight, winding steps. They emerged on the château's east-facing battlements. There, a small group of outlaws, knights and ladies were silhouetted against the lightening dawn sky.

"Jonathon! Miss Cavanagh! Join us!" Bertrand waved them over to the parapet, where he stood with his arm around his betrothed. No one looked askance at Rachel and Jonathon's long absence. No one remarked. The mood was different. This was a gathering of friends after a long night. Winters, Merciers, and one or two other friends.

Emily sat slightly apart from the rest of the group, looking like she was resting her feet after the hours of dancing. Her costume showed all the crumples and creases of a well-enjoyed evening. Her lips twitched with a small, private smile as Rachel took a seat beside her. "Should anyone from England ever inquire, you and I spent the entire evening together."

Rachel released a relieved breath. "Thank you."

"Not that they should have reason to," Emily continued. "For really, you were never in Boulogne at all." She gave Rachel a wink, and Rachel's gratitude grew.

"So what is next, for you and he?" Emily nodded in Jonathon's direction, and Rachel followed her gaze.

The boat captain stood several yards away, his arms braced on the parapet as he spoke with Emily's brother. Not so long ago, those strong arms had held her. He looked relaxed.

To her, he looked beautiful.

"I don't know."

'What next' was a very good question. Like it or not, reality intruded. "First I must return to England. There are matters to which I must attend."

Rossum. She had to speak to Rossum. And to her family. She dreaded both discussions. Thank goodness, her birthday—and her independence—were but a month away.

"One can see Jonathon cares for you very much," Emily said.

Could one? Was it so obvious to others? Of course, Emily had known Jonathon Lecky far longer than she. The thought reminded her of another incident earlier in the evening. "Emily, the man last night. Captain Lawrence. You seemed so shocked to see him." The captain did not number among the group on the château's battlements now.

Immediately, Emily's expression told Rachel she had touched on a delicate topic. Emily shifted in her seat. She glanced away. "I met him once, two years ago. At the time, I was engaged—"

Wait. Rachel blinked. *Emily had been engaged?*

The eldest Winter sister detected her surprise. "Yes," Emily said ruefully. "Unfortunately so."

"But what . . . ?" Rachel felt at a loss.

"Our nuptials were not meant to be. Rachel, the day I met . . . the captain"—she drew a breath—"was a very strange day. The strangest day of my life, I think. And last night . . . after the fireworks . . . last night was strange too."

Rachel frowned. Questions formed on her lips. But before she could select the right one, Emily gave herself a little shake—as though to free herself from old memories—and reached out to clasp Rachel's hands.

"Rachel," she said in earnest. "I am so glad Jonathon brought you to Boulogne. I have enjoyed meeting you so much. I dearly hope we can continue our friendship."

Rachel's heart warmed. She squeezed Emily's hands. "We can," she said fervently. "We shall."

LECKY CAST OFF FROM THE quay several hours later, after both he and Rachel had had several hours of sleep. The return to England was supposed to signal the end to the adventure he'd promised. But now? Now, Lecky no longer knew. Given their late-morning start, he'd have her back at Gravesend at first light, the following morning. He didn't doubt her family would be waiting. But for himself, the thought of depositing her on England's shore and sailing away again suddenly felt a great deal more thorny.

Jonathon, what in hell have you done?

He'd crossed into dangerous territory, that's what he'd done.

He still had Blackburn to consider.

But Blackburn was but a fraction of the problem, wasn't he? A new addition to a decades-old conflict. The woman now at the center of Lecky's quandary sat opposite, once more near the hatch to the cabin, Morgan pressed to her side. Her fingers threaded through the collie's fur. Morgan, with her nestling body and look of contentment, appeared only too happy to be on the receiving end of Rachel Cavanagh's attention.

A hint of strain shadowed his guest's smile. She was quiet. Contemplative. Did that quietness stem from thoughts of the conversations she would have once home? Or the questions she and he were presently avoiding? Questions about what came next once he had returned her to England? Because in the case of the latter, he was damned if he had any answers himself.

Of course, he did know one thing and that was where he wanted her to be at that moment. He was as bad as Morgan, wanting to feel her pressed against his side.

"Rachel. Will the first lieutenant join me at the tiller?"

A question appeared in her eyes as she glanced at him, a question his own look answered. A little smile played across her mouth as she separated from Morgan and moved closer. He gathered her against him, drew her head down and kissed her. She had the mouth of Aphrodite. He wrapped his free hand around her waist and pulled her into his lap. She was warm and soft in contrast to the crisp, salt-laden breeze. Never before at sea had he held a woman close.

Damned if he wasn't beginning to wonder if his choices weren't as irreconcilable as he thought.

OR PERHAPS THEY WERE. THREE hours later, discomfort resurfaced in Lecky's stomach.

A lugger followed their heading. He'd noticed the vessel shortly after they departed Boulogne. He had expected it to change course once out in the channel. It had not.

Of greater concern was that the larger boat should have been gaining on them. It was not.

His years sailing the North African coast had trained him to be on constant guard against attack. Then, one watched for Barbary corsairs. Now, he liked to know the schedule of the MacArthur vessels sailing between London and Cadiz.

A lugger on his heading that didn't gain was not comforting.

THERE WAS NO CHANGE TWO hours later as Lecky's sloop passed through the waters off the coast of the Isle of Thanet, off Kent.

Coincidence? Not likely.

A boat with legitimate business didn't sail for hours behind a sloop half its size. Nor did smugglers cross the channel so early— even though Lecky's gut told him the boat was a smuggler, and he could guess too who owned it. No, his feeling was growing—minute by minute as the sun began its descent—that the lugger's crew had a different objective in mind.

"Jonathon, is something the matter?" Rachel set her hand lightly against his chest, perhaps felt the thrum of his tension. "You've hardly spoken."

He hadn't. He was trying to decide what to do. Experience told him that the crew of the lugger was waiting for the fall of darkness to make its intentions known.

He couldn't outrun the lugger. Nor was outmaneuvering it a possibility: his boat's draught was shallower, but he dared not risk running aground and marooning them on a sandbar. There would be five or six men aboard the lugger to his one.

There was no easy shore escape. Thanet's limestone cliffs rose up from the sea on the port side, and beyond the cliffs lay the marshes. Poseidon be damned, there were no good options. Accounting for Rachel Cavanagh's safety made him acutely aware of every bloody thing that could go wrong.

The only option he had was retaining the element of surprise.

"JONATHON, IS SOMETHING THE MATTER?" Rachel tried again. His heart beat rapidly beneath her palm. Over the past few hours, all signs of the easy, laughing Jonathon had disappeared. He was quieter. The lines of his body were taut. The arm that encircled her had hardened. Rachel straightened to look at him.

"As soon as night falls," he said, "the lugger off our stern will attack."

"*What?*" Rachel twisted in his arms to look at the vessel. She had noticed it on the horizon, of course, but had thought little of it. "How do you know?"

His lips twisted. "Prescience."

She looked at him sharply. He was serious. More than that, he was certain. Her mouth tasted the metallic tang of fear. "What will we do?"

"As soon as night falls, we prepare."

"And until then?"

"We make all haste for Whitstable."

"Rachel, if I ask you to do *anything*, I need you to follow my orders without question."

"Yes, of course." Just minutes before, the sun had slipped below the horizon. The light of dusk was fading. He expected the occupants of the other boat to make a move. She could only pray that he was wrong.

"The whale oil lanterns in the cabin," he said. "Fetch them for me, but don't light them yet." She did as he asked, and he stowed the lanterns in the well at his feet, out of view of the vessel behind.

The mantle of night was beginning its descent over the deck. He had been waiting for this, she realized. This mantle made his movements difficult to distinguish even for her. He set the tiller in the comb, then slid sideways a foot to pry open a storage compartment constructed into the deck. Her heart accelerated at the shape of the object he withdrew. A rifle. Nay, a *double-barreled* rifle. He set it down beside him, then reached into the compartment again.

At first, she didn't recognize the second object. Then, she realized it was a small leather holster, from which he removed a pistol with *no* barrel. Confused, she watched him prime the pan, then carefully set the pistol back in the holster and slide the holster onto his belt.

He looked up at her, his expression grim. He motioned her closer. She shifted forward as he produced a folding knife from his trouser pocket. Her stomach gave a lurch as he pressed it into her hands. "I want you to keep this on you, for your safety. Use it if you have to, but better that you stay out of arm's reach. Rachel...." His gaze settled on her, and she didn't quite know how to describe the maelstrom she saw there. Was it regret? Remorse? Pain?

"*Damn.*" He reached out, grasped the back of her head, then leant forward to kiss her hard.

"Understand," he said vehemently as he set her away, "I *never* wanted this to touch you. I *never* wanted you involved in this."

"Involved in what? What do they want?" Her lips felt bruised, the folding knife cold in her hands.

"My past," he said. "They want me."

THE DECK OF THE SLOOP lay in darkness, the lantern attached to the backstay unlit. The dark, slumbering silhouette of the coastline of Kent lay off the sloop's port side. Ahead—although still some miles off—lay the harbor town of Whitstable. Lecky's heart hammered as he scanned the darkened waves for sails.

Come now, boys, where are you tonight? I've got a smuggler here for you.

Two of the King's revenue cutters were stationed at Whitstable. The question was where did the Revenue's preventative forces patrol tonight.

The only advantage Lecky had was that the lugger's crew needed him alive. They'd only get their reward if Chaloner MacArthur got the opportunity to confront Lecky himself.

Across from Lecky, Rachel sat with her arms hugging Morgan. Her face was pale in the intermittent moonlight that filtered between broken clouds. Off the stern, the crew of the lugger had decided to make their move. Wind filled the lugger's sails as the vessel picked up speed.

They didn't have long.

"Rachel," he instructed. "Light the lanterns and set them back in the well. Make sure they won't fall over." Whale oil was highly flammable. Few things were more dangerous to a boat than fire. He was taking a risk; and, by Rachel's concerned gaze, she was aware of it. Still, she knelt in the well and did as he asked.

Behind them, the lugger was closing the gap. Minutes later, he had the confirmation he'd been waiting for. He recognized the vessel. He'd glimpsed it earlier that week.

Five men lined the gunwale, making a total crew of six including the helmsman. At their centre stood the lugger's owner. *Henri Cox.*

Every man aboard was armed with a rifle. Two also held grappling hooks. Across the gap between the vessels, Cox's eyes shone. The sly old bastard thought he'd found himself a prize.

Not bloody likely.

The lugger sliced through the estuary's dark water and drew alongside Lecky's sloop with a ten-yard separation. With a rifle slung over his back—and noting the position of Lecky's own—Cox spaced his hands on the lugger's gunwale. "Well, now. Didn't realize you'd have company. But now I've got a proper look at her, I can see why. Ripe little piece, isn't she?"

In a protective move, Rachel drew her knees up closer to her chest. Her lips pressed together. Lecky knew beneath the folds of her cloak she clutched the folding knife. Beside her, Morgan released a low, reverberating growl.

"Are you attempting to endear me to you, Cox?" Silently, Lecky slipped the tiller into the comb.

"Ah, know my name, do you? In that case, you probably know what I want." The lugger captain's gaze narrowed. "We can do this the easy way, and you and your lady friend can come sail with us. *Or* we can do it the hard way, 'though I can't promise your lady friend won't get hurt." What his eyes did promise, as they dwelt on Rachel, was deliberately designed to incite Lecky's ire.

The gap between the boats was closing. Ten yards turned to eight. Cox's men were readying their grappling hooks.

Lecky reached down into the well to wrap his fingers around the handle of a whale oil lamp. Eight yards turned to six. Two of Cox's men were preparing to board. "You do realize I'm of no value dead."

Acknowledgment glinted in Cox's eye, although on that point, he didn't deign to respond. "Easy or difficult. You have ten seconds to decide," the lugger captain said.

Six yards became four. He couldn't think about the fear that shone in Rachel's eyes.

His muscles tightened in readiness. A smile sliced his face. "Generous. But no."

Lecky hurled the lantern. It arced upwards between the boats—then plummeted to the lugger's deck only to bounce and skitter.

The damn thing didn't smash.

Cox hissed in a breath, then swung back toward Lecky, eyes narrowed. "Get him!"

The distance between the two boats closed. Sensing the threat, Morgan began viciously barking. Two men dropped over the lugger's side as their crew mates threw out grapples, targeting the fore and aft of Lecky's boat. The sloop rocked violently as each man's weight hit the deck. The grapples scraped across wood. Lecky succeeded in launching himself at the aft grapple and deflecting it overboard before it hooked. On the lugger, Cox's man quickly started to wind the deflected grapple's line in. Lecky wouldn't have long before the man tried again. And the grapple thrown onto the foredeck *had* caught.

On the deck of his sloop, the two boarders were moving. "Rachel, keep out of the way!"

Already she'd scrambled to the opposite side of the sloop, folding knife clutched in her hand, as the first boarder made a lunge for her. The second came for Lecky.

His every sense was heightened to the danger, his body wound ready to respond. Grasping both ends of his rifle like a quarterstaff, he drove the weapon upward and knocked the man back, into the boom. The boat rocked violently. On the aft deck, Rachel gave a cry as she grasped for a steady hold. *Poseidon, please god, don't let her drop that knife.* Her pursuer was knocked off balance and sprawled over the roof of the cabin. At the sloop's bow, the first grappling hook had found purchase, and Cox's man was securing the vessels.

Lecky's attacker recovered to launch himself at Lecky again. Lecky swung hard again and knocked him back, just as he heard the aft grappling hook land again, scrape across the deck and catch. *Fuck.*

At Rachel's side, Morgan's teeth were bared. Her barks rent the air as she launched forward, snapping at the first boarder, then retreating as Rachel scrambled back across the deck toward the bow.

"Free the grapple!" Lecky shouted as the second boarder came at him again. This time, his attacker was swinging his own rifle. Lecky blocked the blow before the rocking of the boat threw them both off balance and Lecky's rifle skidded out of his hands across the deck. He rolled for the weapon—his fingers just grazed the stock—as his attacker came at him again. Temporarily abandoning his efforts to retrieve the rifle, Lecky lifted his foot and kicked his attacker in the knee. He sprang up as the man recovered. This time, he was prepared as the man rushed forward. He grabbed the barrel of his attacker's rifle as the man sought to land a blow. Spinning his attacker around, he grabbed the man by the back of the neck and used the force of the man's thrust and lack of balance to propel him overboard. His attacker toppled over the stern and into the channel. Overbalanced himself, Lecky spilled forward, catching hold of the bulwark and breaking his fall with his hands. His heart came to a momentary stop as his glance came up—and caught on the sight of sails in the distance.

Poseidon, yes! Let that be the good boys from Revenue.

Morgan was still barking as Lecky freed the barrelless pistol he'd readied, which was a tool used by smugglers to signal to their land gangs on shore. He couldn't see either Rachel or Morgan—the sloop cabin and the jib blocked his view of their position.

"Rachel!" he shouted as he leveled the pistol over the side of the sloop. If those sails did belong to the Revenue boys, the flash in the pan would get their attention. Bracing himself, he pulled the trigger. As the gunpowder lit, a blue flash sparked in place of the barrel.

The man Lecky had tossed overboard had come up spluttering and was attempting to swim back to the lugger.

"Jonathon!" Rachel scrambled back onto the aft deck with the first of Cox's men in pursuit. "Jonathon, I couldn't—"

Immediately, Lecky saw she'd been too hard-pressed avoiding the advances of Cox's man to free the grapple on the bow. Morgan's barking and growling had reached frenzied levels. She had leapt onto the roof of the cabin, lunging and snapping at Rachel's pursuer as the man tried to follow Rachel to the aft deck. Their attacker had had enough of the dog's scrapping.

"I'll fix you," he snarled, and Lecky's heart almost exploded as the man swung the butt of his rifle and smashed it across Morgan's jaw. Morgan's surprised yelp was echoed by Rachel's frightened cry as the blow sent the collie spinning across the cabin roof. She crashed through the open hatch and tumbled down the companionway into the cabin below.

Morgan! But he couldn't go to her now.

Fear and rage brought pinpoint focus. "Rachel, the lantern!"

As Lecky positioned himself between Rachel and her pursuer, she lunged for the well, understanding what he wanted her to do.

"No!" shouted Cox. "You!" he screamed at one of the men holding the lines. "Don't let the bitch—"

But it was too late. Rachel had grasped the lantern and flung.

Notus be damned, she had a good arm.

The lantern smashed against one of the lugger's masts and shattered, falling to the deck. Whale oil ignited.

Lecky made use of the distraction to repay Morgan's attacker by driving his rifle into the man's jaw. As the man's head reared back, Lecky grabbed him by the hair and slammed his skull into the boom. The man's body sagged and Lecky rolled him over the side.

"Put out the fire! Quick!" Cox shouted, his fury palpable as he rushed toward the blaze.

The aft grapple slackened as the man holding the other end of the line abandoned his position to respond. Rachel immediately freed it and let it fall overboard. *Now for the bow.*

"Rachel, take cover!" The lads on the lugger were still armed. Lecky glanced towards the distant sails as he grasped the sloop's mast and slid across the cabin roof. With any luck, the spiral of smoke now rising above their position would capture the attention of the other boat. Flames began to lick up the lugger's mast as their attackers attempted to beat out the blaze.

Lecky fell to his knees on the bow and loosed the second grapple, which had caught on the coiled lines hanging on cleats near the bow. Using the butt of his rifle like a pole, he pushed the sloop off the lugger's side. A gulf began to widen between the two boats.

"Don't let them get away!" Cox shouted.

But Cox was helpless, his crew occupied with the effort of preventing the spread of flames as fire licked the bottom of the spar, threatening to ignite the lugsail.

"Arghhh!" their attacker bellowed furiously, as the gap between the two boats opened.

Lecky's pulse hammered, his every sense heightened. A quick glance assured him that Rachel had taken shelter on the port side of the cabin. He raised his rifle again and this time took aim at the lugger's own boat lantern. Steadying his breath, he pulled the trigger. The recoil of his rifle thudded into his shoulder as the lantern shattered, causing a whoosh of blue flame as the volatile oil flared up. Burning droplets of oil spilled from the shattered lantern onto the deck, increasing the chaos as Cox's men realized they were now dealing with a second blaze.

Good, but *blast it.* He needed to get them away before the

lugger's rigging went up. He swung across the cabin roof, dodged the boom and grasped the tiller, seeking a current that would help carry them away.

The chaos on the lugger's deck continued as they drifted apart.

In the distance, sails had turned their way.

CHAPTER SIXTEEN

A man at sea becomes acutely aware of the vastness of the world. He is also made to stare into the face of his every vulnerability.
—*The Memoirs of Rhys Cavanagh*

"Rachel, take the tiller for me. Hold this heading." He had to get to the cabin.

Rachel came forward, thankfully understanding the direction of his thoughts now that they were a safe distance from the lugger.

Poseidon, help him. His chest constricted and his throat closed over at the sight of Morgan lying still on her side at the bottom of the companionway. As if realizing Lecky was above, his collie let out a low whine. Her tail gave a soft thump against the deck.

He was down the steps in a second.

Swiftly he stepped over her body and knelt. "Here, girl, what happened to you?" With a whimper, she tried to lever herself up on her elbows. Immediately, he was reaching out to stay her and press her back down. "No, girl. Shhhh. There's no getting up." Then he was inspecting her, running his hands over her body. After a moment of gentle, albeit frantic searching, his panic began to subside. She'd been knocked hard. She'd *fallen* hard, yet nothing appeared broken, not even her jaw. Still, she flinched away and whimpered as his fingers gingerly explored it. *Thank the gods.*

Releasing a breath, he buried his hands in her long coat and pressed his forehead to her side as he strove to reassert an iron grip on his rampaging heart.

Morgan remained still for a moment, then gave a concerned prod at his ear with her wet nose. Once, twice. *That's a girl.*

And the woman above. She too could have been so easily hurt.

She still *could* be hurt through her association with him. She didn't know the dangers. Poseidon and Notus and Zephyrus *damn* him for his selfishness.

No. *Zephyrus* damn him, for thinking for a moment he might have a right to anything like her. Anything gentler, softer, so damn brave and fine.

RACHEL CLUNG TO THE TILLER. She had no idea what was happening below. She felt sick, horrifically nauseous and heartsore. She could still hear the crack of their attacker's rifle across Morgan's jaw. She could still picture the collie's subsequent, helpless tumble through the hatch. Morgan had been protecting *her*.

Her heart bled for the collie. And for Jonathon, too. *Please*, she sent a fervent wish to God. *Please, let Morgan be all right.*

Across the water, the lugger was burning. The sails were now alight; and every sailor knew once the rigging went up, the fire would be near impossible to put out. Smoke curled into the sky. Flames reflected in the water.

As she sucked in a breath and tried to reassemble her shattered thoughts, she realized another boat was approaching at speed from the west. Dread surged again. Her mouth went dry.

Just as she prepared to call to Jonathon, the breeze caught the vessel's ensign. It was red, with a Union Jack in the canton and a regal crown supported by a star in the right-hand half.

Her nerves calmed a notch.

The approaching vessel was a revenue cutter.

The sloop rocked as Jonathon re-emerged on the deck with Morgan in his arms. The collie was curled against the boat captain's chest. She gave a little lift of her tail at the sight of Rachel. *Oh, Lord.* She looked so huddled and wretched, Rachel's heart bled all the more.

"Is she badly hurt?"

Jonathon grimaced. "More frightened than damaged."

She wasn't damaged .... A little of Rachel's anxiousness eased. Nonetheless, the collie's look of vulnerability wrapped round and tugged on her soul. Clearly, Morgan did not wish to leave her master. Rachel could empathize. The scared part inside—the part she was trying to batten down—wanted the boat captain's arms encircling her too.

He turned to wait for the revenue cutter's approach.

There were at least a dozen crew on board, half of whom were armed. The officers in charge relaxed at the sight of Rachel. Or perhaps it was the sight of Jonathon, holding the collie in his arms.

"What goes here?" one of the two officers aboard called.

"My wife and I were attacked by that smuggling lugger."

The younger officer exchanged a glance with his captain. "How do you know she's a smuggler?"

"We've come from Boulogne-sur-Mer. The vessel is known there. You may contact Elijah Winter, of the Winter Trading House in Boulogne, if you require confirmation."

The officer's lips thinned. "Do you carry papers?"

"I do." His arms were full of Morgan. "Rachel, will you fetch my satchel from the bunk below?" Rachel dropped the tiller in the comb and went to fetch the item.

"What interest did they have in you?" She heard the officer ask as she climbed down the companionway.

"I fear I got on the captain's bad side back in Boulogne," came Jonathon's reply.

Rachel spotted his satchel, grasped it up and returned to the deck. She handed it to him unbuckled, and he slid a page out. "Please, hand that up to the officer."

She passed the page to the officer, who reached over the cutter's gunwale to take it. The officer glanced over the page. "The Winter Trading House in Boulogne, you said?"

"Yes. I'm the company's ship's agent in Boulogne." Jonathon grimaced. "Forgive me. My wife has had a terrible fright. My dog has been wounded. Permit me to see my wife to her family in Gravesend, and I will return to speak with you at Whitstable tomorrow. I'll be happy to go over all the details." He gave a nod in the direction of the burning lugger. "Besides, I rather think they need you."

The officer handed the page back to Rachel. "Give me your direction, and you can go."

Jonathon supplied the name of the Lord Nelson Inn and Owen Griffith as contact. "The proprietor always knows how to reach me."

"But we will see you tomorrow?"

"Yes."

The officer nodded, and the revenue cutter sailed on. Rachel realized she was still holding the page in her hand. Quickly, she picked up the satchel that Jonathon had set down at his side. "Here, let me put this away." Her hand began to shake as she tried to slide the page inside. She was forced to slow down and focus as she fumbled to put the page away, then to secure the buckle. She hugged the satchel to still her hands.

They were safe but... she was at as big a loss to understand what had transpired as the Revenue officers. A weighty silence encased the sloop's aft deck. "What... what happened back there? Why did they want you?"

He had turned his attention back to ensuring his canine companion was all right. His expression hardened. "Someone was of a mind to profiteer."

"Profiteer how?"

He laid Morgan carefully on the deck, despite the collie's whimper of protest, and looked toward Rachel. Glinting and angry, his gray eyes brought to mind quicksilver. His steely look thrust her back to the Lord Nelson Inn five days before, following the attack in the yard. She knew, both then and now, his anger wasn't directed at her. But the lugger's attack held a significance she didn't understand, a significance that had caused him to erect this wall.

When angry, Jonathon Lecky pushed her away. She didn't want to be pushed away. She feared too greatly the consequence.

"The less you know, the safer you are," he said. "Excuse me."

Abruptly, he left the deck.

She was left, clutching the satchel.

And just as the less than pristine waters of the river Thames flowed out to the English Channel to commingle with the sea, so too did a sense of foreboding flow through Rachel's heart.

HER APPREHENSION INCREASED THE LONGER Jonathon remained below. Five minutes, ten, fifteen . . . she held the tiller. No sounds came from the cabin. When the burning lugger was but a speck in the night, she placed the tiller in the comb and ducked beneath the boom, headed toward the hatch. Morgan gently thumped her tail as Rachel approached. Her heart went out to the battered collie. "There's a girl; you're a good girl." She paused to give Morgan a pat, then moved to the hatch.

Jonathon Lecky was standing in the center of the cabin, an elbow braced against the overhead lockers, his face pressed to his arm. He stood still, his rifle slung over his back. It was his very stillness that exposed him in a way nothing else might. Rachel's throat went dry. *What did he carry inside?* She felt the wall of his past as though it were a physical barrier between them.

He heard her and lifted his head to look up at the hatch. Silver eyes met hers. "There's trouble above? Have the Revenue boys returned?"

"No." She shook her head. "I wanted to know whether you were all right."

"I'm perfectly fine." Straightening, he came toward the companionway and quickly mounted the steps to the deck. "You're relieved of tiller duty."

She shuffled back out of his way. "Is there something more I can do to help?"

"Nothing. You need not do anything." Moving back to the tiller, he opened the deck compartment and stowed his rifle and the barrelless pistol. He looked up at her. "You still have the knife?"

"Yes." She extracted it from the pocket of her pelisse and passed it to him.

She wanted to believe the barrier she felt was purely a reaction to the attack. Her instincts told her it was more. *Just wait*, her sense of self-preservation urged. She settled back against the cabin and watched him in the darkness.

He said nothing as he steered the sloop closer to the darkened stretch of coast. Rachel sat taut, one hand covering one of Morgan's front paws. It was perhaps a comfort as much for her as it was for the collie. After a time, the sloop passed the British army garrison at Sheerness. Cloud obscured the moon. The occasional owl hooted. Throughout, Jonathon was silent.

Oh, she understood what was happening. Two gulfs were widening here. The first lay between the sloop and its attackers. The second was the one opening between Jonathon and herself. He was pushing her away.

The night was cool, yet that was nothing compared to the chill of uncertainty and apprehension that found entry into her blood.

LECKY WATCHED AS THE SKY began to pale with the first hint of pre-dawn. A blustery easterly filled the sails, speeding the sloop's passage to Gravesend. They would arrive soon. Soon, Rachel Cavanagh would be safe.

Safe away from him.

How had Cox known who he was? How had he been exposed? That was the question he needed to answer.

Rachel Cavanagh was distressed. It showed in her drawn, pale face and dark, fear-filled eyes. He knew she wanted reassurance, but there was none he could provide. Yet her hurt—nursed in silence and searching looks as they made their way to Gravesend—gnawed powerfully on his conscience.

The masts of the ships anchored off Gravesend rose up through the early morning light. With the exception of a few fishing boats setting out, the shore appeared quiet. Normally, Lecky would have taken a visitor's berth at the pier. Instead, he again retrieved his rifle, slung it over his shoulder, and drew alongside the Three Daws jetty. He was not in the mood to wait for customs.

The Three Daws Inn was the biggest smuggling den and gin-swilling cavern in all of Gravesend. That said, any patrons still left at this hour were likely passed out over their cups.

Lecky secured the stern and bow lines, then extended his hand to help Rachel Cavanagh onto the jetty. "Come."

Looking up at him from the centre of the aft deck, she didn't budge. Rather than fearful, she looked mutinous. "You are going to leave me here, aren't you?"

"No. The Three Daws has the worst reputation in town. I want you safe. We're going to the Lord Nelson."

She looked no more pleased with his words. "And *then*?"

"Rachel, we always planned to bring you back."

"Yes. That *was* what we planned. To set sail for five, possibly six days. Enough time to give me a taste of a different life." Rejecting the offer of his hand, she lifted her skirts and climbed up onto the jetty, then whirled to face him. "But you and I both know you are lying to yourself, Jonathon Lecky, if you think to just leave and wave goodbye. You have the same questions I do."

Such as do you belong in my arms? Do I want to be at your side to see your face light up, when you're standing before all the places you've always wanted to go?

Can I let you go, and not be there to protect you from sinking ships and shifty, no-good types?

Of course, he bloody well wondered that.

He stared back, his teeth gritted. That was *all* he could do. Because inside, his gut was being slashed with great, burning talons. *He was a danger to her.* He'd told Owen he'd watch out for her, and he'd almost failed.

Across from him, Rachel Cavanagh's chest heaved with fury.

They were at a standstill.

Finally, jaw still clenched, he jerked his head toward High Street. "Let's go. Morgan, you stay here." He didn't want the collie exerting herself while she was still so bruised. With a mournful look, she flattened her ears and lay down on the jetty.

Lecky set off. Rachel caught up to him with several quick paces and doggedly stuck at his side. Her silence and the flashes of dark, coffee-colored eyes beneath dark lashes were more accusing than if she'd spoken. She was furious. *Enraged.*

It wouldn't do either of them any bloody good, he wanted to snarl. Because he was furious as well. *At himself.* For wanting things he had no damn right to claim.

He grasped her upper arm and marched her around the corner into King Street. She bristled and tried to wrench her arm free of his grip. Although revolted by his own high-handedness, he held on. He didn't want to risk her balking in the middle of the street. He wanted her inside the Lord Nelson, where Owen Griffiths would keep her safe.

They passed beneath the archway into the coach yard of the inn. Several coaches stood in the yard; otherwise, it was vacant.

Lecky started toward the door, only to have the woman at his side stop short in a sudden, frozen halt. He turned, prepared for one hell of a holy row. Then his stomach clenched and his thoughts recoiled as he saw her face—suddenly, terribly pale.

She looked so at sea, for a moment he thought she might faint. He followed her gaze toward one of the coaches, a large barouche with a coat of arms emblazoned on the door.

"Jonathon, *stop.*" Now she was clutching him, grasping hold of his forearms, preventing him from going further. "Please, don't do this again. Don't just leave . . . again."

"Again?" he asked.

"Like Dunkirk," she said.

Like the panic in her eyes, the reminder slammed into him. The image of her—the softness of her lips, the surprise and confusion in those dark eyes, the way she had *flinched*, when, in the guest room of the Hotel Patrice, he had dismissed the notion of contact between them.

Poseidon help him. He had to get back to his boat.

"Rachel, let me go."

She shook her head. "Don't do this. Please." Appeal, distress— he hated to see either writ on her face. "For us to meet again, here in Gravesend, was pure chance," she said. "I don't understand what happened at sea, but please, can we—"

"*What?*" he demanded. "Can we *what?* Sail away together after you've dealt with Rossum?"

He might as well have struck her, by her pained rush of breath. Poseidon be damned, he wanted to garrotte himself for hurting her. As he watched, she gathered herself up, as though gathering together fragments of herself that someone had so carelessly caused to break.

"Tell me, Jonathon Lecky, if 'sailing away together' were what we both wanted, is there something that might prevent that?" she asked.

Damn. His throat closed over. *Damn.*

Blackburn. Cox. Jonas and Chaloner MacArthur. Behavior too long gone unthwarted.

"Tell me, Jonathon. Be honest."

He held her gaze. He felt divided within himself. He felt as though he was looking into the still surface of a lake, where the words and thoughts he needed were minnows darting beneath the surface, too quick and slippery to grasp.

Even if he *could* grasp them, they were more than he could share.

He told her the only reason she might understand. The only one he could manage to enunciate.

"Rachel, I can't keep you safe."

A frown formed on her brow as she stared at him. Questions formed on her lips. She began to shake her head slowly.

Behind him, the heavy inn door slammed.

"Oh, Lord. Rachel!" a woman cried.

Lecky turned, to be flooded with a fierce, swift sense of impending debacle. Oh, yes. Notus was laughing.

"Rachel? She's here?"

The Marquess of Rossum stood before the inn's oak door with an impeccably dressed young woman on his arm. By her coloring, it didn't take Da Vinci to guess she was a Cavanagh—Rachel's sister, perhaps. The young woman's gaze flashed to Lecky, full of questions and shock. As she took in how close he stood to her sister, the young woman blanched.

He could feel Rachel's horror in her paralyzed grip. He could see it, too, in her ashen face. Of course, it was in her nature to care about hurting the Marquess. It was also evident, by her response, that the exchange her sister and the Marquess had stumbled upon was an intimate one.

It was also clear that the other Miss Cavanagh had taken one look at Lecky and not liked what she'd seen. Her lips pressed into a line.

Desperately, Rachel looked his way. *Please*, those eyes begged. *Please, there is more to say.*

"Rachel?" The Marquess asked. "Faith .... Why the silence?"

There was a stricken note in the Marquess's tone. Stricken and bewildered and suffused by the awareness there was more he couldn't see.

Not a single voice answered.

Rachel's gaze whipped toward Lecky again. Her eyes begged. *Don't go.*

Sometimes words didn't make a difference. Not even 'I'm sorry'.

Still, for a few moments, that's what he allowed his look to convey.

Then he turned and forced his feet to move.

He felt the sting in the back of his eyes as he strode into King Street.

He *couldn't* keep her safe. Not least, because one would not find the birth of Jonathon Lecky recorded in the parish register of St. Philip's Church in Charleston, South Carolina, in October, 1787.

No, there one would find one Jonathon Matthias Prescott MacArthur, the youngest son of Jonas MacArthur, owner of the shipbuilding and trading firm, MacArthur and Sons of London.

And nowadays, also of Spain.

CHAPTER SEVENTEEN

Patience and equanimity are the domain of the experienced, for they are often only learned with time.
—*The Memoirs of Rhys Cavanagh*

BORN IN CHARLESTON, SOUTH CAROLINA, during one of his parents' visits to America, Jonathon Matthias Prescott MacArthur resided at the MacArthur family estate in Surrey until the age of eight. An enterprising child from the first, he had driven his nanny, and later his governess, half-mad with his propensity to escape both nursery and classroom and disappear on various boyish adventures. He built dams and floated sailboats along the stream that ran through the family estate. From old barrels he constructed rafts, which he captained down the stream while fending off attacks by dangerous pirates. Then there were times when he played the role of pirate himself.

Jonas MacArthur's leniency toward his second son's behavior became a significant source of disgruntlement among Jonathon's siblings, not least his brother, Chaloner, who was older than Jonathon by eight years.

"But, father, he is spoilt," Chaloner would complain, only to be silenced by the quelling look of Jonas MacArthur's silver eyes.

"The boy shows initiative and won't back down from a challenge. These are excellent qualities to have in business." Then Jonas MacArthur sprinkled the seeds that would sow his eldest son's hatred: "It is a shame that *you* see every bump on the road as an impediment."

At the age of eight, Jonathon MacArthur was sent to boarding school at Harrow. In summer and over the holidays, he returned to rove the dappled woods and fish the Surrey streams and toil alongside his father's men at the MacArthur shipyard at Deptford, on the Thames, southeast of London. Few things were more enjoyable to a young boy than wielding caulking mallets or caulking irons alongside his father's shipwrights. At the age of ten, he had not fully understood what it meant: that the ships they were fitting out would be used to transport slaves.

Jonas MacArthur had been pleased with his younger son's industry. "It's good for a boy to understand manual work." The patriarch of the MacArthur family had also been pleased at the time Jonathon spent poring over ships' plans and drawing his own. "Shipbuilding runs in that boy's blood."

At Jonas's back, his elder son, who had no interest in lifting either a mallet or a stylus, had seethed.

Jonathon had been twelve years old when he saw Chaloner break their mother's heart.

Olivia Freya MacArthur had been born a baron's daughter. Her marriage to Jonas MacArthur had been arranged, without regard for her feelings, by her father. She had been as helpless to prevent her own marriage as she had been to prevent her dearest friend and lady's maid from being thrown out of the baron's home for falling pregnant to Olivia's brother—a relationship the young serving woman had also not chosen.

Olivia Freya had been devastated the day she learned that her own son, Chaloner, had forced himself on one of the chambermaids.

Three years later, to Jonas MacArthur's everlasting grief, Olivia Freya was gone. Claimed by lung fever, she left behind a husband, two sons, and five daughters.

One son, through his callousness, had continued throughout those three years to break her heart over and over and over again.

LECKY STOOD WITH HIS BACK to the wrought-iron fence that encircled Hanover Square as the early afternoon traffic of carriages, pedestrians and riders flowed by along the cobblestone street. On the opposite side of the street, through the throng, stood the

Cavanagh townhouse.

There is more to say.

Rachel Cavanagh had been right five weeks ago in Gravesend. He couldn't just leave her and wave goodbye.

He didn't want to leave her at all.

Although where that left the pair of them, he still didn't bloody know. He'd watched the newspapers for engagement announcements to see if she'd gone back to Rossum. He'd seen none.

He needed to speak to her. He owed her an apology. And honesty. Of course, that didn't mean she would want to hear from him.

Tell me, Jonathon Lecky, if 'sailing away together' were what we both wanted, is there something that might prevent that?

Aye. He'd turned his back for too long. He needed to see this thing with Blackburn done. And he didn't yet know what the outcome would be.

But right now, he had the opportunity to speak to her without putting her at risk.

From behind bars in Canterbury, Henri Cox and his crew awaited their appearance before the courts of assize. Following the attack, Lecky had established, through inquiries in Boulogne, Kent, and Le Harve, that Cox was a former slaver. Years before, the man had worked for Chaloner MacArthur; Cox had recognized Lecky as MacArthur's missing brother. He'd hoped to take Lecky in the Channel, sink his boat, and cash in on 'seeing Lecky home'. It was, after all, far easier for Lecky to 'vanish' at sea than to disappear leaving his sloop tied to the quay at Boulogne. And Chaloner MacArthur *would* pay to get his hands on his mutinous younger brother—he'd made no secret of that.

Thanks to the Revenue boys, Cox had had no opportunity to cash in on his information. For the time being, the former slaver wasn't a threat. Lecky was banking on the fact that Cox would keep his mouth closed. From what he'd heard, the former slaver wasn't the type to want any other black-hearted bastard profiting from the information he'd uncovered.

Lecky wasn't sure how long that would be the case.

He was playing a waiting game with Blackburn too. A game in

which timing was key. Lecky and Blackburn had to wait until the last possible moment to force MacArthur and Sons to back out of the company's shipbuilding and delivery contracts—and hence face ruin. Talk was rife that the King of Spain would shortly sign a treaty with the British, promising to consider means to abolish the Spanish slave trade. How likely that was to occur, Lecky didn't know. But it helped to make a great many merchants, bankers and insurers nervous.

Lecky crossed the street and was about to raise his hand to the knocker when he caught a glimpse of the open-top barouche rolling down the street. His breath caught at the glint of butterscotch hair, visible beneath a jaunty bonnet.

It wasn't her, he realized, as the carriage clattered to a halt. It was her sister. The young woman from the yard of the Lord Nelson.

He knew her name now. Miss Faith Cavanagh. A lady's maid, a coachman and a young groom, a boy of no more than ten, accompanied her.

Her eyes widened in surprise as they lit upon Lecky standing on the doorstep.

She looked away just as quickly, her lips setting in a sudden, determined line. The lass sure as hell didn't like him.

Her servants' looks were curious.

Lecky waited as the boy leapt down from his seat by the coachman to help Faith Cavanagh and her lady's maid alight from the carriage. The youngest of Rhys Cavanagh's granddaughters was a concoction, all right. Her bonnet alone was a creation unto itself, heaped with feathers and wreaths of ribbons and flower-shaped ornaments made of cork. Ah, well, at least if she fell in the Thames, she wouldn't sink.

He didn't know much about fashion but gathered Faith Cavanagh was dressed to the height of it.

Once on the ground, she wasted no time in telling him what she thought. "You are not welcome here."

"Well, I didn't expect heralds and a fanfare, but you can stand down from the executioner's block."

She shot him *a look* as she grasped her umbrella. "You are crude."

"Forgive me. I received the impression we were skipping the pleasantries."

She didn't deign to respond. She crossed to the door. Unfortunately, he was in her way.

"Move aside, please."

"I wish to speak with your sister."

"I'm sure." She looked over him with distaste. "My sister is rich, is she not?"

Oh, that was what she thought, was it? Lecky's lips tipped up. "Since you seem to care about such things, how can you be sure that I'm not?"

Faith Cavanagh's eyes flashed to his and narrowed. "Excuse me."

He shifted to allow her and her maid to past. The maid cast Lecky an uncertain look and knocked on the door for admittance.

"Perhaps we might offer your sister the choice whether to see me?" Lecky said.

"Of course, we *might*," Faith Cavanagh replied, as the butler swung open the door. "*If* my sister were here, which she is not. Good day." She turned on her heel and crossed through the entry behind her maid. "Jenkins, please close the door. Our visitor is not coming inside."

The gods be damned. Faced once again with the closed door, Lecky took a step back. Was he to believe her or not?

Several feet away, the coachman let out a breath. "My, didn't you just set a bee in Miss Faith's latest bonnet?"

Standing by the carriage door, the boy smothered a giggle.

"Jack, son, get back up here," the coachman instructed gruffly. Even so, the man appeared amused as the boy scrambled back up beside him. He also seemed to guess Lecky's quandary. "It's true, lad. Miss Rachel went to America a week ago. A week after her twenty-first birthday."

"*America?*" The word hit like a jolt. "For how long?"

"Don't know rightly. Five, mayhap six months?"

Poseidon be damned. Lecky stood for a moment in shock. Then, a bark of laughter escaped him.

Girl, I'm proud.

The coachman gave him an odd look.

He didn't know what his situation would be in five or six months. Certainly, the ship he was constructing in Boulogne would be finished. Possibly, too, his business with Blackburn would be done.

That was assuming *she came back.* Damn, he didn't want to think about the possibility of her *not* returning.

"I need a favor," Lecky said.

The coachman shook his head. "Sorry, lad. You've picked the wrong man."

Which was code for 'I'm loyal'. Lecky stepped closer to the carriage. He saw then what he should have noticed immediately. The coachman's gloves protruded from his coat pocket, and a small tattoo of a mermaid was visible on the back of the man's right hand as he held the reins. "You're Cobham, aren't you? You were one of Rhys Cavanagh's men."

The coachman glanced at his tattoo and squeezed his fist. "Aye. So I am."

Lecky knew that tattoo from Cavanagh's memoirs. "You were the boatswain aboard the *Artful* when he took the French schooner *Chandenque* off the coast of Alexandria." Cavanagh's raid on the *Chandenque* had been one of the Welsh privateer's most risky—and most brilliant.

"Seems you know my captain's memoirs, all right."

"I've spent time in North Africa," Lecky said. "I know what it's like. Miss Rachel wants to visit Alexandria, too. She wants to walk where her father did, see the last things he saw." That brought the coachman's attention round. A frown creased the man's brow.

"I want her safe as much as you do. I want to keep her safe," Lecky said, in no uncertain terms.

Looking down on him from the driver's box, the coachman's gaze narrowed and grew evaluative. He appeared to consider his own words before he spoke. "You know, lad, I've seen you before. You were with Miss Rachel in that coach yard at Gravesend. You're the one that in truth rescued her and the Marquess."

Ah. Below stairs gossip had been rife. What fodder had arisen after Rachel returned from Boulogne?

"I saw you walk out of that coach yard," the coachman said.

Fair play, Lecky thought. "Yes. Now you see me standing in front of her house."

The men regarded one another. The coachman's expression told Lecky that the man still wasn't won. That was a good thing; Lecky wouldn't trust the man otherwise. "If you doubt me, wait and see. When Miss Cavanagh returns, she'll want to go to Alexandria."

Still, Rhys Cavanagh's man regarded him.

"I'll leave you my details," Lecky said. "Send me word when she returns. I'll make it worth your while."

CHAPTER EIGHTEEN

We go away to return with more.
—The Memoirs of Rhys Cavanagh

Glamorgan, Wales
March 1818

WALES. AFTER NEARLY SIX MONTHS abroad, Rachel was home. Very soon, she and her maid, Ruby, would arrive at the Cavanagh estate.

Ruby was resting. The day had been long, first with their arrival in Bristol on the brig that had conveyed them from New York, then with the voyage on a much smaller vessel across the Bristol Channel to Cardiff, where they met the Cavanagh carriage. Rachel had hoped her family would greet them in Cardiff, but the overjoyed face of Jack Cobham—the coachman's ten-year-old son—helped make up for their absence.

Rachel propped her elbow on the window frame of the carriage and rested her chin on her hand. Outside the carriage window, the road she knew so well wound along the Glamorgan coast. Across the Bristol Channel, in a view so familiar to her heart, the last light of dusk was fading.

Wales. When it came to seeing her family again, she was both nervous and hopeful. It would be wonderful to hear their news. Juliet was due to give birth soon, having fallen pregnant almost immediately after her wedding. And Rachel too had dozens of stories to share. How interested they would all be, she wasn't certain. She *hoped* that time may have helped them to accept her decision not to marry Rossum.

At first, they'd been furious. Rachel had weathered a barrage of recrimination, not least over the 'coarse brute' in whose company Faith had discovered her at the Lord Nelson. The situation had not improved when they learned the 'coarse brute' was in fact responsible for saving her life. Her mother's fury turned to iciness, cold stares and disapproval.

It hurt. It hurt a great deal.

After a month, that disapproval had showed no sign of abating. Once more, she'd felt Ariene's absence acutely.

Then Elizabeth Wilston's heart-twisting letter had arrived, thanking Rachel for sending word of her daughter's death.

The daughter Elizabeth Wilston had never known. And at that moment, Rachel knew where the path she had chosen would start.

She declared her intention to travel to America. *To meet Ariene's mother.*

She would be forever grateful that she had.

With Ruby for companionship, Rachel had boarded the New York–bound brig one week after she turned one and twenty. On the other side of the Atlantic, she had met a woman who had been forced by her controlling husband to make an impossible decision.

The decision between leaving four children forever, or remaining with one.

Such had been the legacy of the young Elizabeth Wilston's affair with a dashing ship captain who—unlike her much older husband—had shown her warmth. In the years since the affair, the grief of not knowing her youngest daughter had long grafted its place in the American woman's heart.

It was grief Rachel had not been prepared for: the realization that *every day* for thirty-five years, Elizabeth Wilston had thought about, wondered about, the life and well-being of the daughter she had never known.

Rachel was no substitute for Ariene. Still, she hoped that the many stories that she had shared with Elizabeth of Ariene's life had brought the American woman some happiness. Certainly, sharing those stories had helped Rachel. It had been ... a celebration ... to share those moments with someone so avid, so hungry to absorb each and every snippet of the life that Ariene had lived. It had been a celebration that, in totally unexpected ways, felt so *right*.

THE LAST LIGHT OF DUSK

It had felt right because it had helped turn Ariene's death into something else. Something less focused on tragedy and far more wondrous. For each story was a reminder of all the ways Ariene had *lived*.

A feeling of wellness and love lodged in Rachel's heart.

It was difficult to explain how the last seven months had changed her. There was a confidence that came with making all her own decisions, of course; but what she felt went beyond confidence. Within, she felt settled. The months she had spent in New York with Elizabeth Wilston had been some of the most wonderful of her life. She had met Ariene's half-brothers and half-sisters and their extended family and friends. She had visited museums and art galleries and attended social engagements. She had completed dozens of sketches of the buildings and the port and the markets and the city's inhabitants.

She had completed those sketches in her journal, which featured a patchwork cover, sewn from a mix of pecan and rosewood leathers. A journal she'd acquired in France.

There were moments, too, down by the docks, when she caught a glimpse of a black and white dog. The first time, her heart had given a start—but it wasn't Morgan. The boat captain and his collie had not come after her. But she refused to dwell on those thoughts. She would *always* be grateful to Jonathon for broadening her horizons last summer; she would not let thoughts of 'what might have been' narrow them.

If he *wanted* to be part of her life, he would be. If he did not, then she was grateful for the things they had shared. The things that ultimately had led her here. From Gravesend to France and America and back.

Whether she was exploring New York or roaming the ships that had conveyed Ruby and her across the Atlantic, she had used every day to learn something new.

What more would she learn, she wondered, when she traveled to Alexandria? She knew now it was no longer a choice. She *had* to visit her father's final resting place. She felt that pull inside.

The offer made to her by the American diplomat, Mr. Johnston, played on her mind. She had met Mr. Johnston and his daughter, Henrietta—or 'Etta' as the young woman preferred to be called—

on her homeward voyage. Etta and Rachel were the same age, and swiftly the two became friends. Etta was accompanying her widowed father on his diplomatic posting to Egypt. When she had learnt of Rachel's desire to travel to Alexandria, Etta had begged Rachel to join them, an offer her father supported. "I would *so* love the company of another woman," Etta had explained. "And it would be perfect for you. You will be a member of our party. You will fall under Papa's protection. No one can question the appropriateness of your escort."

Indeed, traveling with the Johnstons *would* be perfect. Not only would she have companionship, she could also learn a great deal. She could not assume control of her portion of the Cavanagh shipping interests for another four years, yet in that time, there was much she could learn. The American diplomat's position was such that accompanying Mr. Johnston and his daughter would provide hereto unknown insights into the world of international commerce. As Etta had said when Rachel talked to her about her desire to actively participate in the family business, "Father has so many business contacts vying for his attention, you cannot help but benefit."

The only thing that had stopped Rachel from accepting was timing. The Johnstons were to depart from London in a month, following a short stay in England. Rachel needed to spend time with her family and hopefully repair the rift.

The carriage slowed to turn off the country road and pass through the Cavanagh gates. Gently, Rachel nudged Ruby awake. She smiled as Ruby rubbed her eyes and sat up quickly, the maid's drowsiness quickly replaced by excitement. Ruby too had grown up on the Cavanagh estate. Her father had been one of Rhys Cavanagh's men.

"You must go to your mama and papa as soon as we arrive," Rachel said. "And tomorrow, you must take the day off to spend time with them."

"Thank you, Miss Rachel." Ruby clasped Rachel's hands and gave them a squeeze, her big, cornflower-blue eyes thankful and conveying a message both women understood. Ruby was Mary's younger sister, and her parents would be relieved by their youngest daughter's safe return. Struck by the moment and thoughts of

THE LAST LIGHT OF DUSK

Mary, Rachel returned the squeeze. She saw the sheen of tears spring to Ruby's eyes and felt moisture in her own. Then both women broke away to look out the carriage window, waiting for their first glimpse of the Jacobean mansion that was home.

At first, Rachel had been reluctant to take Ruby with her. She hadn't thought she could bear the guilt should misfortune befall them. But it was Ruby's mother who told Rachel to put such thoughts from her head. "Just like you, Ruby grew up hearing talk of all the wondrous places her Pa sailed with Captain Cavanagh. I know what you're thinking, Miss Rachel, and I thank you for it. But don't deprive my girl when she so wants to go."

The carriage came to a halt in front of the house. Rachel craned her neck up at the fanciful pilasters that, in the soft glow of lantern light, framed the entrance way.

Her heart filled as the warm sense of returning home flooded through her.

This might not be where I end up. But it is where I am from.

Her brother strode down the steps as Rachel and Ruby alighted from the carriage.

"Rachel! Welcome home."

At the sight of her elder brother, the fullness in her heart felt ready to burst. "Hugh!"

She buried her face against his chest as he enfolded her in a hug.

Finally, he rested his hands on her shoulders and set her at arm's length. "Let me see if America has changed you." He looked her up and down, then smiled. "Well, you still *look* like my sister. If anything, a more dashing version, perhaps. Faith will covet that cloak."

Rachel smiled in turn. Her new, dark plum woolen cloak was indeed very dashing. "Have you heard how Juliet is progressing?"

"Well, by all accounts. She still has a month before the little one is due." Hugh smiled at Rachel's lady's maid. "Hello, Ruby. Welcome home."

"Hello, Mr. Cavanagh. Thank you." Ruby bobbed in a curtsey.

"Ruby!" The cry came from Ruby's mother, who spilled onto the steps, followed by her father. "My little girl is home!"

"Mama!" Ruby cried, as she was gathered up in her parents'

arms.

Tears stung the corner of Rachel's eyes as Ruby, swamped by her parents, simultaneously laughed and cried.

Hugh smiled and slid his arm around Rachel's shoulders. Together, they watched Ruby and her family's reunion. "Rest assured that Juliet is in good hands," Hugh said, "with so many of Kersley's female relatives to fuss over her."

Sir William *did* have a lot of female relatives.

"And Andrew? How is he?" Of all her siblings, she knew her youngest brother would have most loved New York. She had received one letter from him while she had been away, describing his first impressions of university, which he'd commenced the previous autumn.

"I should like to *think* he is studying," Hugh replied. "But I don't rightfully know. Shall we go inside?"

"Let's," Rachel concurred, and Hugh wheeled her toward the main door. She craned her neck as they entered the entry hall to take in the high ceiling and the grand mahogany staircase, which, at the first landing, broke into two staircases—one that rose to the right and one that rose to the left. How many times had she returned home to see her grandfather casually leaning over the balustrade, shouting some instruction down? Or heard Ariene and her sisters' laughter echo in the entry hall? That inexplicable feeling hit her once more, the feeling of home. But it was more than that. She had walked into a hall filled with the spectres of history—the spectre of memories. She could picture all of them there. Ariene and Rachel's sisters with their parasols, ready to take a summer's stroll to the beach. Rhys Cavanagh making his way down the stairs, laughing with his old seafaring friends. Lady Georgiana hurrying through the hall, headed for her coach. Those moments lived in this hall—they lived over and over again—whether their manifestation was still of this world or not.

Speaking of which, there was some of this world she still had not seen. "And mother and Faith?" Rachel asked. "They are here?" She peered hopefully toward the top of the stairs, but Hugh stopped and slid his arm from her shoulder, looking surprised.

"No. Did Cobham not tell you? Mother and Faith received an invitation to the Earl of Aspinall's house party in Herefordshire.

They accepted, naturally."

Yes. *Naturally.* Rachel was pierced by a swift shaft of disappointment. Lady Georgiana and Faith had known she would be arriving home, and while ship schedules were not precise... Rachel and Ruby *had* reached Bristol on schedule. "Will they return soon?"

"Not for a sennight at least," Hugh replied. "The party only began today."

This time, she felt his words as a slap. *Today*? The party began *today*? In Herefordshire, only two counties away? Could they not have delayed their travel by *one day* to see her?

She felt as though she'd just tasted a bad apothecary's remedy.

"Not upset, are you?" Hugh eyed her. "Mother expected you to understand."

"Oh, I understand." That didn't lessen the hurt. *You knew the consequences of your choice*, she had to remind herself. *You knew it would be difficult for them to accept.*

But would it always be like *this*? Was this what she must trade for choosing her own path? Suddenly, she appreciated Hugh's presence all the more. "Thank you for being here, Hugh."

Hugh laughed. "Thank the Earl of Aspinall. Had I been included on the invitation, you might have found the place empty!" Her expression must have betrayed her dismay, because he added, "Oh, come now; I was *jesting*. Shall we adjourn to the drawing room and partake in a glass of Madeira to celebrate your homecoming?"

"Yes." Rachel released a pent breath. She had been too sensitive to his jape. "I'd enjoy that."

Hugh took her arm and began leading her up the stairs. "Your room has been made up."

"You mean Ariene's cottage?" In Rachel's last letter home, she had asked her mother to have the staff air the cottage she had inherited.

"No." Hugh's brow creased. "Mother thought you'd be more comfortable staying with the rest of the family."

Indeed. With the rest of the family. *Who weren't at home.*

Take a deep breath, Rachel. Don't be upset. She knew she should have sent the request direct to Mrs. Pymble, the housekeeper. Instead she had hoped . . . .

She had hoped that if her mother issued the instructions, it might just be a sign of acceptance.

"I see. Thank you, Hugh." She would not criticize Lady Georgiana in front of Hugh. Nor would she tell Hugh that she would not sleep in her old room. The feelings her mother's decision aroused she would deal with later, in private. She smiled and slipped her arm around his waist as they continued up the stairs. "I can't wait to hear about everything that has happened while I've been gone."

"I HEARD YOU INTEND TO open Ariene's cottage after all. Do you plan to hire staff?"

Hugh's voice sounded from behind Rachel as he entered the breakfast room. His words were spoken casually . . . . Still, Rachel tensed. Briefly closed her eyes. She had known that it would not take long for her instructions to Mrs. Pymble to reach him.

They had spoken long into the previous evening. It had been a good conversation. Even so, she doubted her decision would be popular.

Steeling herself, she turned from her place by the window, where she had been nursing her warm cup of tea as she gazed out over the Bristol Channel. She had always loved the view offered by this room: the dip of the green fields and woodland of the Cavanagh estate plunging down to the rocky coast.

"Good morning, Hugh." She watched as he poured a steaming cup of coffee from the pot on the buffet and settled at the breakfast table. "To answer your question, yes, I intend to live there."

"I see." Hugh frowned as he picked up a spoon and stirred sugar into his coffee.

She had stayed up half the night coming to terms with Lady Georgiana's absence—her mother's very clear message of disapproval. It was no wonder Rhys Cavanagh and Lady Georgiana's relationship had been so abrasive. The privateer had always been one for direct confrontation. The daughter of the Earl of Whittlesey preferred to relay her messages by more oblique means.

Well, the Cavanagh blood in Rachel was coming to the fore. "Is something the matter, Hugh? Is it a problem that I should live in a cottage I inherited?"

Her brother glanced up, again with a frown. He was clearly debating his words.

"I didn't want to say anything last night, but we are ... concerned for you, Rachel."

"I would prefer that you were happy for me."

"You rejected the finest match you are ever likely to make. Rossum *loved you*, for goodness sake." He dragged the newspaper across the table toward him in apparent frustration. "I am dreading the day you realize you made a mistake."

Mistake? Hugh still thought she'd made a *mistake*? After everything she had told him about her trip to meet Elizabeth Wilston? About what New York had meant?

She tried to rein in her anger. Still, her teacup clunked against the saucer as she set both down on the breakfast table. "I love Rossum as the dearest of *friends*. That's why it would have been a mistake *had* I married him."

Hugh expelled a breath. "I don't see the problem." He came to his feet slowly, as though he carried a great weight on his shoulders. He rested one fist against the breakfast table as he set his shoulders back. He was, after all, the head of the family.

"God above, Rachel. *Someone* has to say this to you. We all know how close you were to Ariene. We know how hard you took her death. But you don't need to forego your own happiness because *she* died."

Blood rushed to her ears. Her mouth dropped open. How could Hugh *say* such a thing? Is that what he really thought?

"Rachel," Hugh continued. "You don't need to emulate her life because she didn't have the opportunity to live hers to the full."

Ariene *had* lived her life to the full; it was the duration that had been cut short. But that was not the point. "Is that what you think I've done? Laid myself on the sacrificial alter of grief? Denied myself a life as a marchioness out of *guilt*?"

"Haven't you?" Hugh asked. "Rachel, you traveled to America to meet Ariene's mother. You intend to move into Ariene's cottage. I can only presume—since you rejected Rossum—that you intend to live as a spinster, too."

The raft of pain in her breast came fast and hard. For a moment, she couldn't breathe. Had they listened to her six months ago when she had explained how important it was for her to go to America? Had Hugh listened, *truly listened*, to what she said last night? Or had everything she'd said been disregarded, presumed to be the product of grief?

Suddenly, she had a keen and entirely desperate desire to accept Mr. Johnston and Etta's offer to join their party to Egypt.

"I would be delighted to marry"—she strove to keep her voice level—"but it would be wrong of me to marry Rossum."

"Rachel, you are beautiful, dashing, kind and rich. None of us wishes to see your life made harder than it needs to be. You saw how Ariene was received. For every person she charmed, three more—" Apparently, he thought better of his words. "Well, they didn't understand her," he finished.

Neither did you or mother, Rachel thought.

"The ability to charm a quarter of the population is hardly disappointing," Rachel pointed out. "Half the members of Parliament only dream of charming so many."

Hugh made an exasperated sound. "What I am saying, Rachel, is that you don't need to continuously carry this . . . this . . . *guilt* or whatever it is. You don't need to live someone else's life."

His words ricocheted inside her, ripping small wounds. She took a deep breath. It was temporary balm to the hurt she suddenly needed to absorb in private. "No, Hugh. You are right. I wouldn't wish to live *somebody else's* life." She snatched up her shawl, which was hanging over the back of one of the dining chairs, and drew it around her shoulders. "You'll excuse me. You've given me so much to think about."

"Rachel—" Hugh began as she started for the door.

She spun around, her palms held up. "Hugh . . . *don't*. I'm telling you . . . just *don't*."

CHAPTER NINETEEN

*To sail anywhere, man must catch the right wind. But how far will
we let that wind take us?*
—*The Memoirs of Rhys Cavanagh*

RACHEL STARED AT THE MISSIVE she had received from her mother that morning. Lady Georgiana had made her wait four days for a response to the note Rachel had sent, which was far longer than it *needed* to take, given Cobham had been waiting at the Earl of Aspinall's estate to return with her mother's reply.

> *I am pleased to hear you are home. Your sister and I will be continuing directly from Herefordshire to Oxfordshire to await the birth of Juliet's child, following which we will remove to London. You are welcome to join us in London for the remainder of the season.*

Rachel could read between the lines. The expectation was that Rachel *would* join her mother and Faith for the season. Now that Rachel had had her American adventure, she was welcome if she accepted the role Lady Georgiana planned for her.

Her wrist fell slack against the arm of the drawing room sofa. Her mother's words never failed to hurt, yet her blood was beginning a slow boil. Her mother was asserting her dominance. She would be pleased to have Rachel's company so long as Rachel conformed to Lady Georgiana's expectations.

Lady Georgiana might believe exclusion would wear Rachel down and bring her back into the fold. In reality, her mother's tactics were having the opposite effect. Mr. Johnston and Etta's offer had played over in her mind the past four days as she roamed the Cavanagh estate. She loved home, its memories, and the view to the Bay of Bristol and the estate's rocky shoreline and stands of broad-leaved woodlands.

She'd flicked through her sketchbook, too. At the beginning, always, were the drawings she'd completed in Boulogne. The market by the Church of St. Nicholas. The Château de Boulogne-sur-Mer, with its decorative archway that led to the moat bridge. There was a picture of Emily sitting on the château's battlements in her medieval gown at sunrise, which Rachel had drawn from memory. So too, a certain Boulogne-sur-Mer shipyard.

She'd never been able to bring herself to sketch the boat captain whose ship was being built there. Not after what had happened in Gravesend.

Next in her sketchbook came shipboard life, then New York, then shipboard life once more. There were drawings of sailors performing various tasks and of the Johnstons relaxing on the deck with the other passengers. As she gazed upon those drawings, she could feel their expanded horizons as though she were still there.

It lived within her chest, that feeling of standing before miles of sea, beneath the open expanse of sky. The sense of belonging to a little patch of shipboard life in the midst of a grand ocean.

Rachel set the letter from her mother down. She had no intention of participating in the remainder of the London season. Against her every hope, it seemed that, other than bowing to Lady Georgiana's plans, she could do nothing to improve relations with her mother. Meanwhile, she had the opportunity in three weeks' time to accompany an established party to Alexandria; a kind, generous party from whom she could also learn a great deal about international diplomacy and commerce. That too was a unique opportunity—one she would not have at home under her elder brother's tutelage.

Boulogne and New York still lived within her.

She wasn't yet ready to give up her sense of the world as a larger, expanded place.

She stood and moved to the writing desk to compose a letter to the Johnstons.

Two days later, she canceled her plans to reopen Ariene's cottage and traveled to Oxfordshire to see her elder sister, Juliet. She arrived in the midst of an uproar—Juliet's baby had decided to come early.

"Rachel is here?" Juliet cried, when she heard. "I want to see her!"

Sir William's female relatives had scrambled to do her bidding, and Rachel spent the remainder of Juliet's labor at her sister's side.

Afterwards, Juliet was exhausted.

Her son was small but perfect.

Notification was dispatched to Lady Georgiana in Herefordshire, to advise of her daughter's early labor and her grandson's safe arrival.

Over the following days, Rachel spent much time talking to her sister as Juliet nursed her new child. Juliet, ever the peacemaker of the family, wanted to know what had happened in Gravesend. To date, everything Juliet had heard had come from Lady Georgiana and Faith. To say such an account was slanted redefined geometry.

Rachel began with the sinking of the *Castalia* and the true means by which she and Rossum had been rescued. She spoke of how unsettled she had felt in the months after the shipwreck and how she had struggled to come to terms with owing a man her life. She described the attraction that had sparked between her and her rescuer when they met again and the horrific moment in the coach yard of the Lord Nelson Inn, when Rachel, Jonathon, Rossum and Faith had stood in such horrible, horrible silence . . . and Jonathon had turned and departed.

Rossum had heard the sound of his footsteps moving away. "Who was here? There was someone else just here?" His tone had grown frantic. "*Rachel?*"

Rachel could remember Faith's look at that moment. The youngest Cavanagh sister might have been one of the King's Lancers, ready to run Rachel through. Livid, Faith's eyes had bored into Rachel's, demanding an explanation. Yet Rachel had known that to reveal all at that moment would only wound Rossum more. "We should go inside," Rachel had said. "We can speak inside."

Rossum, of course, knew her too well. It was unlike her not to provide a blow-by-blow description tailored especially for his benefit. Her deflection spoke more than words. "No!" he said. "What just happened here, Rachel? Your mother, your sister and I have been worried sick. Who was just here?"

Rachel's glance had flickered to Faith. Her sister's lips were set in a firm line. Rachel may as well have been floundering at sea in a dinghy, miles from shore with no wind and no oars. Finally, because they were both waiting for her answer, she'd said, "The boat captain who rescued us from the *Castalia*."

At that, the color had drained from Rossum's face. "Jonathon Lecky?" His words emerged as a whisper. "These past six days, you've been with him?"

Faith had not waited to hear Rachel's answer. She had dropped Rossum's arm and walked off. The oaken inn door slammed behind her as she disappeared inside. That slam had had the same effect as the recoil of a thirty-six pounder. It spoke of rejection. Disgust.

And Rossum—"

"How did . . . have you . . . kept in touch?"

The hurt had been plain in his voice. Not just because of his offer of marriage but because of their friendship, too. He had wished to understand whether she had kept something so significant to both of them from his knowledge.

"No." The word had sounded raw. There had been no moisture left in her throat. "No, I didn't. We met again by chance. Cauis"—his first name had come to her lips—"it's not what you think—"

Wasn't it? Even she'd had to ask herself that.

"I think you've been gone for six days. Six days during which you originally intended to be at Atherton Court. What am I to think, other than that I had a part in your . . . delay?"

Even now, seven months later, it pained her to think of the look on his face at that moment.

It pained her to speak of it to Juliet.

"You care for Rossum still," Juliet observed.

"Of course." That went without saying. "He is the best of men. But I am not the right wife for him."

"Will you see Rossum before you depart with the Johnstons?" Juliet shifted her son's weight, cooed to settle him, then looked at Rachel with concerned eyes.

"If Rossum will meet with me, yes." Rachel would offer the Marquess that choice. Whether Rossum would wish to see her was another matter. Their friendship had not avoided the rift that came with her refusal of his offer of marriage. They had not corresponded during her time in America, which was perhaps for the best. She did not want Rossum to love where that love—the same kind of love—was not returned.

"LADY GEORGIANA AND FAITH HAVE arrived, Miss Rachel," Cobham, the Cavanagh family's coachman, advised several days later when she returned to Sir William's stables following an afternoon ride.

"Thank you, Cobham," she replied, grateful for the warning. She had been steeling herself for this meeting since receiving her mother's letter in Wales. Even so, knowing she would face her mother's knives couldn't wholly prevent the hurt that would come each time her mother decided to throw one.

She wondered how they compared with African throwing knives.

She found Lady Georgiana in Juliet's sitting room, smiling and clucking as she held her first grandchild. Faith, who was perched on the sofa at Juliet's side, stood at Rachel's entrance and came to press a cool kiss to her cheek. "Rachel, welcome home."

"Rachel." Lady Georgiana motioned Rachel closer in order to do the same. Her cool lips met Rachel's cheek. With her grandson in her arms, she did not rise. "Juliet said you were here. You have decided to join us for the season, after all. I am pleased."

Rachel's gaze flickered to Juliet, who gave a minuscule shake of her head. *No, I have said nothing of your plans,* Juliet's look said. Now, however, was not the time to broach the topic. Rachel leant down to touch her finger to her nephew's cheek. "I see you have met little Thomas, mother. Is he not gorgeous?"

Despite Rachel's avoidance of the topic, it did not take long for Lady Georgiana to make her feelings known. Indeed, the topic of the London season arose the following morning as the women gathered again in Juliet's sitting room for breakfast, which enabled Juliet to rest.

"I hope you intend to call on Rossum when we reach London," Lady Georgiana said. "We have seen so little of him these past months, your sister and I miss him dreadfully."

Then you ought visit him yourself, Rachel thought.

"I hope to see him, yes," Rachel said.

"Good." Lady Georgiana poured tea into her cup. "I hope you will apologize too. What you have put that man through.... We must commission Madame Schurter to prepare your new wardrobe."

Juliet's gaze snaked to Rachel. There was no good time, Rachel was coming to realize, to inform her mother of her intentions. Nor did she want Lady Georgiana to become too caught up in plans that would never materialize.

Rachel dabbed her mouth with her napkin, then placed the linen on the table. "Mother, Faith. There will be no need to engage Madame Schurter. My visit to London will be short."

Faith grew very still. Lady Georgiana's hand paused, teacup halfway to her lips.

"Oh?" Rachel's mother asked.

"I have been invited to travel to Alexandria with an American diplomat, Mr. Johnston, and his twenty-one year old daughter, Miss Henrietta Johnston. The Johnstons journeyed aboard my ship from New York, en route to Mr. Johnston's new diplomatic posting. They have stopped this past fortnight in London and in another fortnight will travel on to Egypt via Spain."

"Is that so?" Lady Georgiana said, in a way that implied she clearly did not like what she heard.

"I wish to see where father was laid to rest, and Mr. Johnston and Henrietta are excellent—and very respectable—companions. I have accepted their invitation."

Lady Georgiana's lips drew into a line. Without saying a word, she set her teacup down, stood and left the room.

"She thought you had come to your senses," Faith said. "That you would seek to make amends with Rossum. Do you see what you have done?" Faith too stood and departed.

"Rachel, I'm sorry," Juliet said, into the silence of the sitting room.

Rachel could do naught but smile sadly. "So am I."

THE LAST LIGHT OF DUSK

ONE WEEK LATER, MATTERS HAD not improved. *She would have been better off riding in a prison cart to London,* she couldn't help but think, rather that endure the silence and stilted conversation that pervaded the Cavanagh women's carriage. To Lady Georgiana, her plans may as well have been criminal.

However, Rachel had come to realize it was not her participation in the London season that her mother wanted. It was Rachel's reconciliation with the Marquess. Lady Georgiana would not be satisfied unless Rachel had done all in her power to win Rossum back. To elevate herself to the status of marchioness and, thus, Lady Georgiana to the status of the mother of a marchioness.

Or perhaps, even more importantly, the mother-in-law of the much-loved Marquess of Rossum.

There were days Rachel couldn't help but think how much easier it would have been for them all had Rossum grown to care for Faith.

Still, she wanted to call on him—if he would receive her.

Upon their arrival in London, she dispatched Cobham with a note to the Marquess's residence in St. George's Square to ask whether her visit would be welcome. A reply came in the affirmative.

She gathered her nerve and Ruby as her escort and called at Rossum House the following day.

"Miss Cavanagh," Rossum's butler greeted her. "My lord is expecting you. He asked me to escort you to the conservatory."

Rachel parted with Ruby and followed Rossum's butler to the conservatory. She was surprised. In her mind, she'd envisaged meeting him again surrounded by the stern woodgrain paneling of the drawing room, not in the garden room where Rossum was most relaxed. The conservatory was Rossum's favorite place. He knew every plant by touch—be it the texture of a leaf or a delicate stem—or by scent. He knew their genera better than she.

She spotted his blond head behind a profusion of blooms. Suddenly, her throat turned very dry.

"Miss Cavanagh, my lord," the butler announced.

Rossum turned toward the doorway as her announcer withdrew. He was . . . Rossum. Tall, broad, perfect yet imperfect. The sight of him wrenched her heart.

"Rachel?"

"I'm here." She came forward, her footsteps on the stone floor helping him to locate her. "Good day, my lord."

He released a slow breath. "How are you?" he asked. "How was your trip?"

"All that I hoped. More than I hoped. I met Ariene's mother."

"Was she as you expected?"

"No. No, she was very different." She had learned it was perhaps too easy to judge a woman who had given her child away. "Elizabeth was...thoughtful and gracious and kind." And wounded and loving and strong. Rachel had been able to see in the older woman what Rhys Cavanagh had loved in the younger one. But those were discoveries she didn't want to elaborate on. "I...I needed to go. It was the right thing to go."

"I understand," Rossum said.

Did he? Was that possible? Of all the things Caius Atherton, the Marquess of Rossum, could have expressed, she was unprepared for *understanding*. Perhaps because part of her still carried so much guilt. She felt at a loss. Wished things could be as they were...before his proposal.

She cast about for something to say. "The geraniums are lovely." The mauve blooms overflowed from a box by the conservatory window.

"The oak-leaf geraniums? Yes. Rachel, please." He took a step forward. "I sense what you are not saying. Or perhaps, what you *want* to say."

What she *wanted* to say? She wanted to apologize. Not for the decision she'd made—her decision had been the right one. But certainly for all those aspects that she'd handled badly.

"Cauis, I am so sorry. What happened seven months ago—"

"Rachel, I know you." Rossum cut her off. "I know the dreams your head and heart hold. You are fortunate to have the resources—and courage—to chase them. Rachel, I don't want to stand in your way. And I would have, of course, because you are compassionate and loyal; and because of that, if we wed, you would never feel that you could leave me, even if I said you could."

He was right. As his wife, she wouldn't leave him.

"The last thing I would ever want to do is to limit you, Rachel.

Limit who *you* are. We both know that is why you could not marry me. And no—I don't think it is because I am blind. It is because I am beholden. To my position. To this." He raised a hand to indicate their surroundings and all that came with it.

Rossum House. The House of Lords. Each one of the marquessate's entailed estates.

While all were important, they weren't important to *her*. Not important *enough*.

"Perhaps, too," Rossum said, "you felt something stronger... with another."

Rachel frowned.

"You're frowning, aren't you? Because you don't want to agree with me, but you do?" His lips curved ever so slightly. Quietly, he asked, "Did he find you again, Rachel? The boat captain?"

"No," she said. "No. He hasn't found me again." There had been one month before she departed for America in which he might have changed his mind. He had not. When she had boarded the brig for New York, her disappointment had become resignation.

"I sensed something, even aboard his boat. There was a moment, was there not, when I came out onto the deck, the morning after the shipwreck? I interrupted something between you?"

"Conversation only."

"When a man is blind, Rachel, he becomes very attuned to the air. The air when I came onto the deck that morning was thick. Did you know I had words with him? I thought he might... take advantage. I implied he wasn't good enough for you. He said that morning that he didn't want you, but he did. Oh, he did. The same thickness lay in the air that morning in Gravesend. I don't doubt he wanted you." Rossum paused. "I don't know what his business is. I do know *both* of us are alive, due to him. But if he loves you, Rachel, and doesn't seek you out? In that case, he doesn't deserve you."

"I know." And she did. She wanted someone who would be as staunch at her side as she would be at his. Jonathon Lecky had walked away before she could ever truly know him.

That's not true, another part of her argued. Part of her

understood exactly who he was.

Before she could think twice, she reached for Rossum's hand and squeezed it in her own. "The right woman is out there for you. I am sorry I cannot be her."

Rossum returned the squeeze. "Rachel, she is very difficult to see." He sensed her frown. "A bad pun?"

"A little," she agreed.

"Ah, but that is the reason I trust you. You never lie to me. You have always remained true to yourself. No one can doubt your heart, your intentions."

"I have never wished to cause hurt."

"No. But you cannot help how people feel for you. There is much to love." He paused again. "Rachel, I've had time to think, these past months. I now know, too, as you have always done, why marriage between us would not be right. I can offer much, enough to satisfy many, but you were born with your grandfather's blood. The husband you need will unfurl the sails for you and help you catch the wind. What you have already—what you can achieve by yourself—will only expand. Your horizons will broaden, not narrow."

Was it possible for one's heart to expand and contract at the same time? How was it, Rachel wondered, that he could describe exactly the feeling she carried inside? The sense that a bigger world lay in wait for her, if she was only courageous enough to follow that path?

She had never believed Rossum would compromise her. She did believe that, with him, she would compromise herself.

"I know the challenge you face with your mother," Rossum said. "Don't let her stop you, Rachel. Unless you are Faith or Juliet, you will never please her."

"I know."

"It is fear, you realize. The feeling that things are out of her control. She couldn't stop her father from gambling the Whittlesey coffers empty. She couldn't prevent the death of your father. And she couldn't countermand Rhys Cavanagh's legal guardianship of her children. In you, she sees too much of the Cavanagh spirit. It is the same reason she is closer to Hugh than Andrew, though Andrew is a son, and so it is easier for her to blame his youth and male vigor for his waywardness." He took a breath. "Rachel, I suspect she has never felt as though you were truly hers. From the first, you were drawn away with tales of adventure the like of which she's never known nor ever wanted. Adventure brings uncertainty. Your mother strives for certainty. She can't control you, and the only weapon she ever chose to master was disapproval." He paused again. "You won't please her, Rachel. But in her own way, she will always love you. The fault doesn't lie with you. Just be you."

"Caius." Tears stung behind her eyes. Every time she'd thought of Rossum these past months, she'd felt a thick, crushing weight of guilt on her chest. Now, that was replaced with a far greater weight of *gratitude*. Gratitude that she had not been the only one to survive the loss of the *Castalia*. "Cauis Atherton," she said, "I think Jonathon Lecky granted the world a very great gift when he ensured you remained upon it."

Rossum's expression softened. "Rachel. Thank you. But I'm certain the greater gift was you."

THE NIGHT WAS OVERCAST. CLOUDS blanketed the moon and the stars. To the south of Lecky's position, the district of Deptford slumbered. The area's diffuse and silent sprinkle of lights glittered beyond the reach of the Thames, while docks spread along the waterfront. The royal dockyard, with its warehouses and five slips for building warships, lay at one end. The MacArthur and Sons shipyard lay at the other. Six miles to the west was London.

The Thames lapped quietly against the river bank and the slipway where Lecky and Blackburn stood. The vessels anchored nearby in the river were quiet, most of their crews abed. It wasn't the response of those ships Lecky or the man beside him needed to be concerned with.

No, the swiftest response would come from the adjoining shipyard, which belonged to the Navy.

"That's her?" Blackburn asked.

"That's her," Lecky agreed.

The Star.

He knew the silhouette of her masts and her rigging as though the knowledge flowed in his blood. She'd been built here. Named here. The brigantine, once fitted to carry slaves, was the pride of the MacArthur fleet. Notus knew his brother, Chaloner, had spent plenty of days and nights aboard.

Lecky had seen the vessel in action once in West Africa. He'd watched the slaves led from their pens at Bance Island and forced into rowboats for transfer to *The Star's* hull. For many, it was their death voyage.

Usually, he could appreciate all sailing vessels; he knew too well the effort it took to see them crafted and launched, how they could come to inhabit one's soul. Wanton destruction was a crime against her builders and Poseidon.

But then, in addition to his benevolence, Poseidon was known to wield brute force at times too.

The sight of *The Star's* timbers filled Lecky's gut with revulsion.

Now her hull loomed above them, her tall masts stretching like false ladders to heaven. There was no beauty there. Just the vestige of old curses, soaked into the timber decks by blood and vomit and piss and shit that had long since been washed away.

The ship had been out of the water for refit for weeks. Her timbers were dry. The shipyard's watchmen would be found later, furious and nursing bruised skulls, thanks to Blackburn's men.

And Jonas and Chaloner MacArthur and the authorities would know it was arson.

"Let's have this done," Blackburn said, and signaled to his men.

Lecky and Blackburn remained on the slipway as Blackburn's men set the brig alight from the inside, then torched her cursed decks. The flames kindled and greedily spread.

Lecky and Blackburn watched as the flames licked out the brig's gunports and climbed the base of her masts.

Lecky's nostrils filled with the acrid scent of the accompanying whorls of thick black smoke. The fierce, radiated heat of the blaze washed over his face and body, prickled his exposed skin and heated his clothes. His fingers curled. His hands became fists. The inside of his wrists began to ache with a phantom throb.

Years of memories spilled forth as he watched *The Star* burn. The boat designs he'd completed as a boy and proudly shown his father. The pride he'd taken on this dock as he hammered away with a caulking mallet. The confusion he had felt at Harrow, the first time he'd picked up an abolitionist pamphlet, which had then led him to read about African societies in the proceedings of the explorers of the African Association. Call him young or boyish or ignorant, but until that time, he'd never given much thought to his family's 'trade'.

Then there was the time he'd found his mother crying and heartbroken, when she discovered Chaloner had taken advantage of one of the young women of her staff.

There was his father's stony face when his heartbroken wife died.

So many, many moments.

The destruction of his idealism the following year in South Carolina, when he witnessed Chaloner's complete disregard for his own bastard child.

The discovery of what acts his father would permit in the name of 'business'.

The year he had spent traveling down the west coast of Africa to see for himself the truth of his father and brother's business practices. Practices they had expected him to continue.

Yes, like the past reenacted before him, he saw all those things through the thick shimmer of heat and smoke.

MacArthurs didn't forget. They didn't let go. They were not the kind that one scored a victory over. *Ever.*

It was a trait all MacArthur men shared. Jonas MacArthur had done his job well—with both his sons.

Poseidon be damned. He felt the blood pulse behind his scars as self-realization came, swift and condemning. He drew a breath, a breath that in no way compared to the shudder he felt inside.

Blast it! Elijah Winter was right.

For almost fourteen years, this feud had governed his life.

Its presence had always lain in the background, always a thought away.

He'd bought many men's freedom during his years in North Africa. Europeans, but where he could, Africans, too. But the number he'd saved wouldn't even amount to one voyage of *The Star*, carrying full cargo. He could only hope that, on some ledger, the years he'd spent and the men whose lives he'd spared had counted.

He'd purged himself of his family name and taken a new one. But never had he left his family behind. That tie led men like Henri Cox after him.

It drove those he loved away.

But then, perhaps he'd wanted it to. He hadn't wanted anyone that close. He'd been set on his path, a path that had begun on a South Carolina plantation where he had been sent following his mother's death fifteen years before. It was a path that, in the fifteen years since, had brought him back across the Atlantic to England, then to Africa, only to return to England again.

It had also been his excuse. An excuse he had clung to.

Beside Lecky, Blackburn said, "Satisfying as it is, it doesn't bring her back." The man spoke of his daughter.

No. No, it didn't. And yet Lecky had had to do this.

Their attack had been carefully planned. Not least, it had required patience.

"You made me wait a long time for this, Mr. Lecky."

Yes. Because this way, MacArthur and Sons had no options, no salvation. The damage to the Deptford Shipyard and loss of *The Star* meant they would have no choice but to renege on shipbuilding and delivery contracts they could not afford to renege on. Coupled with the uncertainty arising from the Spanish treaty to abolish the slave trade by 1820, financially, Lecky and Blackburn's act would spell the MacArthurs' destruction.

"How do you feel destroying the life's work of a dying man?" Blackburn asked. "Destroying the life's work of your *father?*"

In the MacArthur family's Spanish villa overlooking the Bay of Cadiz, Jonas MacArthur lay dying. The patriarch of the MacArthur family had removed there for the warmer clime several years ago, after the British had driven the French from Spain's borders.

How did Lecky *feel?*

"I can't see that it's a life's work to be proud of." Britain's role in the transportation of slaves had never ended, no matter the legislation passed in 1807 or the subsequent enforcement efforts of government. Even now, the British goods MacArthur and Sons shipped to Cadiz ended up in the hands of the African chieftains, traded by the Spanish in exchange for slaves to transport to their colonies. No, the MacArthurs had never gotten out of the trade.

They, like a number of other British merchants, had simply ... adapted.

Aye, let them adapt now.

The smoke of *The Star's* burning timbers grew thicker in the sky.

The MacArthurs might scrape by for a time, attempting to hold the pieces together, but they wouldn't 'adapt' to this.

How did he feel? He felt ... everything, and nothing, all at once.

He felt sated ... yet at the same time, vastly empty.

A sense of completion, yet no satisfaction.

His ship, named for his mother, *Freya*, had now launched, with Ian Lawrence at her helm. *The Star* would be no more. It was fitting that the two vessels never sailed the same seas.

It was restitution.

Perhaps it was that that he felt most deeply.

Of course, the man at his side didn't share those connections. Blackburn wanted more. The taste of reprisal had roused the look of hunger in his eyes and his jackal's smile.

He'll get his revenge regardless of whether you abet it. Such had been Winter's words.

Blackburn had agreed to wait months longer than a less cunning man might have, because he wanted to see Chaloner MacArthur suffer. And he had known this act would make Chaloner suffer. Blackburn was the type that liked to bring a man to his knees before Blackburn stood over him.

Chaloner MacArthur was on borrowed time.

Those details Lecky didn't want to know.

"Your intentions regarding Chaloner," Lecky spoke in a low voice. "I can't help you with those."

Beside him, Blackburn stilled. Then, hard and unflinching, Blackburn's gaze met his own. "Good," the man said. "Because I'm not willing to share."

Shouts rose from the direction of the naval dockyard.

"It's time to go," Blackburn said. "Lads!" he shouted to his men. "Be sure to light the warehouses as we go."

Ringing through the night from the adjacent naval dockyard, a fire bell began to toll.

LECKY'S SLOOP WAS MOORED FOUR miles downriver at Woolwich. At his return, Morgan bounded up to him, tail wagging, as though not a damned thing had changed along the stretch of Thames between London and Gravesend.

Yet everything had changed.

The scent of the burning brig still permeated Lecky's nostrils and clothes as he untied the sloop and pushed off from the mooring. With Morgan settling by his side at the tiller, he put several more miles' distance between their position and the shipyard at Deptford. Once satisfied, he dropped anchor in the Thames, then lowered his head to his hands.

Pain, quickened by a whitewash of anger, crushed his chest, squeezed his lungs, ached through his arms up to his wrists. Anger—for the young boy who had grown up building dams and floating sailboats and not understanding all that fed and clothed him. Anger—for the young man who'd traveled half the world home, clinging to beliefs, *ideals*, about his father, only to see them destroyed as surely as his mother's had been destroyed. Anger—at hurt perpetuated, at hurt he'd never been able to stop. And anger—finally—at all the ways he was just the bloody same.

"Damn it, Morgan. Damn it, girl." Some acts remained no matter how one scrubbed or what one reduced to cinders.

He slung his arms around his dog and buried his face in the fur at her nape. She twisted, concerned, and wet his ear with her nose. When she realized he just needed her to be still, she settled.

He stayed that way for a long time, breathing deeply, as years of dredged up feelings—anguish and hopelessness, detestation and loathing—washed over him. All feelings that had come before, yet this time with the benefit of hindsight—and foresight.

Finally, he released Morgan and sat up. He took another steadying breath and turned over his wrists.

The white scars shone there.

He'd been young and burning with anger. Filled with fury that had driven him down the coast of Africa, that had some-bloody-how *not* gotten him killed and—as he had told Rachel Cavanagh in Boulogne—had made him impervious to Berber daggers and African throwing knives.

Time and again down the African coast, he'd seen men and

THE LAST LIGHT OF DUSK

women in European slave factories led forward to have the marks of others burned into their skin with hot branding irons.

He'd seen it, and he'd hated from whence he came.

He'd seen it, and he'd wanted the reminder.

The reminder of what *he would not be*. What his hands *would not do*. What they *would not take*.

Already, he had taken enough.

In one single, premeditated act in a blacksmith's forge in Sierra Leone, he had seared that reminder into his skin. A reminder he'd thought he would always want.

He'd even paid the stunned blacksmith a shilling, presented him with the shiny, laureated head of King George, for the privilege.

Once again, Lecky clenched his fists.

He would always have those marks. He could never have back that smooth, unpuckered skin. The bands of white scored across the insides of his wrists had long since become a story of his life. Not the only story—but one.

One he wanted to leave in the past. Not forgotten—never forgotten—but behind. He hadn't realized that, deep within, those scars had sealed in poison.

In his Spanish villa on the Bay of Cadiz, Jonas MacArthur was dying. Lecky wasn't interested in amends or apology. Nor did he want reconciliation.

He did want one arabica-eyed, butterscotch-locked Welshwoman in his future.

In that respect, there was one thing he could do.

Notus, have mercy.

He needed to see Jonas MacArthur.

FIRST, HE RETURNED TO THE Lord Nelson Inn, where Owen Griffiths was expecting him. Busy moving casks behind the counter, the innkeeper straightened as Lecky entered the public room. He wiped his hands on the cloth that was slung over his shoulder and directed his gaze at Lecky.

"So . . . ?" Owen said.

Lecky set his hands on the closest table to the counter and sank into a chair. In the pre-noon hour, the public room was otherwise empty. "So." Morgan settled at his feet.

Owen studied him. "You look like hell and smell worse."

"Hell is where I've come from."

"Ale?"

"Yes."

Owen took up a tankard, moved to a cask and turned on the tap. "Is Blackburn happy?"

"I would say Blackburn is feeling somewhat avenged."

"And you?"

The look Owen cast his way was keen.

How was *he*? How did one answer that? Lecky gave a little snort and rested his chin in his hand. "Where's that ale?"

The innkeeper came around the counter and set the tankard down. "A letter came for you."

Caught off guard by the tidings, Lecky sat a little straighter. "Oh?"

Few contacted him at the inn, and there was only one he was waiting on.

"Aye. It came this morning." Owen presented an envelope.

The innkeeper watched as Lecky cracked open the seal and extracted the page inside. His glance went first to the signature at the bottom.

Joseph Cobham. Rhys Cavanagh's man.

Lecky's pulse accelerated. Swiftly, he read the content of the letter.

Poseidon be damned.

At first he sat in stunned silence. Then a laugh rose in his throat.

Weren't the fates bloody apt?

Poseidon and Notus and Zephyrus be damned.

All roads led to Cadiz.

CHAPTER TWENTY

It's a man's deeds, not his name, that determines who he is.
—*The Memoirs of Rhys Cavanagh*

"Rachel, Rachel! We're to make port in two hours!" In an effusion of the latest fashion, acquired during the Johnstons' month-long London stay, Etta Johnston arrived at the ship's rail, a parasol over her shoulder. Beneath her bonnet, strands of midnight-brown hair escaped and her large, blue-gray eyes shone. Enthusiasm was, after all, a sentiment the American diplomat's daughter regularly dispensed. Any person stuffy enough to find her jubilance unrefined was quickly charmed by the receptiveness of her smile.

"I can't wait to arrive in Cadiz!" The skin at the corner of Etta's eyes crinkled as she looked down to see what Rachel was working on. "Oh, let me see! Another drawing of father and I? That one is *lovely*. They're *all* lovely. I shall have to buy them from you, you know."

"You needn't buy a single one," Rachel laughed up at her. "This is what traveling is all about. Meeting new friends."

"Show me the picture of your English friend again," Etta said.

Rachel flicked back through the pages to the sketch of Emily, sitting on the battlements of the Château de Boulogne-sur-Mer in her medieval gown.

"That one is my favorite," Etta said. "She's breathtakingly beautiful, yet you've captured something more. Something solitary and wistful."

"Yes." Rachel pressed her hand to the page. She thought of

Emily often. They had exchanged letters, but Rachel hadn't received one for some months. She'd written to Emily before she left London, but her stay in the city was so brief, there was no time to receive a reply.

Sometimes opportunities happen so unexpectedly, chances are missed.

She had told Emily of her plans. She'd even listed the ship she and the Johnstons would sail aboard and the dates and the hotel at which they intended to stay in Cadiz. As she'd addressed the envelope and waited for the seal to set, she couldn't help but wonder if part of her hoped Emily would pass that information along to a certain master shipbuilder and boat captain.

If he loves you, Rachel, and doesn't seek you out? In that case, he doesn't deserve you.

It was up to Jonathon Lecky to decide whether he wanted to be a part of her life . . . . And if he didn't, well, she reasoned, the fates had something else in store for them.

She tucked a stray strand of her own wind-whipped hair behind her ear and, with it, brushed such thoughts away. Summoning a grin, she looked up at Etta, who smiled softly, then turned to look at the bow.

Rachel followed Etta's gaze as the breeze skated over her skin and ruffled the cloth of Etta's parasol and the trimmings of both women's gowns and bonnets.

Yes, she had made the right decision to come. She needed the open space and air around her. Air that had grown warmer, even though it was still spring, as their ship traveled south, past the tip of Portugal and toward the Strait of Gibraltar.

She thought of the letter she had received from her younger brother, Andrew, on the morning of their departure from England. In stark contrast to the rest of the family, he'd expressed his 'untold jealousy' at her next adventure. She was so grateful that his missive had arrived in the nick of time. It was nice to know that at least one of her siblings truly understood.

In two hours' time, this leg of the journey would be over. Rachel and the Johnstons would spend the next week in Cadiz, where Mr. Johnston would meet with various traders and dignitaries while they awaited the ship that would take them onward to the Mediterranean and Alexandria.

"Ah, Andalusia," Etta breathed, twirling the handle of her parasol. "I cannot wait to see the watchtowers of Cadiz. How many flags do you think will be flying, Rachel? A hundred? More?"

There were more, they discovered an hour later, when the Andalusian city came into view. The flags of the merchant families of Cadiz flew atop watchtowers that crowned the city, the architecture of which had been influenced by North Africa.

But these were not municipal watchtowers. No, these watchtowers decorated people's homes. There were dozens of them, square in shape and symbolic of prosperity. From the watchtowers' heights, their merchant owners could watch the arrival of their ships in port without the need to leave the comfort of home. The watchtowers provided a distinctive silhouette to a city whose prosperity truly derived from international commerce. Affluent, opulent, Cadiz lay at the heart of Spanish trade with Africa and the West Indies.

Of course, there was a dark side underlying such opulence. For while British- and American-owned ships no longer carried slaves, the trade continued in Spain.

For another two years that was, assuming Britain's recently signed treaty with the King of Spain to abolish the slave trade was upheld.

"Who is greeting us today, Etta?" Mr. Johnston asked, arriving at his daughter's side.

"Mr. MacArthur, father. A relation of mother's cousin William. You will recall he is the one who owns the large English shipbuilding and trading firm, whose shipyard we visited in London." Etta had taken over the role of hostess and keeper of her father's schedule since the death of her mother, five years before.

"Ah. The brother of cousin William's wife, am I correct?"

"Yes. Quite."

Mr. Johnston winked at Rachel. "Such is the life of a dignitary, my dear. There's always someone to welcome you in every port."

"Yes, there's always *someone*," Etta agreed, her tone holding an uncharacteristic lack of enthusiasm, "whether one likes it or not."

"Oh, now, tut-tut, my dear," Mr. Johnston said. To Rachel he explained, "My wife, Caroline, Etta's mother, was from the South.

Her cousins own several large plantations in South Carolina, near Charleston."

"Mother's cousin William married an Englishwoman. The daughter of one of his business associates," Etta added. "Her brother now lives here in Spain." The young American woman noted Rachel's curious look. "If I appear less than enthusiastic, it is because I don't particularly like William's wife. So I doubt I will particularly like the woman's brother."

"You haven't yet met the man, my dear. It's quite unlike you to be so judgmental," Mr. Johnston said.

"True. Perhaps it's just that I don't like the way they do things in the South. If not for the fact William is mother's cousin, I doubt I would wish to spend any time with him either."

"My daughter is very much the abolitionist," Mr. Johnston told Rachel. He looked at Etta fondly. "Ah, my girl, it is a good thing you are a diplomat's daughter. Especially here."

Here, where so many livelihoods were derived from the trade of human merchandise, Mr. Johnston meant.

"A diplomat's daughter?" As she gazed upon her father, Etta's expression softened. "I am that, Papa. And I shall be on my best behavior, of course." She looked out over the port to the city to release a sigh. "There is no denying that Cadiz is magnificent."

RACHEL AND THE JOHNSTONS DISEMBARKED, accompanied by Mr. Johnston's valet and the women's two lady's maids, among whom an excited Ruby numbered. "Oh, no, miss! You're not going off on another adventure without me!" Ruby had declared, when Rachel had told her three weeks ago that she had accepted the Johnstons' offer. Now, the two women exchanged a grin; and Rachel, feeling a rising tide of excitement, turned to scan the dock.

With its North African and Mediterranean influences, this dock looked and felt and smelled different from the docks of London, or France, or New York. This dock brimmed with native Andalusians and foreigners: Genoese, French, English, Dutch . . . .

But it was the sight of the man pushing through the throng towards their small party that suddenly left her breathless and immobilized with shock.

Her heart locked in her chest. At first, she thought it was Jonathon Lecky.

But it wasn't, she saw as he drew closer. This man was older. Eight, perhaps ten, years older than Jonathon. Yet for all his trimmed hair and shaven face, the likeness was powerful. His eyes met hers, and his eyes widened as he detected her reaction—her shock and surprise impossible to disguise. As his gaze moved over her, she saw a sudden, undisguised, masculine flare of curiosity.

It caught her off guard, his likeness to the boat captain and the look she saw in his eyes.

Etta noted her distress. "Is something the matter?"

The man was too close. There was no time to answer before he came to a halt before them and graced them with a smile.

"Mr. Johnston and party, is it? In the correspondence I received, I was told to look for an exceptionally good-looking senior gentleman with a penchant for blue waistcoats."

Mr. Johnston cast a look from under his wooly brows at Etta, who smiled, unapologetic.

"You do have a penchant for wearing blue waistcoats, father."

"This is true. And I should be grateful that my daughter thinks me exceptionally handsome. However, I think you are taking quite a chance, my dear, in hoping others will identify me by that descriptor." Mr. Johnston turned back to the newcomer. "Mr. MacArthur, may we presume? Brother of Amelia?"

The man before them smiled again. "That is so."

The men bowed their heads to one another.

MacArthur.... The name lodge in Rachel's mind. She found herself compiling his every similarity to Jonathon as Mr. Johnston introduced him to Etta.

My eldest sister married a South Carolinian, a business associate of our father's. The rest spend their time between England and Spain.

The rest?

My father, brother, and four other sisters.

This man's sister had married a South Carolinian. This man resided in Spain. *MacArthur*, the Johnston's had called him. They were different in name, yet so strong in resemblance. Surely, the two men had to be some manner of relation? Was the man before her Jonathon's brother?

Although similar to the boat captain in height and looks, this man was refined where Jonathon Lecky was rugged. His skin was not so deeply tanned, his build slimmer albeit still fit.

This man, Rachel sensed, was a businessman, an administrator. Not a sailor or master shipbuilder.

They both had gray eyes that were equally sharp. Yet as he exchanged pleasantries with Mr. Johnston and Etta, MacArthur's failed to convey the same warmth. The creases at the corners were not etched as deeply as those of another man she knew. Oh, MacArthur had charm; it was there as he smiled at the American dignitary and his daughter, yet she couldn't shake the feeling it was window-dressing, rather than something that ran deeper and surfaced naturally.

His was not the type of magnetism that had radiated from Jonathon Lecky when she first saw him in the sloop's companionway, disheveled from the bluster of wind and the spray of waves, compelling and alive and elemental.

No, this man's magnetism—if you could call it that—felt crafted.

Do they want to find you?

Oh, yes, sweetheart. They want to find me. Very much.

I can't keep you safe.

She missed whatever her companions were saying. Missed it, that was, until Mr. Johnston turned her way. "Mr. MacArthur, may I introduce you to Miss Cavanagh, a family friend who is traveling with us?"

"You may."

His silver gaze swung to her, and suddenly she was filled with a feeling of cold like the whip of the wind off the Bristol Channel. Her legs felt remarkably unsteady. She clutched her reticule before her. "Mr. MacArthur, how do you do?"

Although she tried not to betray herself, she knew by the sharp light of his eyes that he'd again noticed her lapse of composure. "I am delighted, Miss Cavanagh. May I ask... you are not any relation to *the* Cavanagh family, are you? As in, Rhys Cavanagh, the famous privateer?"

"I am. Rhys Cavanagh was my grandfather, Mr. MacArthur."

THE LAST LIGHT OF DUSK

There was no way around it. She knew with that response, her value—and his interest—climbed upwards.

"We must talk more, Miss Cavanagh. But, of course, you are here for a week, and so we shall have the opportunity. Mr. Johnston, I trust your party can still attend dinner on Thursday evening?"

Mr. Johnston cast a look to Etta, the keeper of his diary.

"Indeed, Mr. MacArthur. That is what we had planned," Etta replied.

"Wonderful." MacArthur gave a nod. "Now, let me escort you to your lodgings. The Hotel Argantonio is an excellent establishment. Please, I have a coach waiting and a cart for your baggage." He led them through the throng of merchants, travelers and sailors to a medium-sized coach, whose coachman opened the door as they approached. "Please, ladies, Mr. Johnston, make yourself comfortable," Mr. MacArthur said. "It is only a short distance to your hotel."

Rachel accepted the coachman's hand up, following Etta and Mr. Johnston into the carriage. As she settled into her seat, her glance was caught by a commotion developing on the dock behind their escort. From the direction of the street, a young woman was pressing through the throng towards the carriage.

She was not the only one who noticed.

"My goodness, look at that poor girl." Etta frowned. "She looks terribly upset."

Rachel, Mr. Johnston, and Mr. MacArthur looked toward the girl.

Etta was right. She did look upset.

She was also exceedingly pregnant.

More curious was Mr. MacArthur's response. A flash of something—anger?—passed over his features. "I'm sorry," he told Rachel and the Johnstons. "Excuse me for one moment." He turned and pushed through the throng to intercept the girl. She halted at the sight of him. For a few seconds, her expression collapsed into one of relief.

Then he spoke. His back was to the carriage, his words low and out of earshot. One second later, all that relief was gone.

Whatever he said left her stunned, a portrait of stillness amid the bustle of the port. A portrait of *distinctive* stillness as MacArthur turned away, for the girl was most assuredly British. Unlike the Andalusian women with their olive skin and dark hair, she was exceedingly pale, small and blonde. In her crumpled day dress, alone and pregnant in the midst of the Spanish port, she didn't belong.

Etta was frowning more deeply. "Do you think that girl needs help? Papa?"

"I don't know, my dear." Mr. Johnston's expression matched that of his daughter.

The girl looked ready to faint. Rachel's fingers curled around the door frame. "She certainly needs help of some kind."

Mr. MacArthur's shadow fell over the carriage doorway. "I am sorry for the interruption," he said as he climbed inside and pulled closed the door. "Let us carry on."

"Mr. MacArthur, what is the matter with that girl?" Mr. Johnston asked.

"Ah." The Englishman's glance passed over Rachel and Etta. "I did not wish to say, but she believes one of my sailors is responsible for her condition. Unfortunately, she is not above making a scene."

"*Was* one of your sailors responsible for her condition?" Etta asked.

Despite promising to be on her best behavior, at times, the diplomat's daughter displayed all the brashness Americans were so famed for.

MacArthur bestowed upon Etta a patient—and Rachel thought somewhat patronizing—smile. "Forgive my words, Miss Johnston, for they are hardly delicate—I understand any number of men could have been responsible for her condition."

"You are quite correct, Mr. MacArthur. That is hardly a delicate thing to say." Etta's glance flickered back to the girl. "Look at the poor lass. She's barely out of the schoolroom. Does she have food? Lodging? Do you know if there is something we might do to help her?"

"A philanthropist, are you, Miss Johnston?" Mr. MacArthur smiled. "How very American."

"I should like to think I am a good *Samaritan*, Mr. MacArthur," Etta replied. "That girl might have her baby at any moment. She is

THE LAST LIGHT OF DUSK

clearly under great stress."

The girl in question was staring at the carriage as though its departure meant the end of her hopes, the end of her life. Her glance met Rachel's, and the agony that flashed across her delicate features pierced as keenly as a whetted blade, a blade that carried her pain.

Rachel's gut lurched. No one could see that look and not act. She grasped the door handle. "We need to stop—"

Outside the carriage, the pregnant girl had already placed a supporting hand beneath her belly and was shouldering her way back through the crowd.

"We need to go after her," Etta said.

But the girl was gone.

"CADIZ TRULY *IS* MAGNIFICENT," SAID Etta several hours later. Weary from exploring the city, the young American woman and Rachel slid their bodies into the empty chairs at Mr. Johnston's table at the small, street side restaurant adjoining their hotel. "Alas, I cannot help looking for that young girl everywhere we go."

Mr. Johnston lowered his newspaper to look at his daughter. "The pregnant girl from the port?" he clarified.

"Yes," Etta replied as she dragged off her bonnet and set it on the table. "The look on her face after Mr. MacArthur spoke to her. I cannot get it out of my mind. Such absolute dejection and . . . shock. I think he must have been quite cruel."

They are not nice people, Rachel. Jonathon's words came back to her.

"I see Mr. MacArthur has not helped his cause," Mr. Johnston said.

"My disinclination to like him, you mean? That's true." Etta frowned. "I thought his response quite odd, to not lend aid to a young countrywoman. But then, one only needs to consider his family's history, and I *am* predisposed to dislike him. How did he strike you, Rachel?"

It had been MacArthur's likeness to Jonathon that had struck her. A likeness that had left her puzzled and distracted as she and Etta explored the narrow streets and plazas of Cadiz. Puzzled and distracted and *upset*, but not yet ready to confide in Etta.

The man had, after all, walked out of her life eight months ago.

Where are they now? she had asked of his family when she was with him in Boulogne.

The rest spend their time between England and Spain.

Spain. She had never asked what his family's interests were in Spain.

"What is Mr. MacArthur's family history?" Rachel asked Etta. "You said earlier they are shipbuilders and traders?"

"Yes," Mr. Johnston responded. "The MacArthurs own a large shipyard at Deptford, outside London. Cousin William arranged for us to tour it while we were there."

"It was unpleasant," Etta said. "They used to build ships for the slave trade. And trade in slaves. That was how William met Amelia MacArthur. Her father supplied their plantations."

Sudden coldness filled Rachel's core. And here she'd thought as privateers her family's reputation was black. The MacArthurs were former *slavers*?

Jonathon Lecky's family had traded in slaves?

"I have a particular dislike for the deprivation of freedom," he had said.

"Yes, well, they've had to diversify," Mr. Johnston said. "The British Parliament ended that."

"Yes, well, it might help explain why Mr. MacArthur had so little consideration for his countrywoman," Etta pointed out. "It is not as though they have turned *away* from slaving, given their interests in Cadiz. The very idea that the British ship captains and merchants have separated themselves from the slave trade is laughable. Transportation by British ships may be over, but the supply of goods to those countries that continue to partake is very much alive. Plenty of British traders are only too happy to sell gunpowder, cheap Scottish guns, copperware and cloth to Spain for the Spanish merchants to trade with the Africans. Mr. MacArthur, we both know, is one of them. Meanwhile, the British Foreign Office is busy negotiating search and seizure treaties with Spain and the Arab tribes to very little effect, other than increasing the cost of insurance for remaining slave vessels."

"Do you see why she is my secret weapon?" Mr. Johnston said

to Rachel. "My daughter leaves me in no doubt as to her opinions, but in a room full of local and foreign dignitaries, she navigates the different political interests with aplomb. She wheedles more out of them than I do. I do worry sometimes, though, my dear, that you are sacrificing your own happiness to accompany me when you could marry and begin a life of your own."

"Goodness, father! A life of my *own?* This *is* my life. Why would I want another, when we travel and live in such interesting places? Besides," she teased, "perhaps in Egypt I shall be swept up in a delicious romance with a handsome sheik."

"I do not think so, dear girl," Mr. Johnston replied. "Although I shall not object if you find yourself enamored of another diplomat, presuming he is American or English, of course." He looked at Rachel and sighed. "I hope she *will* marry someday, 'though I fear only another with a wandering soul shall capture hers. I am responsible for this, you see. All her life, I have moved us from one country to another and another."

"Which you know I would not have had any other way," Etta said. "Besides, since we lost mother, you need me, father."

"I do. But should you wish to forge a new life, I will make do."

His views were so different from her family's, Rachel thought, with a deep pang in her chest. How wonderful it would be for Lady Georgiana to say such a thing, to be so willing to let her choose her own life.

Mr. Johnston turned to Rachel. "Did you decide on some locations to sketch while you were exploring?"

Rachel nodded. "I did. Speaking of which, if you intend to sit here for a time, I think I will browse in the bookstore across the street."

"*I* intend to sit here for a time," Etta said. "I need to rest my feet."

"You will need them again this evening," Mr. Johnston put in, glancing down at her boots as he flapped over a page of his newspaper. "You'll recall Mr. Simons is a fiendish dancer."

Rachel smiled. Mr. Simons, the American envoy to Cadiz, was hosting their party for dinner that evening.

"Mr. Simons is a fiendishly *bad* dancer," Etta said. "In which case, I don't just need to rest my feet. I need steel plates grafted to every bone. Last time I had the pleasure of dancing with Mr. Simons, I nearly *lost* my toes." She sent a pointed look her father's way. "Do not for a moment think I may become 'enamored' of our envoy to Cadiz."

"I wouldn't dream of it." The amusement that played along Mr. Johnston's lips abruptly dissolved when he looked down at the newsprint. "Oh, dear Lord."

Etta's brow creased at his note of concern. "What is it, father?"

"You recall the brig we saw in dry dock at the MacArthur shipyard? There was a fire. The vessel has been destroyed."

Etta looked less than impressed. "The former slave ship? I should say that was the best thing for it."

"Someone else thought so, too," Mr. Johnston's tone was dry. "The authorities have deemed it arson."

Rachel went still. Arson at the MacArthur shipyard? The feeling of cold within her intensified. Alongside it, bloomed a suspicion.

No, Rachel. No, she berated herself. *Why even* think *Jonathon might be involved?*

"I'm surprised Mr. MacArthur didn't mention it earlier," Etta said.

"Perhaps he did not know yet?" Mr. Johnston hypothesized. "Then again"—he checked the date on the front of the newspaper—"this newspaper is nearly ten days old."

Rachel pushed to her feet. She needed a distraction. "I think I'll go to the bookstore now."

"If you spot any American newspapers from the past month or so, do bring them back," Mr. Johnston said.

"I will."

A FEW OTHER CUSTOMERS BROWSED in the bookstore as she entered. Rachel smiled politely at the storekeeper, then turned to gaze at the framed sketches of Cadiz hanging near the door, needing a few moments to settle her mind. *Drat him. Stop thinking about the confounded man.*

Two sketches depicted different watchtowers, whereas the third sketch showed a cathedral that Rachel and Etta had passed earlier. She was glad to have a week here. The North African–inspired architecture left her itching to draw.

The shop was much larger than it appeared from the outside. She moved further along the shelves, drawn toward the small collection of English books tucked by the back wall. The polished wood of the bookshelves was smooth as she absently skated her fingertips along the shelves, occasionally pausing to trail down the spine of a book as she trawled their titles. She plucked one volume from the shelf—an English traveler's guide to Madrid. After flipping it open and leafing through the pages, she slid it back into place. Her fingers paused over the next title as she experienced a little thrum of surprise . . . *Boulogne-sur-Mer.*

"Oh, for goodness sake." Surely there must come a day when coincidences would not lead her thoughts back to him?

Her skin suddenly prickled. She heard the creak of the floorboards behind her. She looked down as a black shape rushed toward her legs. *What—*

Rachel spun around, boxed against the bookcase—her back to the shelves—as a man's hand shot out, further boxing her in.

And then her breath caught. She couldn't breathe because he was right there, right before her. Morgan was happily wriggling and getting tangled up in Rachel's skirts, the collie's nose snuffling in greeting. Still, Rachel could not look anywhere but into Jonathon Lecky's eyes.

Clear, gray, intent and unflinching. Those eyes—and his mouth—were but inches from hers.

She was stunned to silence, too. Frozen by surprise. Her hands clung to the frame of the bookcase behind her. Her fingernails pressed hard into the wood.

His gaze raked her face. As direct as that look was, she saw something more. Something softer, unguarded and vehement.

Lord above, he was *so close.*

"I should not have left you, Rachel Anwen Cavanagh. Not for a minute. Because there hasn't been a moment in the past eight months—hell, the last *eighteen* months—that you have left my mind."

Her chest seized up at his look, at his words. For a second, she thought he intended to kiss her.

Instead, he clasped her hand. It was completely swallowed by his own. "Come."

A surprised noise leapt from her throat as he drew her through a passageway and into the narrow alley behind the stationer's store. "What are you—" He was pulling her along. She snapped to her senses and hug her heels in. "Wait, no, stop! Where are you taking me?"

He turned back to her. She saw the flash of awareness in his eyes, the realization he'd been too heavy-handed. *Indeed, he had, as he would shortly find out.*

"I'd like to go somewhere we can talk."

Her instincts recoiled. He could not just reappear in her life and have his way so easily. She wrenched her hand from his grip. "I am not going a step further. My party is waiting for me. If you wish to speak, you will have to do so here."

He glanced up the alleyway. "I would prefer—"

"I don't care what you'd prefer."

His gaze jerked back to hers.

It was a lie, of course. She cared a great deal. Her anger evidenced that. But regardless of what they had shared, she would not just meander off with a man whose very name she was now not even sure of. "I met a gentleman at the port today. A Mr. MacArthur." Jonathon's features hardened. She reminded herself that it was as Rossum had said: if Jonathon wanted her, he would seek her out. But she must have the truth. "The likeness between Mr. MacArthur and yourself is striking. Are you related?"

She held her breath.

And saw the shift—the thawing—in his eyes as he realized what she was asking.

"We are related," he said. "Chaloner MacArthur is my brother. I was born Jonathon Matthias Prescott MacArthur, but I am Jonathon Lecky now. Rachel, I am Jonathon Lecky in every way that counts."

"You changed your name?" There was a note of disbelief in her voice.

"It's easy enough to do, and I had no wish to be known by the alternative." Lecky watched her throat work as she absorbed his words. Notus knew, even angry, she was lovelier than he remembered.

No, it wasn't that she was lovelier than he remembered. She was in fact *lovelier*. Eight months had passed since he had walked away from her in England. Her face had a new thinness. Thinness that spoke of experience and gave her a richer, more sophisticated beauty. Experience that—between when he saw her last and now—had smelted her down and rebonded her into something fiercer, stronger, more passionate. He could sense that new strength.

"I owe you an apology," he said. "I want to explain what happened at Gravesend."

Her smile was quick, sharp and edged with fury. "I think, if you wish to continue our acquaintance, *Mr. Lecky*, you have more to explain than that. Why are you in Cadiz?"

"For the same reason I went to Hanover Square seven months ago."

His words met silence. Then, her smile slipped. "W-what? Did you just say ... Hanover Square? But—"

Clearly, her sister had not mentioned his visit. He wasn't surprised. "You had already left for America. I spoke to your sister, outside on the square. Rachel," he added, "I was wrong."

She blinked. "You spoke to *Faith*? She never mentioned...." She seemed suddenly uncertain. But then, as though deciding to deal with the information about her sister later, she fixed him with a dark, appraising look. "You said you couldn't keep me safe."

"I was wildly afraid you would be hurt." He took a breath. "I still am."

A flicker of emotion crossed her face. "Yet your solution was to walk away."

"My solution, which was entirely logical at the time, was to separate you from the danger."

"You refer to yourself."

He half-grimaced, half-smiled. "Proximity to me was the danger. 'Though is seems danger has found you anyway."

Her brow creased. "Your brother?"

"Meet with me and let me explain." In her eyes, he saw the vestiges of anger and still much doubt. He also saw hesitation, temptation to accede. "If not now, then tonight. I will come to your hotel and escort you. Will you meet with me?"

She caught her lower lip between her teeth. Her hesitation was a sign of how badly he had damaged her trust. Still, uncertainty was better than outright refusal.

"I'll not put you at risk," he said. "On that, I give you my word."

She regarded him, and he found himself unable to read that dark gaze.

"Not tonight," she said finally. "Tonight I'm to accompany my traveling companions to dinner. Tomorrow. Eleven in the evening. I'll meet you by the gate to the stables. You understand, I would prefer to keep our meeting discreet."

"Yes." The gods be thanked, she'd agreed. The wrought-iron stable gate was located on the narrow street that ran down the hotel's west side.

She turned to go then. Before she stepped back into the bookshop, she paused to look at him once more.

Behind her, at the end of the alleyway that dipped away toward the port, the late afternoon sun had turned the sea to shimmering gold. With her face turned half in profile, her entire silhouette backlit by the warm afternoon glow, her loveliness stole his breath.

This was his future. *This* was what he wanted.

She spoke. "Emily told you where I was, didn't she?"

"Emily?" *What?* Her words momentarily confused him. He shook his head. "I haven't seen or heard from Emily for over a month."

His confusion was now hers. "But I wrote—" All of a sudden she stopped, as though reluctant to say more. "If not Emily," she said, "how did you find me?"

He felt his expression soften, feeling a sliver of hope. Could she have written of her plans to Emily, hoping Winter's sister would pass the details on?

"I forged an ally in Cobham," he said. "I told him you would want to go to Alexandria when you returned from America. And I told him I would keep you safe."

CHAPTER TWENTY-ONE

She gave me more than she ever knew. And I thank every guiding star that I realized it.
—*The Memoirs of Rhys Cavanagh*

I SHOULD NEVER HAVE LEFT you, Rachel Anwen Cavanagh. Not for a minute. Because there hasn't been a moment in the past eight months—hell, the last eighteen months—that you have left my mind.

Jonathon Lecky's words swirled in her mind for hours, wreaking havoc on her concentration. Somehow, she managed to hold a conversation with the American diplomat, Mr. Simons. Thankfully, for the most part, she needed only to nod and smile, while Mr. Johnston and Etta kept up the flow of conversation. Thankfully, because her thoughts kept returning to a certain boat captain.

He said he'd gone to Hanover Square, that he'd spoken with Faith. Alas, Rachel believed him.

All these months, she had thought he'd walked away. This afternoon, his gray eyes conveyed something different. His eyes told her he'd never left at all.

They told her, too, that he was sorry.

An English friend of Mr. Simons was also present at dinner. Quite handsome, the man was perhaps a half dozen years older than Rachel. She could tell, by his straying glances across the table, his circumspect smile and the question in his eyes, that she had piqued his interest.

A few days ago, even a few hours ago, she might have flirted and—if he offered—accepted his escort around Cadiz.

Now she was too shaken.

You were born with your grandfather's blood. The man you need will unfurl the sails for you and help you catch the wind.

Why did she feel, deep in her bones, that that man was Jonathon Lecky? Why did she feel he would understand her best?

One part of her, the fearful part, warned she would be opening herself up to the same disappointment as Dunkirk and Gravesend if she allowed her feelings to become engaged again. That part told her to swivel her chiffon-clad self toward Mr. Simons's handsome friend and ply her smile for all it was worth. To thrust away all thoughts of one roughly handsome boat captain.

But heaven help her. The way he'd looked at her, with all the same intensity as the night at the château in Boulogne, beneath the storm....

Rossum was right. Jonathon Lecky wanted her.

He'd come to Cadiz for her.

Now, she wanted to hear what he had to say.

HE WAS WAITING FOR HER, alone and swathed in a dark gray cloak when she arrived at the gate at eleven the following evening. "Where is Morgan?" she asked, as he held open the gate for her.

"With my boat."

She regarded him. "Are we going to your boat?"

"No. You remember Martine Winter's fiancé, Bertrand? His family owns a house in Cadiz. It will be a private place to talk. Is that acceptable to you?"

Yes, she wanted privacy. At her nod, he motioned her forward. "Please. This way."

The Spanish evening was cool. Certainly cool enough to don a cloak, but not so cool as to deter the merchant elite of Cadiz from enjoying the spring night. Music and light spilled from the rooftops as Jonathon led Rachel through the narrow alleys and streets below.

"Here. This is the one." Jonathon stopped before a darkened doorway. Turning a key in the lock, he let them quietly inside. "The house is closed, but we may have use of it."

Rachel looked about the darkened interior of the entry hall as

THE LAST LIGHT OF DUSK

Jonathon Lecky removed a lantern from the wall. "Are you certain it is all right for us to be here?"

"Yes. A housekeeper and her husband, the steward, maintain the house. They're abed now but knew we were coming. I told them we would not need anything. Have you been inside one of Cadiz's watchtowers yet?"

"Not yet."

"Good. Come this way."

She followed him up the stairs. One flight, then two. For a moment she felt as though she had been thrust back in time... back to the night in France when she'd followed him up the staircase to the battlements of the Château de Boulogne-sur-Mer. But that wasn't the case. He was here in Spain, when she had doubted she would ever see him again.

At the top of the fourth flight of stairs, he opened a door onto an expanse of flat rooftop. He indicated she should proceed him, and she stepped outside to a glittering vista of lantern-lit, white- and ecru-colored rooftops.

"The watchtower." He tilted his head toward the square, two-storey tower that rose up on one side of the roof, then led her to the entrance and again held open the door.

Beneath a ceiling some twenty feet high, the first chamber of the watchtower contained large divans in gold and red jewel-colored fabrics. Octagonal side tables in various sizes, featuring different geometric patterns, were positioned by the divans and around the room. A large rug covered the floor, while soft light spread from metal lanterns and sconces. It was a quite glorious space for entertaining.

"Would you like to see the view from the top of the tower?" Jonathon asked.

"Yes." She followed him up yet another narrow flight of stairs to the tower roof, which was enclosed by a chest-high parapet.

The view drew her across the rooftop to the parapet. A maze of narrow streets and pale buildings spread before her to the harbor. There, the masts of dozens of ships with sails furled rose up like a leafless forest against the inky sky. The air was salty, balmy, and carried the hint of foreign spices. In the night sky, above it all, the moon was an auriferous medallion, the reflection of which shone a silver-gold path over the open sea and revealed several ships at distant anchorage.

It was beautiful. Yet she didn't just feel its beauty *out there*, a pretty view to pass her eyes over. Instead, there was something impalpable about the view that went deeper, that seemed to absorb into her soul.

She felt Jonathon's gaze upon her.

She turned to him. "Did you bring me up here to steal my breath away?"

Perhaps she expected his usual, swift, laughing, amused smile. To her surprise, what she received was something different. He dropped his gaze and looked back to the sea. She glimpsed the barest quiver of his lips. A quiver, not just of self-deprecation, but of vulnerability.

"I had no motive other than to show you the view."

She sensed he spoke true. He'd hoped to share the beauty of it with her. Now that he had done so, he was uncertain. She had never seen Jonathon Lecky look uncertain before.

"Is your boat down there?" she asked, turning back to the parapet.

"Leftmost jetty." He pointed.

She searched in the direction he indicated. "I see." She identified the vessel among several fishing boats, then looked back to him.

The wind lifted a little. He pushed back the hood of his cloak. "I have things to tell you."

She waited but said nothing. There were many things she wanted to understand.

"You know now who my family are." He cast her a look that was part apology, part acerbic, and she let her eyes say she was sorry, too. "I took their money, Rachel. Every guinea I could get my hands on. The lion's share of the American accounts. For a time, the loss caused significant damage to their trading operations."

Oh, Lord. Her chest tightened. She had thought Jonathon Lecky and his family merely estranged. His grim expression left her in no doubt about the magnitude of what he had done.

"The amount was not insubstantial," he said.

"But . . . when?" she asked. "And . . . *how*?"

"Fourteen years ago. I was seventeen years old. After my mother died of lung fever, my father wanted me to attend university. I refused. Learning more from books while sitting in cloisters held no appeal to me. By then, the things I needed to understand . . . I needed to see with my own eyes. I was sent to live with my eldest sister, Amelia, in South Carolina."

She was almost afraid to ask. "What did you need to understand?"

"How my father and elder brother and their sharply dressed colleagues could sit in our drawing room and furiously debate the political difficulties the 'rabid' abolitionists were causing their commerce, while outside, on the street and in parliament, men and women called for transportation to end. My father has and always will be about profit. Profit was placed above *all* else. His children. My mother." At that admission, his lips twisted in a look of disdain.

Disdain that she could see bore the trace of old hurts. Her heart gave a squeeze.

"I attended public boarding school—" he continued.

"Which one?" she interrupted.

His gaze leveled on her. "Harrow."

Harrow was second only to Eton. The sons of many successful men attended.

She had struggled to assemble the boat captain's background. She could feel the pieces of the jigsaw beginning to fit together as he told her his story.

"We were educated," he said. "Occasionally encouraged to think. From the time I was twelve, I read books, pamphlets, newspapers. I knew the arguments on both sides—both ethical and economic. My father made it clear he did not appreciate my . . . *initiative* . . . when it came to understanding the alternative side of the argument. Similarly, whenever I raised the topic with my mother, she became . . . distressed. After she died and I finished school, I needed to see the practice. I needed to see what my family's commerce was built on."

He wouldn't have been more than fifteen or sixteen. A schoolboy at an eminent school. A schoolboy caught in the middle of one of the greatest political and moral debates of their times.

Rhys Cavanagh had died when Rachel was fifteen. She couldn't help but make a comparison to her own experience at that age. *They had both been so young.* "What happened?" she asked.

"I met my niece."

Rachel frowned. "Your eldest sister's daughter?"

"No. My elder brother's daughter. At six, she was already hard at work in my sister's rice fields, beside her mother."

It took Rachel a moment to understand. "Wait. Your niece was a *slave*? On your sister's property?"

"*Is* a slave. And she *was* my sister's property. Or Amelia's husband's property, at least. I can't imagine that has changed."

"But your brother.... He was involved with a slave woman?" In her mind, she was fitting the image to the man she had met at the dock. The man who had behaved so dismissively to a young, pregnant countrywoman.

"I don't believe 'involved' is quite the right word. My brother has always tended to use his position of power to get what he wants."

"You mean—" She didn't know quite what she was asking or whether she even *wanted* to ask. Because the hard look in Jonathon's eyes, coupled with his words, told her there was no gratification to be found in the story.

"How did you discover the child at your sister's property was your niece?"

"The story was coaxed out, after the girl's mother cringed away from me, thinking I was my brother."

Rachel swallowed. She could only imagine what that feeling must have been like for him. And for the woman.

"I took my complaints to my brother and sister," he said. "When we did not see eye to eye, I caught a ship and returned to England to confront my father. I turned seventeen the day I landed back on English soil."

"How did your brother and sister respond to your desire to return to England?"

"I didn't ask their permission, if that is what you mean. I simply took my things and left."

Yes, she could see Jonathon doing that, even at sixteen. "How did your father react when you confronted him?"

THE LAST LIGHT OF DUSK

His jaw firmed, the look in his eyes as hard as she'd ever seen. Harder than at the Lord Nelson. Harder than when they'd been attacked off the coast of Kent.

"His response was... disappointing. He is the head of the family, Rachel."

That was the greatest betrayal, she realized in a moment of clarity. What his father stood for, the decisions his father chose to make, defined them all.

And Jonathon Matthias Prescott MacArthur had refused to be defined that way.

"I thought he must not have known about my brother's... approach to management. I expected that he would make his displeasure known. Not for my sake: I thought he would do it for my mother. He had grieved when she died. Until then, I had never realized how much he loved her. I thought her memory would make the difference. I thought he would know what it would have meant to her."

"But he didn't?"

Jonathon's lips twisted at her question. "Oh, he did. But he chose business instead." Moonlight and the shadow of the parapet played across his features, as though each were vying to envelop the most.

"My mother's name was Olivia Freya," he said, turning his face to the moon. "She was a baron's daughter, married at eighteen to my father, who was many years her senior. She was innocent in many ways, except in the way in which men in positions of power were able to abuse women in a position of none. Her lady's maid, a girl she had grown up with and was very close to, was cast out of my mother's family home for falling pregnant to my mother's brother. He had also... abused his position of power. My grandfather forbid my mother to have anything further to do with her childhood friend. It wasn't until my mother married that she was able to help, and by then, the woman's son had been born." He paused. "My father knew how mother felt about the abuse of women. You cannot imagine how devastated she was the day she discovered her own son—my brother—had followed in her brother's footsteps and taken advantage of a young woman in her employ."

Rachel's stomach recoiled. "I'm so sorry." Again, her mind summoned an image of the man she had met at the dock. She could see that window-dressing of charm, turned on a young woman.... She took a breath. "Your father... what did he...?"

"He gave the girl money and sent Chaloner out to the MacArthur fleet."

The slice of his glance told her what result *that* had produced.

In the fleet, there had been no one to police him. Chaloner MacArthur had been able to do as he liked.

LECKY HAD ALWAYS THOUGHT THAT, in a fairer world, Olivia Freya would have wed a gentler man, a man who would not have put her values in conflict. She was, in the truest sense, 'a lady', as the name *Freya* meant.

He could see her in his mind even now, how fragile and still she looked that day when he had come upon her. Her arms had been crossed over her chest, her fingers digging into her elbows, as she stared sightlessly over the estate from behind the mullioned windows of the family's drawing room. He had known, that day when he saw her, that something had changed irrevocably.

He came to understand, as the years passed and the sadness never quite left her smile, that what had changed had been her will to continue. Her desire to fight.

"My mother was a beautiful woman, Rachel. But she was another one of my father's transactions. His personal and business lives were separated. In the greater scheme of shipbuilding and trade, he didn't listen to her. My mother's thoughts, wishes and feelings counted for naught." He looked out to the sea, but it was his mother, fragile before the mullioned window, that he saw. "In her own way, she was as powerless as any one of those women she cared about, while I... I was idealistic."

"It took me three months to get home," he said. Three months due to storm damage to his ship off the coast of Africa, during which Chaloner had time to notify their father of Jonathon's departure. Jonas MacArthur had had a week to fume before Lecky presented himself in Deptford. "Part of me is glad she was never privy to that conversation." He had been so certain that, for the memory of his mother, his father would act. However, the news of Chaloner's conduct had come as no surprise to Jonas MacArthur.

He had never felt sicker in his life than during that audience. Jonas MacArthur had swept away his every last illusion and filled the void with nausea and disgust. Disgust that coalesced into a hard wedge of fury as his father's indifference became undeniable.

"I was given a lesson on 'a few hard facts of business' and told to spend time thinking about the things I had to thank for my education and opportunities. My father's men, you see, kept in better spirits if they had access to the female merchandise."

He glanced at Rachel. Her expression held all the discomfiture he expected. No, it wasn't a gratifying tale. Nor was his own behavior upstanding.

"In the process of 'thinking' about the source of all the things I had to be 'thankful' for, I found myself in the possession of a large number of the company's bills of exchange." He could still see those bills sliding from the envelope into his hand as he searched his father's desk. Bills that represented the revenue from the last three shipments of transatlantic trade.

Those bills had not been his objective. But his objective had been to make a powerful and pointed statement. He had gazed down at them for several minutes before he tucked them deep inside his coat pocket. "I exchanged those bills for hard currency," he said.

"Your father knew that it was you?"

"The banker was a close friend of my father and an investor in the trade. He assumed when I presented those bills that I was acting on my father's behalf. The loss of those funds almost crippled the company." Almost, but it had not *quite* been enough.

"It corresponded with a particularly difficult time," he continued. "First, the company lost a ship and had difficulty claiming insurance; and within eighteen months, the Slave Trade Act had passed. Of course, my father had plans in place to deal with the end of transportation, but it wasn't long before the British were at war with the Americans and the company's traditional trade routes to America were closed. The company was able to rise to prominence again through several lucrative Navy shipbuilding contracts in Deptford during the war... and through trade with

Spain. Nevertheless, my actions made circumstances... harder than they needed to be. My family holds me responsible for that."

In the difficult years after Lecky had taken the money, a number of assets had had to be sold off. That included the Surrey estate, where the MacArthur children had grown up.

A frown now marred the space between Rachel Cavanagh's brows. He wanted to smooth it away. He wanted to close his eyes and breathe deeply, knowing that she was here and that he'd found her again. He wanted to pull her against him, cup the smooth skin of her jaw beneath his hands and lean his forehead against hers.

Whether those things were still possible, he didn't know. She seemed wary and rightfully so. He had let her go. Twice in her view—if one counted Dunkirk. Because even then, something had begun between them. Something he had not been willing to acknowledge, even though, on a deeper level, she had already sensed and understood and questioned it after both Dunkirk and Gravesend.

Then life took a sharp turn. Brought a man face to face with things he never thought he wanted to have. And it was in those moments a man came to realize he never wanted life to turn back.

"Would you have told me all this," she asked, "if I had not already met your brother?"

"I would have told you in London seven months ago, if you had not already set sail for America. I should have told you in Boulogne."

He *should* have told her before he'd so much as kissed her. He should have done away with all omissions then. He clenched his fists, feeling the phantom throb of the scars that marred his wrists.

"Rachel," he said. "I'm sorry. I am sorry."

Arabica eyes blinked and looked away. He couldn't tell whether she believed him. Poseidon's trident twisted in his chest.

She appeared to muster herself. "The money you took. Do you still have it?"

"The money is gone. It went a very long time ago. To women like my mother's lady's maid." He had considered that fair given what his father allowed. "Rachel, I don't find anything to be proud of in my heritage. I don't like that I grew up with opportunities at the expense of others' misfortune."

"So you spent almost eight years in Africa, saving others from misfortune?"

Meeting Enrique Barillis in Mogadore had changed everything. "Seems only fair, does it not?"

Her gaze was steady. "You were punishing yourself."

"No." He shook his head. "Not punishing. *Repenting*. Balancing the scales. For a long time, I didn't appreciate what I took." He pushed his sleeves up and turned his wrists over to expose the twin bands of white. "This," he said, "this was to make sure I would never forget."

Her glance flicked to his wrists then returned to his face with a look of uncertainty. "I-I don't understand. Your scars . . . ?"

"Are a reminder. They remind me what I will not take."

Her eyes widened. Again, her glance went back to his wrists. "You mean . . . ." She swallowed. "You mean . . . *you* did that?"

"At the time, a tattoo didn't seem quite sufficient."

Her look snapped back to his. His tone held humor, but it was true. He'd needed something he would feel. Something that reflected, in some small way, the suffering he had seen. The suffering upon which, for almost eighteen years, his life had been formed.

Decoration wasn't enough.

"These marks were a promise to myself. But it wasn't until I reached Mogadore that I knew what I had to do."

"Your work for the Vice-Consul."

He drew his sleeves back down. "Yes."

Mogadore had turned something angry into something good.

She studied him. "In the newspaper, there was a report of a ship being burned at the MacArthur shipyard. The authorities deemed it arson."

By the question in her gaze, she had guessed his involvement already. "It was. I didn't hold the torch, but it happened at my instigation. My family's company is presently at a weak point. Their line of credit is stretched thin. I helped a man to exploit that weakness, after Chaloner destroyed both that man's business and his daughter. Now, Chaloner faces the same, at least with respect to his business."

"How did Mr. MacArthur—Chaloner—destroy the man's

daughter?"

"The same way Chaloner has hurt many people's daughters."

Her troubled look told him she had grasped his meaning.

"This time, the daughter took her own life, and the father has a particularly vengeful streak," Lecky said.

"She took her own *life*? Good Lord! How horrific!" His tidings had clearly left her shaken. Resting her fingers atop the parapet, she turned to face the sea, her dark eyes disquieted, her expression perturbed.

"What will your family do if they find you?" she asked quietly.

"My brother has long had a bounty on my seizure. That's what Cox was after when he attacked us off the coast of Kent."

"But not a bounty on your head?" Once more, that dark gaze swung to his. Questioning, but in a way that made him want to tell her everything, for evermore, even when that truth was hard to speak. Because, the gods knew, he didn't want to risk losing her again.

"Not until it can be established whether I still have that money."

"And once that is established?"

He smiled, ever so softly. "Neither forgiveness nor self-examination runs particularly strong in MacArthur blood. For all my brother's reserved manners, I'm quite certain he would be pleased to know mine had bled out, my throat slit, in a back alley of Cadiz."

Her breath hitched, and she caught her lower lip between her teeth. He hoped that was a good sign. A sign that his fate mattered to her.

"But you." Her dark eyes once more searched his. "You're not like that."

"No. I'm not like that." He curled his hands into fists. Notus knew, it was all he could do not to reach out and touch her. "I think, Miss Cavanagh, when it comes to blood, I got my mother's."

A GIRL HAD DIED; HIS brother wanted him dead. And that was before the ship had been burned.

His scars ... what they meant.... Those scars represented a

lifetime. The beginning of and the direction of a life.

Rachel's thoughts churned, and fear rose in her throat. "It's dangerous for you here."

"Yes," Jonathon said.

Yet here they stood in this watchtower, with its view over Andalusia's oldest city. Spain's oldest city. And he had come for her.

Suddenly, she couldn't look at him. She had to look down and away to Cadiz's lantern-lit port. His gaze had become too intense, and she feared to give too much away.

Because it mattered that he had come. It mattered that he had apologized.

"Cadiz must have been the last port to which you wished to sail," she said, with no small amount of irony.

"Rachel." The low, rough sound of her name sparked a ripple of yearning that started and ended in her heart.

"Sweetheart," he said, "as soon as I learned where you were bound, Cadiz was the only port to which I wished to sail."

Furnished with such words, she had to look at him. He also needed to hear the truth.

"Jonathon, I went on without you."

For a moment, he was still, quiet. Then—slowly—he raised his hand. Her skin tingled as he brushed the back of his fingers down her cheek, all the while following the motion with his gaze. "You know you were right to. You had no knowledge of my intentions." When his touch reached her chin, his gaze moved up to again look into her eyes. I want for you everything that you desire. I can only ask, Rachel Cavanagh, that I might again be your escort, to any and all the places you desire to go."

Her breath stilled in her throat. She pressed her hand against the parapet to steady herself. Was he truly saying these things?

Yes. Here they were, lit by moonlight, the lights and rooftops of Cadiz below. His body angled towards hers, his hand upon her cheek, intimate in this vastness of space.

The breeze gently played with the dark, tangled hair that rested against his collar and hood.

"When I look at you," he said, "I see something that is both real and that transcends the things I know, and I don't know where it leads."

She raised her hand to cover his. It was warm and callused beneath her own. "You make me sound dangerous."

"Mayhap I just don't have the charts for this part of the sea."

Oh, that prompted a small smile. "Surely you've sailed without charts before?"

"Aye. Plenty of times. However, some stretches are more precarious than others."

She sobered to ask, "What makes this stretch precarious?"

His gaze softened to become almost reverent, to skate her features as exquisitely as devout fingers might stroke sensitive skin.

"This stretch?" he asked. "I'd say it's the need I have to see you smile. To wake up to the sight of you at the first glint of dawn, then watch the last light of dusk play across your face. I want to end each day with you in my arms at night."

She barely knew what to say. "That is what you class as precarious?"

"For a man like me, yes." Beneath her hand, he spread his fingers to cup her cheek.

She grew serious. If she were to understand this, there was more she needed to know. "Precarious in a way that might see you leave again?"

"Not by choice. Not again."

Looking into his eyes, she believed him. There she saw this wasn't the man who, in the vacuum of space between her sister, Rachel and Rossum, had walked away in Gravesend. No, the man before her had decided what he most wanted—and he was looking at her.

Rising up on her toes, she leant forward. He was still as she lightly brushed her mouth over his.

His lips felt firm, roughened by wind and sea. She pulled away to meet his gaze.

"Rachel." Her name was a breath. His eyes were a churning, cinerescent gray. He leant forward, captured the back of her head with his hand and rested his forehead against hers. This close, she could feel the warmth radiating from his body.

"Finding you has made me realize there are things I want to be free to look forward to and things I want to leave behind." He brought his hand forward to stroke her cheek again, then caught her hand in his own, his fingertips angling her wrist. Then, ever so slightly, he turned his head and pressed a kiss to her palm. Her throat went dry, her breath suspended.

"Thank you, Rachel Anwen Cavanagh," he said, "for my life."

With that gesture, those words, she was transported back to the guest room of a Dunkirk hotel, to the chink of glasses and the sound of laughter filtering up the stairs from below.

Her voice was hoarse. "Putting aside the use of one umbrella stand, I haven't saved your life. Not as you saved mine."

"Oh, I don't know. You proved apt at setting a smuggling lugger alight." His words held a smile before his tone grew serious again. "Rachel, you changed my course. Meeting you showed me a new one. I want to take you to Alexandria. I want to be there for you to turn to when you visit the places your father and grandfather stood and when you discover new places of your own. Every sketch you do, I want to see."

Her heart clenched. She set a steadying hand on his chest, her fingers curling against his cloak. It was as though they had come full circle since that day in Dunkirk. A full circle that had demanded their paths diverge in order to bring them back together at this moment, on this rooftop, with these understandings.

"But what of your ship?"

"My ship? Ah. The *Freya* is launched. Ian Lawrence is at her helm."

"The *Freya?*" In light of his story, her heart washed out to sea. In his eyes, she could see he understood she'd grasped the significance. "You said you always knew her name."

"I always did." Quietly, he said, "I wanted, always, to see wind in her sails. I wanted that freedom for her."

"That's beautiful."

"It is what it is."

"It's *beautiful*," she said firmly.

These were the depths that drew her to him. That she'd sensed from the first and which drew her back. "And what of... what I might bring you?"

He released a shaky exhalation. Then his arms were around her shoulders, and he was hauling her closer, enfolding her tight and flush against him, as though he would never again let her go. His scent surrounded her, warm and salty and male. She could feel his strength. Her lashes drifted shut as her hand tangled in his cloak. It felt so good to be held. Her body relaxed against his.

She felt a frisson as his mouth brushed across her cheek.

"Zephyrus," he breathed.

"Zephyrus?" He had said that name to her once before. She didn't understand.

"You," he said. "This." His lips left another gentle trail of sensation across her cheek. "Rachel, I just want you."

CHAPTER TWENTY-TWO

Justness never tastes as one expects.
—*The Memoirs of Rhys Cavanagh*

RACHEL FELT NO EXPECTATION IN his touch. Just tenderness, humbleness, and perhaps—in no small part—*gratitude*. She sensed that, at that moment, he would be satisfied simply to hold her, with the light of the moon on the sea and all of Cadiz spread out below them.

As he pulled back to look at her, he wove his fingers through hers. "I love you, Rachel."

Oh, Lord. Her throat constricted. *How had they come from nowhere to here?* Just yesterday morning, she would not have dreamed.... She felt heart-warmed and heartsick at the same time. She clenched his fingers between her own. "Jonathon... I loved you in France."

He smiled softly, not missing the distinction. "But not in Spain?"

How did she say that she wasn't a woman who would cling to love in a place no love was returned? "For the past eight months, I have been of the understanding there was no future for us. I had no idea you came to see me in London. I don't... I'm not..." She drew a breath. "I've keep my feelings for you ... in check."

"What a man *does* matters. I know I have much to prove. Rachel, I don't expect you to fall into my arms." He looked down, his words prompting a wry smile, likely on account of the fact she *was* standing in the circle of his arms. "You need to know my words carry weight."

That was true. "Sailing to Cadiz was a good start."

"It's a beginning," he agreed. His expression sobered. "You're traveling with an American diplomat? A Mr. Johnston and his daughter?"

His knowledge caught her off-guard. "How did you...?" Then realization came. "I hope you compensated Cobham well," she said. "I would love to know how you persuaded him to disclose my plans."

"With coin?"

"Cobham is loyal. We both know that it would have taken more than coin."

"I've read your grandfather's memoirs." His look was pointed. "The *Chandenque*."

"Ah. So you stroked my coachman's ego?"

"Perhaps. For the most part, I appealed to his protective nature. Of you."

"He didn't tell me."

"Perhaps he wasn't entirely certain I'd still come."

Suddenly, a warm feeling of gratitude flooded through her, overflowing from a deep well in her chest. Gratitude and affection for Cobham. Thankfulness for the man before her. She looped her arms around his neck. Fiercely, she said, "I'm glad of it."

"Are you? By the gods." His gaze softened. "I want to kiss you right now."

Her heart gave a little stutter. "You may."

He shook his head and smiled ruefully. "There's one more thing I have to do. I have to see my father."

The beat of her heart faltered. "But... surely that is dangerous?"

"It is. But there are things I can do to reduce the risk."

"Such as?"

"Retaining the element of surprise. Ensuring Chaloner is nowhere nearby."

He had all but said his brother wanted him dead. "The Johnstons and I are to have dinner with your brother tomorrow evening."

His gaze sharpened. "Where?"

"Here in Cadiz, I believe."

"Not across the bay? Not at the villa?"

Rachel frowned. "No. No one has mentioned a villa across the bay." She and Etta would certainly have spoken of that.

"Good," he mused. "Perfect, in fact. Currently"—once more, one of those wry smiles came—"my father owns both a townhouse in the city and a villa across the bay. If Chaloner is dining with you at the townhouse . . . ."

"He will not be at the villa." She did still not see how that helped alleviate the threat. "Will your father not—"

"My father is dying, Rachel. He moved to Spain for his health. Physically, it's his minders I have to worry about."

His father was *dying*? Her breath rushed out. Of all the things she could have imagined him saying, she'd not imagined that. "*Wait*. Your father is *dying*? How long have you known?"

"For some time." He read the question in her eyes. "There was never going to be a deathbed reunion, Rachel. It was always my intention to hear, one day, in some foreign place, that he had died. I wouldn't go except—" He stopped, as though his gaze had stuck on her.

"Except?" she prompted.

He set his hands on her hips. "All these years, I've thought there were no circumstances under which I'd go back. But I need to be free of them. I need to come to *you* free of them."

She could see in his eyes how important that was.

Besides, she needed time to think for herself about all that he'd said. "When will I next see you?"

His mouth formed a line as he considered. "You're having dinner with Chaloner tomorrow evening. While I would prefer to know you weren't anywhere near him, with the Johnstons you'll be safe. Rachel, don't trust him. And don't spend a moment with him alone."

"I understand." She also knew—they *both* knew—the man standing before her would be safer if his brother's whereabouts were accounted for. "Jonathon, Mr. Johnston has cast himself in the role of my guardian for this trip. I hope you will not object if I speak to him of you?"

"Tell them what you think is best. As to when to meet—the day after your dinner? Friday? I'll come for you at dusk. We can talk then about what comes next." He reached for her hand and pressed a key into her palm. "Take this key. Should anything worry you before you see me next, come here. Bertrand's staff will help."

THE MACARTHURS' SPANISH VILLA, SITUATED across the bay from Cadiz, had been purchased twenty years before to entertain business associates away from the company's operations in the city center.

There were certain similarities between the MacArthur villa and the Jacobean mansion house purchased by Rhys Cavanagh in Wales. Both fronted the sea. Both stood as testament to the riches their owners had acquired through their respective trades.

Both were accessible by beach under the cover of darkness.

Lecky would have preferred the direct approach, but better to keep surprise on his side. Remaining deep in the shadows, he stowed his rowboat behind a nearby outcrop of rocks, then waded a short distance back to the beach. He used the passage of clouds that intermittently blotted the moon as a cloak to weave his way up from the beach to the villa, then slipped into the shadows of the extremity of the building.

The villa's layout was familiar. The main suite was located front and centre, one story above the ground, and featured a balcony that overlooked the sea. He could remember standing on that balcony as a boy, on the one or two times he'd visited. He could still picture the view across the bay to Cadiz on a sunny day, gleaming in all her ecru- and white-walled glory. For a long time, Cadiz had stood at the centre of a mercantile empire, the heart of Spanish trade with the Americas and the most important Spanish port. With the British hold on nearby Gibraltar, the Royal Navy had also had a strong presence. The melting pot of foreigners that had so fascinated him in Cadiz as a boy was perhaps part of the reason he had felt so comfortable in North Africa.

He expected to find Jonas MacArthur in the main suite of the villa.

At the rear of the villa lay an enclosed courtyard. Lecky was silent as he made his way along the walls, then pulled himself up onto a low, flat, single-story roof. He inched forward to overlook the inner courtyard, which featured cloister-style terraces and a central fountain. The rear doors of the villa were thrown open. Occasional voices drifted from within—voices speaking English. Members of his family were home.

He lowered himself from the roof into the shadow of the terrace.

A young woman appeared in the doorway. "I'll just be in the courtyard," she called to those indoors. Wisp-thin, with a clear complexion and a mass of dark golden-brown hair dressed atop her head, she stepped outside onto the terrace. Resting a hand against one of the stone arches, she tilted her chin up, her gaze upon the clouds that masked the moon. The light from the windows of the villa fell across her face.

A sudden sheen of tears glimmered in her eyes. Quickly, she sought to brush them away.

Gods above. She looked, in that moment, so terribly like his mother.

Then he realized. She was his baby sister, Margaret. Born just eighteen months before their mother had died, she had been no more than three years old when he saw her last. His chest seized—tightened—as the vastness of the time he had spent away hit him. His sister had grown up—she had lived almost her entire life to now—in the years that he had been gone.

In the next moment, misfortune favored them both. The light of the moon emerged through the clouds just as she glanced toward his hiding place. A small frown formed between her brows. She looked searchingly, bothered by something she'd glimpsed. Lecky pressed back against the wall and held his breath.

But she stepped forward to peer deeper into the shadows.

Mirroring eyes met. The lass's widened. She let out a frightened gasp and stumbled back.

Lecky moved fast. He grasped her and spun her around. He stifled her cry with one hand while he trapped her slim form against his chest. "Shhh," he murmured, close to her ear. "I'll not hurt you. Listen, Margaret. I'll not hurt you."

His hand still clamped over her mouth, her eyes widened. She renewed her struggles—possibly panicked further by his use of her name. Blast. Notus knew he didn't want to frighten her.

The occupants inside had heard her cry. Footsteps rushed forward. Lecky spun towards the doorway, his grip on the lass secure despite her struggles.

"Margaret." Older, thinner and grayer than Lecky remembered, a man appeared on the terrace. Phillips. His brother-in-law. His second-eldest sister Ann's husband. His eyes widened at the sight of Lecky. "Ann—stay back."

Ann had already come forward. She spotted Lecky. "*You!*" she denounced.

"I came to speak to our father," Lecky said.

In Lecky's arms, but for the quick rise and fall of her breath, his younger sister stilled. Shock, he expected. He doubted she'd realized who he was.

"I want to let Margaret go, then I want to speak to our father," Lecky repeated.

Ann seethed. "What do you think gives you the right to make *any* demands?"

In manner, his second eldest sister was Chaloner in female form. Savage and self-serving. *Notus knew he would prefer not to do this.* Unfortunately, he also knew where in the MacArthur family the real power lay, and it wasn't with his sisters. He removed his hand from Margaret's mouth and withdrew a pistol concealed in the pocket of his cloak. He raised it in the direction of Phillips and cocked the hammer. His brother-in-law visibly paled. "I'm the man with his pistol pointed at your husband, Ann."

A tense second passed. "You bastard," Ann spat.

His smile came swift and cold. "Oh, we both know there are plenty of *those* in this family. We also know I am not one of them."

His sister's lips pressed together in a white line of fury. "You betrayed this family."

"That argument has interesting nuances. How about I have it with our father?"

Ann's lips thinned further. "Damn you, you cur."

"The powers that be will already have a plan for that. Are you going to take me to him, Ann?"

His question met terse silence. Against his chest, Margaret's breath had turned shallow. Ann stood unmoving on the terrace, trapped in a stalemate of fury. Her husband, however, was a businessman. Tight and straight-laced, Phillips was not the type to dabble in the dirty ends of trade. The pistol pointed in his direction was causing the man to fray.

"For heaven's sake, Ann," Phillips bit out. "You know your father wants to see him."

Did he, now? Lecky grimaced. "You. Take me to him," he told Phillips, without lowering his weapon.

Phillips's gaze flickered to his wife with a clear message. *I am doing this. Do not defy me.* He turned and moved inside.

With his eyes on a mutinous Ann, Lecky urged Margaret forward. His youngest sister gave a little, choked whimper. "I'm not going to hurt you," he murmured again. "Just walk with me to our father."

"Are you going to hurt papa?" His youngest sister's hands clung to his arm where he had her trapped. He had no idea what she had been told of him, but he sensed deep fear. Fear that he would hurt her papa.

Suddenly, he understood it had also been fear that had driven her to the courtyard and caused her tears. Her papa was ill, and she was afraid she would lose him soon. Irrespective of what Lecky thought of Jonas MacArthur, this girl loved her father.

"I'm not going to hurt him."

Still, he could feel the uncertainty that thrummed through her.

He looked again at Ann. None of his sister's fury had abated.

"Ann, come." The instruction was issued by her husband, who had entered the villa and turned to look back at the three members of his wife's family.

Ann didn't speak as she spun in front of Lecky and followed behind her husband—placing herself in the line of Lecky's pistol. Phillips waited for Ann to reach him, then grasped his wife's hand to walk side by side with her up the villa's staircase to the second floor.

They reached the doorway to the main suite. Lecky's brother-in-law rapped on the wooden surface, then glanced over his shoulder at Lecky. The door cracked open.

Barrymore. Lecky's father's valet. The man must have served Jonas MacArthur for over forty years. He was older, grayer, more lined—but just as recognizable. By the widening of the older man's eyes and the catch of his breath, it seemed Lecky was too.

"Master Jonathon," Barrymore breathed.

The address sounded strange to Lecky's ears. Perhaps all the more strange for the lack of anger—the lack of any negative emotion—on Barrymore's face. No, even noting the pistol in Lecky's hand, the older man's expression appeared to be one of... *relief.*

Barrymore opened the door wider. "Please, Master Jonathon. Come in."

"You can lower your weapon," Phillips said. "No one here is armed."

Lecky loosened his grip on Margaret, and she immediately slipped from his hold. Sinking onto a sofa set outside the doorway to the master suite, she pressed her hand to her mouth. Her narrow shoulders shook as fright caught up to her. She began to sob.

"Please, come forward." Barrymore motioned as Lecky lowered his pistol, holding it down by his side.

"Ann can proceed me." Lecky trusted his sister less than he trusted Phillips.

With a searing glare, Ann raised her chin and turned.

"No!" Margaret leapt to her feet. Barging by them all, she rushed into the room. Lecky tilted his head, indicating that Ann and her husband should follow.

It took a moment for Lecky's eyes to adjust to the dim interior of the suite. Candlelight flickered up the walls. A canopied bed stood at the far end. Margaret MacArthur flung herself down at the side of a bundled shape. "Papa!" She threw her arm across his torso and buried her face in his blanketed side. "Papa."

"Margaret, my child." Her name emerged as a weak, concerned utterance, one that was followed by a cough as Jonas MacArthur struggled to sit up. "Barrymore, what is going on?" He set a hand upon Margaret's shoulder as he sought to peer across the dim room. His eyes lit first on Ann and her husband, then shifted to Lecky.

His lips parted. His expression froze.

"Sir... it's Master Jonathon."

"Jonathon...."

Even at this distance it was possible to see the toll of Jonas

MacArthur's illness. The sunken cheeks, the pale face. But those eyes.... His father's eyes hungrily scoured, then traced, then softened with the glistening of tears. Tears that spoke of a deep churn of emotion.

"Jonathon...."

Lecky gave no reply. He couldn't. Whatever the response he had expected from his father, it was not this.

He didn't care for the man. A wedge had existed between them for a long time. Still, his chest tightened. His throat clogged. Only once before had he seen a glistening of tears in Jonas MacArthur's eyes.

Ann wasn't happy. His sister's voice rose. "He forced his way in here with a pistol aimed at my husband. And look at Margaret. He scared her half to death."

"Ann." Jonas MacArthur's voice was gently chiding and flecked with knowledge of his grown daughter. "Why did he have to force his way in?"

"Father—" Tears of mutiny, tears of betrayal, sprang to Lecky's elder sister's eyes. Phillips clasped her against him even as Ann attempted to brush off her husband's grasp.

"Margaret." Jonas MacArthur gave his youngest daughter's shoulder a squeeze. "Margaret, I need you to sit by the fireplace. There, my child, off you go."

Margaret clutched him tighter. "He has a pistol, papa."

"Come now. I don't think he's here to hurt me." This time, the look Jonas MacArthur cast Lecky was searching. "It's not the money you have brought back to me, is it?"

"No."

"Ah." Jonas MacArthur's head fell back against the pillows. He blinked rapidly, then placed his hand over his daughter's. "Margaret, come now. To the sofa by the fireplace."

Margaret reluctantly came to her feet. She brushed the tears from her cheeks with her palms as her gaze flickered to Lecky. She didn't trust him, this stranger of her blood.

"I knew you would come back," Jonas MacArthur said.

There was no superiority in his tone. None on his face. No, just the raw passage of emotion as Jonas MacArthur's features scrunched, he pressed his hand over his mouth and he squeezed closed his eyes.

"Sir—" Barrymore spoke out in distress.

Jonas MacArthur shook his head and held up a quietening finger. "I'm fine— I need—" He gestured to the vacant space beside him on the bed. To Lecky, he said, "Come forward. Sit."

Lecky came forward. Feeling uncomfortable, he perched on the edge of the bed but didn't let down his guard. At this level, they sat eye to eye.

Jonas MacArthur's gaze drank him in. "You've seen the elements. They've graven your skin."

"There are many things I've seen. Many I've been graven by."

Framed newspaper articles hung on the wall by his father's bed. Some Lecky recognized. Old articles, published before he had left, now yellowed with age and sunlight.

There were newer articles, too, reporting on the establishment of the Royal Navy's West Africa Squadron, the rise of impressment and the War of 1812.

Noticing the direction of Lecky's attention, Jonas MacArthur pushed a copy of a newspaper toward him. The *Morning Post*. "I have a new article to add to my collection," the head of the MacArthur family said. His finger dabbed at an article at the top of the page. "This article. Here."

His hand trailed away while Lecky read the headline. *The Star burned in shipyard fire.*

"It was a fine ship. A fine shipyard, too. It will be impossible for us to deliver on our contracts now. This will spell the end of the company. Ninety years of business . . . over."

His father's eyes were on him. Lecky said nothing.

"We will have to sell the other ships. Chaloner will lose—" His father broke into a fit of coughing.

Barrymore hastened forward. "Sir—"

Shaking his head, Jonas MacArthur waved his valet back as he began to recover. "No . . . I'll manage." He looked back at Lecky. "But that—the company—is not why you are here."

"No." The tightness in his chest remained, unwanted and unexpected.

Jonas MacArthur regarded him. "Then let us not dwell on it."

Nearby, Ann made a shocked, disbelieving sound. "My God!

But surely he is responsible—"

His father's voice cut her off, gravelly with hope. "There are things you've kept, too, are there not?"

"Yes." Lecky reached into the inside pocket of his cloak and withdrew a small, oilskin pouch. Following Lecky's action, Jonas MacArthur's brow creased, and he drew a ragged breath as he pressed his hand over his mouth. His eyes swelled with tears.

"What is it?" Ann demanded.

Lecky placed the pouch down and slid it across the bedsheet. With shaking hands, Jonas MacArthur picked up the pouch, opened it and pulled out the small, cloth-bound item inside. His aged fingers brushed the protective cloth away.

A tear spilled to run down his cheek. Then another.

Jonas MacArthur stared down at the miniature portrait of Olivia Freya MacArthur, his dead wife. The miniature portrait that had been commissioned by Lecky's mother as a gift to her fiancé, following their engagement.

It was the only picture of Lecky's mother that existed.

Lecky had taken it from its keeping place in his father's drawer—it had been what was searching for—the day he had found the bills of exchange.

His father's gaze drank in the small painting. More tears slipped down his cheeks.

"What is it?" Ann demanded.

"Your mother."

"The missing miniature? *He* took it?"

Ann's shock was real, thus sparking Lecky's own. *Had his father never told them? Had he nursed Lecky's blow in private?*

Even now, Jonas MacArthur ignored Ann's question. His focus was on his son. He reached out and set a hand upon Lecky's wrist. In reflexive recoil, Lecky balled his hand against the bed.

"I knew you would bring this back."

Jonas MacArthur regarded him with an intensity and a degree of understanding that shook him.

How had his father known such a thing? He didn't want to ask, because he'd told Rachel the truth. He had never planned to have a deathbed reunion.

His father answered regardless. "All you have ever wanted is freedom. And for that, at this moment, I am grateful." Returning his gaze to the miniature, his voice broke. "Olivia, I am sorry." He covered the lower half of his face with his hand as he clutched the miniature to his breast.

The passage of years lay in those four words. Years Lecky thought would never have made a difference. But it was there—reverberating in that raspy voice—a vast store of apology. Layers of pain and self-blame, felt and known deeply.

"What about the money?" Ann exclaimed. "What about the damage he has done?"

"He has returned what matters most." Jonas MacArthur's voice was quiet and steady.

"But don't you *care*? The pain he has caused—"

"Cannot *all* be laid at his feet. This"—Jonas MacArthur clutched the miniature—"this is what I wanted most. I have felt the pain of being deprived of this. But that pain has been compounded, knowing what my actions cost my daughter. Margaret." He looked toward his youngest daughter. His voice cracked. "My dear, I am so sorry."

Margaret's face was etched with confusion and distress. "Papa—"

"You have never seen this. You have never known your mother's face. I have it now," he said, almost as though he were reassuring himself. "My son has brought it back."

Poseidon be damned. Vast and expansive, a cavern opened in Lecky's chest, with cavities he had never known were there.

Margaret's voice choked. "Papa—"

It was Jonas MacArthur that Lecky had sought to hurt when he took the miniature. Young and furious at seventeen, he'd not thought of Margaret, the child who would grow into a young woman in their mother's image.

"Come here, my dear. Come see how much you look like her."

Lecky shifted and came to his feet as Margaret moved forward. Her face was still tear-streaked. She perched next to their father—shy, yet lovely. Very much like their mother.

With his weakened arms, Jonas MacArthur tucked his youngest daughter against his side. "Look, you see? How the shape of your face is just the same? And your lips?" Margaret's hands curled against his chest as she looked down at the miniature. "How many times have we seen that smile?" Jonas asked. "It is just like yours. Don't you think we have seen that smile before?"

He nudged her, coaxing a little tear-streaked smile. "Yes," she agreed with a sniffle, as he held her slender shoulders. She lifted a finger to touch the tiny frame and trace her finger around the edge of it, then looked up at Lecky. Perhaps as curious about her long-gone brother as she was about their mother.

Jonas MacArthur's gaze followed, yet it conveyed something more complex, more faceted. It was the gaze of a man who, looking toward the end of his days, had narrowed down the things that mattered most in his mind—and culled all else.

"You did the right thing," he said. "I knew you would."

No words came to Lecky's throat. There were none he could give.

Yet that too seemed understood.

"You have done what you came for, haven't you?" Jonas said.

"Yes."

"I would like you to know Margaret one day."

Lecky's glance flickered to his youngest sister. She looked at him with equal uncertainty.

"One day," Jonas MacArthur repeated. "One day it might be possible. She deserves to hear about the life of her brother, too."

"No!" Ann protested.

"Ann." Their father's warning.

"*No!*" This time, she wouldn't be quietened. She thrust away her husband's cautioning hand and stepped forward. "No, *damn you!*" Her chest rose and fell with angry breaths. "I love you father, I do. But for once, in *this*, I wanted to see you proved wrong. I wanted to see your damnable faith in *him* shattered." She turned on Lecky. "And instead, what do *you* do? *You prove his words right!* You prove his damnable faith in you *right!*" She pointed her finger at him, herself a mass of turmoil and fury, the expression in her eyes dark and bruised. "He may have forgiven you, but I can't. Not for what you did to us. Not for what you took. Not for coming here today. And I'm sorry, father, but I *never* wanted you to see him again. We all know that he didn't come here for you. He didn't come here for any of us."

"Oh, Ann." Jonas MacArthur gazed upon his daughter with a greater measure of understanding than Lecky could ever have anticipated. It was the way of the MacArthurs to cling to grievances and to punish. Yet he could see what his father had done. Jonas MacArthur had let go of the bills of exchange and the difficulty their loss had caused. He'd even accepted the unraveling of his company after the fire at Deptford and the destruction of *The Star*.

Lecky would not have recognized that letting go had he not wanted to be free himself. He was just glad it hadn't taken until his own deathbed before he understood.

"My dear girl," his father said. "He came here for a better reason. He came here for himself."

CHAPTER TWENTY-THREE

Decide carefully who to love, then rip your saber from its scabbard, raise it in the air and shout "Aye, me hearties!"
—*The Memoirs of Rhys Cavanagh*

"WE READ THE TERRIBLE NEWS of the Deptford fire yesterday," Mr. Johnston said to Chaloner MacArthur, who was seated across from the American diplomat at the dining table. "The newspaper speculated the cause was arson. Have you heard whether the authorities have identified any perpetrators yet?"

Rachel's hand froze momentarily on the way to her wine glass. Recovering, she lifted her glass to take a sip and cast a glance at their host. Chaloner MacArthur was seated diagonally across from her. Displeasure pinched his lips.

"The cause *was* arson, Mr. Johnston," he said. "The guards were attacked and tied up."

"Ah. That is a fairly good indicator. No lives were lost, I hope?"

"No, no lives were lost. We may be grateful for that. However, the authorities have been of very little assistance. It is difficult not to question their competence."

Rachel swapped a glance with Etta seated opposite, at their host's side.

"Ah. A difficult situation, truly," Etta's father agreed. "Do you have your own suspicions?"

"Given your own delicate line of work, Mr. Johnston, I'm sure you'll appreciate that a businessman like myself cannot help sometimes treading on toes. Unfortunately, I can think of several people with a base enough nature to behave so despicably."

Rachel found it necessary to reach for her glass again. She had decided to wait until after their dinner to speak to Etta and her father about Jonathon. She did not want Chaloner MacArthur to suspect they had any knowledge of his brother.

Mr. Johnston dabbed his mouth with his napkin. "Might you engage your own investigators, Mr. MacArthur?"

"It is a distinct possibility. I fear the difficulty lies not so much in the perpetrators' identity but in the ability to locate them."

"It is extremely disappointing when people go unpunished for their crimes," Mr. Johnston observed.

"I agree. Unfortunately, this is the second difficulty to beset us in eight months. Last year, we lost the lading of another ship, *The Helena*, during a storm. The vessel has required substantial repairs." He smiled as he lifted his own wine glass. "On a more pleasant note, my sisters are of the view that it has come time for me to take a bride."

Yes, the addition of a bride's dowry would help a great deal right now, Rachel thought wryly.

"Surely your sisters have been urging you in that direction for some time, Mr. MacArthur?" Etta's voice carried all the diplomat's daughter's tact.

"They have, Miss Johnston. But I attest, I've been difficult to make settle. However, a woman with beauty, as well as riches, and the potential to forge a strategic business alliance . . . . Now that is very attractive."

A little smile hitched the corner of his mouth. He didn't need to glance at Rachel for all present to grasp his allusion. He stopped short of saying he needed an inpouring of dowry, Rachel noted. She managed a pinched smile.

"Miss Cavanagh, how did you come to travel with Mr. and Miss Johnston?" he inquired, shifting back to safe territory. To that question she was happy to reply, to explain she had made a voyage to America and now wished to visit Alexandria to see where her father lay buried. Chaloner MacArthur listened with interest, and she realized he was bolstering his efforts to charm her.

Which was fine, if it kept his thoughts from his brother.

As it was, she was doing her best not to think of Jonathon herself, lest she worry.

"You were involved in a shipwreck yourself, were you not?" Chaloner MacArthur asked as servants removed their empty plates.

"I was. A year and a half ago now." This was not a topic she wished to discuss with him. "I hope you understand I do not like to talk about it."

"Of course," he agreed. "It was harrowing, I'm sure. There was a great deal of speculation about you and the Marquess of Rossum after the event."

It was a question, albeit not asked as such. "It is very common for newspapers to get these things wrong," Rachel said. "The Marquess and I are extremely good friends."

"I see." MacArthur smiled.

The evening progressed until finally it was time to go. Their host stopped Rachel by the door, just as she was about to follow the Johnstons down the steps to the waiting carriage. Despite her gloves, it was very difficult not to recoil as he raised the back of her hand to his lips.

His gaze left her in no doubt about his interest. "I would like to see you again before you leave Cadiz, Miss Cavanagh."

She withdrew her hand carefully so as not to cause offence. "I'm afraid that will be quite difficult, as the remainder of the Johnstons' schedule is quite full."

"I've no doubt. Permit me to speak to Mr. Johnston. Surely there will be opportunity for you to be excused."

She offered another pinched smile. There surely *wouldn't* be. She would make certain of that. "Good evening, Mr. MacArthur."

Jonathon's brother smiled. "Good evening, Miss Cavanagh. But I shouldn't think goodbye."

"Ugh," Etta said, as their carriage wound back through Cadiz's streets to the hotel. "Mr. MacArthur does not improve upon acquaintance."

Etta's sentiments echoed Rachel's own. "There is something I need to tell you both when we get back to the hotel," she said.

ALTHOUGH SHE'D ENDURED CHALONER MACARTHUR'S attention for a good cause, his overtures nevertheless left her feeling sullied.

They made Etta angry. The American woman was already

pacing by the window of Mr. Johnston's hotel suite, having heard Rachel's story. The hour had grown late.

"And Chaloner MacArthur had the *nerve* to call someone who burned his slave ship despicable!" Etta exclaimed. "I should say that's just deserts! Truly, Rachel, I don't know how you didn't throw a plate at his head."

Rachel had spoken of the shipwreck and her rescue, Jonathon's role in helping her to find her proper course, the work he had undertaken in Africa, and, finally, his rift with his family and how he had come to find her again. She thought it best—for the time being—not to disclose the true fate of *The Star*.

"I like the sound of this Mr. Lecky, Rachel," Mr. Johnston said. "Tell me what help you need."

"I'm not certain yet, Mr. Johnston. He is meeting with his father tonight. I . . . I don't know what the outcome will be."

"When will you see him again?"

"Tomorrow evening he intends to meet me here."

Mr. Johnston gave a nod. "Remember, Rachel. Whatever help you need."

THE SULLIED FEELING THAT CAME of her association with Chaloner MacArthur continued the next day, almost as though it crawled over her skin every time she thought of the man. She would have thrown her gloves away, except, in the unfortunate event that she *did* have to meet him again, she didn't want him to have any contact with a second pair. As soon as she sailed from Cadiz, the gloves that his lips had touched would be the first thing overboard.

But more than Chaloner MacArthur, she thought of Jonathon. Was he *safe*? What had happened the previous night? Those were the thoughts that kept repeating in her mind. She'd barely been able to keep track of the conversation during the visit she and Etta had paid to the French envoy's wife that morning. That didn't bode well for more chit-chat with the British diplomat's wife that afternoon. Thankfully, Etta had detected her distraction and, in her typical, artful style, steered the conversation. Rachel, meanwhile, had found herself palming the key that Jonathon had given her, almost as a measure of comfort.

THE LAST LIGHT OF DUSK

Of course, what she'd told him *was* true. She *had* moved on. Although at times she'd *hoped*, she had never truly considered he would change his mind. He'd walked out of her life twice. However, knowing that he'd come for her.... It seemed her feelings where one particular boat captain were concerned could all too quickly rekindle. She looked down at the key in her hand as the carriage she and Etta were riding in clattered along. Would Jonathon be at Bertrand's townhouse? Would he return there before he came to see her?

She realized it didn't matter. There was only one place she could be right now. "Etta, may I meet you back at the hotel?"

Etta's look was first quizzical, then understanding. "Of course. Where should we drop you?"

"Señor Lecky, there is a English señorita here for you," Bertrand's steward informed Lecky when he arrived back at the townhouse.

"An English señorita?" His breath stilled as every damn thing that could have gone wrong flashed through this mind. *Why was she here?*

"*Si.* She is waiting upstairs, in the watchtower. Will you need anything, señor?"

"No. *Gracias.*" Lecky took the steps to the roof two at a time. He strode across the roof to the watchtower and dragged the door open.

Rachel Cavanagh twisted away from the window alcove in surprise as he strode inside. With the sunlight streaming through the window behind, her butterscotch hair shone.

"Are you all right?" He was almost breathless.

"Yes." She must have read his fright, realized what he thought. She clutched her hands together in front of her skirt. "I . . . I didn't mean to scare you."

He crossed the room, his heart still beating a panicked tattoo. "Why did you come? I was going to meet you at the hotel tonight."

She shook her head. "I couldn't wait. All morning, all I could think about was whether you were all right."

Relief slid through him. He relaxed and pulled her against him, wrapping his arms around her shoulders as the tension eased from his muscles. "I thought something had gone wrong. Your dinner with Chaloner last night—"

"Nothing went wrong." She wrapped her arms around his middle and buried her head against his chest. "'Though I can't say I like your brother."

He choked back a laugh. "Sweetheart, *I* don't like my brother." He pressed a kiss to the top of her head, then drew a deep breath. *It felt so good to hold her.* For a moment he allowed himself that. No discussion. Nothing else. Just Rachel Anwen Cavanagh.

Finally, he asked, "Did Chaloner do anything particular to earn your dislike?"

She grimaced. "Apparently your sisters are urging him to marry."

Lecky let out a hiss. Of course, an influx of funds was the only thing that might save MacArthur and Sons now.

"He finds the idea of a woman 'with beauty, as well as riches, and the potential to forge a strategic business alliance' very attractive," she added.

Notus be damned. "I'll kill him if he touches you," Lecky said.

"No, *I'll* kill him if he touches me."

Her vehemence broke through his anger and brought a little smile to his lips. "Ah. Bloodthirsty." Even so, he hated that it had helped *him* to have her anywhere near his brother.

"Let's not talk about my dinner. Did you see your father?" She leant back in his arms to survey him from head to foot. "You are still in one piece."

"Yes, I saw him."

"And?"

"It went differently to what I expected." He saw her querying look. "He wanted to see me. He was ready to let the past go."

"Truly? But that's wonderful!"

"Aye. But Chaloner will want his revenge. He'll know by now that I'm in the city. Or close by."

Her brow puzzled. "What ought we do?"

Strangely enough, Lecky felt calm. It was as Winter had said. Sometimes things have a way of catching up with a man. Blackburn was likely to catch up with Chaloner MacArthur soon. "Lay low until we depart. I may remove to Gibraltar rather than tempt the fates. Your ship to Alexandria sails in three days?"

"Yes. What will you—"

"I intend to speak to Bertrand's contacts. Determine what my options are. Whether it's better to sail in my sloop to Alexandria or to accompany you, in which case I'll need a safe berth for my boat." Leaving the vessel in Cadiz would be tempting fate. News of Lecky's visit to Jonas MacArthur was likely to have reached Chaloner by now. "I also need to bring Morgan," Lecky added.

"But what about . . . what about your shipbuilding? Can you leave Winter?"

"There will be plenty of time for more ships." And there would be.

The woman he loved softened in his arms, her arms still looping his waist. Her coffee-brown eyes had the look of melted chocolate. "I can't believe it."

"Can't believe what?" He smiled.

"You. Here. When I set out from London with the Johnstons, I never dreamed . . . ."

"I did," he said. "Every night."

Then—because the little smile that blossomed on her lips was so sweet—he leant forward to brush his mouth over hers. "Mmmm." Pulling back, he set his hands on her waist to survey the rest of her. He looked down at her outfit, a chocolate-colored pelisse perfectly tailored to mould her curves. *He'd get himself in trouble if he wasn't careful.* "This is pretty. Best you step away, Miss Cavanagh. My resistance goes down in direct proportion to the rate your desirability goes up."

Her eyes shone with laughter. "Perhaps in that case I need to work on my desirability. Tell me, Mr. Lecky, how might I convince you to kiss me again?"

"You probably need to keep looking at me just as you're doing." Hell, he'd welcomed trouble plenty of times before.

"Are you certain? Looking at you doesn't seem to be doing enough."

"Miss Cavanagh, it's doing plenty."

She threw her head back and laughed.

Trouble, yes. With her lips tipped up, he kissed her. Her mouth stirred the Leveche in his blood.

There were other names he might call that wind, too. The *xaloc* in Catalan. The *xlokk* in Maltese. The *sirocco* in Italian. He knew all its names. But instead of originating in the Sahara, this warmth spread from her touch.

And damn, but it wasn't just lust. As she stopped laughing and started kissing him, she damn near shredded him. For months, he hadn't known if she would receive him. Now she was here in his arms.

His focus shifted to the feel of her hands on his chest and the flare of her hips beneath his own. She moved her lips along his jaw. Then, her mouth was on his again as she slid her palms up his chest to his shoulders. She made his thoughts loose, heady. At the same time, those thoughts were stirring into something honed, silken, and altogether red-blooded.

He skated his hands up her back, while within, some deep, inborn, knowing place flared hot and satisfied and possessive at the involuntary shiver that passed through her. *His. His always.*

He caught his breath, closed his eyes, as she slipped her fingers beneath the open neck of his shirt and brushed her fingertips along the length of his collarbone. *Steady, Jonathon.* They weren't yet wed.

By the gods, listen to him. *Wed.*

"Jonathon." Her voice was like smooth whisky, an intense blend of peat and smoke. A heady draught absorbed by his senses. "Jonathon, this time . . . don't stop."

His heart jarred, his throat went dry—even while the rest of his body recognized and reacted to her invitation.

He cupped her face to force the attention of those glorious, arabica eyes and make certain they both understood. "Rachel, I had no expectation. We can wait."

"Wait for?"

"Anything you wish. Marriage."

"Marriage?" Once more, her eyes were laughing at him.

"I realize, Miss Cavanagh, that the word is not one that would typically be associated with me. But, Rachel, I want you."

She smiled. Not only did her smile show his words had touched her, it also held a small measure of teasing. "You want me and you wish to wait until marriage?"

"Well . . . ." There was no stopping the self-deprecating twitch of his lips. "That depends on which part of me you ask, but that's my mutiny to deal with. Head trumps. Rachel, I'm not leaving—but I wish you to be secure in that knowledge. I've had a long time to think about this."

She regarded him, then stirred every one of his senses again as she leant forward to brush her mouth over his.

Whisky once more at his jaw, she spoke, her voice low. "I know you're not leaving. Don't stop."

His heart slammed against his ribs. If that was the case—if she was sure—then he wasn't going to rush this.

He rested his weight against the window seat beneath the window alcove, then with one hand on her waist, drew her to stand in the space between his thighs. He brush the back of his fingers across her cheekbone, to graze across her mouth. "May I take down your hair?" He wanted to see all those butterscotch tresses loose, falling about her shoulders and breasts.

"Yes." She began to raise her hands to the pins holding her hair.

He stopped her by placing one hand over hers. "Allow me?"

She paused, gazed into his eyes, and saw perhaps everything he intended her to see. Her hands fell away. "Yes."

He smiled softly. He was aware of her gaze on his face as his fingers found and slowly withdrew the first pin.

As the second pin came free, a hint of shyness flickered on her lips. The same shyness, the same vulnerability, he knew flickered on his own.

"My comb," she said. "It's at the back. Holding my hair at the back."

His fingers found it, grazing over filigree and pearls. For a moment, he stilled, then he carefully extracted the comb and brought it forward.

In his palm, inlaid in filigree, lay five round, perfect Tahitian black pearls. The most prized kind of all.

The sight produced a pang that constricted every chamber of his heart. *Notus and Poseidon and Zephyrus, thank you for keeping her for me.*

He looked back at her, hurting at her loveliness. The coils of her unwound hair curled down her back and over her shoulders.

"I was mad," he said. "Mad to leave you. Never again. By the gods, never again." He set the comb on the window seat and buried his hand in silken tresses.

Everything he hoped and wished to give, he poured into his kiss.

ALL HIS LONGING, ALL THE pent up emotion of the past months, all the time he'd waited for her—she felt all of those things in his kiss.

She felt a *lifetime* of longing in that kiss.

His words hadn't been born of a whim. He was here because it was the most important place he could be.

She found herself leaning into him dizzily as his lips shifted to brush the skin of her throat, above her collar. She clutched his shoulders, fingers digging into the wool of his cloak. But it was *him* she wanted to feel. The warmth of his skin. Straightening, she brought her hands up to the clasp of his cloak. "May I?"

His lips curved. "You think I would say no?"

Her smile surely mirrored his. "No."

She unclasped the cloak and pushed it back from his shoulders to bare his white shirt. His eyes darkened.

Then she lifted her hand to her own throat where the long line of black buttons that adorned her pelisse began.

The expression in his eyes told her that he knew exactly what she intended. The silken note in his voice permeated through her. "I can get those, too."

Her fingers stilled on the top button. "You would like to?"

The grin she loved slashed his features, with its usual lethal effect. "With my teeth if I have to."

"Maybe next time. Right now, I would be happy with your hands." She smiled, then sobered again, as he raised his fingers to the long row of buttons. Slowly, while she watched him, he freed each button from its fastening.

Watching her, he peeled her pelisse back across her shoulders, to reveal her rose-colored walking dress. He set the pelisse down on the window seat next to her comb. His hands returned to brush the length of her arms. A little shiver ran through her.

She felt the appreciation of his gaze as he looked over her. "You are beautiful, Rachel Anwen Cavanagh."

He took her hand and inclined his head toward the divans.

"Yes," she said to his wordless question.

He led her to stand before a divan. Then wove his fingers through hers as he drew her against him, thigh to thigh, hip to hip. His grip was firm. Her name was a whisper. "Rachel."

His mouth dipped, claimed hers. Oh, surely there had to be a word that described his kind of appeal. One that summed it all up. If it didn't exist now, then surely someone would create one. A word that conveyed his ruggedness—coarse and handsome at once—coupled with his wicked intelligence and humor.

Then, too, there was his physique. She remembered how it felt to be held against his chest, layered muscle enfolding her, his bare skin against hers. She wanted that again.

"Please," she breathed against his mouth.

"Please?" There was an amused note in his response.

Her hands went to his waistband and dragged free the hem of his shirt. The catch of laughter in his throat quickly became an indrawn breath as her fingers hooked over his waistband, skimming the soft skin inside.

The passage of her hands was stopped by his grasp upon her wrists.

"Surely you don't plan to stop me this time?"

"Oh, no." He was pressing her back onto the divan. Back onto her back, precisely where she wanted to be, as he came down above her. He dragged his shirt off over his head. Again, she was rewarded with the vista of his broad chest, the muscles in his shoulders and arms.

"How does this come off?"

He spoke of her dress. Sweeping her hair over her shoulder, she promptly rolled away from him onto her side, to present him with the row of buttons that ran down the back of her gown. He settled alongside her, but his fingers didn't go straight to her buttons. No, first his hand stroked the curve of her shoulder, then stroked forward and down. Through her dress, he cupped her breast—eliciting a hitched breath and a corresponding ache between her thighs. Next, his hand moulded her waist, her hip.

"Rachel." His mouth brushed the back of her neck, sending another spike of wanting straight to her womb. She kicked off her slippers and he worked loose the second set of buttons, revealing her stays and shift. He kissed the back of her shoulders as he peeled the gown down her arms. Her short stays loosened next, and she twisted to help him pull her shift over her head. Once done, she turned naked in his arms. The expression in his eyes intensified as he looked down upon her.

"I've dreamed of this. Of you." Sliding his hand over her chest, he bent his head and drew one of her nipples into his mouth. He gave it thorough attention before switching to the other, as the cool air from the tower window brushed over her skin. God of the Sea— or whoever it was that had so long laid claim to him—she wanted him for herself.

"Rachel, I want you."

Once more, her hands strayed to his waist. He watched her, his eyes that incredible, churning gray, as she drew a finger over his hip, just inside the band of his trousers. She waited for his response. She loved his response. "You're not stopping me," she pointed out.

"No."

Boldly, she splayed her hand across the front of his trousers. He drew a savage breath.

"And now?" she asked.

"I said I wouldn't stop you. But you might like to think about how quickly you want to be bedded."

Taking confidence from his reaction, she ran her hand over his length. "Are you saying that me doing this will hasten the experience?"

"What I'm saying is the rate of onset is likely to increase." He leant forward to kiss her throat. "I do, however, want you to be ready."

She understood what that meant. "Perhaps you might like to . . . check?"

"Ahha." She felt his smile against her throat. "Perhaps I should. Sweetheart . . . ." She parted her thighs a hand's width, then had to bite down hard on her lip as his palm brushed the soft inner skin of her thigh and his fingers found the wetness there. "You may send me mad, Rachel Anwen Cavanagh, in a very good way."

"I don't want to send you mad." Her breath hitched as his fingers teased.

"No? You're already doing a good job of it." He slid a finger inside her, then groaned and pressed his own body harder against her hand. "I would say you are very nearly perfect."

"Yes." It was difficult to think as his fingers continued to tease and part and slide. She reached again for the waistband of his trousers, wanting them gone.

This time he helped her, shoving the waist down over his hips and shifting so he could remove footwear and trousers entirely. Her gaze passed over his thighs, over his.... She blushed. Jonathon Lecky's lower body matched his upper body in terms of powerful physique. He rose up over her, caught her hands and wove his fingers through hers as he pressed her onto her back, one large, muscled thigh between hers.

"Are you certain this is what you want?"

His skin against hers, from chest to hip to thighs? "If you mean you, then yes."

He gazed down upon her. "I know this is a gift."

"From each to the other?"

He smiled. "Yes. From each to the other." He shifted, and suddenly she was biting her lip again as he nudged her thighs apart and settled between them.

He didn't enter her immediately. He pressed at her entrance as his mouth claimed hers, once more sweeping her away and stealing all thoughts bar one. Between her legs, her body hungered for more. "Jonathon," she managed, when he broke their kiss. She gathered he had a very good idea of what his restraint was doing, of what longing he was causing.

He raised himself to look down into her eyes as he slowly pressed forward.

The feeling was new.... It felt.... She tensed as he reached her barrier. He slid his hand beneath her buttocks.

"Rachel." He thrust forward.

Her fingers dug into his shoulders at the swift pain. It receded as he remained still, allowing her to become accustomed to the feel of him inside.

"Are you all right?"

"Yes."

"Is this all right?" He shifted inside her. Withdrew a little, then delivered another stroke.

This time, she bit her lip because it felt good. "Yes."

He too seemed to understand that her response was not one of pain. She was not sure, however, if the delicious feeling of his body sliding within hers was meant to be survived.

"And this?" His next move withdrew further, stroked longer.

She released a little breath. "Keep going."

That brought a smile. One that once more smoothed to seriousness, as he withdrew, then penetrated just as deeply. But more slowly, more languorously. Then again.

And again, and again, and again.

Leaving her in no doubt that he loved her.

SHE WAS BARE AND SILKEN and open. Warm and responsive. Coltish curves and thick butterscotch curls and eyes the rich hue of coffee. She was everything he wanted. Everything he could wish.

He wanted to spill his soul into her and, in turn, know her inside and out.

He watched her face. The depths of her eyes hid nothing as she took his body inside. There, her depth of feeling mirrored his own. She gasped, and he took satisfaction in the flush of her skin and the parting of her lips and the downward sweep of her lashes. Somehow, he managed to concentrate on that. Not just her wet heat around him—no, then he would be lost. He watched for the little signs that told him she was beginning to unravel.

Her escalating, short catches of breath as he delivered stroke after stroke. The catch of her lips on his name. The splay of her hands across his chest. Her attempts to pull him closer, thighs parting to draw his thrusts deeper.

He went down on his elbows to gather her in the curve of his arms. Zephyr and Leveche in one.

The little pulses that rippled inside her, around him, were his undoing.

At the last moment, he pulled away, finding release outside. For long moments, he could do nothing. One breath would not do it. Not ten. Not one hundred. He'd ached for her for months.

"Jonathon—"

She seemed to understand he'd held part of himself back. But he was not about to complicate her hopes and dreams with a pregnancy she had not planned. "Shhh," he said. "Just until we take other precautions." He stretched out beside her, gathering her against his chest. "Already, you've given me everything I hoped."

She'd given him the chance to love her. To lie beside her, to reach out a hand and convert a gentle stroke to a more knowing, deeper touch.

Damned if he knew whether he deserved her. He did know now there was more than one way to be blind. Beliefs could limit sight as much, if not more, than the eyes could. Mayhap he'd been blinder than the Marquess, in his own way.

Surrounded by the scent of the ocean and the smell of her soap and skin, he sent a silent thanks to the gods for granting a man wisdom when he needed it.

And to a beautiful, courageous woman, who had a heart large enough to offer the right blind man a chance.

Their limbs tangled, and she appeared warm and content, settled in his arms.

"How long can you stay?" he asked, as she burrowed against him.

Her lashes drifted shut as her lips smiled. Her fingers came to rest on one of his wrists.

"Forever," she replied.

CHAPTER TWENTY-FOUR

It's a man's deeds, not his name, that determines who he is.
—*The Memoirs of Rhys Cavanagh*

LECKY RETURNED RACHEL TO THE gate to the hotel stables later that evening. There, they paused in the shadows of the buildings that lined the narrow street.

"I won't come into the hotel," Lecky said. Discretion was called for, at least until they were safely away from Cadiz. "What are your plans for tomorrow?"

"In the morning, Mr. Johnston, Etta and I are meeting with the Marquise de Pentejos at the Café Apolo on the Plaza San Antonio," Rachel said, naming one of Cadiz's leading hostesses and one of the most powerful political figures in the city. "In the afternoon, I had planned to further explore the city and sketch. What of you?"

"I'm going to see Bertrand's contacts to determine what options Morgan and I have." By the gods, he didn't want to leave her. "Rachel, you'll stay away from my brother?"

"I'll do my best. And you? You'll be careful?" Moonlight and shadow flickered across her face, her dark eyes full of concern. Concern that was understandable. Among the traders of Cadiz, his MacArthur features were easily recognizable.

"I promise," he said. "I'll meet you here, tomorrow evening at nine?"

"Please," she said, and with that, he kissed her goodnight.

"What a fascinating woman!" Etta exclaimed to Rachel and Mr. Johnston outside the Café Apolo. They had just exited the coffee house, which stood on one side of the Plaza de San Antonio, the main square of Cadiz. The plaza was otherwise dominated by the San Antonio church with its twin belfries and a series of mansions constructed in neoclassical architectural style.

"The Marquise has seen a great deal," Mr. Johnston said.

"Yes," Etta agreed. She cast a sideways glance at her father. "She was very circumspect in how she spoke of the King."

"The Marquise did not gain—or retain—the power she has by being anything less, my dear. She is not the Queen of the 'Cortes Chicas' for nothing."

'Cortes Chicas' was the public's name for the coffee house, which meant 'Little Parliament', on account of the Spanish elite who had gathered there during the war.

Lord knew, however, the situation with the King was difficult. The Spanish Parliament had operated from Cadiz during the years of French occupation, during which time the nation's new constitution had been established. Upon the Spanish King's reinstatement, Ferdinand VII had set aside the new constitution. Not all parties were happy.

The three came to a stop beneath a tree in the plaza. "I know father, but—uh oh." Her gaze caught something over Rachel's shoulder. "Mr. MacArthur is approaching. We should have anticipated that, with his residence so close." Continuing to look over Rachel's shoulder, Etta's lips curved up in a forced smile.

"Quite right, my dear." Mr. Johnston agreed. He turned. "Ah. Mr. MacArthur! Well met."

"Indeed. Good day, Mr. Johnston, Miss Johnston, Miss Cavanagh. You've been at the Café Apolo?"

"Enjoying tea with the Marquise de Pentejos, yes," Mr. Johnston replied.

"Ah, I see. A very interesting woman, I hear. I intended to call on you yesterday. Unfortunately, unexpected business arose that prevented me."

"Oh? How terrible." Etta's brows rose. Her glance flickered to Rachel. "It has been taken care of now, I hope?"

"One day. Unfortunately, it is a recurrent problem that causes no end of grief. I look forward to the day it is finally taken care of."

"Well, I am glad we ran into you," Mr. Johnston said. "I wanted to thank you again for dinner on Thursday evening. It was most enjoyable."

"I also enjoyed your company. Indeed, I found myself most inspired and hoped to speak to Miss Cavanagh of a range of business prospects that may be of interest to her. I hoped you would allow me to steal her away for an afternoon or evening before you leave."

How could the man look so much like Jonathon, yet make her skin crawl so? Thank goodness she had spoken to Mr. Johnston and Etta of her dislike.

Mr. Johnston frowned. "I really don't know.... I believe the rest of our days are quite booked?"

"They are, Papa," Etta responded. "'Though perhaps, if Mr. MacArthur is not in a rush, we might all take a turn about the plaza now?" Etta's glance moved expectantly from her father to Rachel, then landed on Chaloner MacArthur. "That way, Mr. MacArthur may share his ideas with Rachel, while you and I may enjoy the sun? We have a half hour to spare before our next engagement."

It was likely, Rachel thought, that they all wanted to tell him to go to the devil, but in lieu of that, Etta's ploy was artful. Rachel sent the American woman a silent look of thanks.

Chaloner MacArthur's lips pressed together. "Of course. Miss Cavanagh?" He offered his arm and turned toward the centre of the plaza.

It was a good thing she'd not thrown away her gloves. "Thank you." Reluctantly, she placed her arm atop his, then glanced over her shoulder at the Johnstons. Mr. Johnston's lips twitched in a little message of reassurance. A message that promised he and Etta would be right behind.

"Miss Cavanagh, I had hoped we might spend some time alone."

So he could what? Compromise her?

"Mr. MacArthur, I must advise in that respect I cannot be persuaded. You may thank my mother, who was determined to ensure no daughter of hers would wed in scandal. Her lessons have sunk deep."

Every word was true. During her first two seasons, she'd desired to avoid marriage at all costs. Observing propriety had been one of the very few of Lady Georgiana's demands to which Rachel had had no difficulty acceding.

That was until Jonathon.

"Unfortunately," she said, "more men in London claim to be gentlemen than can truly be accounted for."

MacArthur smiled. "Then how, Miss Cavanagh, might a good man woo you?"

With a buccaneer's kiss on a cobblestone street in Gravesend, with her hand pressed to his heart.

Truly, how could these men be *brothers*?

San Antonio church rose up over the plaza to their fore. All manner of people congregated in the square. Some strolled, some visited the church, others hawked wares. Yet amid the movement, her eyes caught a glimpse of a familiar cloak, worn by a man entering the plaza from the avenue beside the church.

Jonathon.

Immediately, she stiffened. Her pulse picked up pace. *No, Rachel.* She had to relax.

Thank goodness Jonathon had seen her. Seen his brother.

He fell back into the shadows of the church as Rachel halted. Sliding her arm free from Chaloner MacArthur's, she twisted to face him, to draw his attention away from the facade of the church.

"How might a good man woo me? Are *you* a good man, Mr. MacArthur?"

"Would you believe me if I said I was very nearly perfect?"

"I would ask whether that claim was tongue in cheek."

"Do you doubt perfection, Miss Cavanagh?"

"I am suspicious of any who believe it applies to themselves."

A slow smile spread across Chaloner MacArthur's face. "I have a great deal to offer, Miss Cavanagh. Strategically and otherwise."

From several feet away, Rachel heard Etta gasp.

Jonathon.

Such was her immediate thought, but it wasn't the case. As Rachel twisted again, she saw a young woman had stepped into their path. The same young woman that she and Etta had been keeping watch for these past few days. Tears streamed from the girl's huge green eyes.

Her face was thin, her arms waif-like and delicate. Her hands were buried deep in the pockets of her coat, a too-small, tattered coat that fell open over her pregnant belly.

Etta's gasp had brought Chaloner MacArthur's attention round, too.

"Leah," MacArthur said sharply. "Good Lord. What are you doing?"

With a glance, one could see the girl was on the verge of hysteria. "I'm trying to speak to you. I was waiting outside your house. I followed you here." Her eyes were filled with agony as her glance flickered to Rachel. "Who is she? Is she your new woman? Is she your *fiancé*?"

"No," Chaloner MacArthur said. "Leah, unless you leave, I will be forced to call the *policia*."

"You say that every time!" She burst into tears. "My babe is about to be born!"

"This is . . . ." Chaloner MacArthur gave a dismissive motion of his hand. He looked embittered, repulsed.

The girl sobbed and wiped her eyes with the back of one hand, then withdrew a pistol from the pocket of her coat. Her hands shook as she took aim at Chaloner MacArthur's heart.

"Good Lord." MacArthur's sentiment echoed Rachel's own. Both he and Rachel took surprised steps back. "Leah, what are you doing?"

Across the plaza, Jonathon had pushed back the hood of his cloak and taken a panicked step forward. Other occupants of the plaza had paused to stare.

Was the pistol loaded? Had the girl loaded it?

"I told you!" the girl cried. "I just wanted to talk!"

Chaloner MacArthur put up his hands. "Very well. Now put the pistol down. We'll talk."

The girl was in too much of a state. Too panicked and hurt. "As you talked to me at the dock?" she cried. "No! Look at what you've done to me! You said we would be married! But you haven't come! Not since I told you about the babe. Did you not read my letters? And Pa, my Pa, he thinks—"

"There now, lass—" It was Mr. Johnston who took a step

forward.

The diplomat's intervention seemed to frighten the girl more. "Don't come near me!"

"Lass, you need to put the pistol down. I'll make sure Mr. MacArthur resolves your concerns."

Rachel's glance darted to Jonathon again. Across the distance, his eyes told her to *get the hell back*. Taking a breath, she began to inch away.

Meanwhile, Chaloner MacArthur had grasped Mr. Johnston's intervention. "That's right, Leah, sweetheart. Put the pistol down and we'll all go away and talk."

Sudden fury steadied the girl's hand. "*Sweetheart*? Don't call me that! How can you call me that? You're lying!"

"I haven't lied to you," MacArthur said soothingly. "I didn't receive your letters. I misunderstood your predicament."

He *was* lying. Every man, woman and pigeon in the plaza could see it.

"Don't treat me like a fool! I'm not a fool!" she cried.

"You are certainly behaving like one. Look at what you're doing! Look at the number of people you are offending! You can't shoot me, Leah. Do you know what will happen if you shoot me? The *policia* will put you in jail. You'll have your baby in jail. They might even hang you. Now put the pistol down."

"You've done this to me!" she cried.

His lips firmed. Again, revulsion shone in his eyes. He made a sudden lunge for the pistol.

The girl leaped back as his hand closed over hers and sought to bring the gun down. "No!" she squealed. She was flustered and scared witless. "Don't—"

The pistol discharged.

Shocked cries echoed around the square.

Oh, God. Rachel couldn't breath. The girl started to howl.

Her cries were nothing compared to Chaloner MacArthur's agonized screams.

Jonathon Lecky's brother sank to one knee, then toppled over, still screaming.

The girl fell into silent shock. The pistol tumbled from her fingers to thump on the ground.

Both Jonathon and Mr. Johnston were already rushing forward. Others in the square were running for the *policia*. A short distance away, the Marquise de Pentejos stood outside the Café Apolo with her entourage of ladies, her hand clasped over her mouth.

"Where is he shot?" Mr. Johnston asked.

Rachel could already see. Blood was spreading out from his groin. Or rather, his upper thigh, just to the left of his groin.

"By God, his artery." Mr. Johnston fell to his knees at Chaloner MacArthur's side. The American diplomat dragged off his cloak to use as a compress and battered MacArthur's panicked hands away as he sought to apply pressure to the wound. "Rachel, Etta, look after the lass." Etta was already moving as Mr. Johnston pointed to a man frozen nearby. "Señor, quickly! Fetch one of those carts. We need to get this man to an infirmary."

On the ground, Chaloner's eyes widened as Jonathon arrived at his side. "You," he hissed.

Mr. Johnston looked up, although he kept pressure firm on the wound. "You're his brother."

"No," Chaloner spat from the ground. "He and I—we are *not* brothers."

"I can help," Jonathon said.

"No," Mr. Johnston said, taken aback by MacArthur's viciousness. "Not you. If there's bad blood between you, better that no one can say you killed him." He looked around. "God help us. This man is going to bleed to death."

"Oh, God!" A young man had torn into the plaza, his expression clearly panicked. Like the pregnant girl's, his coat was tattered and his appearance suggested good board and lodgings were hard to come by. He sprinted forward, only to skid to a halt before them. His gaze took in Jonathon, Mr. Johnston, Chaloner MacArthur losing blood, Rachel, Etta, then finally the girl.

He thrust his hand through the black hair that flopped over his brow.

"Shit from heaven, Blackburn! What in the blasted hell have you done?"

CHAPTER TWENTY-FIVE

Who chooses our fate? Why and for whom?
—*The Memoirs of Rhys Cavanagh*

BLACKBURN? LECKY'S GAZE SWUNG TOWARD the girl. Suddenly, matters became very clear. Or at least clear enough.

By the gods, the lass wasn't dead. She was, however, in Cadiz.

"It was an accident," the girl cried.

An accident? Oh, yes, it was an accident. One that had clearly had a helping hand from Chaloner. Poseidon be damned; the girl was barely older than their sister Margaret.

"Oh, Jesus, Blackburn." The young man moved forward, and Etta surrendered the lass to his arms. The girl curled into him, balling her hands against his chest and burying her face against his throat as she cried.

Across the plaza, men were shouting and tugging on a cart. On the ground, Chaloner MacArthur was rapidly losing blood.

He noted the direction of Lecky's gaze through his pain. "Look at you," he fumed, between breaths. "You . . . you probably think this is justice."

The tide had gone out in Lecky's stomach, leaving a vast, empty, scoured shore. His throat was equally dry.

Justice? For years of selfish taking? For caring naught for the hurt he caused and never changing course?

Justice, arriving in the form of the pregnant daughter Blackburn believed was dead, yet who was alive and hysterical in a Spanish plaza with a gun?

"I think," Lecky said, "that is for you to decide."

333

He saw his brother's hatred for him then. It was like seeing into the bottom of a blackened chasm. In its the depths sat a cauldron, its boiling contents spilling over to flood the cracks of the chasm floor and seep deeper still.

That hatred was there before Chaloner MacArthur heaved his final breath ... and the light went out in his eyes.

There was a moment of shocked silence.

Then Lecky felt Rachel slip her hand into his own.

"You accompanied the girl to Spain?" Mr. Johnston asked. "That was your pistol?"

In the study of Bertrand Mercier's townhouse, the American diplomat and Lecky faced the young man who had arrived in the plaza. Lecky put the boy at seventeen or eighteen years of age. Upstairs, in one of the guest rooms, Leah Blackburn was asleep, her welfare overseen by Rachel, Etta Johnston and Bertrand's servants.

The young man's eyes flashed. "It was her father's pistol. I was minding it. I didn't know she'd taken it."

"Where have you been staying?" Mr. Johnston asked. "How long have you been in Cadiz?"

The young man looked aside and wouldn't answer.

The streets. The lad didn't have to say it.

Mr. Johnston sighed. "Lad, we want to help you. But you're making it damned difficult when you refuse to speak."

The young man stuck his chin toward Lecky. "He's MacArthur's brother. Look at him."

"They're estranged."

The lad remained stubbornly silent.

"What is your name?" Mr. Johnston tried again.

Moments passed before the young man answered. "Ariel."

"Ariel what?" Mr. Johnston said.

Again, a resentful pause. "Maitland."

"Well, then, Ariel Maitland, how do you know Leah Blackburn?" When no response was forthcoming, Lecky guessed. "You worked for her father."

Ariel Maitland glowered.

Lecky crossed his arms over his chest as he rested his weight against Bertrand's heavy oak desk. "Did you know that her father thinks she is dead?"

"She wanted him to."

"Why?"

"*Why?*" The lad bit out. "Because she had a crazy notion—" He silenced himself.

"A crazy notion that Chaloner MacArthur would want her?" Lecky supplied, and Maitland's lips again set in a line. "Why did you help her?" he asked. "Why didn't you just go to her father?"

Maitland narrowed his eyes. It was then Lecky saw. "You love Leah Blackburn." It was there in the lad's hostility. In his defensiveness. In the savage flame that burned in Maitland's eyes.

The lad scoffed, but it was a feint. "Crazy chit would have run away to Spain no matter what. She thought he didn't get her letters. Someone had to protect her."

So this lad, still growing into manhood, riled and impassioned with his smooth features and unkempt black hair, had acted as her guardian on a journey from England to Spain. *Notus have mercy.* In a way, Ariel Maitland reminded Lecky of himself.

"Blackburn's men destroyed one of MacArthur's ships. Leah's father is on his way to Cadiz, with the intention of seeing Chaloner MacArthur dead."

Maitland watched Lecky from beneath distrusting brows. "Best he get here soon then. Before they dig a hole."

"I'm sure Blackburn will be pleased that you looked out for his daughter," Mr. Johnston said.

Maitland snorted. "You don't know Blackburn. As soon as he hears, he'll want *me* dead, too."

"But you've supported her. Taken care of her," Mr. Johnston pointed out.

Lecky could well guess what Ariel Maitland had done. The lad would have scraped his knuckles raw working and stolen if need be to keep food in their bellies and some form of shelter over Leah Blackburn's head. Lecky suspected Maitland had done every damn thing he could to keep the girl safe.

"Taken *care* of her? Not to Blackburn's way of thinking, I haven't. And not—" Again, the lad fell silent. His lips twisted in an expression Lecky recognized. It was one of self-disgust.

Unfortunately, Maitland was probably right. Blackburn *wouldn't* forgive the lad for helping his daughter to run away and for allowing Blackburn to believe she was dead. He wouldn't see what Maitland has done as 'help'.

"Will she be all right?" Maitland asked. Some of his bravado had slipped. "Will they come for her? The *policia*?"

"No. I'll speak to the *policia*," Mr. Johnston said. "Then we'll make sure Leah Blackburn is returned to her father in England, if he doesn't arrive in Spain first. *After* the babe comes, of course. It would be too taxing to send her back to England now."

"You can both remain here in this house," Lecky said. "When the time is necessary, the staff will fetch a midwife."

Maitland loosed a ragged breath, which sounded a lot like relief. Likely, the lad had been worried about Leah Blackburn giving birth without assistance. "You said... her father is on his way?"

"Yes."

"Good." Even so, the lad looked pained. "And you promise she won't go to jail?"

"That shouldn't be a problem. However, if it looked like one, we'd smuggle you both out of the city."

"It's not me that I'm worried about."

"The lass will be fine," Lecky repeated.

His jaw firming, the young man gave a nod. Even so, Lecky couldn't shake the feeling Ariel Maitland was biting back tears.

THE LATE AFTERNOON SUN WAS descending over the Bay of Cadiz when Rachel found Lecky on the roof of the watchtower. Beyond the tower, the sea glimmered from the port to the horizon. Below, the shadows on the east side of the city's white- and ecru-colored walls were deep. After the events of the day, he'd needed a few moments of solitude and salt-laden breeze.

Solitude, that was, except for Morgan. He'd brought the collie to Bertrand's townhouse that morning, before the events in the plaza. Now the collie lay on her belly on the rooftop, her head resting atop one of her paws. The light gusts of wind ruffled her black coat.

He was standing by the parapet with his arms crossed when he heard footsteps on the stairs. He turned as Rachel appeared in the doorway beneath the small cupola that capped the stairway.

Coming to a stop as she spotted him, she rested one hand against the doorframe. "Jonathon, Mr. Johnston said the young man—Ariel Maitland?—is gone. Mr. Johnston just went to find him, and the servants looked, too, to no avail. They found the servants' door slightly ajar. Do you think . . . ?"

Did he think Ariel Maitland was gone? The news of Maitland's disappearance didn't surprise him. Not when Maitland realized Leah Blackburn's father was coming. Lecky felt a stab of heartache for the lad. In their brief audience, too much about Maitland reminded Lecky of himself. Fourteen years before, full of noble intentions, he'd escaped his sister's plantation in South Carolina and crossed the Atlantic, only to discover all his efforts were for naught. Or, if not for naught, his impassioned pleas and youthful naivety had at the time failed to produce a happy ending—or at least the ending he'd hoped for.

"While you were tending to Leah, I told Maitland that Leah's father is en route to Cadiz."

Rachel's brow furrowed. She dropped her hand and came forward. "En route already? But how . . . ?" Then she realized and came to a halt before him. She tipped her head up. "Blackburn wanted retribution. He intended to come for Chaloner himself, believing his daughter was dead. You knew."

"Yes, I knew." Lecky was quiet for a moment as she absorbed this. He wondered how it made her feel, to realize he'd known another man planned to kill his brother. Truth be told, Lecky didn't rightly know how he felt about it himself, even though he had known that same brother would happily see *him* dead.

He *had* known he wanted no further part in it. It was as Elijah Winter had said: *These things usually have a way of catching up with a man. Let him orchestrate his own doom.* Chaloner had done that.

"Is that why you chose to avoid Chaloner in Cadiz?" Rachel asked.

"Yes." If Blackburn accomplished what he had hoped to do, Lecky would no longer have to look over his shoulder. "But if he'd found me, threatened me, that would have been different. If he'd touched *you*, that would have been different." Notus knew, it had been bad enough seeing Leah Blackburn brandishing that pistol. By the gods, he'd been afraid Rachel would be hurt.

"But you were otherwise prepared to walk away?"

"Once I'd seen my father, yes." It was Jonas MacArthur he'd had to settle with. It was with others that his brother had held accounts.

When he had set out on this path, he'd wanted to see both Chaloner and his father brought low. He'd wanted to strip them both of everything they'd used to gauge importance, all of which had been built on the back of others' suffering.

Irrespective of the regrets his father may have had, the truth was the man had never done anything to curb his eldest son's ways. As Jonas MacArthur grieved for his first born, as he considered the nature of his son's death, Lecky hoped he considered that.

He also wanted to smooth away the crease that had formed between the brows of the woman standing before him.

"I wish I could say I'm sorry about your brother but, knowing the hurt he has caused . . . ." She pursed her lips. "Jonathon, I don't understand why the young man—Ariel—has left? Isn't he worried for the girl?"

Oh yes, Ariel Maitland would be worried. He'd be driving himself *mad* with worry. Yet the lad would believe he'd done the right thing by leaving. "In Blackburn's view," Lecky explained, "Maitland won't have helped his daughter."

"But he *did* help the girl. And her father is not here yet. Why not wait?"

Oh, this Lecky understood all too well. He rested his weight back against the parapet, arms still crossed. "Because, Miss Cavanagh, the longer Maitland stayed, the harder for him it would be to leave."

"Oh." Soft light of understanding entered her eyes. She stepped within arm's reach and tipped her head up, wearing a little smile. "Is that why *you* left Dunkirk so swiftly, Mr. Lecky? And Gravesend? Were you afraid it would become harder to leave the longer you stayed?"

He was happy to take the bait she dangled, looking up at him as teasingly as she was. He set his hands on her hips and drew her toward him. She melted against him, looping her arms around his neck.

He leant his forehead against hers and gazed into those pools of coffee-brown temptation.

"Well?" she prompted.

Because he knew it would drive her mad, he didn't answer.

Her lips nipped up. "Jonathon, what are you thinking?"

He was thinking about one half-drowned, infamous privateer's granddaughter, capable of felling a drunken thug with an umbrella stand. He was thinking about a travel journal filled with sketches of Boulogne, prepared by a woman who had sat on his companionway wearing medieval garb and asked if he would debauch her. He was thinking about the woman he'd so madly left and the woman who'd welcomed him back—and one very comfortable Cadiz-watchtower divan.

He was thinking about not having to watch over his shoulder.

They still had an hour or two before dusk, and the sea glimmered in the light of the sun.

"What am I thinking?" he repeated. "I'm thinking about the beach. I want to take off my boots and roll up my trouser legs and feel the sand between my toes. I want to throw a damned stick for Morgan."

At the word 'stick', the collie raised her head and thumped her tail.

"Rachel Anwen Cavanagh"—he smiled because the woman in his arms was so damn beautiful—"will you join me?"

EPILOGUE

As captain, it was a favorite duty of mine to marry a couple at sea.
  —The Memoirs of Rhys Cavanagh

ALEXANDRIA. ONCE THE PEARL OF the Mediterranean, in its heyday the city had been as significant to the Greco-Egyptian world as Cadiz now was to Spanish trade with the New World. But as the years passed, wars and purges had destroyed it. First it fell to the Sassanid Persians, then to the Ottomans. The once-glorious city shrank to a town. Twenty years before, it was stormed by Napoleon's troops and then, two years later, bombarded and besieged by the British. Alexandria was a city with a long past, and that past had touched the life of the woman before Lecky intimately.

Rachel Cavanagh could have come by herself. She had the courage, the intelligence, the determination and the means. But he'd wanted to be here, too. He wanted to hold her not because she needed to be held, but rather so she could feel his arms around her. So she knew he was here.

He watched from the shore as she moved further along the pier. The light breeze plucked at her skirts and sent them rippling around her half-boots. He'd waited behind as she went ahead, sensing she needed the first few moments here alone.

Morgan, of course, couldn't be stopped. She padded along at Rachel's side. Then, as Rachel halted a few yards from the end of the pier to cross her arms over her chest and gaze out to sea, his collie sat vigilantly upon her hindquarters, a sentry at her side.

It was calm today. Serene. There was nothing to indicate that, sixteen years before, this pier had been teeming with the crews of British warships and munitions. Then—tragedy. A chance explosion. Twenty-seven men dead, James Cavanagh and his captain included.

Taking Rhys Cavanagh's son, a woman's brother, a woman's husband and the father of five children.

Lecky watched as she stood. He understood what it meant for her to come here. There was her father, yes—a man she had barely known.

She had also meant to share this moment with her aunt.

It was nearing two years since the day he had plucked Rachel Cavanagh from the sea.

Backlit by the glint of sun off the water, she turned her head in profile.

It was nearing two years since she'd become embedded in his life, curled up against his cabin in the pre-dawn, exhausted and vulnerable and brave.

His wife now.

His path after all.

When she glanced back to him, hand raised to the brim of her bonnet to shield her eyes, he approached. Morgan gave a thump of her tail at his arrival.

With the heat of the afternoon sun kissing their faces, he stood between her and the wind. She leant back against his body as he set his hands upon her shoulders.

He could have lost her. Let her slip through his fingers as easily as Poseidon could have claimed a filigree comb inlaid with Tahitian black pearls.

In a split moment, his path could have changed as easily as the outcome of any of the sieges of Alexandria, or his own chance meeting with a former Spanish slaver on the streets of Mogadore. Instead, he'd secured the greatest prize of all.

She raised a hand to rest her white-gloved fingers against his bare ones.

"It barely feels real that this was the last place he stood. The last land that he saw. I wonder what he felt when he looked back to shore. Do you think he felt far from home? Far from us?" She turned her head then to look beyond Lecky's shoulder to the row of

Egyptian stalls along the quayside and the great medieval citadel that rose up behind.

"You know that land wasn't the last thing he saw," Lecky said.

She tilted her head and redirected her gaze to him. Morgan looked up at him, too.

"No?" Rachel asked.

"In his mind, it would have been you. Your mother. His children."

Her eyes softened and misted, the warmth of appreciation in their depths. Her smile was just slight enough to make her lips quiver. "You believe that?"

"I have no doubt." He paused, just long enough to raise his finger to brush the softness of her bottom lip, to lose himself in those eyes. "I know my wife will be the last thing I see."

Her lips parted on her little indrawn breath and arabica darkened to whisky, a combination that showed she was at once deeply moved by his words and made vulnerable. "Jonathon . . . ."

Nearby, Morgan gave an indignant little huff, sparking Lecky's smile. He took Rachel's hand and turned her to face him. Bringing her hand up between both of his, he pressed a kiss to the base of her palm. "Not yet. Not for very long time."

The *khamaseen*—the wind of fifty days—the hot wind was called here. Blinding, abrasive, destructive and dust-laden, it drove the land's inhabitants to take refuge in their dwellings or pits in the earth when it scoured the land. For so long, the *khamaseen's* hot blast had called. Yet the wind that brought life—that nourished, that replenished—didn't lock a man up inside or in place. It didn't obscure the territory that spread out before him. No. That wind filled sails, occasionally lifted and carried, cooled and supported. It refreshed and brought calm after its harsher counterparts tore through.

Like that wind, the smooth slide of this woman's arms, the glimpse of her smile, carried the soft promise of calmness and warmth.

There would be times, too, when harsher winds would blow and it would be she who needed a sheltered cove, a place where she was safe. Regardless of whether it was her direction or his they sailed, it was within him to defend, to turn buccaneer-fierce in a moment. Yet as rugged as he was, as coarse as his seafaring, shipbuilding hands were, he could still gently cup a treasure.

Aye, it just so happened, what Zephyrus called for, this man could give after all.

ABOUT THE AUTHOR

I first fell in love with romance in the back seat of a rental car crossing midwest America.

Twenty years ago, during our first-ever overseas family vacation, we were visiting friends in a small rural town outside Detroit, Michigan, when the unthinkable happened: I ran out of books to read. Our host, Nora, pulled out a huge box of old, dog-eared historical romances with the generous offer, "Take what you like."

Now, inspired by the emotions evoked by my all-time favorite novels, I seek to create my own rich and exciting historical worlds. My desire? To write stories that carry depth in which people find themselves, become whole, or, at the very least, find true strength, fearlessly hold themselves to account, lift, inspire and rebuild themselves, and do so with an undiminished heart. And what better way to do it, than with a big plot and a grand adventure?

www.joannelockyer.com

CPSIA information can be obtained at www.ICGtesting.com
Printed in the USA
LVOW07s1517220115

423935LV00001B/97/P